I0580481

Beyond the
Carrying Capacity

By

Paul A. Fell

Dedicated to my darling wife Sarah for her support and appreciation.

Carrying Capacity, **Noun**

"The maximum, equilibrium number of organisms of a particular species that can be supported indefinitely in a given environment."

"Humanity as a whole, driven by an unyielding need to survive and prosper, will always strive to overcome their most horrific and petrifying futures, regardless of the impact on fellow humans and the ecological systems around them."

Prologue

Over fifty years ago from the present just before the year 2100, humanity entered a new era of health and well-being. It was propelled by unprecedented advancements in medical science and technology. Diseases and illnesses that had once plagued humankind were mostly a distant memory. Humanity had forged ahead into a future of unprecedented longevity.

With breakthroughs in genetic engineering, regenerative medicine, and nanotechnology, the average human lifespan had extended far beyond what was once thought possible. Once considered old age in the early part of the century now seems like little more than middle age in present times. Human's physical ages belied their actual ages as individuals were capable of routinely living well into their second century and beyond.

With the eradication of many diseases and illnesses, the quality of life for people of all ages physically improved dramatically. Gone were the days of suffering and pain, replaced by a newfound sense of vitality and vigour that permeated every aspect of society.

The elderly had once been relegated to the side lines of life. They now found themselves involved as active participants in a world that better valued their wisdom and experience. Centenarians and beyond had been celebrated for their contributions to society. The longevity of the human form was seen as a testament to the triumph of ingenuity over the forces of nature. Newfound longevity brought its own set of challenges. As the population continued to age, the need for luxury support services and resources became increasingly pressing. Governments and organizations around the world scrambled to adapt to the changing demographic landscape. Large sums of credits invested in programs and initiatives designed to support the needs of an aging but healthy population.

The history of humanity is a tale of growth, innovation, and progress. From the humble beginnings, it flourished and multiplied, spreading across the globe, and leaving its mark on every corner of the Earth. In the early twentieth century, the world's population stood at a mere one billion people. This was a fraction of what it would become in the centuries that followed. Advances in medicine, agriculture, and technology transformed the way humanity lived. Numbers swelled, reaching six billion in 1999, seven billion by 2011, and eight billion by the year 2023. Humanities growth continued unabated throughout the twenty first century, showing no signs of slowing down. Life expectancy increased and infant mortality rates declined. More and more people were born into the world, each adding to the ever-expanding human family.

By the year 2100, the world's population had reached a staggering fifteen billion. It was a figure that would have been unimaginable to our ancestors of just a few generations earlier. Cities stretched skyward, vast urban sprawls teemed with life, and every corner of the Earth was touched by the presence of humanity.

With such a vast number of people to care for, the challenges facing society were greater than ever before. Resources were stretched to their limits, ecosystems strained under the weight of human activity, and the delicate balance of life on Earth hung in the balance. Feeding fifteen billion people required an intricate web of agricultural systems. Vast industrial farms produced food efficiently topped up by small-scale subsistence agriculture. Fields stretched for miles, producing crops to feed the hungry masses. Even with advanced farming techniques and genetically modified crops, there were times when food shortages occurred. Millions of people often went hungry through to starvation. Food and water, the most fundamental requirements for life, were not infinite. While agricultural advancements and irrigation techniques had boosted yields, there was a point where the Earth's capacity to produce sustenance reached its peak. Every acre of arable land, every drop of freshwater, had a maximum yield beyond which further exploitation led to diminishing returns.

Water became the most precious commodity in a world where demand far outstripped supply. Desalination plants worked overtime to turn seawater into drinkable water. Rivers and aquifers were drained to irrigate thirsty crops. Despite these efforts, clean water remained elusive for many, leading to sanitation crises and outbreaks of new diseases. Humans multiplied becoming reservoirs of water themselves, their bodies comprising approximately seventy percent of this vital substance. With each new inhabitant, more water is diverted from the natural cycle, stored within the confines of their bodies. The water being permanently removed from the dwindling reservoirs within the seas and oceans.

This shift in water distribution had far-reaching implications for all life forms. As the water is drawn from natural sources to meet the needs of human populations, ecosystems suffer, with rivers running dry, wetlands shrinking, and wildlife struggling to survive in an increasingly parched landscape.

Natural resources were stretched to their limits to meet the demands of so many people. Forests were cleared for timber and agriculture. Minerals were mined from the earth, and fossil fuels were burned to power industries and transportation networks. The environmental toll of such exploitation was immense. Habitats were destroyed, ecosystems disrupted, and pollution levels soared beyond control.

In the face of such challenges, governments and organizations around the world scrambled to find solutions. Initiatives were launched to promote sustainable agriculture, conserve water resources, and develop renewable energy sources.

Technological innovations, such as vertical farming, hydroponics, and solar power, offered glimpses of a more sustainable future.

In the vast expanse of the cosmos, Earth was a tiny blue dot, teeming with life yet bounded by finite resources. Despite humanity's ingenuity and technological prowess, basic mathematics and science dictated that the planet could only support a population of a certain size before reaching its limits.

The basic numbers around population growth were straightforward. As the number of people increased exponentially, the demand for food and water followed suit. With the Earth's resources growing at a linear pace, they were constrained by factors such as land availability, climate variability, and ecological balance. Eventually, the gap between supply and demand widened to a critical point.

At this juncture, the concept of carrying capacity came into play. Carrying capacity referred to the maximum population size that a given environment could sustain indefinitely without degrading its natural resources. Beyond this threshold, an ecosystem becomes overstressed, leading to depletion of resources, environmental degradation, and collapse. There are ways to increase, or at least hold off the limits of a planet's apocalyptic threshold. These included increasing resource availability, better technology for terraforming, and resource extraction. These efficiencies would incorporate adaptation to different environmental factors and even more sustainable infrastructure. Eventually, no matter how efficient and effective policies become, the depletion of a lifeform becomes the only way forward. The growth much of secondary importance or even an unwarranted effect to survival itself.

For Earth, with its finite landmass, finite water bodies, and finite atmospheric capacity, there existed a clear limit to how many people it could support. Beyond this point, further population growth would only lead to scarcity, competition, and conflict over dwindling resources.

Reality forced humanity to confront a sobering truth: there was a line in the sand, a threshold beyond which population growth could not continue unabated. To exceed this limit was to court disaster, risking the collapse of the natural world, the destabilization of societies, and the potential extinction of the human species.

As time progressed beyond the initial heralding of living longer, there was a realisation that there needed to be a mandatory retirement age so that it could allow those younger people a chance to contribute to society. This would allow them chance to fill in the roles occupied by those older citizens. Conversely, this gave the old stalwarts of society a chance to relax and enjoy fruitful years having fun whilst they were still fit.

This is why at the beginning of the current government rule the mandatory retirement age was set at ninety years old. This forcibly made people retire from any jobs they had and disappear from visibility to enjoy their pinnacle years in luxury. Over time this age was reduced to the benchmark of eighty years which it is today in the year 2123. To this end, there are no longer any people of over eighty years left out in the public on planet Earth, as they have been sent out for retirement. Due to aggressive measures of the governments in the last twenty to thirty years the rate of population growth had slowed significantly. It was now estimated that only around sixteen billion people were currently living on Earth...... if you can call the constant battle and competition for essential resources as "Living"

Chapter 1: The World's Hunger

In the year 2123, London was a sprawling metropolis, stretching far beyond its historical boundaries. Towers of steel and glass pierced the sky, casting long shadows overcrowded streets where hovercars zipped by in a symphony of electric hums. The city pulsed with life, yet beneath its vibrant facade lay a hunger that gnawed at its very core.

Jayden knew hunger all too well. Born into a world where natural food and drink were scarce luxuries, he had grown up in the heart of London's concrete jungle. His childhood memories were not filled with the laughter of picnics in green parks or the taste of freshly picked fruit, but rather the metallic tang of synthesized meals and the sight of endless queues outside ration dispensaries. As the son of a struggling single mother, Jayden learned early on the art of survival in this unforgiving urban landscape. His days were spent navigating the streets, scavenging for scraps to trade or sell in exchange for credits to buy the essentials: water, nutrient supplements, and the occasional treat of synthetic protein bars. On one particularly sweltering afternoon, Jayden found himself trudging through the bustling crowds of Covent Garden. His stomach aching from hunger and growling in protest. His mother had fallen ill from hunger, and their meagre rations were dwindling fast. Desperation clawed at him as he weaved through the throngs of people, his eyes scanning the faces for any opportunity that might offer a reprieve. It was then that he spotted a familiar figure standing by a makeshift market stall nestled between towering skyscrapers. Mr. Patel, the old shopkeeper from the corner of their block, was hunched over a crate of wilted vegetables. His hands were wrinkled after sorting through the sparse offerings.

Jayden approached hesitantly, his heart pounding in his chest. "Mr. Patel, do you have anything... anything at all?" he asked, his voice barely above a whisper.

The old man looked up; his eyes clouded with sorrow. "I'm sorry, Jayden. The drought has been cruel to us all. There's nothing left."

Despair threatened to consume Jayden as he turned away, his thoughts swirling in a maelstrom of hopelessness. How could they survive another day, another week, in a city where even the most necessities were beyond reach?

Just then, as if by some miracle, a voice cut through the clamour of the crowd. "Hey kid, you hungry?"

Jayden turned to see a girl about his age, her dark hair pulled back into a messy ponytail, offering him a small package wrapped in brown paper. He hesitated for a moment, then reached out to accept it, his fingers trembling with anticipation.

"Thanks," he muttered, his voice choked with emotion.

The girl grinned, her eyes sparkling with mischief. "No problem. Just pay it forward, yeah?"

With a nod of gratitude, Jayden unwrapped the package to reveal a small but simple sandwich, its contents a mystery to him. As he took his first bite, he tasted something he had not experienced in years: the unmistakable flavour of real food. He wrapped up the remaining food and saved it as he would share it with his mum later on. For a moment, amid the chaos and scarcity of the city, Jayden's world was filled with the promise of possibility. As he looked up at the endless expanse of towering buildings that loomed overhead, he dared to hope that, just maybe, there was still a chance for a better tomorrow.

As he rounded the next corner, Jayden stumbled upon a scene that brought his heart to a standstill. A group of protesters had gathered in front of the towering gates of a government building, their voices raised in a chorus of anger and desperation. Banners waved defiantly in the air, their slogans a rallying cry for change.

Curiosity piqued, Jayden edged closer, straining to catch snippets of conversation amid the cacophony of noise. The protesters spoke of inequality and injustice, of a world teetering on the brink of collapse while the elite few lived in luxury behind fortified walls.

For a moment, Jayden felt a flicker of hope stir within him. Could this be the catalyst for the change he had long dreamed of? As quickly as it had come, the hope was extinguished by the weight of reality. The odds were stacked against them, and Jayden knew that true change would not come easily.

In despair he turned away from the protest and continued his journey, his footsteps echoing in the empty spaces between the towering skyscrapers. As the sun dipped below the horizon, casting the city in a wash of fiery hues, Jayden could not help but wonder what the future held for him and for the world he called home.

With the population reaching its maximum sustainable level and natural resources dwindling to critical levels, humanity faced a daunting challenge unlike any before. In response, a new world order had emerged. It was one governed by a centralized authority that spanned the entire planet. Gone were the days of national borders and independent governments; the world now operated under the watchful eye of the Global Governance Council (GGC); a body of elected representatives tasked with overseeing the collective welfare of humanity.

The GGC loomed large over the world, its authority extending like the shadow of a colossus across every continent and disappearing ocean. Formed in response to the myriad crises facing humanity. The GGC was heralded as a beacon of hope. A unifying force that promised to steer the course of civilization toward a brighter future.

In theory, the GGC's rule was intended to alleviate the suffering wrought by decades of exploitation and neglect. Its directives aimed to ensure the equitable distribution of resources, the preservation of the environment, and the promotion of social justice. Indeed, some lauded the Council's efforts, pointing to improvements in living standards and advancements in technology as evidence of its benevolent stewardship.

The GGC's influence permeated every aspect of daily life, from education to healthcare to employment, shaping the very fabric of society in its image.

Jayden and his best friend Arianna separately sat in front of their holographic screens; their faces illuminated by the soft glow of their virtual classroom. Outside, the world was a quiet with heavily polluted skies. Within the confines of their digital learning environment, they were transported to a world of knowledge and discovery.

The Global Governance Council had long since taken control of the education system, implementing a strict syllabus designed to meld young minds according to their own agenda. Schooling was now delivered entirely remotely, with students attending virtual classes from the comfort of their own homes.

In this virtual classroom of the future, students are greeted not by flesh-and-blood teachers, but by lifelike AI holograms that guide them through their lessons with precision and expertise. These digital educators are programmed to adapt to each student's unique learning style, providing personalized instruction and support that caters to their individual needs and abilities. With the aid of advanced technologies such as virtual reality and augmented reality, students are transported to immersive learning environments that bring their studies to life in ways never before possible. From exploring ancient civilizations to dissecting virtual organisms, the possibilities for interactive and engaging learning experiences are endless, limited only by the bounds of imagination.

In these futuristic communities, children found companionship and camaraderie not within the confines of their school classrooms, but within the familiar streets and corridors of their own neighbourhoods and buildings. Friendships were almost always forged by the close geographic proximity of their homes. They formed through sports and interest groups that are mostly within the confines of their residential complexes. Bonds were forged that are shaped by shared experiences and common surroundings.

In this world where technology reigns supreme and virtual classrooms are the norm, the physical landscape of the neighbourhood becomes the backdrop for all social interaction and connection. Children gather in parks and playgrounds attached or on top of their buildings. These are the only places where they have chance for real human social interaction with children of their own ages.

These close-knit neighbourhood communities foster a sense of belonging and solidarity among children. Comfort and support is provided within the familiarity of their surroundings. Whether exploring hidden corners of the neighbourhoods, embarking on outdoor adventures, or simply enjoying each other's company. These lasting bonds that endure long after the final bell of the school day has rung, and the virtual classroom closed. In the towering residential skyscraper that loomed over the cityscape, two families occupied neighbouring floors. Jayden's family were on floor 114 and Arianna's family on floor 112. For as long as they could remember, their lives had been intertwined, their families bound by a shared history and a sense of kinship that transcended the concrete confines of their towering abode. In this world the word 'family' seemed to exhibit new definitions as it was not just those people genetically related to each other; but a family was people who lived almost every part of their existence together separated by one or two walls. Whether they were born of the same kin, creed or race was irrelevant as they were family in every sense of the word.

Jayden and Arianna had grown up in the shadow of their skyscraper, their childhood memories filled with the sights and sounds of life in the bustling metropolis. From their respective floors, they had watched the world go by. Their lives intersected in unexpected ways as they navigated the complexities of growing up in the heart of the city. Jayden and Arianna had always felt a close connection. The bond was forged by the shared experiences of their families and the unspoken understanding that they were more than just neighbours. From impromptu playdates in the communal spaces of the skyscraper to chance encounters in the elevator, their paths had crossed countless times over the years. Each interaction leaving an indelible mark on their hearts. Arianna and Jayden both lived with their mum's, and both had similarly lost their dads at a young age. Arianna's dad had been a high powered GGC engineer who had left a visual holographic note one day for her mum detailing how he had moved onto another relationship. Jayden's dad had passed away when he was just a few years old and was not something he liked to talk about. The similarities between them were endless.

For Jayden and Arianna, the GGC education reality was the only learning reality they had ever known. From the moment they were born, their lives had been carefully guided and shaped by the directives of the GGC, their every thought and action dictated by the curriculum they were taught. In the ever-evolving landscape of education, the emphasis on traditional skills such as handwriting has waned, giving way to a new era of learning that prioritized technological literacy and practical skills over outdated methods of communication. For Jayden and Arianna, growing up in a world defined by innovation and automation, the art of handwriting was but a relic of the past. It was but a skill taught only in the most basic form, relegated to the annals of history. They were taught the essentials of numeracy and literacy, but with a twist. While basic arithmetic and reading comprehension were still fundamental components of their education, the focus shifted towards mastering tools and technologies that could perform these tasks with greater efficiency and accuracy.

Instead of spending hours practicing penmanship, Jayden and Arianna learned to navigate digital interfaces and manipulate data using advanced software programs. They honed their problem-solving skills through interactive simulations and real-world applications, leveraging technology to tackle complex mathematical concepts and analytical challenges with ease.

In place of traditional textbooks and worksheets, they were provided with access to vast digital libraries and online resources. Any information they needed or wanted was just a few keystrokes away. From virtual laboratories to immersive learning experiences, the possibilities for exploration and discovery were endless, limited only by the bounds of imagination.

As they progressed through their education, Jayden and Arianna became adept at using these tools and technologies to enhance their learning experience. They leveraged AI assistants, augmented reality, and virtual reality to expand their horizons and deepen their understanding of the world around them.

When they sat through their lessons, Jayden and Arianna could not help but feel a sense of unease creeping over them. They knew that their education was not just about acquiring knowledge, it was about indoctrination, about instilling within them a set of beliefs and values that served the interests of the GGC above all else.

Despite their misgivings, they knew better than to question the status quo. Dissent was not tolerated in this brave new world, and those who dared to challenge the authority of the GGC risked swift and severe punishment. The post-education landscape of had undergone a profound transformation. With advancements in technology, shifts in labour markets, and an ever-increasing human lifespan, the boundaries of learning had expanded far beyond what previous generations could have imagined.

One of the most significant changes was the rise in the compulsory education age to twenty-three. In the early decades of the 21st century, the notion of lifelong learning gained traction as societies grappled with the complexities of a rapidly evolving world. The traditional model of education, which had once culminated in a degree or diploma obtained in early adulthood, no longer sufficed in preparing individuals for the challenges of the modern workforce.

Gone were the days of job hunting and endless interviews. It was a relic of a bygone era replaced by the efficiency of algorithmic assignment. In this brave new world, potential employers no longer relied on outdated methods of recruitment, such as advertising and interviews, to fill vacant positions. Instead, they turned to the vast repositories of data that lay at their fingertips, mining through educational scores, accomplishments, and personality profiles to identify the ideal candidate for each role. It was a world where ones curriculum vitae was established by the system itself and the opportunity to embellish and rephrase areas of life that needed a bit of whitewashing were no longer possible. If you had been in trouble with the authorities or had failed in a key subject, then any potential employer would at best see this flagged out in front of them. Most likely though, the settings on any applicant search would hide the 'criminal record' or 'failed subject' flag and many doors would be closed immediately. Minor transgressions would affect life paths as never before. The doors that would remain to such data 'poor' students would be the kind of doors that most would not choose by their own free will. Those jobs that have little value, high risk and no reward would seek them out. With an almost unlimited pool of possible workers and a relatively small pool of jobs then this had simply become the way of the new world.

For Jayden and Arianna, this system of algorithmic assignment had been an integral part of their lives from a young age. From the moment they entered the educational system, their academic achievements and personality traits were meticulously catalogued and analysed, forming the basis for their future career prospects.

As people graduated into the workforce, they found themselves thrust into roles that had been chosen for them based on the data that had been collected throughout their lives. For Jayden, whose aptitude for analytical thinking and problem-solving had been recognized from an early age, this meant a career in data analysis was likely; a role perfectly suited to his skills and temperament.

As for Arianna, whose creativity and interpersonal skills had been her greatest assets, this meant it highly likely that a career in marketing awaited. A role that would allow her to leverage her talents to their fullest potential.

While the system of algorithmic assignment had its benefits, it was not without its drawbacks. For some, the lack of autonomy in choosing their career path was a source of frustration, a reminder of the limitations imposed by a society governed by algorithms and data. As automation and artificial intelligence reshaped industries and occupations, the demand for highly skilled workers surged. Jobs that required repetitive tasks or routine manual labour became increasingly scarce, while those that demanded critical thinking, creativity, and adaptability rose in prominence. To thrive in this new landscape, individuals needed not only foundational knowledge but also the ability to learn continuously. People would need to acquire new skills and to reinvent themselves throughout their lives.

The decision to extend the compulsory education age reflected this shift in societal priorities. No longer was education seen as a finite period of instruction followed by a lifetime of work. Instead, it was recognized as a lifelong journey, an ongoing process of discovery and growth that continued well into adulthood and beyond.

Some did not make it all the way to the end of the compulsory learning. Arianna and Jayden grew up with a girl called Mandy who was exceptionally gifted and bright and always scored higher than anyone they had ever known in engineering and mathematical subjects. She was taken away from the educational system at the age of just Thirteen and assumed to be assigned some role in society due to her sheer intelligence and potential. On the other end of the scale there were peers to Jayden and Arianna who were rather lost to the educational world. It was hard to envisage a bright future in any way post-compulsory education had drawn to a close.

As their final year of schooling drew to its end, Jayden and Arianna found themselves grappling with a sense of uncertainty about their future. They had been conditioned to believe that success in life was synonymous with obedience to the GGC. Deep down, they could not shake the feeling that there was more to life than what they had been taught.

For now, they had no choice but to play along, to toe the line and conform to the expectations placed upon them. In a world where every aspect of their lives was controlled by an all-powerful government, rebellion was not an option. As they logged off from their virtual classroom and prepared to face another day in the dystopian reality of their existence, Jayden and Arianna could not help but wonder what lay beyond the confines of their digital prison. Was there still hope for a better future, or were they destined to remain forever trapped in the clutches of the GGC, their dreams of freedom nothing more than a distant fantasy?

Chapter 2: The Silent Exodus

For all the GGC's promises of progress and prosperity, there lingered an uneasy undertone. It was a whisper of dissent that dared to question the Council's motives and methods. Rumours circulated in hushed tones, tales of dissenters disappearing in the dead of night. Tales of protests violently suppressed, of secrets buried beneath layers of propaganda and misinformation.

Jayden went for a walk to clear his head and made his way through the bustling streets of London; he could not shake the feeling of unease that gnawed at his conscience. The city thrummed with the energy of progress, its skyline ablaze with the lights of progress and innovation. Beneath the surface of prosperity lay a shadow; a shadow cast by the omnipresent gaze of the GGC. Its watchful eye ever vigilant and ever unyielding. For all its promises of unity and harmony, the GGC's rule marked by a chilling sense of control. It was a control that reached into the very depths of people's hearts and minds. Their thoughts and desires shaped to fit the Council's vision of the world. Though the streets may have been seen to be free from crime and poverty, they were also devoid of freedom and autonomy, a trade-off that many were willing to make in exchange for the illusion of security.

Everyone lived under the shadow of the GGC, its influence shaping his world in ways both seen and unseen. As Jayden looked to the horizon, where the sun dipped beneath the skyline in a blaze of fiery light, he knew that there must be more out there than they had been told and many things to discover. If there were those who dared to defy the Council's tyranny, there remained a glimmer of hope. A hope that one day, the people of the world would rise and reclaim their destiny from the grasp of those who sought to control it.

Beneath the veneer of prosperity and progress, a clandestine directive lurked within the depths of the Global Governance Council (GGC). It was hidden away from the prying eyes of the populace. Rumours whispered of a shadowy underworld operation; a macabre practice known in the shadows as the "Silent Exodus." It was a chilling truth shrouded in mystery, an unsettling reality that sent shivers down the spines of those who dared to contemplate its implications.

Among the whispers that echoed through the alleys and corridors of the city, none were more sinister than those concerning the fate of those deemed to be at their retirement age. Those whose presence deemed a burden upon the carefully balanced scales of resource allocation and population control. It was said by some that upon reaching the age of eighty, individuals would vanish without a trace. Their existence erased from the collective consciousness as if they had never existed at all. This of course was a completely opposing view and picture to that of the GGC whom explained and advertised the retirement process at every opportunity.

Jayden had heard the rumours, of course. Those of tales spun by the desperate and the disillusioned, whispered in hushed tones behind closed doors. Like so many others, he had dismissed them as nothing more than the fevered imaginings of a society haunted by the spectre of uncertainty. The GGC conveyed its own message about being the age of retirement for people to go to their own utopia and enjoy their later life days, but some people still doubted this as is the nature of questioning minds.

One day, as he made his way through the streets around old Canary Wharf where Jayden stumbled upon a scene that would shatter his illusions and plunge him into a world of darkness from which there would be no escape. It was a quiet alley, tucked away from the prying eyes of surveillance cameras and patrolling guards. It was a forgotten corner of the city where the whispers of the past lingered like ghosts in the shadows. There, amid the crumbling facades and rusting metal, Jayden stumbled upon a group of figures huddled together in the darkness.

At first, he hesitated, his heart pounding in his chest as he watched the clandestine gathering unfold before him. As curiosity overcame caution, Jayden edged closer, his senses attuned to the faint murmur of voices that drifted through the air like a haunting melody. What he witnessed in that alley would haunt him for the rest of his days. It was a chilling tableau of secrecy and subterfuge that revealed the true extent of the GGC's reach. Before his eyes, a group of elderly individuals were led away by masked figures clad in black, their frail forms disappearing into the depths of the night like wraiths fleeing the dawn.

Intrigued by the mysterious scene unfolding before him, Jayden narrowed his eyes and leaned in closer, his curiosity piqued by the enigmatic figures and their secretive demeanour. Who were they, and where were they taking the elderly individuals? Why the need for masks and secrecy? Jayden's mind reeled as he struggled to comprehend the gravity of what he had witnessed. Was the silent exodus no mere rumour? Was a horrifying reality, a twisted manifestation of the GGC's insidious agenda? What fate awaited those who were taken, he could only guess, for the truth remained shrouded in darkness, obscured by layers of deception and deceit.

"Don't worry son...," said a well-dressed businessman who saw him looking on.

"I know those people and they were all late to the retirement processing facility. Those guards are just ensuring that they do not miss their transport."

"But why all the masks and dark clothing?" said Jayden.

"Would you want anyone to know that you worked for the GGC? It helps them keep anonymous in society so they can continue amongst us all," the man explained.

Upon this wisdom, as he stood frozen in the alley, the weight of the revelation and the man's thoughts were settling upon his shoulders like a heavy cloak, Jayden did not know what to believe. Were the events good for these people or was it something else, he just did not know. Jayden decided to go home and chat with his Mum.

As Jayden hurried through the night-time streets of London, his mind raced with conflicting thoughts and emotions. His heart pounding in his chest with a sense of urgency and uncertainty. The image of the masked figures leading away the elderly individuals lingered in his mind, casting a shadow of doubt over his perception of reality. With each step, the darkness seemed to close in around him, enveloping him in a shroud of uncertainty and fear. Was what had been witnessed real, or merely a figment of his imagination? If it was real, what did it mean for the future of the city, and indeed, the world?

Racing against his beating heart, Jayden's thoughts swirled with questions and doubts, his mind consumed by the weight of the unknown. He felt that he had to act quickly if he were to uncover the truth behind the silent exodus but did not know where to turn or how to get the answers he sought. With each passing moment, the city seemed to grow more ominous, its streets lined with shadows and secrets that whispered of hidden dangers lurking just beyond the edge of perception. Jayden's senses were heightened, his every instinct screaming at him to turn back and flee from the darkness that threatened to consume him.

As Jayden approached his towering apartment block, a sense of unease settled over him like a suffocating shroud. Every shadow seemed to leer at him with malevolent intent, each whisper of the wind carrying a sinister undertone that sent shivers down his spine. He cast furtive glances over his shoulder, half-expecting to find himself pursued by unseen forces, but the streets remained eerily deserted, devoid of any signs of life. With a quickening pace, Jayden entered the lobby of the apartment block, his heart pounding in his chest with each step. The fluorescent lights overhead flickered ominously, casting strange shadows on the walls that danced like spectres in the darkness. Ignoring the chill that crept up his spine, Jayden hurried towards the elevator, his footsteps echoing in the empty space.

The doors slid shut behind him, Jayden's breath caught in his throat, his pulse quickening with a mixture of anticipation and dread. The interior of the elevator was bathed in a dim, knowing glow, the air heavy with the scent of unpleasant decay and musty carpet. Jayden watched the floors tick by on the display panel, each passing moment bringing him closer to his destination. With each floor that passed, Jayden's anxiety grew, his mind awash with thoughts of what awaited him on the 114th floor. Would he ever find answers to the mysteries that had plagued him, or would he be met with only more questions and uncertainty? He could feel the weight of the unknown pressing down on him like a physical burden, threatening to crush him beneath its weight. As the elevator reached its destination and the doors slid open with a soft hiss, Jayden's fear gave way to elation, his heart soaring with inner glee. He had made it to the 114th floor, the pinnacle of his journey.

As Jayden stepped out of the elevator onto the corridor, his heart raced with a mixture of relief and apprehension. The familiar hallway stretched out before him, bathed in minimal lighting, but there was no time to linger in its familiarity. With hurried steps, he made his way towards his family's apartment, his mind still reeling from the events of the evening.

As he reached the door, Jayden pressed his fingers against the biometric scanner, the device whirring to life as it recognized his unique fingerprint. Further security ensured the authenticity of his iris scan. For what seemed and eternity and with a soft beep, the door unlocked, swinging open to reveal the safety of home beyond.

With a sigh, Jayden sank onto the edge of his bed, his thoughts still swirling with the events of the evening. He knew that he needed to calm his racing mind, to find a sense of peace and clarity amidst the turmoil that had gripped him. Closing his eyes, he focused on his breathing, allowing the rhythmic rise and fall of his chest to soothe his frayed nerves.

Slowly, the tension began to melt away, replaced by a sense of calm and tranquillity that washed over him like a gentle tide. In the stillness of his room, Jayden found solace, the worries and fears of the outside world fading into the background as he surrendered himself to the quietude of the moment.

After a time, Jayden rose from his bed, his mind clear and his heart lightened by the weight of his burdens lifted. He knew that he could not face the challenges ahead alone, that he needed the support and guidance of those who loved him most. With a determined resolve, he made his way to the living room, where he found his Mum sitting alone on the sofa, lost in thought.

As the evening settled around them like a familiar embrace, Jayden found himself seated beside his mother once again, the soft glow of the lamp casting a warm halo over their conversation. Tonight, he carried a weighty question in his heart, one that had been gnawing at him for days.

"Mum," Jayden began, his voice soft but tinged with uncertainty, "I need to talk to you about something... something that's been bothering me."

His mother turned to him; her eyes filled with a gentle understanding that soothed the edges of his worry. "Of course, Jayden," she replied, her voice a calming presence in the quiet room. "You know you can always talk to me. What is on your mind?"

"It's about the retirement program," Jayden confessed, his words hesitant as he struggled to find the right way to explain his thoughts. "You know, the one where people over eighty are sent to live out their days?"

His mother nodded; her expression attentive as she listened to him carefully.

"Well, I've been thinking about it," Jayden continued, his words gathering momentum as he spoke. "And I can't shake this feeling that there's something... off about it. People are disappearing, Mum. They're being taken away, and nobody seems to know where they're going or why."

His mother's brow furrowed in concern, a flicker of worry crossing her features as she processed his words. "That does sound concerning, Jayden," she replied, her voice soft but tinged with unease. "But I'm sure there must be a reason for it. The authorities wouldn't just send people away without cause."

Jayden nodded, his thoughts whirling with a mix of doubt and determination. "I know, mum," he admitted, his voice tinged with frustration. "But what if there's more to it than they're telling us? What if... what if there is something they are not saying?"

His mother reached out, her hand finding his and giving it a gentle squeeze. "I understand your concerns, Jayden," she said, her voice a soothing balm against his worries. "But sometimes, things are not always as they seem. It's important to trust in the system, to have faith that those in charge have our best interests at heart."

Jayden sighed, a heavy weightlifting from his shoulders as he absorbed his mother's words. "I suppose you're right, mum," he conceded, a sense of reluctant acceptance settling over him. "But it's hard not to wonder, you know? To question whether there's more to the story than meets the eye."

His mother smiled; her eyes filled with a quiet wisdom that transcended the confines of their small, cozy living room. "It's natural to have questions, Jayden," she replied, her voice gentle but firm. "But sometimes, the answers we seek are not always easy to find. Sometimes, we must trust in the unknown and have faith that all will be revealed in time."

Jayden's mother was a woman of quiet strength, her gentle demeanour belying the inner turmoil that often weighed heavily on her heart. She had always been a loving and caring presence in Jayden's life, her unwavering support a beacon of light in the darkest of times. Beneath her warm smile and tender embrace, there lingered a sadness, a quiet ache born of dreams deferred and hopes unfulfilled.

Once, she had harboured dreams of a life filled with adventure and possibility, of exploring distant lands and chasing her passions with unwavering determination. Life with its unpredictable twists and turns, had other plans for her, leading her down a path fraught with hardship and disappointment.

Since Jayden's father had had a traffic accident and had passed away a few years after Jayden was born, she had devoted herself wholeheartedly to caring for him, her days consumed by the relentless demands of his illness and the crushing weight of uncertainty that hung over their future. When he had passed away, leaving her to shoulder the burden of grief and loss alone, she had soldiered on with quiet resolve, her spirit battered but unbroken. When Jayden's father, Harry, was killed it was a day like any other, filled with laughter and joy as a young Jayden and his father embarked on a routine trip across the city. In an instant, everything then changed. A space car appeared dangerously spin out of control due to its reckless speed and hurtled towards the ground below with an agonising bang. Jayden's father, his strong and steady presence a pillar of strength in his young life, did everything in his power to protect his son, but it was not enough for him too. The impact was catastrophic, the force of the collision tearing their world apart and leaving Jayden alone in the aftermath, but alive as Harry had sacrificed himself for the future of his son. Jayden never really had chance for a goodbye, just a knowing look from his father as they all knew what was to happen and is something that the five-year-old Jayden passed down to the Jayden of this very day. A haunting picture that the mind would never shake.

In the days and weeks that followed his father's death, Jayden's Mum struggled to make sense of the tragedy that had befallen her family. The loss of her husband left a void in her heart that seemed impossible to fill, a gaping wound that refused to heal. As the years passed, the pain of his loss only seemed to grow deeper, casting a long shadow over her life. Perhaps the most intriguing part of all was the fact that the culprit of the accident was never found. Despite countless investigations and exhaustive efforts to uncover the truth, the circumstances surrounding the accident remained shrouded in mystery, leaving Jayden and his family to grapple with unanswered questions and unspoken fears. Even the space car remains completely disappeared before Harry was officially pronounced dead. It seemed like an accident that took on no blame.

What is more remarkable in the age of constant technology and monitoring systems is that the incident was seemingly never captured on any device, camera or by any witness and is one of a very small number of incidents across the whole of what is still referred to as England, which remained unsolved. Only one memory of that day remained in what was a five-year-old boy's head. That of a very distinctive tree shaped birthmark that he saw when the driver of the car left the death scene in a hurry with a bleeding ripped shirt revealing his bare chest. Jayden often drew the same mark to this very day as it was a thing he could never forget.

For Jayden, the loss of his father was more than just a personal tragedy. It became a defining moment that shaped the course of his life. It fuelled his determination to seek justice, to unravel the secrets of the past, and to ensure that no other family would have to endure the pain and heartache that he had experienced.

Yet despite the hardships she had faced, Jayden's mother remained a pillar of strength and resilience, her love for her son a driving force that propelled her forward through even the darkest of days. She poured her heart and soul into nurturing him, instilling in him the values of kindness and compassion, of resilience in the face of adversity. As Jayden poured out his fears and doubts, his mum listened with a heart heavy with empathy, her own worries momentarily set aside in her devotion to her son. She knew the world could be a harsh and unforgiving place, filled with dangers and uncertainties, but she was determined to shield Jayden from harm, to give him the chance to build a better future for himself. In that moment, as she looked into Jayden's eyes, she felt a surge of fierce determination coursing through her veins. She would gladly sacrifice her own life if it meant securing a brighter future for her son if it meant sparing him from the pain and hardship she had endured. For Jayden's mum, like most mothers, it was a sacred bond, a solemn vow to protect and nurture her child at all costs. She would stand as a shield against the storms of life, a steadfast guardian watching over him with unwavering love and devotion.

Chapter 3: The Visionary's Dilemma

High above the bustling streets of New York, within the hallowed halls of the Global Governance Council (GGC), Reebus Longmuir sat upon his throne of authority. His gaze fixed upon the holographic displays that flickered before him. To the world, he was the visionary leader of a new era. It was a beacon of hope in a time of uncertainty. He was also known only as Reebus to each and all with his surname lost in his descriptive recognition of being above a mere mortal and within the godly sub sphere. Behind closed doors, Reebus grappled with a burden that few could comprehend. A burden born of noble intentions twisted by the machinations of power and necessity.

As the leader of the GGC, Reebus bore the weight of the world upon his shoulders. It was a burden he carried with a solemn determination that belied the turmoil within. For years, he had watched as humanity teetered on the brink of collapse, its resources stretched to the breaking point by the relentless march of progress and population growth. In the face of such dire circumstances, Reebus had made a fateful decision; one that would shape the course of history for generations to come. The silent exodus, as it came to be known, was Reebus's brainchild. It became a radical solution to the existential threats facing humanity. In his eyes, it was an act of mercy and a way to alleviate the suffering of the elderly and ensure the survival of future generations. Though the decision weighed heavily upon his conscience, Reebus remained steadfast in his belief that it was the right course of action for the greater good. Even as he implemented the silent exodus, Reebus knew that the truth could not be revealed, not yet at least. Under the guise of benevolence, the GGC launched a series of elaborate media campaigns, painting a picture of paradise on a nearby residential planet. It was a utopia where the elderly could live out their days in peace and tranquillity.

As Reebus watched the propaganda unfold, a pang of guilt occasionally gnawed at his conscience. It reminded him of the lies and half-truths that he had woven to conceal the dark reality of the silent exodus. With each passing day, the weight of necessity bore down upon him like a leaden shroud, driving him ever deeper into the depths of deception. It was so that Reebus carried the burden of his conscience like a scar upon his soul. It was a reminder of the sacrifices he had made in the name of progress. For though he genuinely believed that he was doing the world a favour by getting rid of the old, the truth remained a bitter pill to swallow. It was a truth that would consume any mere mortal from within.

As he looked out upon the world he sought to save, Reebus knew that the road ahead would be a difficult one. He would not falter in his quest to secure humanity's future, even if it meant sacrificing his own soul in the process. For in the end, the weight of history would judge him not by his intentions, but by the consequences of his actions. Only time would tell whether he had made the right choice. The choice for himself, for humanity, and for the world that hung in the balance.

Reebus, the leader of the Global Governance Council (GGC), was a man forged in the crucible of tragedy. Born in the ashes of what was once known as Chicago, he had witnessed firsthand the unforgiving cruelty of a world in turmoil. A world where hope was a fleeting illusion, torn asunder by the relentless march of fate.

As a child, Reebus had known nothing but hardship and loss. His parents, weary survivors of the chaos that had consumed their city, had struggled to provide for their family in a world teetering on the brink of collapse. Despite their best efforts, tragedy followed them like a shadow, leaving scars upon their souls that would never fully heal.

The turning point came when Reebus was just a boy. It was a day that would forever alter the course of his destiny. A catastrophic event, shrouded in mystery and sorrow, ripped through the heart of Chicago, leaving devastation in its wake.

The day began like any other in the bustling city. It was a vibrant tapestry of life woven through the streets and alleys. The skyline reaching for the heavens like a monument to human ingenuity. For Reebus, a boy of ten, it was a day like any other with the simple joys of childhood. He was blissfully unaware of the storm clouds that loomed on the horizon. As the sun dipped below the skyline in a blaze of fiery light, the world was plunged into darkness that would forever alter the course of Reebus's destiny.

It began with a rumble - a low, ominous growl that reverberated through the streets like a distant thunderstorm. At first, Reebus paid it little mind, dismissing it as nothing more than the echoes of the city's ceaseless activity. As the rumble grew louder, morphing into a deafening roar that shook the very foundations of the earth, fear crept into his heart like a spectre in the night. It was then, without further warning, the sky split open. It was a blinding flash of light followed by a deafening explosion that shattered the tranquillity of the night. In an instant, chaos erupted as buildings crumbled and streets turned to rubble, the city consumed by a maelstrom of destruction and despair. With each step he took, Reebus surveyed the wreckage, his heart heavy with the weight of uncertainty and fear. His parents, his only connection to the world he once knew, were missing. Their fate unknown in the wake of the seismic event that had engulfed the city. Amidst the rubble and debris, Reebus searched for any sign of his parents. He looked for a photograph, a memento, anything that would offer a glimmer of hope in the darkness that surrounded him. The city offered no solace in this search; no answers to the questions that plagued his mind. As he ventured deeper into the heart of the destruction, Reebus encountered scenes of unimaginable horror. He noted buildings reduced to rubble, streets littered with rubble, and the echoes of distant sirens wailing in the distance. No sign of his parents was to be found, which would feed his unwavering resolve in life in an endless quest for answers.

As the hours turned into days and the days into weeks, Reebus's hope began to wane, his spirit battered by the relentless onslaught of despair. With each passing moment, the realization began to sink in. Their chances of finding his parents alive grew slimmer with each passing day. At one point, Reebus stumbled upon a scene of unspeakable horror. He came across a lone survivor, barely clinging to life amidst the rubble, their arm flailing in a desperate plea for help. For a fleeting moment, Reebus's heart quickened with the hope that he had finally found a sign of life, a beacon of hope amidst the devastation that surrounded him.

Then, as he drew closer, the reality of the situation began to sink in. It was a realization that filled him not with compassion, but with a cold sense of detachment. For the survivor before him was not his parent, nor were they anyone he knew. They were a stranger, a nameless face lost amidst the chaos of a city in ruins. In that moment, Reebus felt a surge of disgust, a visceral reaction born not of cruelty, but of disillusionment. For in the wake of the tragedy that had befallen Chicago, he had come to understand the harsh realities of survival. The brutal calculus of life and death that governed the shattered remnants of civilization.

It was then with a nonplussed resignation, Reebus turned away from the survivor, their cries for help fading into the background awaiting their inevitable fate with death. He continued his solitary journey with his own purpose. In the silence that followed, he grappled with the weight of his decision, the echoes of his actions reverberating through the depths of his soul.

The cause and reasons for such a seismic destruction were never really understood or explained and left the entire world asking questions. This was the early days of the GGC throughout the world and the world media seemed to brush the events aside as a mere accident or electrical storm triggering an earthquake. A sense of mystery remained to those who were present especially Reebus himself.

Amid the aftermath of chaos, Reebus found himself torn alone and without family. It was a fleeting moment of panic as he was swept away by the tide of humanity, lost amidst the fear and confusion. When the dust finally settled, he was alone; utterly alone in a world turned upside down. Reebus wandered the shattered streets of Chicago, a ghost amidst the ruins of his former life. The once vibrant city had become a desolate wasteland, its skyline reduced to a twisted mesh of steel and concrete. Within the rubble, he still desperately searched for any sign of his family if nothing else but to give him a glimmer of hope in a world consumed by darkness.

With no one left to turn to, Reebus learned to fend for himself, to navigate the treacherous streets of the city with the skill of a seasoned survivor. With each passing day, the scars of his past grew deeper, embedding themselves into the very fabric of his being. Reebus roamed as a free spirit, his steps guided by the rhythm of the city and the whispers of the wind. Reebus refused to succumb to despair. With a steely resolve born of necessity, he focused all of his energy on survival, channelling every ounce of his strength and determination into ensuring his own existence in a world that had turned against him. For Reebus, every day was a battle. It was a struggle for food and water in a land where such necessities had become scarce commodities. He scoured the desolate streets and crumbling buildings in search of anything that could sustain him, his survival instincts sharpened by the harsh realities of life in the aftermath of catastrophe. With each passing day, Reebus grew stronger, his resilience tempered by the crucible of adversity. He learned to navigate the treacherous landscape of the ruined city with the skill of a seasoned survivor, avoiding danger at every turn and seizing every opportunity for sustenance and shelter. Within this struggle for survival, Reebus was changed forever, with the beginnings of the force of nature he remains to this very day.

His freedom wondering the Chicago streets was short-lived, a fleeting illusion shattered by the sudden arrival of the GGC guards who descended upon him like shadows cloaked in darkness. As Reebus moved cautiously through the desolate streets that day, his senses were alert to any sign of danger. He suddenly found himself surrounded by a group of GGC guards clad in ominous black uniforms. Their faces were obscured by dark masks, their movements swift and purposeful as they closed in on him with menacing intent. With a surge of adrenaline, Reebus instinctively braced himself for confrontation, his muscles tensing as he prepared to defend himself against his would-be captors. As the guards advanced, their numbers overwhelming, Reebus realized the futility of resistance. With a swift motion, the guards moved to restrain him, their hands grasping at his arms with an iron grip that left him powerless to resist. Despite efforts to break free, Reebus found himself overwhelmed by the sheer force of their numbers. His struggles proving futile against their relentless advance. Desperation fuelled his actions as he fought tooth and nail to regain freedom. His mind racing with thoughts of escape back to his reality. Try as he might, Reebus could not escape from the ironclad grip of the GGC guards; their combined strength and determination far surpassing his own. Finally with a merciless hand, they seized Reebus, crushing his spirit as they dragged him away from the familiar streets of his home. In the blink of an eye his life was irrevocably changed. His fate now bound to the whims of those who lurked in the shadows, their motives hidden behind a veil of secrecy. It was a path in which Reebus would eventually succeed and later flourish.

As Reebus swiftly rose through the ranks of the GGC, his past always remained a closely guarded secret. This was a testament to the resilience of the human spirit, and also a reminder of the darkness that lurked within the depths of his soul. He became a man hardened by tragedy. He was a man driven by heartbreak with a hardened stone in place of where a heart once lived.

Soon after his capture, his first role within the GGC was as a lowly guard. He was tasked with enforcing the organization's will with little regard for the consequences. Reebus was not content to remain a mere pawn in the grand scheme of things. He saw an opportunity where others saw only servitude. With each passing day, Reebus honed his skills and sharpened his intellect, learning the intricacies of the GGC's operations and forging alliances with those who could further his ambitions. He worked tirelessly, seizing every opportunity for advancement, and leveraging his talents to climb the ranks of the organization with unparalleled speed and efficiency. As he ascended through the hierarchy of the GGC, Reebus proved himself to be a master of manipulation and strategy, adept at navigating the treacherous waters of politics and power. He cultivated a network of allies and supporters, using his charm and charisma to win over even the most sceptical of adversaries. As Reebus ascended to the highest echelons of power where he became a figure of authority and fear. He was a leader whose ruthless pragmatism was matched only by his unwavering resolve. His decisions were made swiftly, and he ruled with supreme confidence, brooking no dissent or disobedience, for he had seen firsthand the results of weakness and hesitation.

Beneath the facade of strength and certainty, there still lingered a shadow of doubt and regret which haunted Reebus's every waking moment. For as much as he tried to bury the pain of his past, it remained a constant companion, a reminder of the frailty of hope and the harsh realities of a world consumed by chaos.

As he looked out upon the world he sought to govern, Reebus knew that the path ahead would be uneven. He would have many bends and obstacles in the road before him. Though the scars of his journey may never fully heal, they would serve as a testament to the strength of the human spirit; a strength that would endure long after he was gone.

From politicians to labourers, from intellectuals to everyday citizens, there was a sense of collective relief and support of having Reebus at the helm of the GGC. What set Reebus apart from his predecessors was his unwavering commitment to the greater good, his willingness to listen to the concerns of the people, and his determination to enact meaningful change that would benefit society as a whole. To them he did not seem to be driven by personal ambition or greed, but by a genuine desire to make the world a better place for future generations.

Under Reebus's leadership, the GGC had undergone a profound transformation, embracing transparency and accountability in its operations, and prioritizing the well-being of humanity above all else. His policies and initiatives were met with widespread acclaim, as people from every corner of the globe rallied behind his vision for a more just and equitable world. His retirement policy was the political jewel in the crown.

Chapter 4: The Illusion of Hope

In the corridors of power within the Global Governance Council (GGC), whispers of a grand endeavour echoed like a distant melody. It was a symphony of ambition and possibility that promised to reshape the destiny of humanity. It was known as the Space Exploration Program, a monumental undertaking aimed at unlocking the secrets of the cosmos and securing the future of civilization.

For decades, the GGC had poured untold resources into the exploration of space, driven by a singular vision of finding other planets within the solar system capable of supporting life in a manner akin to Earth. It was a quest born of necessity. It was a desperate bid to escape the confines of a world on the brink of collapse and forge a new future among the stars.

Despite the tireless efforts of countless scientists and explorers, the Space Exploration Program had never achieved its desired goal. Time and again, expeditions launched into the void had returned empty-handed, their hopes dashed against the cold, unyielding expanse of space. Within the halls of power, the truth was carefully concealed behind a veil of propaganda and misinformation. The GGC spun tales of successful missions and groundbreaking discoveries, painting a picture of progress and achievement that belied the stark reality of failure.

To the people of Earth, the Space Exploration Program was heralded as a triumph. It was a testament to the ingenuity and resilience of humanity in the face of adversity. After all there had been one very early success in Reebus's time in charge of the program; the remarkable discovery of what was referred to as the retirement planet, 'Serenity 1', back in the early days of its existence. Media campaigns extolled the virtues of exploration and discovery, portraying a future filled with promise and possibility.

Behind closed doors, the truth was far more sobering. The harsh realities of space exploration with the vast distances, the inhospitable environments as well as the countless obstacles, and unknown unknowns had proven insurmountable. Dreams of a new frontier were shattered upon the rocks of despair. The charade continued unabated, driven by a need to maintain the illusion of progress and prosperity. In a world plagued by scarcity and uncertainty, hope was a precious commodity. It was a fragile thread that bound together the fabric of society and kept the darkness at bay.

As Reebus, the leader of the GGC, looked out upon the world he governed, he knew that the Space Exploration Program was more than just a quest for knowledge. It was hope in a world consumed by chaos. Although the truth may have been obscured by lies and half-truths, the illusion of hope remained a powerful force. Something that would endure long after the echoes of deception had faded into the void.

The Space Exploration Program was the crown jewel in the Global Governance Council's ambitious agenda. It was a bold endeavour aimed at unlocking the mysteries of the cosmos and securing the future of humanity. At its core lay a simple yet audacious goal: to find other planets within the solar system capable of supporting life in a manner akin to Earth.

As Reebus, soon discovered, the quest for habitable planets was full of challenges and obstacles that tested the limits of human ingenuity and resolve.

The first hurdle lay in the vastness of space itself. It was a yawning expanse of darkness and emptiness that stretched beyond the horizon of human comprehension. To explore such unfathomable distances required technology beyond anything humanity had ever conceived. A forever daunting task that demanded innovation and sacrifice on a scale never seen. For the people of Earth, the nearest solar system beyond our own, Alpha Centauri. This lies a staggering 4.37 light-years away. To put this into perspective, one light-year is approximately 5.88 trillion miles (9.46 trillion kilometres). So, the distance to Alpha Centauri is roughly 25.6 trillion miles (41.3 trillion kilometres). This immense distance had always presented a significant barrier to human exploration and travel, a challenge that had to be overcome to cement in place the key directives of the GGC.

Even with the most advanced spacecraft at their disposal, the GGC's expeditions into the void yielded few tangible results. These marvels of technology were feats of ingenuity, capable of traversing the vast expanses of space with unparalleled speed and precision. Equipped with state-of-the-art propulsion systems and cutting-edge navigation, they were the vanguards of humanity's exploration of the cosmos. Spacecraft were marvels of engineering, capable of achieving velocities that defied comprehension. Utilizing advanced propulsion methods such as hyper drives and ion engines, they could reach speeds that approached a significant fraction of the speed of light. This allowed traversal of vast distances in relatively short periods, allowing the bridging the gap between distant stars, and unlocking the secrets of the universe. Even these incredible machines were bound by the limitations of technology and the sheer scale of the cosmos. Despite their unparalleled speed and capabilities, they were still subject to the constraints of physics and the immense distances they needed to cover. The vastness of space also posed a formidable challenge to even the most advanced spacecraft, requiring meticulous planning and precise navigation to progress safely through the void. Even then with the best and most comprehensive planning there still remained a large amount of luck with every element of any exploration. It was like throwing darts into the vast expanse of the cosmos, each mission a dart hurled into the void. The hopes dependent of hitting a bullseye on a planet suitable for supporting human life. Considering each dart is affected by celestial objects, weather, malfunctions, and other unforeseen dramatics, it was not a game for the easily downhearted to be a part of. In reality, the universe is such a vast and largely uncharted territory, with countless planets and celestial bodies scattered across the void, each shrouded in mystery and uncertainty. Just like the throwing of darts blindfolded, space exploration is a game of chance, a cosmic lottery where the odds are stacked against you. For every planet that holds the promise of a new beginning, there are countless others that are inhospitable to life. There are limitless barren wastelands devoid of the conditions necessary for survival.

The space experts and finest minds in existence instead used a two-stage approach to exploration. Firstly, establishing and finding possibilities for planets that might have a chance of supporting ecosystems like our own. Second was more based on the old age lottery system; throw the darts in as many directions as you can and just hope that one of them will hit the target.

"If you buy more tickets then you have more chance of winning," as Reebus put it.

While the chances of finding a planet suitable for supporting human life may have seemed slim, the potential rewards are immeasurable. Each new data discovery added to the chances of finding a new home. Hope in the darkness of space, where humanity can thrive and flourish in harmony with the cosmos. Time and again, probes and rovers sent to distant planets returned with data that painted a bleak picture. Data that told of barren landscapes and toxic atmospheres, devoid of the conditions necessary to sustain life as we know it.

The greatest challenge of all lay in the very definition of "habitable." What did it mean for a planet to support life in a manner akin to Earth? Was it simply a matter of physical conditions, temperature, atmosphere, and water, or were there other, more elusive factors at play?

As Reebus himself grappled with these questions, he came to realize that the search for habitable planets was not just a scientific mission, it was a philosophical one as well. For in their quest to find a new home among the stars, humanity was forced to confront the fundamental questions of existence, questions that transcended the boundaries of science and delved into the very essence of what it meant to be alive.

As the GGC's expeditions into the void continued, Reebus found himself caught between the harsh realities of the present and the tantalizing promise of the future. The quest for habitable planets was more than just a desire; it was a symbol of humanity's indomitable spirit, a testament to our boundless curiosity and unyielding determination.

Reebus remained steadfast in his belief that one day, humanity would find its place among the stars. He believed that in the endless expanse of th`e cosmos, there existed a world of possibilities; a world where the dreams of yesterday could become the reality of tomorrow. No matter the challenges that lay ahead, Reebus would stop at nothing to see those dreams realized, for the future of humanity depended on it.

Reebus sat in his office within the towering spires of the GGC headquarters, a sense of gravity weighing upon his shoulders as he prepared to address Imelda Stravus, one of his most trusted advisors. The Space Exploration Program and the silent exodus were topics of immense importance, and Reebus knew that he needed to tread carefully. Imelda entered the room, her expression grave as she took a seat opposite Reebus. She was a woman of keen intellect and unwavering loyalty, qualities that had earned her a place at Reebus's side in the highest echelons of power.

"Thank you for meeting with me, Imelda," Reebus began, his voice measured and composed. "I trust you are aware of the recent setbacks we've encountered with the Space Exploration Program."

Imelda nodded; her brow furrowed in concern. "Yes, Reebus. It is disheartening, to say the least. Our efforts to find habitable planets have yielded little success thus far."

Reebus sighed, a heavy weight settling upon his chest. "Indeed. Yet, we cannot afford to lose hope. The Space Exploration Program is more than just a scientific task, it is a symbol of progress and possibility. It is something that the world needs to look positively on."

Imelda nodded in agreement, her eyes reflecting the same determination that burned within Reebus's soul. "I understand, Reebus. But what about the silent exodus? Are we to continue with the plan, as people are starting to ask a lot of questions?"

Reebus hesitated for a moment, his mind grappling with the weight of his decision. "Yes, Imelda. We must continue with the silent exodus, for the sake of peace and stability on our planet."

Imelda's brow furrowed in confusion. "But Reebus, the truth about the silent exodus, about what truly happens to those who are taken..."

Reebus held up a hand, cutting her off before she could finish. "I know, Imelda. The truth is hard, but we cannot afford to let it destroy the delicate balance we have worked so hard to maintain. The people need to believe that we are doing what is best for them, even if it means keeping certain truths hidden."

Imelda's expression softened, understanding dawning in her eyes. "I see, Reebus. It is a difficult decision, but I trust your judgment. We must do whatever it takes to ensure the survival of humanity, even if it means sacrificing our own ideals in the process."

Reebus nodded, a sense of resolve settling over him like a mantle of steel. "Thank you, Imelda. Your unwavering support means more to me than you know. Together, we will navigate these turbulent waters and lead humanity into a new era of prosperity and progress, as we see fit." As Reebus and Imelda reflected on the evolving landscape of their responsibilities, they came to a key mutual decision. The time had come to shift their focus towards more pressing and urgent matters, and that someone else should take the reins of the Space Exploration Program.

"It's time for a change," Reebus remarked, his voice tinged with a sense of resolve. "The Space Exploration Program has served its purpose, but now, I need to prioritize efforts towards more immediate concerns."

"We need to escalate our plans in other areas whilst we still have chance. We need new blood to help focus the minds and thoughts of the people of the Earth.," added the mysterious Reebus.

Imelda nodded in agreement; her eyes alight with determination. "Christina Sandstrom has proven herself time and time again to be a capable leader," she added. "She has the vision and the drive to guide the Space Exploration Program into the future, while freeing up your time and public glare for the crucial tasks that lie ahead."

"I've been giving it a lot of thought too, and I agree." Reebus began, his voice measured as he addressed Imelda. "Christina Sandstrom is the right choice to lead the Space Exploration Program."

Imelda and Reebus nodded as one. "She certainly has the qualifications and experience," she replied. "Christina is also respected and believed by all in the public world who hang on to everything she says."

Reebus considered her words carefully, weighing the pros and cons of their options. "Christina may not have the charisma of a natural-born leader," he conceded. "But she has proven herself time and time again with her dedication and expertise. In times like these, we need someone who can deliver results, not just empty promises."

Imelda nodded; her expression thoughtful. "You make a valid point," she conceded.

"Christina's track record speaks for itself. She has a proven track record of success, and I have no doubt that she would excel in this role."

So, with a sense of willing, Reebus and Imelda sought out Christina with their proposal.

In the heart of the GGC headquarters, Reebus, Imelda, and Christina gathered around a sleek, polished desk, the weight of their shared mission heavy in the air. As they sat in contemplative silence, the gravity of the moment hung over them like a shroud, each of them keenly aware of the significance of their discussion.

Reebus broke the silence, his voice steady and resolute. "Christina, we've come to a decision," he began, his gaze unwavering as he addressed the woman before him. "We have a lot of faith in you, and we believe that you are the right person to lead the Space Exploration Program."

Christina's eyes widened in surprise, a mixture of emotions flickering across her face. She was full of pride, determination, and a hint of trepidation. Christina had spent her entire career preparing for this moment. Imelda reached across the desk, her hand resting reassuringly on Christina's shoulder. "You've proven yourself time and time again," she said, with her voice soft but firm. "And we have every confidence that you will lead the Space Exploration Program with the same dedication and expertise that you have demonstrated throughout your career."

Christina flung her black hair back and her brown eyes glistened with desire as she knew that this was a purpose she had always dreamed about. She thought for a while, not because she did not know her answer but because she did not want to seem over keen or desperate to the choice that lay before her.

To their delight, Christina then accepted the challenge with enthusiasm and determination, her eyes again shining with excitement as she prepared to take on the mantle of leadership.

"I am honoured to accept this responsibility," she declared, her voice ringing out with conviction. "Together, we will continue to push the boundaries of human exploration and pave the way for a brighter future for all."

Later that day a formal ceremony followed with media in tow and was blazoned across world media channels and holographic presentations everywhere. Christina was very much a golden girl, the one talk of town and everyone wanted to seek discussions with her. News stories broke, adverts were run and the whole world knew of her purpose and role before there was time to blink. Prior to the ceremonial handover occurring it was almost old news. The world's focus had been shifted away from any chatter of worry, distrust, or concern across other parts of the GGC's policies, just as Reebus had planned.

For decades, Reebus had been the unwavering figurehead of the Space Exploration Program. His unerring leadership and hope in humanity's quest to explore the cosmos. As the years had worn on and the weight of all his responsibilities grew heavier, he knew that the time had come to pass the torch to a new generation. He had to entrust the future of space exploration to those who would carry the mantle forward. Amidst the backdrop of a world on the cusp of a new era, Reebus stood before the assembled crowd, his gaze steady and his heart heavy with emotion. Beside him stood Christina Sandstrom, a brilliant and ambitious scientist whose passion for exploration mirrored his own, her eyes alight with determination as she prepared to assume the reins of leadership.

With a solemn nod, Reebus extended his hand to Christina, the weight of decades of history passing between them in the space of a single gesture. In that moment, the world knew that he was entrusting not just the future of the Space Exploration Program, but the hopes and dreams of countless generations yet to come.

"As I stand before you today, I am reminded of the countless hours we have spent together, working towards a common goal," Reebus began, his voice steady despite the swell of emotion threatening to overwhelm him. "But now, as we stand on the precipice of a new chapter in humanity's journey through the stars, it is time for me to step aside and make way for the next generation of explorers."

Turning to Christina, he continued, "Christina, you have proven yourself time and time again to be a worthy successor, an inspiration to all who have had the privilege of working alongside you. I have every confidence that you will lead the Space Exploration Program with the same passion and dedication that has guided us thus far."

With a sense of reverence, Christina accepted the mantle of leadership in front of the world, her eyes shining with determination as she addressed the crowd gathered before her with a carefully worded speech that had been put together with Reebus's aid. "It is an honour and a privilege to accept this responsibility," she declared, her voice ringing out with conviction. "Together, we will continue to push the boundaries of human exploration, to unlock the secrets of the cosmos, and to chart a course towards a future filled with endless possibilities. We have already discovered one planet capable of supporting out existence for retirement, but I hope to lead us to many more."

The whole world turned its metaphorical gaze towards Christina Sandstrom, with glowing media appearances and unwavering write ups soon to appear in almost every press and media outlet in the world.

So, with a sense of purpose and resolve, Christina embarked on a new chapter in her personal journey. It was a journey that would see her lead the Space Exploration Program into the future, guided by the wisdom and experience of those who had come before her.

At the end of the speech Reebus and Imelda took her aside in private.

"So, Christina, there is something you need to know about 'Serenity 1'...." as Reebus continued with a dulcet tone. Reebus then laid out all the real truths about the lies that Christina had never before been privy to. Christina came out of the conversation with eyes watering and demeanour depressed as truths and half lies had now become her problem and role ahead. It seemed that she had not just taken on her dream role in life but has been indoctrinated into the reality of horror and become a key part in the lie before it was too late to realise.

Chapter 5: Shadows of Doubt

Underneath the dim shine of a flickering streetlight, Jayden approached his best friend Arianna and found themselves huddled together in the secluded corner of an alley, their voices barely rising above a whisper as they discussed the events that had unfolded before Jayden's eyes.

"I'm telling you, Arianna, I saw them take those people away," Jayden insisted, his voice trembling with urgency. "They were elderly, just like the rumours said. Those masked figures... there was something off about them."

Arianna frowned, her scepticism plain in the furrow of her brow. "Jayden, I know you believe what you saw, but you have to consider the possibility that it was just a misunderstanding. The GGC has been clear about their policies regarding the elderly, that they're being transported to a nearby residential planet for a life of luxury."

Jayden shook his head, frustration simmering beneath the surface of his calm demeanour. "That's just it, Arianna. It does not add up. Why all the secrecy? Why the masked figures? And why haven't any of those elderly people ever returned to tell their tale?"

Arianna sighed, her gaze darting nervously around the alley as if expecting someone to be listening in on their conversation. "I don't know, Jayden. But we must be careful. If what you're saying is true, then we could be in danger just by talking about it."

Jayden's jaw clenched in frustration, his fists balling at his sides as he struggled to contain his emotions. "I know.... but we cannot just ignore what is happening. We have to do something, even if it means risking our own safety."

Arianna reached out, placing a reassuring hand on Jayden's shoulder. "I understand, Jayden. I am here for you, no matter what. But we must be smart about this. We need to gather more information before we make any rash decisions."

Jayden nodded, a sense of determination flickering in his eyes. "You're right, Arianna. We need to find out what is really going on, no matter the cost. If it means uncovering the truth about the GGC's actions, then so be it. We owe it to those who have disappeared without a trace and to those who have been silenced."

As Jayden and Arianna sat in Arianna's small apartment, their minds abuzz with the weight of their conversation, they knew that they could not afford to wait any longer. The time had come to put their plan into action, to uncover the truth behind the disappearances that had plagued their city for far too long.

"I've been thinking, Jayden," Arianna began, her voice low and determined. "My grandad is turning eighty next week, and he's been talking non-stop about how excited he is to be taken away for his retirement. He's convinced that he'll be living in luxury on that supposed residential planet."

Jayden's brow furrowed in thought as he considered Arianna's words. "Do you think he's being truthful, Arianna? Or is he just repeating what the GGC wants him to believe?"

Arianna shrugged; her expression troubled. "I'm not sure, Jayden. But it is worth finding out. That's why I think we should follow him when he goes to meet with the GGC representatives next week."

Jayden nodded, a sense of determination settling over him like a cloak. "I agree, Arianna. We need to know what is really going on. But how do we do that without raising suspicion?"

Arianna smiled, a glimmer of mischief dancing in her eyes. "I have an idea. We can place a tracker inside his coat when he is not looking. That way, we'll be able to follow his movements without him knowing."

Jayden's eyes widened in realization as he grasped the brilliance of Arianna's plan. "That's genius, Arianna! But where will we get a tracker?"

Arianna reached into her bag, producing a small device no larger than a coin. "I've already taken care of that, Jayden. This is a mini-GPS tracker which I borrowed from my cousin, who works in tech. We can attach it to the inside of my grandad's coat when he's not looking."

Jayden grinned, a sense of excitement coursing through his veins. "I'm in, Arianna. Let us do this. We'll finally uncover the truth behind the silent exodus and put an end to the lies that have plagued our world for far too long."

As they clasped hands in a silent pledge of solidarity, Jayden and Arianna also knew that they could not turn back now. Especially not when the fate of their loved ones and the future of humanity hung in the balance.

Arianna's grandad settled into the familiar comfort of his living room on Earth, anticipation fluttering in his chest as he prepared to connect with his old friend, Zelko, through the visual holograph communication system. It had been a couple of years since Zelko had been relocated to the retirement planet which had recently been given the name 'Serenity 1', and the longing to see his lifelong friend once again weighed heavily on his heart.

With a touch of a button, the holograph system hummed to life, and before him materialized the holographic image of Zelko, his face radiant with a warm smile. "Well, well, well, if it isn't my old buddy!" Zelko's voice crackled with excitement as he greeted Arianna's grandad.

Arianna's grandad could not contain his joy at the sight of his friend. "Zelko, my dear friend! It is wonderful to see you," he replied, his voice tinged with nostalgia.

The two friends exchanged pleasantries, their conversation flowing effortlessly as they reminisced about the days of their youth and the memories they had shared together. Despite the gulf of space that separated them, their bond remained unbreakable, a testament to the enduring power of friendship.

As they chatted, Arianna's grandad felt a pang of longing wash over him, a yearning for the simpler times when he and Zelko had spent their days exploring the world around them and dreaming of the future. In that moment, it felt as though they were young boys again, with the universe stretched out before them, brimming with endless possibilities.

Their conversation meandered through topics both profound and mundane, from the mysteries of the universe to the intricacies of everyday life on 'Serenity 1'. They laughed and reminisced, sharing stories and swapping jokes as if no time had passed at all.

Beneath the surface of their light-hearted banter lay a profound sense of longing, a yearning to bridge the gap that separated them and to once again be in each other's presence. For all the wonders of modern technology, nothing could replace the simple joy of spending time with an old friend, of sharing a laugh and a smile face-to-face.

As their conversation drew to a close, Arianna's grandad felt a bittersweet mix of emotions wash over him, for the memories they had shared, and the ones they had yet to create. As he bid farewell to his friend, Arianna's grandad knew that their bond would endure, transcending the vast expanse of space to stand the test of time. For in the end, it was the connections we forged with others that truly mattered, with the bonds of friendship and love that gave meaning to our lives and made the universe feel just a little bit smaller. They would once again see each other in the next few days.

The day before Arianna's grandad was due to leave for the new planet the family had decided to throw a leaving and celebration party as was the expectation throughout the world these days.

Arianna's family home buzzed with excitement as relatives and friends gathered to celebrate a momentous occasion and the impending retirement of Arianna's grandad. As Arianna moved through the crowded rooms, her heart heavy with mixed emotions, she could not help but marvel at the atmosphere of joy and anticipation that filled the air.

Her grandad, a sprightly man with a twinkle in his eye and a spring in his step, greeted each guest with warmth and enthusiasm, his excitement palpable as he prepared to embark on his journey to what he believed to be a paradise among the stars.

The party was a whirlwind of laughter and conversation, punctuated by heartfelt speeches and well-wishes for the future. Arianna watched as her grandad basked in the love and affection of those gathered around him, his smile never faltering as he regaled them with tales of his adventures yet to come.

As the evening wore on and the party reached its peak, Arianna found herself drawn to her grandad's side, a sense of melancholy settling over her like a shroud. She knew that this would be the last time she would see him before he embarked on his journey that would take him far from the familiar comforts of home and family.

"Are you okay, sweetheart?" her grandad asked, concern etched into the lines of his face as he noticed the sadness in her eyes.

Arianna forced a smile, masking her inner turmoil beneath a facade of cheerfulness. "I'm fine, grandad. Just a little emotional, that's all."

Her grandad chuckled, a twinkle of mischief in his eyes. "Ah, emotions are what make life worth living, my dear. Do not worry about me, I am off to live the dream! A life of luxury among the stars, can you imagine?"

Arianna nodded, her smile faltering slightly as she struggled to contain her emotions. "I'm sure it'll be amazing, grandad. I'll miss you."

Arianna sat with her grandad in the cozy confines of the room, the gentle trace of conversation filling the air as they discussed the prospect of his impending journey to the retirement planet. Despite the events Jayden had witnessed, Arianna could not help but feel a sense of bittersweet excitement at the thought of her grandad embarking on a new adventure among the stars.

"It's hard to believe that you'll be leaving soon, grandad," Arianna said, her voice tinged with sadness as she glanced at her grandad's face, illuminated by the soft shine of the evening light.

Her grandad smiled warmly, his eyes twinkling with anticipation. "Yes, it is quite surreal, isn't it, my dear? I cannot deny that I am looking forward to the journey ahead. The retirement planet sounds like a paradise beyond compare."

Arianna nodded, a sense of pride swelling in her chest at the thought of her grandad embarking on such an extraordinary adventure. "It does sound amazing, grandad. The best part is that you'll be able to stay in touch with us even from across the vast expanse of space."

Her grandad's eyes lit up with excitement at the mention of staying in touch. "Ah, yes! The wonders of modern technology never cease to amaze me. Can you imagine being able to chat through space, my dear? It is like something out of a science fiction novel!"

Arianna could not help but laugh at her grandad's enthusiasm, her heart warmed by the genuine joy in his voice. "It does sound incredible, grandad. Think about it. You will be able to keep in touch with us for years to come, even as you live hundreds of years on the retirement planet without aging much."

Her grandad's smile widened at the thought. "Indeed! It is a comforting thought, knowing that we will be able to share our lives with each other no matter where we are in the universe. Distance may separate us physically, but our bond will remain unbreakable."

As they sat together, Arianna and her grandad found solace in the knowledge that their love and connection could transcend the vast expanse of space. As they prepared for the journey ahead, they knew that no matter where life took them, they would always be together with a technological call allowing them to connect through the galaxy itself.

"Hey Arianna, do you like my new jacket? I am going to wear it tomorrow.," said Grandad as he held it up for her to see.

"Of course I do Grandad!" as she knew exactly where she would place her tracker when he turned his back.

With a keen eye for detail, he carefully selected the completions for his best outfit. It was a sharp, tailored jacket in a rich shade of navy blue, adorned with intricate stitching and embellishments that spoke to his refined taste. Paired with crisp trousers and a neatly pressed shirt, it was a look that exuded elegance and sophistication. No ensemble would be complete without the perfect accessories, and Arianna's grandad spared no expense in selecting the finishing touches to complement his jacket. He perused his collection of shoes, each pair meticulously polished to a gleaming shine, before settling on a sleek pair of leather loafers that added a touch of refinement to his look. Next came the shirts. A rainbow of colours and patterns that danced before his eyes, each one vying for his attention. With a discerning eye, he selected a crisp white shirt with subtle pinstripes, its fabric soft to the touch and its fit impeccable. It was a testament to his commitment to sartorial excellence. As he surveyed his reflection in the mirror, Arianna's grandad could not help but smile with satisfaction. His outfit was a masterpiece of style and sophistication. It was an accurate reflection of his personality and taste, and a testament to the timeless elegance that had become his signature.

With one final adjustment to his collar and a satisfied nod of approval, Arianna's grandad was ready to step out into the world, or more appropriately universe, his outfit a testament to the power of fashion to elevate the everyday into something truly extraordinary.

Her grandad's expression softened, his gaze filled with a warmth and tenderness that brought tears to Arianna's eyes. "And I'll miss you too, sweetheart. This isn't goodbye, it is just the beginning of a new adventure."

As Arianna watched her grandad mingle with the guests, his laughter ringing out in the darkness, she knew that he was right. This was not goodbye; it was merely a stepping stone on the path to a brighter future. Though her heart ached at the thought of saying farewell, she also knew that she could not begrudge her grandad the chance to pursue his dreams. It was a chance to reach for the stars and grasp them with both hands, just as he had always taught her to do. At least that is what he hoped was going to happen.

The following day arrived for Arianna's grandad's meeting with the GGC representatives at the space transportation warehouse. Jayden and Arianna found themselves on the outskirts of the city, hidden among the shadows of towering warehouses and industrial complexes. Their hearts pounded with anticipation as they prepared to put their plan into motion, the weight of uncertainty hanging heavy in the air.

Arianna's grandad, unaware of their intentions, left his home dressed in his attire picked with great thought the previous day, a sense of excitement evident in his every step. Little did he know that the jacket he wore concealed a small GPS tracker, silently transmitting his every movement to Jayden and Arianna's device.

As he made his way through the bustling streets, Arianna's grandad consulted his map, plotting his course with precision and care. Though he had made this journey many times before, today felt different. It was the beginning of a new chapter in his life, and he was determined to make the most of it. The city bustled with activity, its streets alive with the hustle and bustle of daily life. Amidst the chaos, Arianna's grandad remained focused, his eyes fixed on the horizon as he navigated the maze of streets and alleys that led to his destination. As he walked, memories of days gone by flooded his mind. The memories captured a life well-lived, filled with laughter, love, and adventure. As he stood on the precipice of a new adventure, those memories took on a new significance, serving as a source of inspiration and strength as he embarked on this journey into the unknown.

Finally, after what felt like an eternity, Arianna's grandad arrived at the GGC space transportation warehouse facility. Its towering hangars loomed overhead, casting long shadows across the landscape as they reached for the sky. With a sense of anticipation coursing through his veins, Arianna's grandad made his way inside, his heart filled with excitement at the possibilities that lay ahead.

Anxiously, Jayden and Arianna followed at a discreet distance, their senses attuned to the rhythm of the city as they navigated its bustling streets. The journey was long and arduous, punctuated by moments of tension and uncertainty as they skirted the edges of danger. They remained at a distance out of range to her grandad's senses as the tracker allowed a good degree of error in their approach. They still wanted to have visuals on him as a tracker is good for following but does not tell the whole story of what might be happening. It was a delicate balancing act.

As they neared their destination, a sense of foreboding settled over them like a shroud. The GGC space travel warehouse loomed before them, its imposing facade a stark reminder of the power and influence of the GGC. Security personnel patrolled the perimeter with vigilance, their watchful eyes scanning the area for any signs of trouble.

"We have to be careful, Jayden," Arianna whispered, her voice barely audible above the din of the city. "If we're caught, who knows what they'll do to us."

Jayden nodded; his jaw set in determination as he peered through the darkness at the warehouse before them. "I know, Arianna. We cannot turn back now. We've come too far to let fear dictate our actions."

With a silent nod of agreement, Jayden and Arianna pressed on, their footsteps echoing in the stillness of the night as they approached the warehouse's entrance. The security presence was formidable, but they were determined to uncover the truth, no matter the cost.

The night air was thick with tension as Jayden and Arianna crouched behind a row of dumpsters, their hearts pounding in their chests as they surveyed the imposing structure of the space processing warehouse looming before them. Security guards patrolled the perimeter, their watchful eyes scanning the area for any signs of intruders.

"We'll never get past those guards," Jayden whispered, his voice barely audible over the din of the city. "They're too alert, too well-trained."

Arianna shot him a determined look, her eyes blazing with resolve. "We'll find a way. We have to."

With that, she set to work, as Arianna started to action her pre-formulated plan to outsmart the guards and gain entry to the warehouse. After a few moments sly grin spread across her face as she looked at Jayden.

"We need a distraction," she murmured, turning to Jayden with a mischievous glint in her eye. "And I think I know just the thing. You will need to do what I say."

On Arianna's instruction, Jayden slipped out from their hiding spot and crept towards the nearest security guard, his movements silent and stealthy.

Meanwhile, Arianna made her way to the other side of the warehouse, her heart racing with excitement as she prepared to unleash her distraction. With a quick glance back at Jayden in the distance, she nodded in silent confirmation, signalling that she was ready to proceed.

As Jayden looked innocuous and innocent, Arianna sprang into action, activating a small remote-controlled drone that she had hidden in her backpack.

Arianna stood with her fingers deftly manipulating the controls of her small drone. The drone lifted off the ground, its sleek design blending seamlessly into the shadows as it soared silently through the air. Her mission was clear. It was needed to create a distraction that would draw attention away from the entry to the facility. As the drone darted and weaved through the sky above the warehouse, Arianna knew that she had to act quickly and decisively if she hoped to succeed. With a flick of her wrist, Arianna directed the drone towards a stack of crates at the far end of the warehouse, its onboard camera capturing every detail with precision and clarity as she walked stealthily in the opposite direction, towards Jayden and the entry gate. Then, with a press of a button, she triggered the drone's payload. A small bang ensued which was designed to create chaos and confusion. As the noise reverberated through the outside of the warehouse facility, panic erupted among the guards, their shouts and cries filling the air as they scrambled to investigate the cause.

The guards all left their posts near the gate entrance and were all directed to deal with the investigatory activity, their attention diverted from their immediate surroundings. Seizing the opportunity, Jayden and Arianna darted past the non-secured entrance, their footsteps muffled by the chaos unfolding around them.

As they then slipped inside the warehouse, their hearts pounding in their chests, Jayden and Arianna knew that they were stepping into the unknown. It was into a world of secrets and lies that threatened to consume them whole. They were undeterred, for they were driven by a sense of justice and a desire to uncover the truth, no matter the consequences.

And as they ventured deeper into the secretive world, their resolve hardened like steel, their determination unyielding in the face of adversity. They also knew that they could not turn back, not when the fate of their loved ones and the future of humanity hung in the balance. They found a place at the back of the warehouse away from any direct attention and hidden to all but the most pressing eye for detail.

From their vantage point at a safe distance, Arianna and Jayden watched in silence as Arianna's grandad and the other eighty-year-olds were led into the beautifully adorned room that appeared to be the gateway to the promised land. The sight before them was both enchanting and unsettling. It was a scene straight out of a fairy tale yet tinged with an underlying sense of foreboding.

As Arianna's grandad and the others crossed the threshold into the room, their faces awash with anticipation, Arianna felt a knot form in the pit of her stomach. She knew that what lay beyond the facade of beauty and splendour was far from paradise. It was a trap, carefully laid by those who sought to deceive and manipulate.

"They're going in," Jayden whispered, his voice barely audible above the general chatter of conversation around them. "What do we do now?"

Arianna's mind raced as she considered their options. They could not confront the GGC directly, especially not with so many security personnel around. They also could not stand idly by and watch as innocent people were led into a possible trap.

"We need to follow them," Arianna replied, her voice firm with resolve. "We need to find out what's really going on in there."

With a nod of agreement, Jayden and Arianna set off, their footsteps silent as they made their way through the infinite corridors of the warehouse complex. They moved with quiet and purpose, their hearts pounding with adrenaline as they drew closer to their destination.

Finally, they reached the entrance to the room where the grandad had just entered. There was a heavy door adorned with intricate carvings and adorned with golden filigree. With a silent glance at one another, Arianna and Jayden found a portal viewing hole along the wall, away from the glance of those who might see them.

What greeted them inside the warehouse was a sight that sent shivers down their spines. It was a vast expanse of space, devoid of any sign of life. The room was a hollow shell, its walls adorned with holographic projections of lush landscapes and crystal-clear waters. This was either the beginning of heaven or a cruel illusion designed to lure unsuspecting victims into a trap.

As Arianna's grandad and the others wandered through the room, their faces filled with wonder and delight. Not knowing what was to occur before them, but expectancy that the gateway to retirement was getting closer with each small step. There was gentle chatter and mostly happiness on the faces as the group of around fifteen people progressed in the room.

As Arianna and Jayden watched from their hidden vantage point, the scene inside the departure room unfolded with an eerie sense of calm. Arianna then handed one of her listening orbs to Jayden as the GPS transmitter was also able to provide direct sound from within her grandad's hidden pocket. The 80-year-olds, including Arianna's grandad, stood before a sleek and imposing machine at the centre of the room. It was a pre-departure machine, as it was called by the GGC representatives. With a sense of anticipation hanging in the air, the 80-year-olds approached the machine one by one, their faces alight with a mixture of excitement and trepidation. As everyone stepped inside the machine, a soft echo filled the room, accompanied by a series of whirring and clicking sounds as the machine sprang to life. Strangely, each of the group of people was asked to read the same few phrases before progressing but neither Jayden nor Arianna knew the purpose of this.

Arianna and Jayden watched and listened in fascination as holographic projections enveloped each of the 80-year-olds, capturing their features and sounds with uncanny precision. The holographs shimmered and flickered in the air, creating a lifelike replica of everyone that seemed almost too real to be true.

As the process continued, Arianna could not help but marvel at the technological prowess of the machine. It was a feat of engineering unlike anything she had ever seen before. A testament to the ingenuity and innovation of the GGC.

Beneath the surface of the placid scene, Arianna could not shake the feeling that something was amiss. There was a coldness to this departure machine, a mechanical precision that felt unsettling in its perfection. It was as if the machine itself had a hidden agenda. Its purpose went beyond the mere replication of physical features and sounds.

As the last of the 80-year-olds emerged from the machine, Arianna and Jayden exchanged a knowing glance. They both sensed that there was more to the pre-departure machine than met the eye. Its true purpose lay hidden beneath a veneer of technological sophistication.

As Arianna and Jayden watched in horror from the shadows, the scene before them took a chilling turn. The 80-year-olds, including Arianna's grandad, stood in the centre of the vibrantly decorated departure room, their faces filled with a sense of awe and wonder as they took in their surroundings.

As Arianna and Jayden looked on, a sense of dread settled over them like a heavy fog. There was something unsettling about the room. There was a palpable sense of unease that lingered in the air, despite its outward appearance of tranquillity. All the people in the room were then ushered into one square segment with boundaries defined by simple lines on the ground. The guard directing them made several checks and assurances about their positioning, before, without warning, the unthinkable happened.

With a blinding flash of light, the 80-year-olds began to dissolve before Arianna and Jayden's eyes, their bodies disintegrating into nothingness as if they were mere figments of a cruel and twisted illusion. There was no sound, no warning, just a silent and swift disappearance that left behind only a faint trace of shimmering particles in the air. It was so quick and definite that it was almost an illusion. Perhaps it was?

Arianna gasped in horror, her hand flying to her mouth to stifle a scream as she watched her grandad vanish before her eyes. Jayden stood frozen beside her, his eyes wide with shock and disbelief at the scene unfolding before them.

Within moments, the departure room was empty once more, save for Arianna and Jayden, who stood rooted to the spot in stunned silence. There was no sign of the 80-year-olds, no indication of where they had gone or what had become of them. In the distance, they could hear the next 'batch' gradually approaching to no doubt suffer the same outcome.

As the reality of what they had witnessed sank in, a cold chill crept over Arianna and Jayden, sending shivers down their spines. They had come to uncover the truth behind the GGC's actions, but they had never imagined it would lead to something so horrific and unimaginable.

With those thoughts present they both decided it was time to leave the facility and get away from the live terror before anybody noticed them. They snook away silently and it was many hours before either of them was to utter another word.

Chapter 6: The Enigmatic Reebus

Reebus, a man of sixty-three years, was a figure of undeniable presence and charisma. Standing at a height that commanded attention, he possessed a lean yet sturdy build. It was a testament to years of disciplined exercise and careful maintenance of his physique. His posture was erect, exuding an air of confidence and authority that seemed to radiate from every pore. His face was weathered by the passage of time and bore the marks of a life lived to the fullest. Lines of laughter and wisdom crisscrossed his features, framing a pair of piercing blue eyes that held the secrets of the universe within their depths. His gaze was intense, unwavering in its focus, and he hinted at a mind that was sharp and astute, capable of dissecting the complexities of the world with ease. Reebus's hair, once a vibrant shade of chestnut brown, had faded to a distinguished silver-grey over the years. It was neatly trimmed and styled, framing his face in a manner that accentuated his sharp features and chiselled jawline. Reebus exuded an incredible air of authority and gravitas. Dressed in impeccably tailored suits that spoke of wealth and refinement, Reebus cut a striking figure wherever he went. His wardrobe was a testament to his taste and diligence. Each garment was meticulously chosen to convey an image of power and sophistication.

It was not just Reebus's appearance that commanded respect. He had an aura of quiet confidence and self-assurance that set him apart from the crowd. He moved with a grace and poise that spoke of years spent navigating the treacherous waters of politics and power. His every gesture calculated to convey strength and authority.

Deep beneath the facade of strength and certainty, there lurked a hint of vulnerability. It was a flicker of doubt that belied the steely exterior. Reebus was not immune to the burdens of leadership, nor the weight of his own ambitions. He carried the world's problems on his shoulders. Secrets and responsibilities that threatened to consume him if he dared to falter.

Reebus stood on the precipice of yet another campaign for re-election, he felt ready. He was ready to face whatever lay in store with the same determination and resolve that had carried him through a lifetime of triumphs and tribulations. For Reebus was not just a man; he was a force to be reckoned with. To many Reebus was the true titan of industry and politics whose legacy would endure long after he was gone.

Reebus was a master strategist, a visionary leader, and a force to be reckoned with. His journey into the political arena had begun decades ago, fuelled by a fervent desire to be effective in the lives of his fellow citizens. With each election victory, his influence grew, and his policies reshaped nations. Reebus's name became synonymous with success. From grassroots movements to international summits, he navigated the complex world of politics with finesse and acumen. His ability to forge alliances, bridge divides, and enact meaningful change earned him accolades from visionaries across the globe. Whether the cause was economic reform, social justice, or environmental sustainability. Reebus was always at the forefront, championing causes that mattered most to the people he served.

In the intricate dance of politics, adversaries emerged from unexpected corners, testing Reebus's resilience and resolve. Among them stood formidable figures, once allies turned rivals, whose ambitions clashed with his own. Reebus was embarking on his sixth campaign where he found himself in a clash of ideologies and ambitions. He had faced off against many adversaries who sought to undermine his authority and challenge his legacy.

Killian Tredwell, a mentor turned adversary was embodied the complexities of political loyalty. Once a guiding force in Reebus's ascent, Tredwell's ambitions grew unchecked, leading Reebus down a path of betrayal and deceit. Reebus had confronted his former mentor with a mix of disappointment and determination, refusing to be swayed by Tredwell's calm style. Through a combination of strategic manoeuvring and unwavering principles, Reebus emerged victorious. Tredwell was left with the consequences of Reebus's victory and had been sent out to retirement from that loss and beyond.

Olsen Jones, the American philanthropist with a penchant for power, posed a different kind of challenge. Armed with vast resources and a relentless thirst for influence, Jones waged a campaign of misinformation and sabotage against Reebus. Reebus met Jones's onslaught with a steadfast commitment to truth and transparency, rallying support from grassroots movements and civic organizations. In the end, Jones's attempts to undermine Reebus's authority fell rather short. Jones was left humbled and defeated in the wake of Reebus's triumph.

Pavel Rydek had also been a worthy opponent with charm and charisma casting a spell over the electorate. Reebus had fought tooth and nail to defend his position against the tide of public opinion. It was not just Rydek's charisma that had posed a threat to Reebus's political ambitions. There were many whispers of foul play, of backroom deals and underhanded tactics designed to tilt the scales of the election in Rydek's favour. Reebus had emerged victorious in the end, the scars of that bitter campaign still lingered. A shadow was cast over his conscience and there were corridor chatter suggesting some foul play in the final election results.

Most recently the opponent was Katelynn Lee, the Asian superwoman with a fierce dedication to her cause. She had emerged as a formidable opponent on the global stage. With her unparalleled charisma and unwavering determination, Lee posed a threat to Reebus's vision for the future. Reebus had met Lee's challenge with a spirit of collaboration and cooperation, recognizing the importance of unity in the face of adversity. Through dialogue and diplomacy, Reebus forged a path forward, leaving Lee to reconsider her approach in the wake of Reebus's victory. She challenged his leadership again six years later with a result more damning than before and she had never been seen again.

As Reebus emerged victorious over each of his adversaries, his legacy as a masterful political force was cemented in the annals of history. For Reebus, the journey was far from over, as he prepared to lead his constituents into another new era of progress and prosperity.

The launch of Reebus's sixth election campaign was not merely an event; it was a spectacle, an extravaganza that captured the imagination of the masses. It heralded the beginning of a new era in political campaigning. From the moment the announcement was made, Reebus's presence seemed to permeate every aspect of daily life. His image was plastered across every available surface and his name whispered in every conversation.

As the countdown to the campaign launch began, anticipation reached a fever pitch. Cities across the world were transformed into seas of banners and billboards. Each advertisement bearing Reebus's likeness in vivid detail. Holograph machines projected his image onto skyscrapers, virtual billboards flashed his campaign slogans in neon lights. Even the clouds in the sky were engineered to form intricate patterns in his likeness. It was not just visual displays that heralded Reebus's campaign; his influence extended into every facet of daily life. Foods bearing his name adorned sparse and expensive supermarket shelves. From "Reebus Burgers" to "Reebus Fries," each product a testament to his widespread popularity. For those with any wealth left and who could afford to go to Restaurants, they offered special menu items inspired by his favourite dishes, while cafes brewed "Reebus Roast" coffee blends to satisfy the cravings of his supporters.

The air crackled with excitement as the campaign launch event kicked off in the heart of the city. Thousands gathered in the streets, waving banners and chanting slogans in support of their candidate. Music blared from speakers, filling the air with infectious energy, while dancers and performers entertained the crowds with elaborate routines choreographed in Reebus's honour.

When Reebus took to the stage amidst thunderous applause, his face illuminated by the shine of the spotlight, he radiated confidence and charisma. "My fellow citizens," he began, his voice echoing across the square, "today marks the beginning of a journey towards a brighter future for us all."

The crowd roared in agreement, their enthusiasm fuelling Reebus's spirit as he prepared to embark on the next phase of his journey. A hushed anticipation then fell over the crowd as a sleek, futuristic vehicle descended from the sky, bathed in a soft, ethereal glow.

It was Reebus's luxurious space car, a marvel of modern engineering and design, awaiting him with its doors wide open. It was, ready to whisk him away to his next destination. With a graceful stride he made his way towards the waiting vehicle, his every movement exuding confidence and poise.

Cameras flashed and onlookers gasped in awe as Reebus approached the space car, the embodiment of his vision for the future. Reebus's future was one where innovation and progress knew no bounds, where dreams were transformed into reality. It was a place where anything was possible. With a final wave to the crowd, Reebus stepped into the waiting embrace of his space car, the doors closing behind him. As the vehicle lifted off into the sky, disappearing into the horizon, the crowd erupted into cheers once more, their voices echoing into the night.

Reebus sat in the sleek confines of his technologically advanced flying car, a sense of contemplation coursing through his veins as he embarked on a journey that would take him to the farthest reaches of the Earth. As the leader of the GGC, he understood the importance of connecting with the people globally. He was determined to make his presence known at every key landmark worldwide.

With a flick of his wrist, Reebus activated the car's holographic display, which illuminated with a map of the Earth and a list of destinations stretching from New York to Tokyo, Paris to Sydney. Each location represented a key landmark for his campaign. They were symbols of human achievement and ingenuity that served as a testament to the resilience of the human spirit.

As his car glided effortlessly through the bustling streets of New York City, Reebus appeared on media screens across the world. His image was projected in stunning high definition as he addressed the people with a message of hope and renewal. He spoke of progress and prosperity, of a future filled with endless possibilities for those who dared to dream.

From the Statue of Liberty to the Great Wall of China, from the Eiffel Tower to the Sydney Opera House, Reebus made his presence felt at every turn. His charismatic demeanour and magnetic personality captivating audiences far and wide. He shook hands with the world's finest and famous, kissed babies, and posed for countless photo opportunities. All the time through every speech and meet he sold himself as the saviour of the people. He was the one and only hope in a world filled with uncertainty.

Reebus had risen to power on the promise of a better tomorrow, but his actions spoke volumes about his true intentions. He had a thirst for power and control that knew no bounds.

When Reebus's car made its way through the streets of Tokyo, a sense of unease settled over him like a dark cloud. He knew that his bid for re-election would not be without its challenges. He also knew that some would stop at nothing to see him fall from grace. Reebus was undeterred. He had come too far to turn back now, and he would stop at nothing to ensure his continued dominance over the people of Earth. For in his eyes, he was not just a leader but a saviour, destined to guide humanity into a new era of prosperity and progress, no matter the cost. As he continued his grand tour of the world, Reebus knew that the fate of the Earth lay in his hands alone, even if nobody was aware.

Chapter 7: The Mysterious Challenger

In the wake of past controversies and to ensure the integrity of the democratic process, the GGC had enacted sweeping reforms with the Election Reform Bill of 2096. Among its key provisions was the stipulation that elections must be held at least every five years. This ensured regular opportunities for the populace to exercise their right to vote and hold their leaders accountable. Perhaps the most crucial aspect of the reform bill was the requirement that a rule of no more than three consecutive terms in office for a given representative was removed, almost without anyone noticing. Further addendums to the bill requiring only two nominated candidates to stand for election and defining a very complicated and non-comprehendible selection process had progressed to where society now sits. These provisions were designed to uphold the principles of free and fair democratic voting. They were meant to ensure that citizens had a genuine choice when it came to selecting their representatives. Also, these provided leaders with enough time to fulfil and complete their fundamental changes assuming they were considered successful and elected by the many. Voting had long since been a compulsory activity and one which could be done from the comfort of your own home without prying eyes or broken pencils.

Under this framework, political parties and independent candidates alike were encouraged to put forth their nominees. Each applicant vying for the opportunity to lead and serve their constituents. This requirement not only promoted healthy competition within the political sphere but also prevented any single individual or entity from monopolizing power unchecked. As election season approached, the air was alive with anticipation and excitement, with candidates from across the political spectrum announced their intentions to run for office. Campaigns were launched, rallies were held, and debates were televised, as the electorate eagerly weighed their options and prepared to cast their votes.

A new contender for leadership emerged in a world gripped by uncertainty. Sandronica Sprowl, a champion of progress and reform, had quickly and efficiently risen from the ranks to challenge Reebus in the forthcoming election. She set the stage for a showdown that would shape the destiny of the GGC. As news spread like wildfire across the Earth, Sprowl's supporters erupted into jubilant celebration, their cheers echoing through the streets as they hailed their candidate's selection.

Sandronica Sprowl had emerged out of thin air, a woman of mystery and intrigue who captured the attention of the public with her sudden appearance on the political stage. As the direct opposition to Reebus in the upcoming election, she posed a formidable challenge to his reign. Her presence casting a shadow of uncertainty over his bid for re-election.

Unlike Reebus, whose background and history were well-documented, Sandronica's past was shrouded in the unknown. This mystique only added to her allure and appeal. Little was known about her origins or her motivations, and yet she commanded a loyal following of supporters who hung on her every word with rapt attention. Sandronica was a woman of striking beauty and charisma, with a presence that was impossible to ignore. Her hair, a cascade of lustrous black curls, framed a face that was both elegant and enigmatic. Her eyes were a mesmerizing shade of deep violet that seemed to pierce through the soul. It was not just Sandronica's appearance that set her apart. She had an aura of confidence and self-assurance, her unwavering belief in her ability to effect change and challenge the status quo. She spoke with a voice that resonated with passion and conviction; her words imbued with a sense of purpose that captivated all who listened.

Yet for all her charm and charisma, there was something undeniably unsettling about Sandronica. There was a sense of unease that lingered in the air whenever she was near. Whispers and rumours that surrounded her, whispers of a past steeped in darkness and intrigue, whispers of secrets that she would do anything to keep hidden.

As Jayden and Arianna sat together watching the latest broadcast featuring Sandronica Sprowl, they could not help but notice something peculiar: the absence of her advisors or any members of her team. It was a pattern they had observed countless times before. Whenever Sandronica appeared in public, whether it was for a press conference or a televised interview, she always seemed to be alone. It was as if she were a solitary figure in the vast expanse of the political landscape.

Have you ever noticed how Sandronica never seems to have anyone with her?" Arianna mused; her brow furrowed in thought.

Jayden nodded; his gaze fixed on the screen. "It's strange, isn't it? You'd think someone of her importance would have a team of advisors or aides by her side at all times."

"And yet, every time she's on camera, it's like she's a one-woman show" Arianna added, a note of scepticism in her voice. "It makes you wonder who's really calling the shots behind the scenes."

Jayden could not help but agree. There was something undeniably unsettling about Sandronica's apparent isolation, a sense of mystery that shrouded her every move.

"I've tried looking into her inner circle before," Jayden confessed, turning to Arianna. "But every time I hit a dead end. It's like they don't even exist."

Arianna nodded sympathetically, her eyes narrowing in suspicion. "Maybe that's the point. Maybe Sandronica is intentionally keeping her advisors out of the spotlight to maintain control over her image."

"It's possible," Jayden conceded, though a nagging doubt lingered in the back of his mind. "But it still doesn't explain why they're so secretive. What could they have to hide?"

Before Arianna could respond, the broadcast cut to a commercial break, advertising the joys of the retirement planet, and they were left with nothing but silence and the flickering of the holograph machine.

Sandronica's supporters were a diverse and eclectic group, drawn together by a shared sense of disillusionment with the current world. Unlike those who aligned themselves with the GGC and Reebus, they did not conform to the ideals and norms that had come to define society. Instead, they were individuals who questioned the world around them, who refused to accept things at face value. These were people who dared to challenge the established order. They were the dreamers and the visionaries, the rebels, and the renegades. All were united by a common desire for change. They saw the retirement planet not as a utopia, but as a prison; a place where the spirit of innovation and exploration had been stifled by complacency and conformity. They longed for a world where creativity and individuality were celebrated, not suppressed. For Sandronica's supporters, she was more than just a political figure; she was a symbol of hope. She was the champion of their ideals and aspirations. They believed that under her leadership, they could build a better world. It was one where freedom and opportunity were not just words but lived realities. Having support for Sandronica was not without its risks. In a society where dissent was discouraged and conformity was rewarded, they faced backlash and persecution from those who sought to maintain the status quo. They were labelled as troublemakers, criminals, and liars, dismissed as idealistic dreamers or dangerous radicals. Despite the challenges they faced, Sandronica's supporters retained their belief that change was possible. They knew that they were fighting an uphill battle, but they were willing to risk everything for the chance to build a world that reflected their values and beliefs.

Across the globe, pockets of dissent began to emerge as Sandronica's supporters rose up against the oppressive forces of the GGC. From the bustling streets of Mexico City to the sprawling metropolises of Beijing. From the ancient alleyways of Jerusalem to the once frozen tundra of Russia, people took to the streets in protest. People demanded change and challenged the authority of the ruling elite.

Their cries for justice fell on deaf ears as the GGC swiftly moved to quash the uprisings. Vast military resources were deployed and powerful security apparatus to suppress any signs of dissent. Long used methods of crowd control were still used in situations like this. Hii-tech riot police emblazoned with neutralizing crowd capabilities clashed with protesters, tear gas filled the air, and arrests were made

en-masse as the forces of order sought to maintain control at any cost. Despite the widespread nature of the uprisings, they received scant attention from the mainstream media. Coverage of such events quickly disappearing from the airwaves and social media platforms. Direct footage posted by eyewitnesses was mysteriously removed as soon as it was uploaded, leaving behind only a void of silence and uncertainty. Throughout the last hundred years social media had evolved further into a powerful tool for communication, information dissemination, and social interaction. It was a vast digital frontier where ideas flowed freely, connecting people from all corners of the globe in an instant. As with any tool, social media could be used for both good and ill. In the hands of the GGC, it became a potent weapon for maintaining control and exerting influence over the masses.

The GGC's approach to social media was twofold. On the one hand, they utilized it as a means of disseminating propaganda and controlling the narrative, shaping public opinion to align with their own agenda. Through carefully crafted messaging and targeted advertising campaigns, they sought to portray themselves as benevolent guardians of society. At the same time, they vilified dissenters and critics as dangerous radicals or enemies of the state. Perhaps more insidiously, the GGC also used social media as a tool for surveillance and monitoring. It employed advanced algorithms and artificial intelligence to sift through vast amounts of data in search of potential threats to their power. Every post, every like, every comment was analysed and catalogued, feeding into a massive database that allowed the GGC to track and monitor the activities of individuals and groups deemed to be a threat to the established order. For the average citizen, social media became both a blessing and a curse. It was a means of staying connected with friends and loved ones, but also a digital panopticon where every move was watched and scrutinized by unseen eyes. As the GGC tightened its grip on the digital realm, many began to wonder if there was anywhere left to hide. Was there anyone they could trust in a world where privacy was a luxury few could afford. Dark webs of social interaction did still exist but GGC control over networks, satellites and any transportation media meant that it was almost impossible to keep anything quiet and private for very long. Only ancient communications involving flying pigeons or subtleties of morse code had any real chance of reaching their intended target. Even these were not foolproof with any bird that landed in the wrong spot being an immediate target for often hungry groups of people desperate for a tasty meal for that day.

For Sandronica's supporters, it was an incessant reminder of the power and reach of the GGC. It was a stark illustration of the lengths to which they would go to maintain their grip on power and silence those who dared to oppose them. Even in the face of such overwhelming odds, the spirit of resistance remained alive, there would always be a segment of any regime that had contrarian views and beliefs on any matter, no matter how large or small.

In the heart of Rome, the media circus surrounding the upcoming election reached fever pitch. Reporters and journalists swarmed the streets, their cameras and microphones poised to capture every moment of the unfolding drama. Yet, amidst the chaos, a singular narrative emerged. It was one that seemed to cast Reebus as the inevitable victor, no matter the outcome of the election.

As Sandronica Sprowl's supporters gathered for interviews, their voices drowned out by the relentless drumbeat of the media machine. Questions were rapid-fire, each one designed to reinforce the prevailing narrative of Reebus's dominance and inevitability. Even when Sprowl's supporters attempted to steer the conversation towards her policies and platform, the reporters seemed more interested in discussing Reebus's track record and achievements. It was a frustrating and disheartening experience for Sprowl's supporters, who felt as though their voices were being drowned out by the overwhelming tide of media bias. No matter how hard they tried to make their case, it seemed as though the deck was stacked against them from the start. Despite the overwhelming odds, Sprowl's supporters remained undaunted in their commitment to their candidate. They knew they had a candidate worth fighting for. It was a candidate who represented real change and progress in a world that seemed increasingly dominated by the status quo. As the interviews drew to a close and the reporters moved on to their next story, Sprowl's supporters were left to ponder the uphill battle that lay ahead. There was a glimmer of hope. There was a belief that, no matter how entrenched the forces of the media may seem, the power of the people would ultimately prevail. When the dusts settled and the streets fell quiet once more, the uprisings may have been quashed, but the seeds of dissent had been sown. Sandronica's supporters regrouped and reorganized, they knew that their fight was far from over. As long as they had breath in their bodies and fire in their hearts, they would continue to resist, continue to fight, continue to stand up for what they believed in. In that defiance, they found hope for a better world, for a brighter future, for a tomorrow where their voices would no longer be silenced.

As the election drew nearer, the perceived tension between Reebus and Sandronica reached a fever pitch within the official media. Each candidate was vying for the support of the masses and the upper hand in the battle for power. Sandronica Sprowl did not seem to be someone to be underestimated, for she was a force to be reckoned with. Was she someone who would stop at nothing to achieve her goals? Or was there yet a different narrative to be written about the inevitability of Reebus's victory.

Chapter 8: Unveiling the Truth

Jayden and Arianna sat in Arianna's dimly lit bedroom, the weight of what they had witnessed at the retirement planet complex pressing heavily on their minds. The air was thick with tension as they exchanged uneasy glances, grappling with the unsettling realization that everything they had been told was a carefully constructed lie.

"I can't believe it," Arianna whispered, her voice barely above a hushed murmur. "All this time, we thought they were being sent to live out their golden years in luxury, but... it's all a sham."

Jayden nodded solemnly; his brow furrowed with concern. "It's like they're... disposing of people once they reach a certain age. It's sickening."

As they pieced together the fragments of their shattered illusions, a sense of anger and betrayal simmered beneath the surface, fuelling their determination to uncover the truth behind the Space Exploration Program and the sinister motives that lay hidden within its depths.

"We have to do something," Jayden declared, his voice tinged with urgency. "We can't let them get away with this."

Arianna nodded in agreement, her eyes blazing with righteous indignation. "We need to find out what's really going on behind closed doors. We owe it to all those people who've been... taken."

With a newfound sense of purpose driving them forward, Jayden and Arianna resolved to delve deeper into the mysteries surrounding the Space Exploration Program, determined to expose the dark truth that lurked beneath its glossy exterior.

They would have to tread carefully, for they were up against forces far more powerful than they could have ever imagined. Yet despite the risks, Jayden and Arianna refused to back down. For they believed they had glimpsed the truth behind the facade of lies, and they knew that they could not rest until justice had been served and the innocent had been set free from the clutches of deception.

The light of the holographic communication system echoed through Arianna's room as she and Jayden sat tensely, bracing themselves for the incoming call. Ever since they believed they had uncovered the unsettling truth behind the Space Exploration Program, they had been on edge, their minds consumed by thoughts of the sinister forces at play.

As the holographic image materialized before them, Arianna's grandad appeared, his face illuminated by an eerie blue haze. His smile was warm and familiar, but Jayden could not shake the nagging sense of unease that gnawed at his insides.

"Hello, my dear Arianna, and hello, Jayden!" Arianna's grandad greeted them cheerfully, his voice ringing out with false joviality. "I hope you're both doing well. I just wanted to check in and let you know that I have arrived safely at the retirement planet. I am really enjoying it so far and have had a wonderful first few days so far. Zelko passes on his regards and try not to worry about me as I'm doing fine."

Arianna forced a smile, her heart heavy with dread. "That's great, grandad. How are you finding it so far?"

Her grandad's holographic image beamed with enthusiasm. "Oh, it's simply wonderful, my dear! The scenery is breathtaking, and the facilities are top-notch. I couldn't be happier."

Despite his reassuring words, Jayden could not shake the feeling that something was terribly wrong. It was as if the holographic image before them was nothing more than a hollow shell, a facade designed to conceal the dark truth lurking beneath the surface.

As the conversation dragged on, Jayden's suspicions grew, his mind racing with questions and doubts. How could Arianna's grandad be speaking to them from the retirement planet when they both knew he had been... taken? Was this some kind of elaborate hoax, designed to lull them into a false sense of security?

Before Jayden could voice his concerns, the holographic image flickered and wavered, dissipating into thin air before their eyes. As the room fell silent once more, Jayden and Arianna were left with chills thinking they had been deceived, and the truth they sought was darker and more sinister than they could have ever imagined.

Jayden and Arianna sat in silence, the weight of their revelation hanging heavily in the air between them. The holographic call from Arianna's grandad had been nothing short of unsettling, leaving them both with a sense of unease that refused to dissipate.

"We know this is a lie," Jayden finally spoke up, his voice hushed with concern. "How could he be calling us from the retirement planet when we both know..."

Arianna finished his sentence for him, her voice trembling with disbelief. "When we both know he's... gone. It doesn't make sense."

As they mulled over the perplexing situation, a sudden realization dawned on Jayden, causing him to sit up straighter in his chair. "Wait a minute... what if... what if they scanned him before... you know..."

Arianna's eyes widened with understanding as the pieces of the puzzle began to fall into place. "You mean... they created an exact holographic replica of him so they could... so they could keep up appearances?"

Jayden nodded grimly, his mind reeling with the implications of their discovery. "It would explain how he was able to call us from the retirement planet. They must have scanned him before... before they..."

Arianna's voice trailed off, unable to bring herself to say the words aloud. The thought that her grandad's image could be used as a tool of manipulation was both horrifying and deeply unsettling.

"But why?" she whispered, her voice barely above a whisper. "Why would they go to such lengths to deceive us?"

Jayden shook his head, his jaw clenched with determination. "I don't know, Arianna. But one thing is for sure is that we need to find out the truth behind this holographic technology and for what they are really using it for. If that means digging deeper into the secrets of the GGC, then so be it."

Arianna nodded in agreement, a steely resolve burning in her eyes. "We owe it to my grandad, and to all the others who've been... affected by this."

At that and with a warm smile, Arianna's mother entered the room, her eyes alight with an otherworldly presence that spoke of wonders unseen. "Arianna, darling," she began, her voice tinged with excitement, "I just had the most incredible conversation with your grandad."

Startled from her trance, Arianna turned to face her mother, curiosity dancing in her eyes. "You did? Yeah, we did too."

Her mother's smile widened, a radiant beacon of joy amidst the mundane confines of their world. "Oh, he's doing wonderfully! The transportation was a success, and he's already feeling right at home in his new surroundings."

Arianna's voice responded by instinct and to keep her mother away from any possible deceit and trouble in her mind. "That's amazing! I'm so happy for him."

Arianna's grandad had regaled Arianna's mum with tales of his experiences in the first few days on the new planet, his eyes sparkled with the joy of reminiscence, his voice filled with the warmth of cherished memories. Arianna's mum found the communication she had with grandad and replayed it to the room with glee.

With each anecdote, he painted a vivid picture of life in his new retirement community. It was a world of culinary delights and leisurely pursuits, where every meal was a feast for the senses and every day held the promise of new adventures. He spoke of a sumptuous banquet he had on arrival and gourmet cuisine of fresh produce with things he had not eaten in decades; of flavours that danced upon the palate and left one craving for more. Arianna's grandad had explained to her that he sat on the banks of a tranquil lake, the gentle lapping of the water soothing his soul as he cast his line into the shimmering depths below. It was a scene straight out of his childhood memories. Of a time when the world was simpler, and the joys of nature were abundant. He described that he felt the tug of a fish on his line, a smile spread across his weathered face, his heart filled with a sense of contentment and peace. For here, on the retirement planet, amidst the rolling hills and pristine landscapes, he had found a refuge from the hustle and bustle of the modern world. It was a place where he could reconnect with the natural world and rediscover the simple pleasures of life.

"It's been years since I've been able to fish like this," he had remarked to Arianna's mum, who had taken it all in on face value with her eyes alight with curiosity and wonder. "Back on Earth, the waters were polluted, and the fish were few and far between. It is like stepping back in time to a world where nature still thrives, and the beauty of the wilderness is all around us.", her grandad had expanded.

What is more, as he showed them the amazing images of the planet, with the fields and forests that stretched out before them, alive with the sights and sounds of wildlife. Birds flitting through the air, their songs echoing through the trees, while animals grazed in the fields, their movements graceful and serene.

"It's incredible, isn't it?" Arianna's grandad had continued, his voice filled with awe and wonder. "To think that we've been given a second chance to live out our days in harmony with nature, surrounded by the beauty of the natural world. It's a gift that I'll never take for granted."

It was not just the food, the nature or the animals that had delighted him, there was a sense of camaraderie and community that permeated the atmosphere. It was a feeling of belonging that made him feel truly at home. He spoke of friendly faces and warm greetings, of laughter that echoed through the halls and friendships that blossomed like spring flowers.

Then there were the activities, an endless array of entertainment and recreation that filled his days with joy and excitement. He spoke of his first round of golf on 'Serenity 1' where he played beneath the warm sun, with a gentle breeze which seemed to carry his ball further than ever before. He recounted his first evening spent in the company of old friends including Zelko where he enjoyed live music and dancing the night away beneath a canopy of stars.

As Arianna's mum listened to her grandad's tales, she could not help but smile. There was a sense of warmth and nostalgia washing over her as she imagined the idyllic world he described. For in his stories, she found a glimpse of the happiness and contentment that awaited him in his new home. It was a place where every moment was filled with wonder and every day was a celebration of life's simple pleasures

With a gentle nod, her mother approached, her hand reaching out to brush away the stray wisps of hair that framed Arianna's face. "It truly is. His new home looks fantastic. The holographic projections make it feel like he's right here with us."

Her mother chuckled softly, a melody of laughter that danced upon the air. "In a way, he is. But no matter where he may be, he'll always be a part of our family, connected by the bonds of love and shared memories."

As Arianna's mum left the room, her words about Arianna's grandad still echoing in the air, Jayden and Arianna found themselves enveloped in a heavy silence. This was a silence that spoke volumes of the weight of their thoughts and emotions. In the wake of her mum's departure, Arianna looked at Jayden with a shared sense of despair, their hearts heavy with the realization of life's intricacies and interconnectedness.

"It's like everything is woven together, isn't it?" Jayden remarked, his voice tinged with a hint of resignation. "One moment leads to another, each thread connected to the next in a complex tapestry of existence."

Arianna nodded in agreement, her mind swirling with thoughts of the fragility of life and the delicate balance of the universe. "It's as if every action, every decision, sends ripples through the fabric of reality," she replied, her voice soft with introspection. "And we're just caught in the midst of it all, trying to make sense of the chaos."

"If we were to unsettle people with what we believe is the truth then will we actually help people or hinder them. I think a lot of people will be much better off living the lie.," added Jayden.

As they spoke, Jayden and Arianna found themselves grappling with the profound truths that underpinned their existence. Through the ebb and flow of life, the inevitability of change, and the interconnectedness of all things. In the silence of the room, they found solace in each other's presence, drawing strength from the shared understanding of the complexities of the world around them.

"It's overwhelming, isn't it?" Arianna mused; her gaze fixed on the horizon beyond the window. "To think that every moment, every choice, has the power to shape our lives in ways we can't even begin to comprehend."

Jayden nodded in agreement, his thoughts mirroring her own. "But perhaps," he replied, his voice tinged with a glimmer of hope, "it's in embracing the interconnectedness of life that we find our purpose and when we realize our place in the grand tapestry of existence."

"Sometimes not knowing the truth is a blessing." noted Jayden "Whilst knowing the truth or suspecting the horrors that lie within it is a burden that will drive you to the edge of insanity.," added Arianna. "I think that if we are on the edge of opening a well-guarded Pandora's box of deceit, then it might not be right if we leave it open to everyone else. It is only fair that choice is given to everyone on their own terms. Just look at your Mum. She is happy and content and all is well in her world. If that were to be cruelly taken from her then she may not be able to go on."

Chapter 9: Struggling Through Scarcity

The Earth of 2123 existed in a paradoxical state, where scarcity and abundance coexisted in a delicate balance. Advanced technologies had ushered in an era of unprecedented progress and innovation. They had also exacerbated the disparities between the haves and the have-nots, leaving much of the population struggling to meet their most basic needs.

In the sprawling metropolises that dotted the landscape, towering skyscrapers loomed like monuments to mankind's insatiable appetite for expansion. Beneath the glossy facade of urban development lay harsh realities. Most of the population struggled to eke out a basic existence in the face of overwhelming scarcity.

Among the most pressing challenges that technology grappled with are the essentials of life itself including fresh water, arable land, and the finite confines of geographical space. No matter how sophisticated the algorithms or how powerful the machines, these resources remained elusive. Their scarcity a constant reminder of the delicate balance that sustains life on Earth. A world shaped by the wonders of technology; the limitations imposed by resource scarcity were an ever-present reality. Despite the marvels of modern engineering and the boundless potential of artificial intelligence, there were certain elements of life that could not be replicated or synthesized.

Fresh water, for instance, remained a precious commodity in a world plagued by drought and pollution. Despite advances in desalination technology and water purification systems, access to clean drinking water remained a luxury for many. It was a stark reminder of the inequalities that persisted in a world driven by profit and greed.

The limitations of geographical space posed a challenge to the ambitions of technology, constraining the expansion of urban centres and the cultivation of arable land. With each passing year, the population density of their city had soared to unprecedented heights, driving a vertical expansion that defied the constraints of traditional urban planning. Skyscrapers stretched towards the clouds like monoliths of glass and steel, their towering heights a testament to human ingenuity and ambition.

It was not merely the skyline that had been transformed but the very fabric of society itself. Vertical living had become the norm, with entire communities existing within the confines of these towering edifices. Residential towers reached dizzying heights, their upper floors offering panoramic views of the city below. Commercial and recreational spaces filled the lower levels, creating a vertical tapestry of life and activity that spanned from the heavens to the depths.

Even as the skyline soared to new heights, humanity's ambitions delved even deeper into the Earth itself. Beneath the surface, vast networks of tunnels were being developed with caverns sprawled like the roots of an ancient tree, housing an expanse of infrastructure and industry. Subterranean cities flourished in the darkness, their inhabitants carving out a life beneath the Earth's crust that was as vibrant and dynamic as any aboveground. From underground parks and gardens to subterranean shopping malls and entertainment complexes, the depths teemed with life, their inhabitants embracing the unique challenges and opportunities that came with living beneath the surface.

Despite efforts to harness vertical farming techniques and explore extraterrestrial colonization, the finite nature of Earth's surface remained a barrier to endless growth and expansion. In this world, all agricultural land was constantly under siege, robbed of its precious bounty before the harvest could ever be reaped. Organized crime syndicates and desperate individuals alike would raid fields under the cover of darkness, leaving behind nothing but barren soil and shattered dreams.

Under the cover of darkness, a party of food raiders emerged from the wide expanses of the Canadian countryside and swooped onto the wheat fields. Their acts were motivated by desperation, and their motives were malicious. Over the course of several weeks, allegations had been circulating about illicit activities that were attempting to steal the valuable harvest; but, tonight, those speculations suddenly became a tragic reality. While the raiders proceeded stealthily and discreetly under the cover of night, their attention was fixated on the tall stalks of wheat that were spread out in front of them. Immediately beginning their job with a brutal efficiency, harvesting the grain with reckless abandon. They were completely oblivious to the consequences that would result from their actions. Nevertheless, while they laboured away, a spark lit amid the dry and brittle stalks. A chain reaction followed that would have disastrous results. Burning fields of wheat were consumed by the flames in a matter of minutes, leaving behind nothing but charred ruins in their wake. The flames advanced at an alarmingly rapid pace. The citizens of the nearby towns and cities unaware of the nightmare that was taking place right in front of their eyes as the fire blazed out of control and spread throughout the area. They had little time to waste, so they ran away in order to save their lives, as the ferocious flames burned both their homes and their means of subsistence.

In the days that followed, the true extent of the devastation became painfully clear. Entire communities lay in ruins, their once-thriving fields reduced to smouldering ash. The loss of the wheat harvest meant more than just hunger. It meant the loss of livelihoods, the loss of hope, and the loss of countless lives. Food was a luxury reserved for the privileged few, with scarcity driving prices to astronomical heights on the black market. Those who could afford to pay could feast on gourmet meals prepared by the finest chefs, while the rest were left to scrounge for scraps or subsist on nutrient supplements and synthetic substitutes.

The world bore witness to a haunting silence that would once contain vibrant forests and fertile expansive nature filled plains. It was a testament to the devastating toll that humanity's relentless expansion had exacted on the natural world. Residents of a world shaped by the ebb and flow of technological progress; the disappearance of native animals was a stark reminder of the fragile balance that sustained life on Earth.

Over the past fifty years, native species had dwindled to the brink of extinction, their numbers decimated by the relentless march of progress and the insatiable appetite of humanity. Once-thriving populations of animals had been hunted to the brink of extinction, their habitats destroyed by deforestation and urbanization, their very existence threatened by the encroaching shadows of civilization.

From majestic predators to humble herbivores, no species had been spared from the ravages of human activity. Iconic creatures such as majestic tigers and the elusive snow leopards had vanished from the wild in the early years. More common animals like cows, chicken and pigs would be hunted immediately for food if ever seen in the wild. Any form of life that could provide protein in any way was hunted to such a degree that the wild no longer contained any species or hardly any natural life. Food production and preservation of animals had to always be done behind closed and security laden facilities. Even the humblest of creatures, from the smallest songbird to the lowliest insect, had felt the weight of humanity's presence, their populations dwindling as their habitats were destroyed.

Not only did hunting and the degradation of habitats contribute to the demise of native wildlife, but the absence of native food sources that could feed them also played a key role in the disappearance of these animals. As a result of the devastation of natural ecosystems, a great number of creatures had been deprived of the food and water sources that they relied on for their life, which brought them to the verge of extinction.

At the heart of the Kenyan plains, nestled amidst the vibrant tapestry of the savannah, lay a zoo. It was a sanctuary for some of Africa's most majestic creatures. On another fateful day, the tranquillity of the plains was shattered by an act of unspeakable violence. A brazen attack that would leave a trail of destruction in its wake. Under the cover of darkness, a group of criminals descended upon the zoo, their intentions dark and nefarious. Armed to the teeth, they stormed the perimeter, overpowering the guards with ruthless efficiency as they forced their way inside. As they entered the enclosures, their true motives became horrifyingly clear. They were here for one thing and one thing only: the slaughter of innocent animals.

With callous disregard for life, the criminals set about their grisly task, gunning down the animals in cold blood as they hunted them like prey. From the graceful giraffes to the majestic lions, no creature was spared from the onslaught, their cries of anguish echoing through the night as they fell victim to the merciless killers. As the carnage unfolded and was brought to light, it was a scene of unimaginable horror. It was a senseless act of cruelty that defied comprehension and left a scar on the soul of Africa's wild places. This attack alone brought a number of Africa's species closer to extinction and showed the world once again the brutality and selfishness of some of the human populace. It also showed the lack of food and living standards across the world. When people had nowhere to turn and on the edge of survival itself then anything was possible. Driven to a brutality and unbelievable darkness that unless you had been there yourself would be incomprehensible.

Access to clean, drinkable water was becoming increasingly scarce, water itself was an expensive asset in this bleak and parched world. Those individuals who were sufficiently fortunate to have access to water were compelled to restrict their supply. On the black market, it had become a highly sought-after commodity, and unscrupulous market participants were charging outrageous sums for the privilege of tiny amounts of the precious liquid. Those individuals who were unable to pay were forced to rely on sources that were contaminated, putting them at danger of illness and disease with each sip. The unauthorised usage of mobile desalination machines, which are huge machinery meant to collect vast volumes of water from the depths of the ocean, resulted in the creation of a desolate wasteland in their wake.

At first, the effects were subtle, hidden beneath the surface of the waves. As the desalination machines continued their relentless extraction, the seas began to recede at an alarming pace, revealing more and more reclaimed land across the globe.

The sight was nothing short of heartbreaking. The world watched in horror as entire ecosystems were destroyed, their delicate balance disrupted beyond repair.

As the seas retreated, they left behind a desolate landscape. It was a wasteland devoid of life, where once-thriving coral reefs lay bleached and lifeless. It was also a place where countless species faced extinction. The loss of sea life had far-reaching consequences, rippling through the interconnected web of life that sustained the planet. Droughts ravaged once-fertile lands, crops withered and died, and communities faced the spectre of famine and thirst. Nature itself was beaten and withered away.

Resources once thought to be inexhaustible were now in dangerously short supply, their depletion hastened by decades of unchecked consumption and exploitation. Fossil fuels had long since been depleted, replaced by renewable energy sources that struggled to meet the ever-growing demands of a burgeoning population.

Amidst the rampant poverty and deprivation, there existed a curious paradox. Whilst the necessities of life were increasingly out of reach for the majority, the most advanced technologies were readily available to all at very little cost.

In the gleaming metropolises that dotted the landscape, towering skyscrapers housed state-of-the-art laboratories and research facilities, where scientists and engineers worked tirelessly to push the boundaries of human knowledge. Virtual reality simulations allowed individuals to escape the harsh realities of their daily lives, immersing themselves in fantastical worlds of their own creation.

The pursuit of advancement was a goal for the people who were at the forefront of the titans of the technology sector. It was a lucrative business for them where they received billions of dollars of credits as a result of the demand for their products. From customers who wanted to get their hands on the most recent electronic devices, each of which was more complex and sophisticated than the one before it. As the cycle of innovation churned on, a dark underbelly began to emerge. For every new gadget that hit the market, countless older devices were rendered obsolete, discarded like yesterday's news in favour of the next big thing. With each passing year, the mountains of electronic waste grew higher and higher, threatening to overwhelm the planet with their sheer volume.

Large pits of discarded technology extended out as far as the eye could see in the bleak wastelands that lay outside the bounds of the cities. These wastelands were located beyond the walls of the cities. These enormous graveyards served as the final resting place for millions of outmoded items, which had once been cutting-edge technology but had since become useless and archaic. Their sleek and gleaming exteriors had become tarnished and shattered while their technology had become obsolete. A glaring reminder of the price that must be paid for advancement was the sight of these pits. People watched in disbelief as mountains of electronic rubbish piled up. Each pit contaminated the land and water with dangerous chemicals and heavy metals, whilst posing a threat to the health and wellness of a great number of communities. Housing was crammed into places that were shockingly technologically advanced and efficient, and people had very little space to themselves and their belongings. There were often when families with children were crammed into a couple of rooms that were stuffed with technology and had fold-away mattresses. There were so few jobs available, and incomes were so low. Millions of people were left imprisoned in a loop of food insecurity and hopelessness, with no way out of the circle.

As urbanization accelerated and city populations swelled, the average housing space dropped to under forty square meters worldwide. Gone were the days of sprawling suburban mansions and spacious apartments. Families found themselves crammed into highly technically designed living quarters that made the most of every inch of space.

In addition to being a challenge, the tendency towards living in smaller spaces presented an opportunity. It served as a sharp reminder of the growing pressures that were brought on by urbanisation and overpopulation. On the other side, it presented an opportunity to rethink the way in which cities were planned and constructed, as well as to build and construct areas that were not only effective, but also lively and liveable. Cities and urban sprawl had the opportunity by design to be both welcoming and desirable to all their communities. In the highly technically developed dwelling quarters that were scattered across the urban environment, families enjoyed being surrounded by cutting-edge technology and inventive design features. In maximising space and minimising waste efficiencies made lives as comfortable and efficient as possible. Using a single voice command, smart home systems were able to regulate everything from temperature control to energy usage. Walls were repurposed as storage units, furniture was redesigned to accommodate the shifting requirements of the occupants, and every space could be utilised for multiple purposes. The sense of togetherness produced by compact living was perhaps the most noteworthy part of this living arrangement. Within the close-knit neighbourhoods that emerged in the central business district of the city, residents became like members of the same family. Residents of the same buildings often provided support and looked out for each another in times of hardship. The presence of shared amenities and community spaces fostered social contact and collaboration. A sense of belonging that extended beyond the confines of individual living quarters provided kinship and purpose to otherwise dreary lives. In this world of scarcity and abundance, the true measure of humanity lay not in the gadgets and gizmos that surrounded them, but in the compassion and empathy they showed towards their fellow beings. It was hoped that this spirit of solidarity would eventually determine the fate of the Earth and all who called it home.

Chapter 10: Reebus's Mandate

The halls of the GGC were buzzing with anticipation as delegates from around the world gathered for the highly anticipated Electoral Mandate Summit. At the heart of the summit were two towering figures. In one corner was Reebus, the incumbent leader with a legacy of accomplishment parading like a hero. In the other corner was Sandronica Sprowl, the first-time challenger vying for the highest office.

The atmosphere crackled with tension as the delegates took their seats. Eyes were fixed on the stage where Reebus and Sandronica would soon present their key policies and visions for the future. For both candidates, this moment was crucial. It was a chance to sway the minds of the world's most influential decision-makers and secure their support in the upcoming election.

As the summit commenced, Reebus first and then Sandronica were introduced. Each candidate exuding confidence and gravitas in equal measure. Reebus, dressed in his signature tailored suit, projected an aura of authority and experience. Sandronica was clad in a sharp business attire whilst radiating energy and enthusiasm. Unusually, Sandronica was unable to be there in person as it had emerged that she had experienced a serious personal loss in the previous days. It was a testimony to her resilience that there would be any mandate from her today at all. She was omnipresent in the room as her presence radiated from a media column at the side of the room. Sandronica's every expression could still be seen throughout this meeting. Holographic technology was so advanced in this modern age that it made very little difference whether someone was physically or remotely cast into the room. Holographs allowed people to be view them from all sides and angles; from all locations and have control over viewpoints. In some cases, they can even view the same holographic presence on multiple devices at the same time but from different angles.

As the presentations began; Reebus stood before a gathering of his most trusted advisors with his voice resonating with authority as he issued his mandates for re-election.

"My fellow council members," Reebus began, his tone commanding the attention of all those present. "As we stand on the precipice of a new era of prosperity and progress, it is imperative that we continue to adapt and evolve in order to meet the challenges of the future."

He paused for a moment, allowing his words to sink in before continuing. "To that end, I propose that we reduce the age of transport to the retirement planet from eighty to seventy years old." His concept was simple yet profound. In reducing the retirement age so that people are transported to 'Serenity 1' earlier it would free up valuable space and resources for the burgeoning population. It was a solution that had the potential to address not only the immediate needs of the present but also the long-term sustainability of the planet. In Reebus's mind, the logic was irrefutable. By lowering the retirement age, the GGC could effectively help redistribute resources more equitably. This would ensure that every citizen had access to the necessities of life. This would help alleviate the pressure on Earth's already strained infrastructure, making the everyday battle for food and resources less competitive and more manageable for all. Murmurs of approval rippled through the assembly as Reebus's advisors nodded in agreement. It was a bold move, but one that Reebus believed was necessary to ensure the continued stability of their society.

"As you are all aware, our resources are stretched thin, and the strain on our planet is becoming increasingly unsustainable," Reebus continued. "By lowering the age of retirement transportation, we can reduce some of that burden and ensure that our resources are distributed more equitably among the population."

There was a sense of anticipation in the air as Reebus's advisors absorbed his words, the gravity of his proposal weighing heavily on their minds. It was a decision that would have far-reaching implications, affecting the lives of hundreds of millions of people across the globe. For Reebus, there was no doubt in his mind that it was the right choice. As a leader, it was his duty to make the tough decisions, to chart a course for the future that would ensure the continued prosperity and stability of their society.

He paused for a moment, allowing his words to sink in before continuing. "Also, to that end, I propose a series of mandates that will not only ensure the continued stability and prosperity of our society. Also to pave the way for a future filled with opportunity and promise."

Reebus went on to outline his mandates, each one carefully crafted to address the pressing needs of their society while also laying the groundwork for future growth and development. Among the first was a proposal to increase the budget for transportation and holographic services, recognizing the growing demand for these essential services as more people were likely to 'travel' to the retirement planet.

Reebus updated the room on the latest reports on communication infrastructure between Earth and 'Serenity 1'. The demand for connectivity between the two worlds was greater than ever before, and the existing holographic services were struggling to keep pace with the ongoing need for communication. With each passing day the population of 'Serenity 1' grew, bringing with it a surge in the demand for real-time communication. Loved ones back on Earth along with whole families longed to connect across the vast expanse of space. Friends yearned for the familiar voices of home, and colleagues sought to collaborate on projects spanning the distance between worlds.

"The current holographic services are strained to their limits, unable to meet the ever-increasing demand for bandwidth and reliability. We need to improve this" spoke Reebus. He knew that they needed to maintain a seamless flow of communication between Earth and 'Serenity 1', and improvement ideas would be well received. He spoke with enthusiasm the senate took it all on board, lapping up with a chorus of approval and endless clapping.

Reebus gathered his team and allowed them to present more details in the proposal for additional budget allocation to bolster holographic services. They presented a whole host of data driven information and video presentations. The benefits were detailed including that of enhanced connectivity, improved collaboration on scientific research and strengthened familial bonds across the vastness of space.

As the presentation concluded, Reebus felt a sense of respect from the room. It was a recognition of the vital importance of connectivity in bridging the gap between Earth and 'Serenity 1'. In a universe defined by distance and isolation, communication served as the lifeline that bound their two planets together. This offered hope and solace to all who traversed the expanse of space.

Despite her prominent role in shaping the future of space exploration, little was known about Sandronica Sprowl's personal life. Nobody knew details of her family, or her inner circle of friends. Official media releases painted a picture of a brilliant scientist and visionary leader. She was a woman whose intellect and ambition had propelled her to the forefront of the scientific community. Beyond the carefully crafted image presented to the public, the details of Sandronica's private life remained elusive, hidden behind a veil of secrecy that seemed impenetrable.

Rumours swirled in the corridors of power and the whispers of the gossip mill, with speculation running rampant about Sandronica's origins and connections. Some claimed she was born into a family of influential politicians, while others whispered of clandestine ties to shadowy organizations and secret societies. Even the nature of the personal loss she had experienced in the last few days was cloudy and awkward with nobody willing to dig deeper for the worry of what might be found; or how she or the public might react.

In the heart of the Global Governance Council headquarters, Sandronica Sprowl's lit image beamed before a gathering of her supporter and foes alike. Her voice was steady and confident as she outlined her mandates for election. Being the only direct opposition to Reebus meant that every word she spoke carried weight and scrutiny. She was determined to make her vision for the future known.

"Ladies and gentlemen," Sandronica began in her holographic presentation, her voice ringing out with authority. "As we stand on the cusp of a new era, it is imperative that we chart a course for the future that prioritizes the well-being of all citizens, not just the privileged few."

She paused for a moment, allowing her words to sink in before continuing. "To that end, I propose a series of mandates that will address the pressing needs of our society while also laying the foundation for a more sustainable and equitable future."

Sandronica went on to outline her mandates, each one carefully crafted to reflect her commitment to social justice and environmental stewardship. Among them was a proposal to keep the Transportation age at eighty, recognizing the wisdom of allowing individuals to enjoy their golden years in peace and dignity.

"By maintaining the Transportation age at eighty, we can ensure that our elderly citizens are given the opportunity to live out their remaining years with the respect and care they deserve," Sandronica explained. "It is imperative that we uphold the values of compassion and empathy in all aspects of our society."

She also proposed allocating funds for technological research into new food sources, particularly from various insects, recognizing the potential of these alternative sources to alleviate food scarcity and promote environmental sustainability.

"Insects have long been overlooked as a viable food source, but recent advancements in technology have shown that they hold great promise in addressing our growing food crisis," Sandronica declared. "By investing in research and development in this area, we can unlock new sources of nutrition that will benefit us all."

Sandronica advocated for a more aggressive deep drilling campaign to seek out further water resources. She recognized the urgent need to secure access to clean, potable water for all citizens.

"As our population continues to grow, so too does the demand for water," Sandronica stated. "By expanding our efforts to explore and extract water from deep underground sources, we can ensure that all citizens have access to this essential resource for generations to come."

"I propose we further our drilling campaigns to go deep into the now barren wastelands of the Pacific and Mediterranean shelves where once there stood huge bodies of water" added Sandronica in cementing her argument.

As Sandronica concluded her speech, a sense of mixed feelings filled the room. Her vision for a brighter, more equitable future was resonating with some of those present. Elsewhere most of the delegates who had closer ties with Reebus seemed unmoved. Sandronica appeared to be a leader with some new ideas, and conviction to lead them into a new era of progress and prosperity. Her ideas would appeal to a large portion of the public on the planet. Whether this would be enough to compete with the overall sway of Reebus' new retirement age mandate seemed less likely. Reebus had played a significant drawcard which most of a beleaguered society would see as a possibility to a better future for all.

Chapter 11: A Plan Takes Shape

Jayden and Arianna sat huddled together in Jayden's cramped apartment, their heads bent close as they whispered urgently back and forth. They had spent countless hours poring over their options, weighing the risks and benefits of each potential course of action. So far they had yet to produce a plan that felt right.

"We could just walk right into GGC headquarters and demand answers," Jayden suggested, his voice tinged with frustration. "They can't ignore us if we're right there in front of them."

Arianna shook her head, her brow furrowed with concern. "No, that's too risky. We would be walking into the lion's den unarmed. We need to think this through carefully."

They fell into a tense silence, each lost in their own thoughts as they racked their brains for a solution. It seemed like every idea they produced was either too dangerous or too impractical to pursue. Jayden and Arianna sat in Jayden's room, surrounded by a flurry of notes and diagrams, their minds abuzz with possibilities. As they mulled over their options, they began to explore further avenues for exposing the GGC and revealing the truth.

"What if we try to gather testimonies from people who have witnessed the disappearances firsthand?" Arianna suggested, her brow furrowed in concentration. "We could compile their stories and present them as evidence to the public."

Jayden nodded thoughtfully, considering her proposal. "It's a good idea, but we'd need to be careful," he replied. "We don't want to put anyone in danger by asking them to come forward with sensitive information."

Arianna nodded in agreement, acknowledging the risks involved. Further time passed as neither of them could produce an appropriate idea that had a realistic chance of success. Suddenly, Arianna's eyes lit up with excitement as an idea began to take shape in her mind. "Wait... what if we don't go to them... but instead, we bring them to us?"

Jayden's eyebrows shot up in surprise, intrigued by Arianna's sudden burst of inspiration. "What do you mean?"

Arianna grinned, her eyes gleaming with determination. "Think about it, we don't have to take on the GGC alone. If we can rally enough people to our cause, we cannot be ignored. We just need to find a way to get the word out, to show everyone what's really going on behind closed doors."

As Jayden listened to Arianna's plan unfold, a sense of excitement bubbled up inside him. It was risky, to be sure, but it also had the potential to be incredibly powerful. With enough people behind them, they could make a real difference, they could hold the GGC accountable for their actions.

"Okay," Jayden said, his voice firm with resolve. "Let's do it. Let's tell everyone who will listen, let's shine a light on the truth and expose the GGC for what they really are."

As Jayden paced the room, his brow furrowed with thought, Arianna poured over the countless articles and forum posts that littered their digital domain. Each thread of information was a thread in the tapestry of their conspiracy, weaving a narrative of deception and intrigue that threatened to consume them whole. Jayden and Arianna sat in tense silence, their minds racing with the implications of what they had uncovered. The temptation to share their discoveries with the world. The opportunity to expose the truth behind the silent exodus was almost overwhelming. As they weighed their options, a sobering realization began to dawn upon them: they had no evidence.

"It's just not enough," Jayden muttered, frustration evident in his voice. "Even if we were to post about it on social media, who would believe us? Without concrete proof, we'd just be dismissed as conspiracy theorists." Arianna nodded in reluctant agreement; her gaze fixed on the floor as she wrestled with her own doubts. "And even if people did believe us," she added, "what then? What could we possibly hope to achieve without any evidence to back up our claims?" The weight of their predicament hung heavy in the air, casting a pall over their once-optimistic intentions. For weeks, they had poured over every piece of information they could find, desperate to uncover the truth behind the mysterious disappearances plaguing their society. Faced with the harsh reality of their situation, they were forced to confront the limitations of their knowledge and the futility of their efforts.

"I just don't know what to do," Jayden admitted, frustration and uncertainty etched into every word. "We're so close to the truth, and yet it feels like we're no closer to finding it than when we started." Arianna reached out and squeezed his hand, offering what little comfort she could in the face of their shared despair. "We can't give up," she said, her voice tinged with determination. "Even if we don't have evidence now, we'll keep searching until we find it. When we do, we'll make sure the world knows the truth, no matter what." We must do something," Jayden muttered, his voice tinged with frustration. " We can't just sit back and let them get away with it." Arianna nodded in agreement; her eyes alight with a fierce resolve. "But what can we do? We do not have any evidence. No one will believe us without proof." Their words hung heavy in the air, a silent testament to the weight of their predicament. For all their fervent belief, they were but two voices lost in the vast expanse of the digital wilderness, their cries for justice drowned out by the cacophony of scepticism and disbelief. Even in the face of uncertainty, they refused to yield to despair. With trembling hands, they reached for their keyboards, their fingers dancing across the keys as they sought to give voice to the truth that burned within their hearts. Hours turned to days as they toiled away in their quest for vindication, crafting message after message in a desperate bid to pierce the veil of ignorance that shrouded their world. No matter how eloquent their words, no matter how impassioned their pleas, they found themselves met with only silence.

"Our words will simply get lost amongst the other dissenting social threads and there's no way anyone will believe a thing we have to say," added Jayden. In the end, they were left with naught but their convictions, a flickering flame of hope amidst the encroaching darkness. As they gazed out into the night, their eyes drawn to the distant stars that winked in the heavens above, they knew that their journey was far from over.

Jayden and Arianna sat across from each other, their brows furrowed in deep concentration as they mulled over their predicament. They had come to the stark realization that simply telling the world "Their truth" about the GGC's nefarious activities would not be enough. Concrete evidence was needed to back up their claims.

"It's not enough to just say it," Arianna said, her voice tinged with frustration. "We need proof, something tangible that people can't ignore. If we can find enough proof that my mum will believe us then maybe that is the starting point. Even then we must be careful because the truth could be a dangerous discovery and I do not think that everyone is quite ready for it," she added.

Jayden nodded in agreement, his mind racing with possibilities. "How do we get our firsthand evidence without getting caught? The GGC isn't exactly known for being forthcoming with their secrets."

"What about trying to access classified documents or data from the GGC's archives?" she suggested. "If we could find concrete evidence of their involvement in the silent exodus, it would be impossible for them to deny it."

Jayden's eyes gleamed with excitement at the prospect. "That could work," he said, his voice tinged with anticipation. "But getting access to their archives won't be easy. We'd need someone on the inside to help us, someone who knows their way around their security systems." As they brainstormed ideas and weighed their options, Jayden and Arianna knew that they were treading on dangerous ground. The GGC was a powerful organization, with resources and influence beyond measure, and exposing their secrets would not be without risk.

"The type of information we would need would not be accessible easily and would be sure to be stored behind closed doors," mused Jayden.

Arianna chewed her lip nervously, her eyes darting around the room as she wracked her brain for a solution. "Maybe... maybe we could break into one of their facilities? Find some documents or something that proves what they're up to."

Jayden's eyes widened at the suggestion, both impressed and a little scared by Arianna's audacity. "That's risky, Arianna. If we get caught, we could end up in serious trouble."

Arianna shrugged, a determined glint in her eyes. "It's a risk we have to take. If we want to expose the truth and stop the GGC, we can't afford to play it safe."

With a sense of grim determination settling over them, Jayden and Arianna set to work, meticulously planning their next move. They knew that they had no other choice. The fate of the world hung in the balance, and they were willing to do whatever it took to uncover the truth.

For days on end, they scoured every corner of the digital domain, sifting through mountains of data and decoding cryptic messages in their relentless pursuit of answers. With each passing hour, their efforts bore a few crumbs, leading them ever closer to the elusive truth that lay concealed within the shadows of society.... Or so they hoped. Their search was not without its challenges. Countless times, they found themselves thwarted by the impenetrable digital barriers erected by those who sought to keep the truth hidden from prying eyes. Firewalls and encryption protocols stood as formidable guardians, their presence a testament to the lengths to which their adversaries would go to protect their secrets. Undeterred by adversity, Jayden and Arianna pressed onward, their determination unyielding in the face of immeasurable odds. With each setback, they grew stronger, their resolve hardened by the fires of adversity as they forged ahead on their quest for justice.

Exhausted and disheartened, Jayden and Arianna succumbed to the weight of their frustration, their eyes growing heavy as sleep beckoned them into its embrace. As they drifted into unconsciousness, their minds swirling with doubt and uncertainty, a faint beep echoed through the room, barely registering amidst the haze of their despair. As if by some twist of fate, the sound pierced through the fog of their exhaustion, jolting them awake with a start. Blinking blearily, they turned their attention to the screen before them, where a single message awaited, its sender identified only as 'Affected18.'

Jayden and Arianna quickly rose and sat huddled around their screen; their fingers poised over the keyboard as they awaited the next message from 'Affected18.' The anticipation hung heavy in the air, mingling with the faint noise of the background temperature control devices around them. Suddenly, a further notification appeared on the screen, signalling the arrival of a new message. With bated breath, they opened it, their hearts pounding in anticipation of what they might find. "We have mutually beneficial aims," the message read. "I can help you.", read the message. Jayden and Arianna exchanged a look of disbelief, their minds reeling with the implications of the message. Could this be the breakthrough they had been waiting for. The opportunity to finally uncover the truth behind the silent exodus? In lack of other options this small breadcrumb appeared to offer the best hope of access to be able to find evidence on any hidden data and lies inside the GGC. At the very least it presented an opportunity to learn more. In the depths of the dark web, where shadows danced amidst the flickering glow of forbidden knowledge, Jayden and Arianna found themselves treading ahead. With each keystroke, they navigated deeper down the burrow with minds alight with the promise of revelation.

As they entered a secure channel set up by their contact, they were greeted by a figure cloaked in anonymity, their digital alias a mere whisper amidst the cacophony of voices that echoed through the digital ether. 'Affected18', greeted them, with words laced with a sense of urgency. "I've been expecting you."

With a sense of trepidation mingling with excitement, Jayden and Arianna leaned in closer, their eyes devouring the words that scrolled across the screen. "We need your help," Arianna pleaded, her voice a desperate plea in the darkness. "We're trying to uncover the truth about the Retirement Planet, but we need more information."

Affected18 responded. "I can help you,", with their fingers flying across the keyboard as they accessed a trove of forbidden knowledge hidden within the depths of the dark web. With each passing moment, their connection grew stronger, their minds intertwined in a dance of collaboration and defiance. 'Affected18' revealed secrets long buried beneath layers of deception, shining a light upon the darkest corners of the conspiracy that enshrouded the Retirement Planet.

Amidst the revelations they were offered more than just information; it was a lifeline, a chance to break free from the shackles of the shadows and forge their own path towards freedom.

"I know of a way into the facility," 'Affected18' typed, with words a promise of liberation amidst the chains that bound them. "But it won't be easy. You'll need to be prepared for anything."

With a sense of foreboding burning within their hearts, Jayden and Arianna listened intently as 'Affected18' outlined their plan, each detail a thread in the tapestry of their impending rebellion. They detailed the exact coordinates of the facility, the guard schedule as well as knowledge of the internals of the building that nobody could really know unless they had been there.

"'Affected18': Jayden and Arianna. I can see you are searching out the facility. I can tell you more. Do not worry this message is untraceable. Once you get in the front door you need to enter in 733287 to the keypad to get through the access door into the data room. Also, do not go there in the next few days as there is extra security due to some GGC event, so my advice is to wait till Tuesday next week when there will be less guards and the guard schedule, I sent becomes active."

'Affected18' then sent interactive schematics and plans of the whole facility as if they were the architect of the structure. They were clearly a very powerful and clever individual and someone that was worth knowing, especially if this information helped them out. As they mapped out their plan, their hearts beat stronger and faster, knowing that they were on the brink of something truly momentous. With luck, and a little bit of courage, they might be able to acquire the evidence they needed to expose the GGC's secrets once and for all. The time for talking and planning was over, and it was time that action needed to begin. They just needed a couple more days for the new shift pattern to be active and for them to action their plan.

Chapter 12: The Temptation of the Retirement Planet

Every night, like clockwork, the screens of every household flickered to life, casting a warm glow across living rooms and bedrooms alike. It was time for the nightly broadcast where an interactive media presentation promised to transport viewers to a world of wonder and delight: the retirement planet; 'Serenity 1.'

As the familiar jingle played, images of lush green landscapes and sparkling blue oceans filled the screen, accompanied by a soothing voice extolling the virtues of life on the retirement planet. The presenter, with a winning smile plastered on their face, spoke of endless days spent lounging on sun-soaked beaches, indulging in gourmet meals prepared by world-class chefs, and exploring exotic landscapes teeming with vibrant flora and fauna.

From the bustling streets of New York to the remote desolate villages of Africa, people from all corners of the Earth tuned in, their hearts filled with longing and anticipation. For in the virtual paradise of 'Serenity 1', they found solace and serenity. It was a fleeting glimpse of a world untouched by the chaos and strife that plagued their own. As the program began, viewers were transported to a realm of breathtaking beauty and boundless possibility. They wandered through lush gardens and shimmering lakes, their senses intoxicated by the sights and sounds of this idyllic paradise. They strolled along winding paths and gazed up at the stars, their minds adrift in a sea of wonder and awe. For those who watched each night, 'Serenity 1' was more than just an informative presentation, it was a lifeline, a beacon of hope in a world fraught with uncertainty. It offered a glimpse of a future where peace and harmony reigned supreme, where the worries of the past were but distant memories.

It was not just the visuals that captivated viewers, it was the interactive element of the presentation that truly set it apart. With the touch of a button, viewers could immerse themselves in virtual reality simulations that allowed them to experience firsthand the thrills and joys of life on 'Serenity 1'. They could escape their own realities and swim with dolphins in crystal-clear waters, soar through the sky on a majestic hot air balloon, or dance the night away under a canopy of stars.

Reebus's words would add to the documentary like story, "Nestled among the stars, far beyond the reaches of Earth's atmosphere, lies the retirement planet, the shimmering jewel in the vast expanse of the cosmos. With its verdant landscapes, pristine beaches, and crystal-clear waters, it was a paradise beyond compare, a haven where the cares of the world melted away like dew beneath the morning sun.

For those fortunate enough to call it home, life on 'Serenity 1' is a dream come true. It's the location of a never-ending vacation filled with endless possibilities and boundless joy. For the billions still confined to the confines of Earth, it remained nothing more than a distant fantasy, a tantalizing glimpse of a world of which they could only dream."

Reebus himself then came into the presentation and added more and more substance and hope to entice anyone watching to dream of moving to the planet.

He explained that despite its allure, 'Serenity 1' was not without its limitations. With limited space and resources, there simply was not room for everyone who wished to make the journey. With transportation availability at a premium, only a "lucky" select few were able to embark on the voyage to this idyllic paradise.

Reebus had a vision; a vision of a future where the retirement planet was not just a dream reserved for the privileged few, but a reality accessible to all who dared to dream. As Reebus campaigned for re-election, he promised to make that vision a reality. With his trademark charisma and unwavering appeal, Reebus vowed to increase the frequency and quantity of people who could travel to the retirement planet, ensuring that no one was left behind in the quest for paradise. He spoke of ambitious plans to expand transportation infrastructure, to harness the power of advanced technology to streamline the process, and to forge alliances with other planets to secure additional resources.

As he made his case to the people of Earth, Reebus painted a picture of a future where the retirement planet was not just a distant fantasy, but a tangible destination within reach of all who dared to reach for the stars. As the election drew near, the promise of paradise hung in the air, tantalizingly close yet still just out of reach. With Reebus at the helm, anything seemed possible. As people dared to hope that one day soon, they too would be able to make the journey to the retirement planet and start a new life in paradise.

Jayden and Arianna were still putting together their final plan for the GGC break in they planned on Tuesday, but they dipped into the presentation hoping it would add more information for what they were trying to uncover.

As the presentation reached its climax, a sense of unease settled over Jayden and Arianna who were watching on intently. The promises made by the presenter sounded too good to be true, and after their recent events, for the first time, they found themselves questioning the authenticity of what they were seeing on screen.

"Do you really think it's possible?" Arianna whispered, her voice barely above a murmur.

Jayden frowned, his brow furrowing in thought. "I'm not sure. It all seems so... perfect, you know? Like it's too good to be real."

Arianna nodded in agreement, her expression troubled. "And did you notice how they never show any real footage of the planet? It is all just simulations and CGI. It's like they're hiding something."

"Humanity has a tendency to believe stories and pictures that are described to them, no matter how extreme or unlikely they are, especially if there is an emotional attachment created, or the story is something that they believe is needed within their lives.," added a thought provoked Jayden. "I think we haven't been able to see what is in front of us because the lie is too easy to believe.," he concluded.

Jayden's heart sank further as he realized that Arianna was right. Despite the dazzling visuals and captivating narration, there was a distinct lack of tangible evidence to support the existence of the retirement planet. As he glanced again at Arianna, he could see the seeds of doubt taking root in her mind as well.

Deep down, they both knew that Reebus was a master manipulator, capable of spinning any narrative to suit his own agenda. Whilst the retirement planet seemed like a tantalizing prospect, there was a growing part of them that could not shake the feeling that it was all just an elaborate hoax designed to keep the populace complacent and obedient.

Equally, Arianna still held on dear to the thoughts that her grandad was now on the retirement planet all happy and relaxed and she would one day catch up with him there in real life. Even though she had seen him disappear and evaporate she was of mixed thoughts as to it was just some advanced matter transporter, and her grandad was safe and well. If she were to prove what they both saw at the transportation complex, then she would also be assigning her grandad's existence to the history of time. Even a faint chance that all was well needed to be kept in her heart as the world needed hope and the alternative was too difficult to take in.

As the presentation ended, the presenter's voice took on a note of urgency, urging viewers to start planning for their retirement today. "Don't wait until it's too late," they implored. "Life on the retirement planet awaits, and it's never too early to start dreaming of a brighter future."

And as the screen faded to black, leaving behind a lingering sense of longing in its wake, viewers across the globe felt a gnawing desire stirring deep within them. The retirement planet seemed like a paradise beyond compare, a utopia where all their dreams could come true. With each passing day, the allure of that distant world grew stronger, beckoning them to strive for the day when they too could join the ranks of the fortunate few who called it home. They both believed that the advert had ended as it does every day and people need to focus with the rest of their daily routines. However, today was different, and all around the globe a follow up presentation followed and grabbed the attention of anybody near a holographic or presentation device.....

Among those, across the channel in Paris, France, a large family watched huddled in a small room as their holographic device flickered to life with the new advert which followed. Vincent Henry, a 45-year-old traffic parking enforcer watched with his wife, mother, and father and four children as this added information presented itself.

In shimmering letters, the advert announced a once-in-a-lifetime opportunity: the chance to win an early ticket to the retirement planet, a haven of tranquillity nestled among the stars. Vincent's heart skipped a beat as he saw the details. The retirement planet was a paradise beyond compare, a place where the cares of the world melted away, and every day was a new adventure.

With a trembling hand, Vincent reached out to tap the holographic screen, eager to learn more. Instantly, the advert expanded, revealing more stunning vistas of the retirement planet. Lush gardens stretched as far as the eye could see, their vibrant colours dancing in the gentle breeze. The Crystal-clear lakes again sparkled under the warmth of an eternal sun, inviting visitors to dip their toes in the cool, refreshing waters, it was not just a dream, but it was perfection.

It was not just the natural beauty that captured Vincent's imagination in this new presentation. New images and interactive elements of the retirement planet boasted interactive designs and blueprints of state-of-the-art facilities designed to cater to every need and desire. From luxurious spas to gourmet restaurants, from cultural events to outdoor activities, there was something for everyone to enjoy.

There was the promise of community. The retirement planet was not just a destination; it was a home. A place where like-minded individuals could come together to forge new friendships and create lasting memories. It was a chance for Vincent and his family to leave behind the hustle, bustle of city life, and embrace a slower, more meaningful existence. Several 'residents' then individually came into the presentation each adding more knowledge about the special environment that is Serenity 1. One of the residents talked about the transportation process to the planet and answered a lot of the questions that existed in the darkened corridors of each of Earth's communities. It was if the presentation was designed to allay fears based on grumblings and research around the most sceptical of people. It even went as far as showing a transportation event for one man who went there recently. The transportation seemed smooth and calm and bore no similarities to the events that Jayden and Arianna had seen those weeks before.

As the advert continued, Vincent found himself transfixed, his mind swirling with possibilities. Could he be one of the lucky few to win a ticket to paradise? Was this his chance to finally live the life he had always dreamed of, free from the stresses and strains of the modern world?

Vincent planned he would enter the lottery, throwing his name into the hat for a chance at a brighter future. For in the vast expanse of the cosmos, anything was possible. As he closed the holographic display, a spark of even greater joy ignited within his heart. The retirement planet beckoned, and Vincent was determined to answer its call. Vincent's heart swelled with a smile about this new initiative, one that he knew that Reebus must have led. He like many would be steadfast in their support for Reebus in the coming election.

"The GGC's idea was nothing short of revolutionary, with a comprehensive plan to address global poverty and inequality through innovative economic empowerment programs," he exclaimed, it was a vision that resonated deeply with Vincent, who had long been an advocate for social justice and equal opportunity.

"This is extraordinary," Vincent exclaimed, unable to contain his enthusiasm. "The GGC has truly outdone itself this time. This idea has the potential to transform the lives of millions, offering hope and opportunity where there was once only despair."

"This idea gives us more than just a plan," Vincent continued, his voice filled with conviction. "It gives us hope in a world that can sometimes seem dark and uncertain. With this initiative, we have the power to create a future where everyone has the chance to live a life of dignity and purpose."

Vincent's eyes widened in disbelief as the final part of the announcement continued and echoed further through the room. The GGC unveiled an unexpected addition to their lottery for the retirement. It was an opportunity for winners to bring up to ten members of their family with them. It was a gesture that spoke volumes about the GGC's commitment to fostering unity and strengthening familial bonds.

Vincent felt a rush of emotions welling up inside him, with hope, gratitude, and a profound sense of hope. The idea of being able to share the wonders of the retirement planet with his loved ones filled him with an indescribable warmth. For too long, he had witnessed the struggles and sacrifices of his family, and now, at last, there was a chance for them to experience a life of peace and tranquillity.

As the implications of the announcement sank in, Vincent's heart swelled with gratitude toward the GGC. This was more than just a lottery. It was an opportunity to create lasting memories with the people he cherished most.

With a smile that stretched from ear to ear, Vincent turned to his family, his eyes shining with excitement. "Did you hear that?" he exclaimed, unable to contain his enthusiasm. "The GGC is allowing winners to bring their families with them to the retirement planet!"

As the holographic presentation ended with Reebus himself talking about the idea, more details were given about exactly how to enter and that it was free for everyone to do so, and it all seemed too good to be true.

Vincent sat there, the final parts of the screen jingles illuminating his face as he immediately contacted his closest relatives. He knew what he was about to propose was unconventional, perhaps even audacious, but the allure of Serenity 1 was too strong to resist. With each carefully crafted conversation, Vincent outlined his plan: he would enter his relatives' names into the retirement lottery for Serenity 1, and if he were to win, he would take them with him to the paradise beyond the stars. It was a bold move one that carried with it the promise of a better life for those he held dear. As he completed his final conversation, Vincent felt a surge of anticipation course through him. He knew that the odds of winning the lottery were slim, but the thought of providing his loved ones with the opportunity to escape the hardships of Earth was worth the risk.

Vincent, however had told a few 'untruths' and although he had a definitive and finite set of his nine loved ones and him who he wished to take, he had led maybe thirty people he knew into believing that Vincent would take him should they win. He was so desperate to start a new life that he wanted to take any opportunity he had to readdress the odds to be more in his favour.

Elsewhere in the world, from bustling cities to the smaller desolate villages, from towering skyscrapers to humble cottages, the news of the retirement planet lottery spread like wildfire, igniting a wave of jubilation and excitement that swept across the globe. In every corner of the world, people rejoiced at the prospect of a brighter future, as chance leads to hope and uplifts morale as anything becomes possible.

In the crowded streets of urban metropolises, people gathered in impromptu celebrations, their voices raised in songs of joy and hope. Strangers embraced each other with tears of happiness streaming down their faces, their hearts overflowing with gratitude for the chance to escape the hardships of their daily lives.

In rural communities, where the rhythms of life were dictated by the land and the seasons, families came together around crackling bonfires, sharing stories and laughter late into the night. For generations, they had toiled and struggled to make ends meet, but now, there was a glimmer of hope on the horizon. It was a chance for a better life for themselves and their children.

Back in London, Jayden and Arianna sat across from each other, with the holographic presentation casting flickering shadows on the walls. The news of the retirement planet lottery had come out of the blue.

"I don't know, Arianna," Jayden said, furrowing his brow as he swirled his tea absentmindedly. "It's too good to be true. A chance to leave everything behind and start fresh on some far-off planet?"

Arianna nodded in agreement, her expression mirroring Jayden's concern. "I can't shake the feeling that there's something even further off about the whole thing. I mean, why suddenly are they offering the chance of tickets to anyone who enters a lottery? has something changed?"

"Did you notice Jayden, that, they never even mentioned how many winners there are going to be?" said Arianna perplexed at it all.

"Everyone seems so excited about it," Jayden remarked, his voice tinged with uncertainty. "Maybe we're just being overly cautious. Who would not want a chance at a better life?"

"What about the transportation scene they showed in the presentation?" it was absolutely nothing like what we saw. "Or the information they gave about the collection of 80-year-olds who are late for their transportation, and how the GGC went to help them find their way?", Jayden commented about another scene where various questions were answered throughout in a way that would make almost any non-believer completely fall for the story placed before them. "It seems that the GGC are prepared and aware of whispers in the community out in the wild and have an answer for everything that is thrown in their direction. I think that after tonight it is highly unlikely that anyone would believe anything we were to say about what we saw. We are certainly on the outside now." added Jayden.

Arianna chewed on her lower lip, deep in thought. "I suppose you're right," she conceded. ". It still feels like we are jumping into the unknown when we go to the facility on Tuesday without knowing all the facts. What if there is more to this than meets the eye? What if we get caught?"

"Besides," continued Arianna, "Do we truly know where my grandad is or what happened to him? It just seems like everything is a mystery that is being controlled from above."

Arianna was beginning to doubt herself and what she had seen. The nature of her life and that of many others is that since merely staying alive was a struggle then also it was difficult to truly know what to believe. It was common for people to start imagining and hallucinating due to lack of clean water, or the effects of pollution and disease on their own bodies. Despite the best intentions and clearest thoughts about what they *thought* they had seen, there were still worries about everything and would be until ultimate proof was found. Although he would not say it out loud, Jayden also had a few nagging doubts about what was real and what was not. Irrespective of what people learned and discovered, the misinformation and reliance of distribution of media from the GGC was a life support to many; reliable, trustworthy news sources from the GGC that could not easily but ignored or disbelieved. People needed something to trust, no matter what the repercussions were.

Chapter 13: Into the Heart of the Beast

The air was thick with tension as Jayden and Arianna crouched behind a row of bushes, their breath coming in shallow gasps as they surveyed the looming structure of the GGC facility before them. It was a low-level facility, tucked away on the outskirts of the city, far from the prying eyes of the public. Even so, the security was tight, with cameras and guards stationed at every entrance.

"We have to be careful," Jayden whispered, his voice barely audible over the silence of the night. "One wrong move and we're toast."

Arianna nodded in agreement, her eyes darting nervously around the perimeter as she tried to gauge their chances of success. Even with the schematics, guard schedule and code that Affected18 had provided, breaking into a GGC facility was no small feat, and she knew that they were taking a huge risk by even attempting it. The need for answers outweighed the fear of getting caught, and she was willing to do whatever it took to uncover the truth.

With a silent nod, Jayden and Arianna slipped through the shadows, their movements quick and precise as they made their way toward the nearest entrance. They had scouted the facility for a while, meticulously planning their approach and identifying potential weaknesses in the security system. As they stood on the threshold of their mission, they knew that they had to act fast if they wanted to succeed. The truth about usefulness of Affected18's information was about to be uncovered. They had either helped greatly or misled even more. With practiced precision, they made their way to the designated entry point, relying on Affected18's detailed instructions every step of the way. It was as if they had a guide leading them through the darkness, navigating them through the dark exterior and past the security measures with ease.

As they reached the entrance to the facility, Jayden's eyes caught sight of something glinting in the moonlight. It was a stray security pass, lying abandoned on the ground next to an empty jacket. Without hesitation, he scooped it up, his heart racing with excitement.

"Looks like we just got lucky," he said, a triumphant smile spreading across his face.

Arianna's eyes widened in disbelief as she took in the security pass, her mind racing with possibilities. "Do you think it'll work?" she asked, her voice tinged with uncertainty.

Jayden shrugged; his confidence unwavering. "Only one way to find out."

With a deep breath, he swiped the security pass through the card reader, holding his breath as he waited for a response. To his surprise, and relief, the doors swung open, granting them access to the facility beyond.

As they stepped inside, Jayden and Arianna exchanged looks at each other as, their resolve became stronger than ever. With the security pass in hand, they were one step closer to uncovering the truth behind the GGC's sinister activities.

Jayden was a little suspect by now as although this was not a high-level security facility, it really should not be as easy as it had been. How on earth was a stray entry pass just lying on the floor? How were they so lucky to come across Affected18 and all their advice. If he did not know any better then it seemed someone was watching, or even helping them with their journey from above.

As they then Creeped through the darkened corridors of the facility, Jayden and Arianna's hearts pounded loudly in their chests, their senses heightened as they listened for any signs of approaching guards. The air was thick with tension, each passing moment fraught with the possibility of discovery.

Despite the danger, they pressed on, unwavering as they neared their objective. With the schematic in hand, they navigated inside the building to the data facilities that Affected18 had described, and they were exactly where they had advised.

Finally, after what felt like an eternity, they reached the exterior of their destination. It was a dimly lit room filled with rows of computer terminals; each one alive with the promise of untold secrets.

Peering through the windows Jayden eventually came to the entry door with numerous signs and stickers warning of compliance and danger. This was not a place to get stuck. To this point, Affected18 had provided nothing but valid and useful information, but a code is different. After all, how often would a code get changed, surely the likelihood of this working was minimal? He had read on forums during his research that all GGC facilities change their codes at least once a month, so it would be extremely good fortune if this were to still work.

Jayden depressed the seven key first and slowly moved through the two three's and then a two, an eight and finally pressed the seven. Not knowing whether the door would open or whether this would all be in vain as the final finger landed in position.

"Click, Clunk, Click.," as the mechanism inside the door churned and moved into an unlocked position as the door presented itself open like Aladdin's cave awaiting to show its secrets. Jayden and Arianna glared at each other before entering through the door, creeping silently as they were to continue with the rest of their plan.

With a thoughtful 'hmmm' and a nod, Jayden and Arianna approached one of the terminals ready to start their pursuit on further truth. Jayden's fingers flying over the keyboard as he tried to access the system with the security card reader. It was a race against time, with every passing second bringing them closer to discovery, or to disaster. With bated breath, Jayden and Arianna huddled around the computer terminal, their fingers dancing across the keyboard once more as they delved deeper into the GGC's classified database. The glow of the screen illuminated their faces, casting eerie shadows in the dimly lit room as they worked feverishly to uncover the truth. Arianna kept looking around her and hoping that nobody would see what they were up to. They were both nervous and concerned but knew they had to keep going as they had come too far to turn back. As they navigated through the encrypted files, Jayden's heart raced with anticipation. He knew that they were treading on dangerous ground, but the need for answers outweighed the fear of getting caught.

The encrypted data taunted them, its complex algorithms and layers of security proving to be formidable barriers to their progress. If there was one thing Jayden and Arianna were known for, it was their technical skills and determination to crack any code, which they had learned from a very young age.

With an informal glance, they dove into their work, each tapping into their own expertise to unravel the mystery before them. Jayden's fingers dancing across the keyboard like a silent opera, his mind racing as he attempted to decipher the encryption patterns. Meanwhile, Arianna delved into the depths of her hacking tools, employing every trick in her arsenal to bypass the file's defences. Hours passed in a blur as they tirelessly worked to break through the encryption, their determination growing further in the face of adversity. They encountered firewalls, encryption keys, and layers of obfuscation designed to thwart even the most skilled hackers. Jayden and Arianna remained undeterred; their resolve strengthened by the knowledge that the information hidden within the files could hold the key to unravelling the facility's secrets.

As they delved even deeper into the encryption, they began to uncover fragments of data, tantalizing clues that hinted at the true nature of their discovery. Each piece of the puzzle brought them closer to their goal, fuelling their determination to succeed where others had failed. Just as they thought they were making progress, they hit a wall. A particularly intricate encryption scheme blocked their path, its algorithms unlike anything they had encountered before. Frustration threatened to overwhelm them, and Jayden pulled away from the screen in defeat.

"You have to keep going, Jayden.," said Arianna as she tried to give him motivation. "You are the best code breaker I know, and I know you can do this. I need you to find the truth!"

Jayden sat for a minute and then was pepped by Arianna's words. He knew she was right, and they had to continue as it was not a position they would find themselves in very often, if at all, ever again.

They both redoubled their efforts whilst holding each other's clammy hands when they could so they could add more moral support and show they cared. They pooled their knowledge and expertise when they needed to as it would be easier to tackle the challenge head-on. They flitted between a couple of different screens trying different things each time but still they were not progressing as had been hoped.

With further focus, they launched a coordinated joint assault on the encryption, their synchronized efforts pushing the limits of their technical skills. They dissected the code, analysing its structure and identifying vulnerabilities with precision and skill. Finally, their perseverance was about to pay off with the file and access unlocked.

After decrypting the final file Jayden realised that this was some kind of database which he then loaded through back door meaning that any other passwords required could be circumnavigated. This appeared to be quite an old database; certainly not something they had come to expect in the new GGC world.

Eventually and as he watched the screen flicker to life, a vast people database appeared. It was called the GGC retirement monitoring database. Jayden felt a surge of adrenaline course through his veins as he read this, still not entirely sure what it is true purpose was to be.

"Let's start with me," Jayden said, his voice barely above a whisper as he typed his name into the relevant search fields.

In an instant, the screen filled with a wealth of information about Jayden. This included his personal details, his medical history, and his educational background. It was like peering into a mirror of his own life, each entry a testament to his existence in the eyes of the GGC. It has every educational score he had ever received, his family history and even when his next dental check-up was. Deep inside the data was information about his dad's death and on another tab was a GPS based map with locations where Jayden had bought things in the past few weeks. Further tabs included information relating to his friends, likes, dislikes and pretty much every aspect of a person you could possibly image. This was incredibly scary and very intrusive; much beyond anything Jayden had ever imagined.

Arianna took to the system and started typing in her grandad's name. Her brow furrowed in immediate confusion. "This can't be right," she muttered, her eyes scanning the screen. "There's no record of my grandad anywhere."

Jayden assumed that she has misspelled her grandad's name so kept trying different versions and spellings but there was nothing to be found. They then tried typing Zelko's name too but again this was a complete dead end.

Jayden's heart sank as he agreed what Arianna was saying. It was as if her grandad had never existed, as if he had been erased from the annals of history with no trace left behind. It was a chilling revelation, one that sent shivers down his spine.

"Keep searching," he urged, his voice tinged with urgency. "There has to be something here."

Again, and again they both tried with her grandad's name into the search as if they expected the results to change, but as the screen flashed blank each time, only displaying the same three words, "No results found."

Jayden refused to accept defeat. There had to be a reason her grandad's records were missing, a clue hidden somewhere within the depths of the database. As he stared at the screen, his mind racing with possibilities, he knew that they would not stop until they uncovered the truth, no matter how elusive it may be.

The soft shine of the computer screen illuminated Jayden and Arianna's faces once more. They had been inside the computer facility for over three hours now and had been lucky that nobody seemed to notice their presence. They decided to try something different and start searching for people close to retirement age and see if they could be found or had more details available, but just as they were on the brink of a breakthrough, a sudden blare of alarms shattered the silence, jolting them out of their concentration. Jayden's heart skipped a beat as he realized what had happened, they had accidentally triggered a silent access alarm, alerting security to their presence.

"Run!" he shouted, his voice filled with urgency as he grabbed Arianna's hand and pulled her towards the exit.

Before they could make their escape, the door burst open, and four burly guards stormed into the room, their faces twisted into expressions of fury. They had well and truly been rumbled!

"Hands where we can see them!" one of the guards barked, his voice booming in the confined space.

Jayden and Arianna froze in their tracks, their hearts pounding in their chests as they faced down their captors. There appeared no were out and were trapped, caught in the web of their own making. They were not even sure what they had actually learned and certainly not enough to prove anything to the general public or even conspiracy theorists across the dark information highway.

"Who are you?" another guard demanded; his eyes narrowed in suspicion. "And what were you doing in here?"

Jayden's mind raced as he tried to produce a plausible explanation, but before he could speak, Arianna stepped forward, her chin held high.

"We found this pass outside and thought it would be fun to see what was inside this building.," said Jayden as he pointed to the pass in his hand.

"We decided to just... explore," added Arianna, her voice steady despite the fear raging inside her. "We didn't mean any harm."

The guards exchanged a sceptical glance, clearly unconvinced by Arianna's words. Before they could press the issue further, a voice crackled over the intercom, cutting through the tension like a knife.

"What's going on down there?" it demanded, its tone laced with authority.

The guards exchanged a wary glance before one of them stepped forward, his expression grim.

"We've got intruders, sir," he said, his voice tight with tension. "Two of them, caught red-handed in the retirement database room."

There was a moment of silence as the voice on the intercom processed the information, before finally responding with a single command.

"Bring them to me, I've been expecting them" it said, its tone leaving no room for argument.

Jayden and Arianna were both confused and alarmed as the 'expecting you' comment irked their whole wellbeing. Why would anyone be expecting them when nobody even knew they were coming here. It felt a little bit like they had walked into some kind of perplexing trap.

With a nod, the guards seized Jayden and Arianna by the arms, their grip like iron as they escorted them out of the room and into the unknown. As they disappeared into the depths of the facility, Jayden and Arianna could only wonder what fate awaited them at the hands of their captors.

Jayden and Arianna were ushered into a dimly lit office, the air heavy with tension as they stood before the imposingly dark figure of the facility manager. He sat behind a large desk, his gaze piercing as he studied them with an intensity that sent shivers down their spines. It seemed an eternity before his lips decided to offer guidance.

"Sit," he commanded, gesturing to the chairs in front of his desk.

They obeyed, sinking into the uncomfortable seats as they awaited the facility manager's next move. His brown eyes bore into them, searching for any sign of weakness or deception as he studied their faces with a critical eye.

"Now," he began, his voice low and menacing. "What were the two of you doing in the database room?"

Jayden and Arianna exchanged a nervous glance, unsure of how much to reveal. They knew that they were in a dangerous position, caught red-handed in the heart of the GGC facility with no plausible explanation for their presence.

"We were just... curious," Jayden said, his voice faltering slightly under the weight of the facility manager's scrutiny. "We wanted to see what was in the database."

The facility manager's lips curled into a derisive sneer. "Curious, you say? What exactly did you hope to find?"

The facility manager was not a very attractive man with wispy hair and a crooked face. His nose looked long and as if it had been broken or bent on numerous times before. He was clearly quite an angry and aggressive individual who seemed to scare not just Jayden and Arianna, but all of the guards and staff who worked there who left as quickly as they could. You could imagine the brutalisation he forced upon his staff when outside of the world's watching gaze. It may be that these 'qualities' were a reason that he held his position and worked at a place like this.

Arianna swallowed hard; her throat dries with fear. "We were... looking for information," she said, her voice barely above a whisper. "About... about the retirement planet."

The facility manager's eyes narrowed, his expression darkening with anger. "The retirement planet," he repeated, his voice dripping with disdain. "And what business do the two of you have with that? You are nowhere near old enough to have retirement on your minds!"

Jayden and Arianna exchanged a nervous glance, unsure of how much more to reveal. They knew that they were walking a fine line, teetering on the edge of a precipice with no way to gauge how far the fall might be. Maybe they might be even made to disappear if they were not careful, after all who would know where to look? They were effectively captives in a prison of their own making.

"We just... wanted to know more," Jayden said, his voice tinged with desperation. "We wanted to know if it was real."

The facility manager's gaze bore into them, weighing their words with a scepticism that made their skin crawl. It appeared that he knew more than Jayden and Arianna, and this was a heavily stacked conversation in the facility manager's favour. They were both unsure whether they were about to get beaten up, placed in a cell or worse.

Chapter 14: Caught in the Truth's Glare

Jayden and Arianna exchanged uneasy glances as the facility manager's stern voice echoed through the room. They sat on edge, facing the large monitor on the wall that displayed footage from the previous week. The clear images showed Jayden and Arianna standing in the departure facility, watching as Arianna's grandad vanished into thin air.

"There you are," the facility manager said, his voice a cold reminder of their predicament. "Caught on camera, witnessing a departure. Care to explain yourselves?"

Arianna's heart sank as she watched the scene unfold before her eyes. It was surreal seeing herself on screen, frozen in a moment of disbelief as her grandad disappeared before her very eyes. She had thought that their actions had gone unnoticed, but now it was clear that they had been under surveillance the entire time.

"We... we were just saying goodbye," she stammered, her voice barely above a whisper. "We didn't know what was happening."

The facility manager's expression remained unreadable as he studied them with a critical eye. "And yet, you were present at a highly classified event without authorization," he pointed out, his tone laced with accusation.

Jayden swallowed hard, his mind racing as he searched for a plausible explanation. "We were... curious," he said, his voice tinged with uncertainty. "We wanted to know what was happening to Arianna's grandad."

The facility manager was not convinced. With a snort, he crossed his arms over his chest and fixed them with a steely gaze. "Curious, you say? In a facility that is strictly off-limits to unauthorized personnel?"

Arianna's heart raced as she realized the gravity of their situation. They had been caught red-handed, witnessing a departure that was shrouded in secrecy and deception. There was no denying the evidence laid out before them, no escaping the consequences of their actions.

The facility manager's stern gaze softened for a moment before he spoke again, his voice carrying a weight of authority that sent shivers down Jayden and Arianna's spines. The manager then left the room and locked the door whilst leaving two guards at the entrance and went away without a hint of what was to follow. The room itself was the kind of place that you would like to immediately forget. It was a dark and dingy place not like the advanced and clean places elsewhere around them. It was like the room boundaries were not somewhere that anyone would cross. Even cleaning robots and air purification devices had obviously turned their noses up at the thought of this office and had controls and commands to never enter. There was an inherent musty smell throughout the room and pictures of ancient and bygone days of humanity with pictures upon walls that would be considered unsavoury in the modern day. Scantily clad women from days gone past, schematics of 20th century weaponry and news articles of atrocities that had been committed worldwide all filled otherwise vacant walls. This man was clearly a loner; a despot; perhaps violent and unhinged and someone who existed now at a time where the wider community no longer respected his type. The dregs of humanity all confined in one persona; it was easy to see why he was the leader at this facility.

"What do you think they're going to do to us?" Arianna whispered; her voice barely audible above the pounding of her heart.

Jayden shook his head, his expression grim. "I don't know, but we have to be prepared for anything. We can't let them catch us off guard."

It was a total realization, one that sent shivers down their spines. They had thought they were one step ahead, but they had walked right into another trap. The knowledge that they had been outmanoeuvred gnawed at them, filling them with a sense of helplessness.

As they glanced around the room, their eyes fell on the telltale signs of their discovery. The hi-tech surveillance equipment, the ominous click of locks being engaged – it was all too familiar. They had been so focused on decrypting the files that they had failed to notice the subtle signs of their impending capture. Arianna's hands trembled slightly as she reached for Jayden, the weight of their hopelessness settling heavily on her shoulders. They were facing not just one man, but an entire facility full of GGC guards hell-bent on thwarting their every move. As they stared at each other in silence, the gravity of their situation sank in. The evidence did not look good for them. Not at the retirement facility, and certainly not here. They were outnumbered, outgunned, and outmatched in every way. The odds of escape were stacked against them, and they knew it.

As they paced the room, their minds raced with a whirlwind of possibilities, each more terrifying than the last. Were they to be interrogated, punished, or worse? The thought sent a shiver down Arianna's spine, her hands trembling with a mixture of fear and defiance. They sat huddled together, their minds heavy with the weight of their predicament, but they could not help but be haunted by the tales they had heard about the atrocities committed by the GGC.

The stories were whispered in hushed tones, passed down from one captive to the next like a macabre game of telephone. Tales of torture, experimentation, and unspeakable horrors that sent shivers down their spines. They were stories of lives destroyed, of innocence shattered, and of hope extinguished in the face of unrelenting cruelty. They hoped for once that the tales they have heard were not real and that they were just one of those canaries in a cage sent out to prevent others from following a path upon its death.

For Jayden and Arianna, some of the rumours hit too close to home, of similar people to themselves who had found themselves caught in the direct glare and staring at the enemy and its open gaze. They had heard whispers of one man who had crossed paths with the GGC, only to disappear without a trace, for the stealing of some food from a GGC distribution facility. Others had been lucky enough to escape relatively unaffected but with slaps of wrists and changed attitudes due to repercussions of any type of secondary offence. Some lives would recover, while others had not been so fortunate. It wasn't obvious where Jayden and Arianna would lie on this scale of retribution. On one regards they hadn't done anything, at least nothing with a physical output, but it was not about what they had done; it was about what they had seen, what they had witnessed through closed doors, and what they think they had discovered when their fingers had typed away in accessing a data point.

Hours stretched into eternity as they waited in silence, their nerves frayed and their patience wearing thin. Jayden and Arianna took the opportunity to reassure themselves of being in this together and that no matter what happens they would be there for each other. Just as despair threatened to consume them whole, a faint sound echoed through the darkness, as heavy footsteps could be heard approaching through the corridor beyond. The door slowly began to unlock signalling the arrival of the next stage of fate. With bated breath, they watched as the door swung open, revealing the figure of the facility manager standing in the threshold. His expression was unreadable, his eyes shrouded in shadow as he regarded them with a mixture of curiosity and apprehension. The tension of the room rose beyond palpable acceptance, as Jayden and Arianna's fate was about to be unleashed.

"Jayden, Arianna," he began, his voice a low rumble that reverberated through the room, "you are needed for further questioning. Please come with me."

"I've been instructed by Reebus himself to bring you both to him for a chat with him," he announced, his words hanging heavily in the air.

Jayden's heart sank at the mention of Reebus. The leader of the GGC was not someone to be trifled with, and being summoned by him could only mean trouble. He exchanged a worried glance with Arianna, silently communicating their shared concern.

"Reebus?" Arianna echoed, her voice barely above a whisper. "Why would he want to talk to us?"

The facility manager shrugged, his expression unreadable. "I'm not at liberty to say," he replied cryptically. "But I suggest you follow me. It's not wise to keep Reebus waiting."

With a sinking feeling in the pit of their stomachs, Jayden and Arianna rose from their sticky seats and followed the facility manager out of their recent confines. They left the room that they wished never to return. They walked in silence, their minds racing with questions and uncertainty as they made their way through the corridors of the facility. Their direction changed upwards through a winding staircase. It was unusual that despite their being a lift at the base of the stairs it was decided that walking them around the spiral steps would be a better option. It seemed that the manager was not just an old school monolith of times passed but also a technophobe rejector of almost anything that could help improve the ease of his life. When reaching the top level of the facility his fingerprint opened up a door leading to a landing pad on top of the building. There in front of them was a waiting space car with one of Reebus's guards positioned at each side.

Jayden and Arianna were escorted closer to the car, its sleek design gleaming in the dim light of the facility. As they climbed inside, they were struck by the grandeur of the interior with plush seats, the polished surfaces, the state-of-the-art technology that surrounded them.

"This is amazing," Arianna whispered, her eyes wide with wonder as she settled into her directed seat.

Jayden nodded in agreement, his pulse quickening with excitement. They were about to embark on a journey unlike any they had ever experienced, one that would take them straight into the heart of the GGC's power structure.

The care had four seats like many others and the guards sat in the back row with Jayden and Arianna in front. There would be no need for driving as this was fully automated, so the guards just needed to ensure they watched their prey with the most utmost obedience.

As the space car lifted off the ground, Jayden and Arianna gazed out the windows in awe as they soared through the night sky. The lights of the city below and around them twinkled like stars, casting a mesmerizing shine over the landscape. The car flew close to their own apartment complex with Jayden and Arianna seeing lights turned on where each family were most probably wondering where they were. After a few seconds of contemplation, the car went into a different gear and exploded with speed as they started to make their way towards their destination.

With a sinking feeling in the pit of his stomach, Jayden reached out to the control panel, his fingers tracing the familiar contours of the interface. To his dismay, he found that the controls were locked in place, unyielding to his touch like the bars of a prison.

"No," Arianna whispered, her voice tinged with disbelief. "They've locked us out. We can't change the destination."

Her words hung heavy in the air, a damning indictment of their predicament. Trapped within the confines of the space car, they were powerless to alter the course of their journey, bound by the chains of fate that held them captive. The guards were mere watchers from behind as the car was an effective prison.

With a frustrated sigh, Jayden pounded his fist against the unyielding control panel, his voice rising in defiance. "This can't be happening. We can't just let them take us wherever they please."

No matter how hard he tried, the controls remained steadfast in their refusal, mocking his futile attempts to break free from their grasp. With each passing moment, their sense of helplessness grew, a suffocating weight that threatened to crush their spirits beneath its relentless pressure. The guards behind them simply smirked with gentle laughs as if Jayden and Arianna were fools.

As the space car hurtled through the void of space, its destination still shrouded in mystery, Jayden and Arianna found themselves consumed by a sense of dread that gnawed at the edges of their sanity. What awaited them at the end of their journey? Would they ever be able to break free from the chains that bound them?

Before long leaving London well behind, the towering skyscrapers of what they recognised as New York City came into view, their majestic forms reaching towards the heavens like titans of industry and commerce. At the centre of it all stood the imposing headquarters of the GGC, a gleaming beacon of power and influence that dominated the skyline.

As the space car descended towards the central offices, a landing pad appeared in view from behind a structure. Despite being captive and with no control over the situation they were in, Jayden and Arianna felt a sense of awe wash over them. This was where decisions were made, where the fate of the world was decided by those who held the reins of power. Now they were about to come face to face with the most powerful man of all, Reebus himself.

Chapter 15: The GGC Headquarters

Both Jayden and Arianna exchanged a frightened gaze as the space car touched down on the rooftop landing pad. Their hearts were racing in their chests as they watched the incident unfold. After being captured this way, they were aware that their lives would never be the same again, regardless of what their future held. Moreover, as they exited the space car ready to enter the central offices of the GGC; they braced themselves for the obstacles that were waiting for them in the very centre of authority. The two guards got out first and then ushered first Jayden and the Arianna from their temporary prison that had flown them here. Next, they pointed and directed them both towards a large door just a few metres away. After what seemed like an eternity, the pair of powerful double doors opened. It was guarded by two more imposing security officials. Following the first set of guard's approval, the new GGC guardians in question moved to the side in order to make room for Jayden and Arianna to pass. It was like there was a hierarchy to these men, but it was not entirely clear how that worked.

A towering structure made of glass and steel that loomed over the horizon, its futuristic design and sleek lines serving as a symbol of development and innovation. Jayden and Arianna looked around not quite comprehending the unmatched awe of each direction they looked. As soon as anyone entered here they were transported to a world of unmatched luxury and technical wonders that were more advanced than anything that they had experienced previously. This was on a totally different level to the comforts of their own apartments. The enormous atrium was located inside, and it stretched upwards, bathed in the gentle yet powerful glow of ambient lighting that danced across the polished marble floors. The air was filled with the aroma of exotic flowers, and the vivid colours of these flowers added a splash of natural beauty to the otherwise clean environment.

Every corner of the GGC headquarters was a testament to the heights of technological advancement. It was a symphony of cutting-edge innovation and state-of-the-art design. From the holographic displays that adorned the walls, projecting lifelike images of beautiful landscapes with stunning clarity, to the AI-powered assistants that glided silently through the corridors, anticipating the needs of guests and staff with uncanny precision, every detail had been meticulously crafted to awe and inspire.

These bots here existed as a marvel of modern engineering: the AI serving bot for one was designed with meticulous attention to detail, its sleek metallic frame gleamed under the city lights, a testament to the boundless ingenuity of its creators. What truly set this AI serving bot apart was not its appearance, but rather its capabilities. Unlike its predecessors, which had been designed to mimic human behaviour, this bot embraced its robotic nature with pride. Its creators had deliberately made it look robotic, eschewing the uncanny valley in favour of authenticity. It also helped keep a line between humanity and mechanical deliberately obvious as general humanity had become more worried and concerned by the difficulties in discriminating between real and robotic. Harnessing the differences and enhancing real robotic features created comfort in this environment for all human watchers and participants even if they were still aware that elsewhere it was possible for realistic AI entities to live besides them without being any wiser. Despite its mechanical exterior, the AI serving bot possessed capabilities far beyond anything humanity could imagine. Its processors engrained with computational power, its algorithms weaving intricate webs of logic and reason. It could anticipate the needs of its users with uncanny accuracy, predicting their desires before they even knew them themselves. Perhaps the most astonishing of all were the bot's interpersonal skills. While previous generational AI had struggled to understand the nuances of human interaction, this bot excelled at it having been improved with each iteration over the past century; bugs and inefficiencies mostly eliminated akin to genetic science of humanity to remove genetic cancer causing 'bugs' and crop science enhancing yields, efficiency, and growth time of the essentials of the human food chain. In every area of life, the search for the extra one or two percent gain when repeated on a multi-generational scale eventually shows advanced and efficiencies on a level that cannot be comprehended. The bot could read emotions with pinpoint precision, its sensors detecting subtle changes in facial expressions and body language. It could hold conversations with ease, its responses tailored to each individual user's preferences and personality. As the AI service bot went about its duties, it left a trail of awe and wonder in its wake. People marvelled at its fluency, its grace, and its seemingly boundless intelligence. It was a glimpse into a future where man and machine existed in perfect harmony, each complementing the other in ways previously thought impossible.

The amenities offered within the headquarters were beyond compare, catering to the needs and desires of even the most discerning of guests. Lavish dining halls offered a feast for the senses, with gourmet cuisine prepared by world-renowned human chefs and served with impeccable grace. Alternatively, automated cooking machines could provide exceptional meals with the touch of a few buttons. Spa facilities promised relaxation and rejuvenation, with treatments that melded ancient healing traditions with cutting-edge technology. Health treatments also aided in resolving various ailments from a simple pimple on the skin to a muscular pain, from a scraped knee through to serious migraines and pain. Most health concerns could be remedied almost instantaneously allowing people to remain focussed and sharp for any events of the day ahead. Health technology had advanced so far that long ago when employers required unwell staff to provide sicknotes was replaced by automated employer notification should a condition not be resolved immediately. It was very rare for conditions to run for more than a day or two, assuming that they had a job which gave access to the advanced medical system as least. Those who had little income also by definition had very little access to the rejuvenating technologies that the world had embraced. Instead, they would be confined to their own homes, waiting for illnesses to resolve in the same way as people had done in the distant past.

One visitor to the GGC, a coffee aficionado, was immediately greeted by their personal AI assistant, a sleek device that glided silently beside them, ready to fulfil their every whim. With a subtle gesture, the AI helper sprang into action, summoning a delicious-looking coffee from within its built-in drink dispenser, its rich aroma wafting through the air as it was presented with flawless elegance. The coffee was made to perfection as the bot had access to preferences of every previous coffee they had ordered and drank across a network of establishments worldwide. Not only what was ordered but facial recognition of the gratification and curls of each face was tracked within their own coffee metadata file. With each coffee data point collected, the exact recipe and formulae of the coffee's ingredients had developed into a metadata mapping extraordinaire. These bots now knew what coffee a person liked and wanted more than people did themselves; the information was shared throughout the network of bots and coffee dispensers worldwide that there was no longer a need to ask about what was wanted, or sometimes even when it was wanted. Basic tasks within a human's existence had become routine processes, dissolving the need to think too hard and turning human's more and more robotic themselves. The coffee dispenser was just one attribute of the metadata web that was ascribed to each human, the data network was captured and flowing through choices of food, travel, shopping, entertainment, clothing and just about all weighted decision processes that human's make. Life could be considered much easier, but also lacking in the processing that makes humans think. As many people were concerned by robots becoming more human like, perhaps the bigger concern was humanity becoming robotic and maybe there existed in the middle some entity than was an amalgamation of them all.

Another guest, a fervent sports enthusiast, found themselves engrossed in their work, their mind consumed by the tasks at hand. Even as they focused on their GGC responsibilities, their personal AI helper remained vigilant. It monitored their preferences and interests with unwavering attention. With a subtle notification, the AI helper intercepted their thoughts, presenting them with holographic live images from their favourite sports team's live game. It was a mesmerizing display of skill and athleticism that captured their attention with its vivid realism. Lost in the excitement of the moment, they found themselves transported to the heart of the action, their senses alive with the thrill of the game. The AI understood the guest's preference and desire that the game's progression to them was more important than the work they were completing and interrupted as if a personal lapdog improving their mood and giving a welcome distraction.

As the coffee connoisseur savoured their perfectly brewed beverage and the sports enthusiast revelled in the excitement of the game, the seamless integration of technology and personalized service that defined the GGC experience was clear for all to see, and this was just the tip of the iceberg.

Jayden and Arianna were led through the bustling corridors of the GGC headquarters, their footsteps echoing against the polished floors as they approached Reebus's inner sanctum. The air crackled with anticipation as they neared the door; their hearts pounding in their chests with a mixture of apprehension and fear.

As they entered the room, they found themselves face to face with Reebus, the overlord of the GGC himself. He sat behind a massive desk, his gaze fixed on them with an intensity that sent a shiver down their spines. His room was quite simple but efficient. There weren't really any personal items other than holographic pictures of him shaking hands and greeting various iconic businessmen and celebrities. It was almost like a library; a collection if you will in showing off his power and accessibility to those the world held with esteem.

"Welcome," he said, his voice smooth and commanding. "I've been expecting you."

Jayden and Arianna exchanged a nervous glance, unsure of how to proceed. They had come here seeking answers, but now that they were in the presence of the most powerful man on Earth, they found themselves at a loss for words.

"You've been causing quite a stir," Reebus continued, his eyes boring into them with an unwavering gaze. "Breaking into restricted areas, meddling in affairs that don't concern you... Tell me, what do you hope to achieve by all of this?"

Jayden cleared his throat, summoning his courage as he spoke. "We just want to know the truth," he said, his voice steady despite the nerves that threatened to overtake him. "About the retirement planet, about what's really going on behind closed doors."

Reebus regarded them with a thoughtful expression, his fingers steepled beneath his chin as he considered their words. "The truth," he echoed, his tone contemplative. "It's a curious thing, isn't it? Sometimes it's not as simple as black and white, as right and wrong."

Arianna frowned, her brow furrowing in confusion. "What do you mean?" she asked, her voice tinged with suspicion.

Reebus leaned back in his chair, his gaze piercing as he regarded them with a knowing look. "I mean that sometimes, the truth is not what we want it to be," he said cryptically. "Sometimes, it's better to let certain things remain hidden, for the greater good of society."

Jayden bristled at Reebus's words, his resolve hardening as he spoke. "But who decides what's best for society?" he demanded; his voice tinged with defiance. "Who decides what we're allowed to know, and what we're not?"

Reebus regarded him with a knowing smile, his eyes twinkling with a hint of amusement. "That, my young friend, is a question for the ages," he said, his tone enigmatic. "And perhaps, one that you will find the answer to in due time."

Jayden and Arianna sat opposite Reebus; the air thick with tension as they prepared to broach the subject that weighed heavily on their minds. Reebus regarded them with a patient expression, his demeanour calm and composed as he awaited their questions.

"Mr. Reebus," Jayden began, his voice steady despite the nerves that churned in his stomach. "We need to talk about Arianna's grandad. We saw... what happened to him in the departure facility. He... he disappeared. Completely."

Arianna's voice wavered as she spoke, her eyes fixed on Reebus with a pleading expression. "We just want to know what happened to him," she said, her voice barely above a whisper. "Where did he go? Is he... is he okay?"

Reebus regarded them with a thoughtful expression, his gaze mesmeric as he considered their words. "Your concern is understandable," he said finally, his tone measured. "But I assure you, there is no cause for alarm. Your grandad is... well taken care of."

Jayden frowned, his brow furrowing in confusion. "Taken care of? What does that mean?" he pressed; his voice tinged with frustration. "Where is he? What is happening to him?"

Reebus leaned forward, his expression grave as he spoke. "Your grandad, like many others his age, has been transported" he explained, his voice tinged with sympathy. "It's a place where he can live out his days in peace and comfort, free from the burdens of everyday life."

Arianna's eyes widened in disbelief. "But... but we saw him... disappear," she protested, her voice trembling with emotion. "It was like he was... obliterated."

Reebus shook his head, his expression solemn. "I understand that it may seem that way," he said gently. "But I assure you, what you witnessed was simply the process of transportation. Your grandad is where he needs to be, I promise you that."

Jayden and Arianna exchanged a sceptical glance, unsure of whether to believe Reebus's assurances. As they looked into his eyes, they saw a glimmer of sincerity that gave them pause. Perhaps there was more to this than met the eye, they realized. Perhaps there was still hope that Arianna's grandad was alive and well, somewhere out there in the vast expanse of the retirement planet.

A question burned on Jayden's tongue. Why had they been summoned all the way from London to meet with him in New York City? Reebus, however, seemed to anticipate their inquiry, his gaze steady as he addressed them.

"I brought you here because I believe you have a role to play in the future of our world," Reebus began, his voice carrying a weight that silenced any further questions. "You see, I have been closely following your actions, Jayden and Arianna. Your curiosity, your tenacity... they are qualities that are sorely needed in these uncertain times."

Jayden and Arianna exchanged a glance, their confusion evident. What could their actions possibly have to do with the grand schemes of the GGC and its leader?

Reebus continued, his eyes never leaving theirs. "You have shown a willingness to question the status quo, to seek out the truth no matter the cost," he explained. "And in doing so, you have proven yourselves to be valuable assets to our cause."

Arianna's brow furrowed in scepticism. "Our Cause? Your cause? What cause?" she asked, her voice tinged with suspicion.

Reebus leaned forward, his expression earnest as he spoke. "The cause of progress, of innovation, of ensuring the survival of our species in the face of overwhelming challenges," he replied. "You may not realize it yet, but you have the power to shape the future of our world. I intend to help you fully realize that potential."

Jayden's mind raced with questions, but he held his tongue, sensing that there was more to Reebus's words than met the eye. Whatever the leader of the GGC had in store for them, he knew that it would be no small task. If it meant making a difference in the world, he was willing to see it through to the end. The way that Reebus spoke in almost riddles with his answers not entirely being conclusive stuck with Jayden too.

Jayden and Arianna exchanged further glances as they stood thoughtful before Reebus, their minds still reeling from the revelations he had shared with them. They had hoped to be sent back home to London after their meeting, but Reebus's words hinted at a different fate awaiting them.

"When do we leave?" Arianna asked tentatively, her voice betraying her apprehension.

Reebus regarded them with a knowing smile, his eyes twinkling with a hint of mischief. "Actually, I have other plans for you," he said, his tone cryptic. "You see, I believe that your skills and talents would be of great use to the GGC."

Jayden's brow furrowed in confusion. "You want us to work for the GGC?" he asked, his mind struggling to process the sudden change in direction.

Reebus nodded, his expression serious. "Indeed," he replied. "I believe that you both have the potential to make a significant impact here, to help shape the future of our world."

Arianna's eyes widened in disbelief. "But... what about our lives back home?" she protested; her voice tinged with uncertainty.

Reebus waved a dismissive hand, his gaze unwavering. "You'll find that your new accommodations are quite, 'comfortable,'" he said, a hint of amusement in his voice. "I assure you; you won't be lacking for anything here."

With that, Reebus gestured for them to follow him, leading them down a series of mazy corridors until they reached a pair of ornate double doors. As the doors swung open, Jayden and Arianna's jaws dropped in astonishment at the sight that greeted them.

Before them lay a lavish suite with two bedrooms and complete with luxurious furnishings, state-of-the-art technology, and everything they could ever need. It was unlike anything they had ever seen, a far cry from the modest accommodations they were accustomed to back home.

Reebus smiled at their reaction, his eyes twinkling with satisfaction. "I hope you'll find your new home to your liking," he said, his voice warm with hospitality. "Welcome to the GGC, Jayden and Arianna. I have a feeling that you're going to do great things here. I will let you settle in to your new surroundings.," as Reebus left them behind and willed the to explore their room.

Chapter 16: The Luxury of Power

Jayden and Arianna explored their assigned suite within the GGC headquarters, their breath catching at the sight that greeted them. The room was a masterpiece of luxury and elegance, with sleek modern furnishings and tasteful décor that exuded an air of sophistication.

"Wow," Arianna murmured, her eyes wide with awe as she took in the lavish surroundings. "This is... incredible."

Jayden nodded in agreement, his gaze sweeping over the spacious living area and plush seating arrangements. "I've never seen anything like it," he admitted, a sense of wonder tinged with disbelief in his voice.

As they explored further, they discovered a series of amenities that surpassed their wildest expectations. The bedroom boasted a king-sized bed with silky-smooth linens and a cloud-like mattress that beckoned them to rest. The ensuite bathroom was equally impressive, with gleaming marble countertops, a luxurious bathtub, and a rainfall shower that promised a spa-like experience.

It was the minute details that truly caught their attention. There was the soft lighting that bathed the room in a warm hue. The state-of-the-art entertainment system that offered an endless array of films and music, and the fully stocked minibar that tempted them with an assortment of gourmet snacks and beverages.

At the heart of the entertainment system was a sophisticated holographic projector that filled the room with stunning visuals and lifelike images. It transformed the space into a virtual playground of endless possibilities. With a simple command, they could summon holographic landscapes that stretched out before them in breathtaking detail. It could transport them to far-off worlds and fantastical realms beyond imagination. The entertainment system didn't stop there. It also incorporated virtual reality technology that allowed Jayden and Arianna to step into the immersive worlds they had previously only dreamed of. With specialized headsets and haptic feedback gloves, they could explore virtual environments with astonishing realism. They were able to feel the rush of wind against their skin and the warmth of the sun on their faces. They could journey through digital landscapes teeming with life and adventure. As if that was not enough, the system also featured augmented reality capabilities that brought their favourite characters and stories to life in their own room. Using handheld devices, they could interact with virtual avatars and creatures that appeared to inhabit the physical space around them. The lines between reality and fantasy were blurred in ways that were truly mind-blowing.

There were also settings to enable 5D entertainment. I was a revolutionary experience that engaged not only their sight and sound but also their sense of touch, smell, and taste. In the centre of the room stood a sleek pod. Its smooth contours beckoned them, promising an adventure beyond their wildest dreams. With eager anticipation, they settled into its plush seats, their senses primed for the journey ahead.

With a gentle beep, the pod sprang to life, enveloping them in a symphony of sights and sounds. Their surroundings melted away as they were transported to distant worlds, where towering mountains kissed the sky and emerald forests stretched as far as the eye could see. It was not merely the visual spectacle that captivated their imaginations. As they soared through the ethereal landscapes, a gentle breeze caressed their skin, carrying with it the scent of blooming flowers and fresh rain. Jayden closed his eyes, savouring the sensation as though he stood amidst the verdant meadows himself. Beside him, Arianna giggled with delight, her fingers grazing the holographic displays that shimmered before her. With each touch, she felt the subtle vibrations beneath her fingertips, as though she held the very essence of the digital realm within her grasp. They encountered a feast for the senses unlike any other. The air was alive with the aroma of exotic spices and savoury delights, tempting their taste buds with promises of culinary delights yet to be savoured.

With a mischievous grin, Jayden reached out to pluck a virtual fruit from a nearby tree, its succulent juices bursting forth with each bite. Arianna followed suit, her laughter mingling with the sounds of their virtual feast as they indulged in the sensory symphony that surrounded them.

For Jayden and Arianna, the entertainment system was more than just a source of amusement. It was a gateway to new worlds, to new experiences, and new possibilities. It allowed them to escape the confines of their surroundings and explore the boundless realms of imagination, together.

"This is insane," Jayden muttered, his voice tinged with disbelief as he surveyed their new surroundings. Arianna nodded in agreement, a sense of excitement bubbling up inside her. "I can't believe we get to stay here," she exclaimed, her eyes shining with delight. As they settled and started to relax, Jayden and Arianna could not shake the feeling of being caught up in a surreal dream. It was hard to believe that just a few days ago, they had been ordinary teenagers living in London. Now here they were, living in the lap of luxury within the confines of the GGC headquarters.

Just then Jayden noticed a large machine in the corner of the room. It was an automated food system that was a culinary wonder unlike any other. It consisted of a sleek, state-of-the-art kiosk adorned with a large touchscreen display. You could approach the kiosk, their mouths watering in anticipation of the delectable delights that awaited them. With a few taps on the touchscreen, Jayden was able to browse through an extensive menu featuring dishes from every corner of the globe. From savoury Italian pastas to spicy Thai curries, from mouthwatering burgers to decadent desserts, the options seemed endless. What truly set the Automated Food System apart was its innovative cooking technology. Instead of relying on human chefs, the kiosk was equipped with a sophisticated network of robotic arms and precision cooking appliances. Once an order was placed and selected a picture of their desired dish, the system sprang into action, orchestrating a culinary symphony that unfolded before their eyes. First, the robotic arms retrieved the fresh ingredients from a series of refrigerated compartments, ensuring that every component of the dish was of the highest quality. Next, the ingredients were meticulously chopped, sliced, and diced with surgical precision, guided by algorithms that optimized flavour, texture, and presentation. As the ingredients sizzled and simmered on the cooking surface, the air was filled with the tantalizing aroma of spices and herbs. Jayden and Arianna watched in awe as their chosen dish took shape before them, marvelling at the seamless choreography of the robotic arms as they worked in perfect harmony. With each passing day, the cooking technology learned and adapted, its algorithms evolving to cater to the unique tastes and preferences of its users. For Jayden, who preferred his steak well done, the technology remembered without fail, its precision ensuring that each succulent bite was cooked to perfection. There was no need for him to utter a single word to aid the cooking process. As for Arianna, whose palate craved the delicate balance of sweet and savoury, the technology became a master of subtlety. It adjusted the proportions of sauces and seasonings to suit her every whim. With each meal, it learned and grew, its knowledge expanding with every interaction as it sought to unlock the secrets of culinary perfection. Within minutes, the dish was ready: he had chosen a delicious looking Italian chicken penne, plated with artistic flair and presented to the Jayden with a flourish. Each bite was a symphony of flavours, a culinary masterpiece crafted with the precision and care that only technology could provide. As Jayden and Arianna relaxed around the table, their senses ablaze with anticipation, they marvelled at the wonders that lay before them. It was a feast fit for kings, crafted with care and precision by the cooking technology that had become an integral part of their lives. Not only was this a cooking master chef, but there were no cooking utensils or bowls to wash up afterwards as this was taken care of. The machine internally dealt with any mess caused through mixing and blending cooking recipes with chopping and dicing carried out away from the eyes of the eventual recipient of such food. This was not merely a tool for convenience, it was a testament to the power of innovation to enhance the human experience. It was a bridge between tradition and progress that brought joy and delight to all who ventured into its realm. Once they had both enjoyed and devoured their first proper meals in quite some time they licked clean every morsel of their individual plates. Although more food could be beckoned by the touch of just a few buttons they both decided not to do so as they did not wish to be greedy and wanted to spare a thought for their friends and family with nothing much to eat. Requesting more food on a whim, despite the excellence they had just tasted was a step too far at the moment. They were more than happy to head towards sleep. They both picked up their almost licked sparkling plates and fed them back into the collection tray where the automated machine took them deep inside. In making lots of swishes and watering motions these plates were clearly being cleaned to a deep level of shine and they reappeared partially in translucent plate holder next to the machine. The plate holder itself was sleek and vibrant and added to the furniture of the room. Next to the automated cooking machine there was a button that Jayden decided to press. With a few whirrs of motion, the whole cooking suite was folded into the wall as if it had never even existed. Instead, in its place was a virtual sculpture of times gone by representing Greek civilisations and the gods that had gone before. As Jayden gazed into the sculpture, Arianna cheekily pressed a few buttons on a hand-held device and the Greek holograph disappeared. In its place and elsewhere around the room the whole environment changed. The walls became colourful, paintings turned full of Arianna's favourite cartoon characters and the holograms became heads of famous entertaining busts representing characters that used to drive her youth days with smiles and happiness. Arianna simply wanted to be in a safe and happy place and to her this was her safest place of all. Deep in the centre of the world's decision and authoritative core there they were in a flamboyantly coloured room with cartoons distracting them into smiles and laughter. Perhaps this was the best end of a day they could have imagined especially considering where it began. Lives can change a lot in the period of one day.

The following morning, as they stood before the mirror, their control tablets in hand, they marvelled at the simplicity of the task that lay before them. With the placing of a of a teeth cleaning pill inside their mouths, any decay and plaque which had congregated in their mouths would be dispersed as the pill also issued a minty fresh breath and a minor caffeine intake to prepare them for the day ahead. Gone were the days of cumbersome toothbrushes and messy toothpaste. They were a relic of a bygone era which had been replaced by the elegance of simple but effective technological advancement. When Jayden and Arianna smiled into the mirror, their teeth gleaming with newfound brilliance, they knew that even the most mundane of tasks were transformed into moments of effortless beauty. Their morning routine was not limited to dental hygiene alone. As they stepped into their closets, they were greeted by yet another marvel of modern convenience. With a mere glance at their tablets, they summoned forth a selection of clothing tailored to their individual preferences, personal calendars and the weather forecast for the day ahead as meticulously monitored by the machine itself. For Jayden, whose sense of style leaned towards the casual and understated, the machine selected a comfortable ensemble of jeans and a cozy sweater. It was an outfit perfectly suited to the mild temperatures that awaited him outside. For Arianna, whose fashion sense was as vibrant as her personality, the machine chose a flowing dress in hues of azure and gold, a reflection of the sunny skies that beckoned beyond the window. Not only were these clothes selected on daily factors but as individuals showered routinely their body shapes and fittings were scanned surreptitiously and adjustments with new clothes created for future wear with the most perfect of fittings. Underwear and easy to manufacture items were recycled upon use rather than relying on water intensive cleaning methods. Instead, it was as if every day passed with an entire new wardrobe or functioning outfit in pristine condition for whatever lay ahead. With a sense of satisfaction, they were dressed in their selected attire. Gone were the days of endless deliberation and wardrobe malfunctions. They lived with effortless elegance of a future where technology and style merged in perfect harmony. This was yet another case of life's choices becoming easier and the thought process behind it diminishing with each passing day.

The previous night was spent talking, relaxing, with very little sleep. Jayden and Arianna now stepped outside into the opulent corridors of the GGC headquarters with their eyes wide with wonder as they took in the sights around them. Everywhere they looked, there were signs of wealth and abundance. Gilded fixtures, intricate tapestries, and elaborate displays of artwork adorned each of the walls, while the air was filled with the soft chatter of advanced technology.

"Wow," Arianna breathed, her voice filled with awe. "This place is incredible."

Jayden nodded in agreement, his gaze darting around the vast expanse of the headquarters. "It's like something out of a sci-fi movie," he remarked, his mind racing with excitement. Even for those living in a highly technological world in 2123, the technology within the GGC was simply on a different level again. Occasionally where there were elongated windows letting in the light from outside, the pure magnitude of New York City and beyond could be seen. From the vantage point of such a high perch, the incredible landscape of this futuristic city unfolded like a masterpiece waiting to be admired. As the sun peeped out from the horizon, it casted a golden shine across the skyline, the city came alive with a symphony of light and sound. Neon signs flickered to life, bathing the streets below in a kaleidoscope of colours. Skyscrapers soared towards the sky, their glass facades reflecting the last vestiges of daylight. Some buildings were almost part of the sky itself. From their lofty perch, Jayden and Arianna could see it all; the iconic silhouette of the Empire State Building, standing relatively small amidst a sea of towering structures now beside it; the majestic sweep of what remained Central Park, a small but verdant oasis nestled amidst the concrete jungle that surrounded. Then there was the glittering expanse of the Hudson River with its waters shimmering in the fading light. Central Park itself was much heightened from where it used to be with the land so precious that office and skyscrapers built in a large section beneath it, eventually lifting the gardens and waters of the park over half a kilometre higher into orbit than it used to be. Mid-air corridors and pathways still allowed people access to the park from a multitude of nearby building. The parks usage was intense as many inhabitants used it as their only place to mix with local nature on a relatively open scale. It remained the meeting point of choice for most native New Yorkers.

It was not just the physical landscape that captivated the Arianna's gaze. It was the energy, the pulse of life that coursed through the city streets like a living, breathing entity. From bustling sidewalks to whirring hovercars, from the dense populous moving through the city, New York City was alive with possibility. Jayden and Arianna took in the breathtaking panorama before them, they just stood in silence. This was a city of dreams, where the impossible became possible and the unimaginable became reality. It was a place where innovation thrived, where creativity flourished, and where the future seemed to stretch out before them like an open road. No wonder the GGC had made its headquarters in the core of the heartbeat of the planet.

Wandering through more uneasy corridors, they stumbled upon a series of rooms that seemed to stretch on endlessly. Each room was more extravagant than the last. In one room, they found a fully stocked pantry, brimming with an array of gourmet foods and delicacies from around the world. These ingredients were plugged into wall sockets awaiting food requests from people or machinery around the GGC facilities. In another room they discovered a state-of-the-art gym, complete with top-of-the-line exercise equipment and AI personal trainers on hand to assist them. It was noticeable by this room's emptiness and signs of dust in that nobody appeared to be using it. A slender looking man was positioned just inside the door. He introduced himself as Hugo and seemed to be surprised that Arianna and Jayden had even entered here as it was so rare for him to see people here. After a few irreverent words and smiles Arianna looked again towards Jayden.

"This is insane," Jayden muttered, his eyes wide with disbelief. "I've never seen anything like it.", as they closed the door on the gym and progressed back into the corridors from where they had come. Exploring these corridors and rooms before them was something that would take quite some time and there were sure to be things to be discovered in almost every space they went.

Arianna nodded once more, still in awe of the surroundings, her mind whirling with questions as she turned back to those more pressing questions at hand. What exactly did Reebus have in store for them? Exactly why had he brought them here in the first place?

Chapter 17: Christina Sandstrom

As Jayden and Arianna continued to explore the headquarters, they could not shake the feeling that they were being watched. It was like every move they made was being carefully monitored by unseen eyes. After all, Reebus had brought them here, offered next to no guidance, explanation or penalty for their offences and just seems to let them roam free and do as they want. Despite their unease, they could not deny the allure of the lavish surroundings, or the sense of opportunity that hung in the air.

As Jayden and Arianna explored further, they were suddenly approached by a beautiful woman in her early thirties, her sharp gaze assessing them with keen interest. Her presence commanded attention, and there was an air of authority about her that made Jayden and Arianna straighten up instinctively.

"Excuse me," she said, her voice cool and composed. "I don't believe we've had the pleasure of meeting yet. I am Christina Sandstrom, Reebus asked me to look after you."

Jayden and Arianna exchanged a glance, taken aback by the sudden introduction. They had heard of Christina Sandstrom before. The rumours of her intelligence and capability had circulated through the ranks of the GGC, but they had never expected to encounter her in person.

Christina Sandstrom was now the lead on the Space Exploration Program and must have a wealth of information within her bright mind.

"It's nice to meet you, Ms. Sandstrom," Jayden said politely, extending his hand in greeting. "I'm Jayden, and this is Arianna."

"Please, call me Christina." She replied.

Christina nodded in acknowledgment, her gaze lingering on them for a moment longer before she spoke again. "I've heard a lot about the two of you," she said, her tone measured. "You've certainly made quite an impression on Reebus."

Arianna's brow furrowed in confusion. "What do you mean?" she asked, her voice tinged with uncertainty.

Christina's lips curved into a faint smile, but there was a hint of steel in her eyes as she spoke. "Let's just say that Reebus said that he sees great potential in both of you," she replied cryptically. "And he's not one to overlook talent when he sees it."

Jayden and Arianna exchanged a wary glance, sensing that there was more to Christina's words than met the eye. Whatever her intentions, they knew that they would have to tread carefully around her if they were to uncover the truth about the GGC and its hidden secrets.

Jayden then added, his voice steady despite the nerves that fluttered in his chest. "We were hoping to learn more about the Space Exploration Program and how it fits into the GGC's larger goals."

Christina regarded them with a shrewd gaze, her expression unreadable as she listened to their inquiry. "The Space Exploration Program is a key component of our efforts to secure the future of humanity," she explained, her voice measured. "It's a venture that requires immense resources and careful planning, but it's one that we believe is essential for the long-term survival of our species."

Arianna leaned forward; her curiosity piqued. "What exactly are you searching for in space?" she asked, her voice tinged with fascination.

Christina's lips curved into a faint smile, but there was a hint of mystery in her eyes as she spoke. "We're searching for answers," she replied cryptically. "Answers to questions about the origins of our universe, about the potential for life beyond our planet, and about the resources that may be available to us in the vast expanse of space."

Jayden frowned, his mind racing with questions. "And what have you discovered so far?" with his voice tinged with curiosity.

Christina's smile widened slightly, but her eyes remained inscrutable as she spoke. "I'm afraid that's classified information," she replied smoothly. "But rest assured, our efforts have yielded valuable insights that will shape the future of our world in ways you can't even begin to imagine."

"Christina, we were wondering if the Space Exploration Program has discovered any other planets that are capable of sustaining life," Jayden inquired, his eyes fixed on Christina, searching for any hint of a response.

Christina's expression remained neutral as she considered their question, her gaze thoughtful. "The search for habitable planets is one of the primary objectives of our space exploration efforts," she began, her tone measured. "While we have yet to find a planet that is an exact match for Earth, our explorations have revealed several promising candidates."

Arianna leaned forward; her interest piqued. "Can you tell us more about these candidates?" she asked eagerly, her eyes shining with anticipation.

Christina nodded, her lips curling into a faint smile. "Certainly," she replied. "We've identified several exoplanets within our galaxy that lie within the habitable zone of their respective star systems. These are planets where conditions may be conducive to the existence of liquid water and, potentially, life as we know it."

Jayden's eyes widened in astonishment. "That's incredible," he murmured, his mind racing with the possibilities. "Do you think there could be intelligent life on these planets?"

Christina's smile widened slightly, but there was a hint of caution in her voice as she spoke. "It's certainly a possibility," she conceded. "But it's also important to approach the search for extraterrestrial life with a healthy dose of scepticism. We must be methodical in our investigations and avoid jumping to conclusions based on limited data."

"Christina, we were hoping to learn more about the retirement planet," Arianna began, her voice steady despite the nervous flutter in her chest. "We've heard about it, but there seems to be a lot of mystery surrounding the place. Can you shed some light on what it is really like?"

Christina regarded them with a measured gaze not knowing whether to hit the truth head on or navigate around the subject so not to draw them to deep into the web of lies. Her expression unreadable as she considered their request. "Serenity 1, as we call it, is a unique destination," she replied, her tone carefully neutral. "It was established as a retirement community for individuals aged 80 and older who wish to live out their golden years in comfort and tranquillity."

Jayden furrowed his brow, a hint of distrust creeping into his voice. "But what is it really like?" he pressed, his curiosity getting the better of him. "What do people do there? And why is it so secretive?"

Christina's lips curved into a faint smile, but there was a guardedness in her eyes as she spoke. "Serenity 1 offers a wide range of amenities and activities designed to cater to the needs and preferences of its residents," she explained. "From lush gardens and recreational facilities to gourmet dining and cultural events, there's no shortage of ways to enjoy life on the retirement planet." It was as if Christina's words were read directly from a textbook, or some advertising material and not thoughtful and sharp words from her own soul.

Arianna frowned, her brow furrowing in thought. "But why all the secrecy?" she asked, her voice tinged with suspicion. "Why not be more transparent about what goes on there?"

Christina's smile faded slightly, replaced by a hint of tension in her demeanour. "Serenity 1 operates under strict confidentiality protocols to ensure the privacy and security of its residents," she replied carefully. "It's a place for relaxation and rejuvenation, away from the hustle and bustle of everyday life. While we understand the public's curiosity, we must respect the wishes of those who choose to make Serenity 1 their home."

The discussion then came to an end with Jayden and Arianna saying goodbyes, heading out into the corridor, and heading back to their quarters.

On the way, Jayden and Arianna found themselves alone in a secluded corner of the GGC headquarters. The weight of their conversation hung in the air, but amidst the tension, a sense of relief washed over them.

"I don't know about you, but I actually liked Christina," Arianna admitted, breaking the silence that had settled between them.

Jayden nodded in agreement, a small smile tugging at the corners of his lips. "Yeah, she seemed... different," he mused, his voice soft. "More empathetic, maybe. Like she actually cares about what we have to say."

"It also seemed like she had her words tied and constrained as if she couldn't tell the full story, "Signed Jayden.

"Maybe Reebus is watching her too?" added a wise Jayden.

Arianna's expression softened, her eyes reflecting the sentiment. "Exactly," she replied, a note of agreement in her voice. "It's like she's actually listening to us, instead of just going through the motions like some of the others."

As they spoke, a sense of camaraderie further blossomed between them, forged in the shared experience of navigating the complexities of the GGC headquarters. They were really enjoying spending time together and unlike when at home with family often around, they were well and truly reliant upon each other here.

"I think we should keep an eye on Christina," Jayden suggested, his gaze thoughtful. "If anyone can help us uncover the secrets of this place, it's her."

Arianna nodded in further agreement, a determined glint in her eyes. "Agreed," she replied, her voice resolute. "Let's see what else we can learn from her. Maybe she'll be the key to unravelling the mysteries of the GGC."

As Jayden and Arianna returned to their quarters within the confines of the GGC, a heavy silence hung between them, laden with the weight of their thoughts. The events of the day had left them both contemplative, each grappling with the harsh realities of their existence here. For Jayden there was an additional layer of pain, a wound that cut deeper than any physical injury. As they settled into their relaxing well-lit room, Jayden retreated into himself, his thoughts consumed by memories of his father's untimely demise. With trembling hands, he reached for a sketchpad, the pages filled with a myriad of drawings, each one depicting the same haunting image: the tree birthmark worn by the man who had robbed him of everything he held dear.

For Jayden, the Tree symbol was more than just a mark of identification – it was a symbol of vengeance, a reminder of the debt that still remained unpaid. With each stroke of his pencil, he traced the contours of the mark, his movements marked by a mixture of rage and despair. It was a futile gesture, a futile attempt to make sense of the senseless, but he could not help himself. It was a symbol that Jayden had drawn many times before and would do many times again. Recanting life a five-year-old boy, memories which were so vivid and clear that they would never hide away in the dark for very long. Arianna watched in silence, her heart aching for her friend as he grappled with his demons. She knew that nothing she could say would ease his pain, but she refused to let him suffer alone. With a gentle touch, she placed a hand on his shoulder, offering him silent solidarity in his time of need. Together, they sat in the quiet of the room. For Jayden, the Tree symbol was a constant reminder of the injustice that had been done to him and his family. As he continued to sketch, a steely determination began to take root within him. He refused to let his father's memory be forgotten, refusing to let his death be in vain. Although he deeply loved his mum and appreciated everything she had done for him, he knew that if events had been different then he would be with his whole family and would have enjoyed many more special memories of family life. He knew that as well as his father's death, it was also the day that his mum's heart was broken, and she was never the same again. Although she was always a great mum, she was detached and broken with very few smiles partaking her lips over the years that followed

Over the course of the next few days Jayden and Arianna started to develop a closer friendship with Christina where they were able to dig deeper and deeper into more pertinent questions on their minds. "Christina," Jayden began, his voice steady despite the nervous flutter in his chest. "We were hoping you could shed some more light on why Reebus wanted to see us." Christina regarded them with a thoughtful gaze, her expression guarded as she considered their inquiry. "I'm afraid I can't divulge the specifics of Reebus's intentions," she replied carefully. "But I can assure you that he has your best interests at heart."

Arianna frowned, her brow furrowing in frustration. "But why us?" she pressed; her voice tinged with urgency. "What does he want from us?"

Christina's lips curved into a faint smile, but there was a hint of tension in her demeanour as she spoke. "Reebus sees great potential in both of you," she explained cryptically. "He believes that you have a role to play in the future of the GGC, although he may not have shared the details of his plans just yet." It seemed like they were just dancing in circles and questions would never be truthfully and completely answered.

Jayden exchanged a wary glance with Arianna, sensing that there was more to Christina's words than she was letting on. Whatever Reebus had in store for them, they knew that they would have to tread carefully if they were to uncover the truth.

"Thank you, Christina" Jayden said, his voice tinged with uncertainty. "We appreciate your candour."

With each passing day Jayden and Arianna gradually became more at ease inside the GGC as they watched and learned from everyone and everything going on. As Jayden and Arianna became closer to Christina, she found herself grappling with a difficult dilemma. The burden of secrecy weighed heavy on her conscience, especially when it came to hiding details about the retirement planet from Arianna and Jayden.

Christina, Jayden, and Arianna found solace in each other's company. As they gathered around a cosy table in their shared quarters, the atmosphere was alive with laughter and camaraderie. Despite the weight of their individual burdens, they refused to let despair consume them. Instead, they focused on the simple joy of being together, finding comfort in the warmth of friendship and the promise of better days ahead. With plates of food before them, they dug into their meal with gusto, savouring each bite as if it were a taste of freedom itself. Conversation flowed freely, weaving a tapestry of shared experiences and mutual understanding. They each had a few glasses of the best gin and relaxed away from the worries of their everyday existence.

Christina regaled them with tales of her childhood adventures, her eyes sparkling with mischief as she recounted daring escapades from years gone by. Jayden and Arianna listened with rapt attention, their laughter mingling with hers in harmonious chorus.

In turn, Jayden shared stories of his father's exploits, some which were second-hand told by his mum, his voice tinged with both sorrow and pride as he spoke of the man who had shaped his life in ways he could never have imagined. Arianna listened intently, her heart going out to her friend as he bared his soul to them, and the pain ensued through the tears. Arianna, ever the voice of reason, offered words of encouragement and wisdom, her calm demeanour a soothing balm to their troubled hearts. She spoke of hope and resilience, reminding them that even in the darkest of times, there was always light to be found. As they ate and laughed together, they discovered common interest and focus, their shared passions serving as a foundation upon which their friendship blossomed. They found so ace in each other's presence, drawing strength from the unspoken bond that bound them together. They were stronger together than they were as individuals, and it felt for the first time in ages that the world was full of joy. In that moment, surrounded by the warmth of friendship and the promise of better days ahead, Christina, Jayden, and Arianna knew that no matter what the future held, they would face it together. For in each other, they had found not just companionship, but a sense of belonging that transcended the confines of their surroundings.

During the evening and despite her desire to be transparent with her friends, Christina knew that revealing classified information could jeopardize not only her position but also the safety of those she cared about. Yet, the thought of withholding the truth gnawed at her, creating a rift between her professional obligations and her personal relationships. Christina realized that while she could not divulge everything she knew about the retirement planet, there might be a way to help Arianna and Jayden discover the truth firsthand. She resolved to find a delicate balance between her duty to secrecy and her loyalty to her now friends. She would seek out the perfect opportunity when possible to lead them to where ghosts from previous iterations of the GGC might be able to enlighten them some more, but to equally keep those who watched unaware of the information being shared.

Chapter 18: Like Turns into Love

As the days passed within the confines of their luxurious quarters, Jayden and Arianna found themselves drawn to each other in ways they had not anticipated. What had started as a tentative friendship was slowly blossoming into something deeper, something that stirred within them with each passing moment.

As they sat together, their thoughts drifted to a future where their loved ones could join them in the lap of luxury, free from the burdens that had weighed them down for so long. They dreamed of a day when Jayden's mother and Arianna's family could experience the joy and wonder of a life without struggle, where every need was met and every dream within reach.

With a wistful smile, Jayden spoke of his hope that one day soon, he hoped his mother would no longer have to toil away in obscurity, her days consumed by the relentless demands of life's hardships. Instead, he envisioned her basking in the warmth of the sun, surrounded by the beauty and tranquillity of their new home, her cares and worries a distant memory. Her mum had been subjected to a harsh life always scraping together food and resources in order to survive in the competition for resources. Her dreams had long since turned from hope into acceptance of reality.

Arianna's heart swelled with longing as she imagined her family by her side, their faces lit up with joy as they explored the wonders of their new world together. She yearned for the day when they could laugh and play without fear or worry, their days filled with love and laughter, their hearts full to bursting with the happiness that comes from being surrounded by those they hold most dear. Arianna had always been close to her family and although her youth was not quite as tarnished as Jayden's it was still full of the harsh realities of existence in this world where resources are so limited.

Arianna nodded understandingly, taking a seat beside Jayden on the couch. "I know what you mean. Sometimes, being away from home can be tough."

For Jayden and Arianna, the realization struck like a sudden gust of wind on a calm summer's day – they had not spent a night away from their homes for years, not until they arrived at the GGC on the recent fateful night at Reebus' command. As they sat in the dimly lit confines of their quarters, the weight of this revelation settled over them as if they had not realised until this point and the comfort blanket of their loved ones and their home environments was missing completely. The remembrance of their home surroundings was both calming and suffocating, a reminder of the lives they had left behind. For Jayden, it was the memory of his childhood home, filled with his mum and her love, which seemed now nothing more than a distant dream. As for Arianna, it was the familiar rhythm of her daily routine, the comforting embrace of familiarity now replaced by uncertainty. As they sat in silence, each lost in their own thoughts, they could not help but wonder how they had ended up here, in this place of shadows and secrets. They had been plucked from their lives without warning, thrust into a world they barely understood, with no way of knowing what lay ahead.

Ironically within all this uncertainty, there was also a sense of freedom, a liberation from the constraints of their former lives. For the first time in years, they were free to chart their own course, to forge their own path in a world ripe with possibility. As they pondered the significance of this newfound freedom, Jayden and Arianna found solace in each other's presence. They were no longer alone in their journey, no longer adrift in a sea of uncertainty. Together, they would face whatever challenges lay ahead, drawing strength from the bond that had formed between them.

"Yeah," Jayden agreed returning to the present day after his dreams were interrupted by the reality they now faced. He then started scrolling through digital images and holograms of his mum and friends and the places that were special to him. There were some of his Dad too, long lost images that his eyes had not glanced at in a very long time. Memories and pictures are bound together like strawberries and cream, each improved by the presence of the other. A memory of Jayden's Mum and Dad from when he was very young then came to mind. He could see them happy and dancing away around the neighbourhood; Proud parents laughing and playing with him as if he were the most precious commodity in the world. Then his memories widened further to just last month when he sat with his Mum on the homely couch in their London apartment. They had talked like equals as if her job of motherhood had been completed, leaving Jayden to try and make his own way through the haphazard world before them. He can remember the conversation a vividly as if it were today as his mum was weighing in to discussions about Jayden's education.

"You need to do the best you possibly can Jayden, your education is nearly over, and you will have plenty of time for the rest of your life. Why don't you just spend a bit longer learning rather than chatting with your friends." as her words wormed deep inside his skull like a group of burrowing worms. At the time of the conversation, he can remember being a little irritated as his overbearing mother gave out advice that he did not want or need, but in hindsight he recalled that this was the last full conversation he had with his mum before they were captured at the GGC facility.

Love shone through all these memories in a different way to what was starting to gently take over the room in the present.

"Looking at these pictures reminds me of something important."

"What's that?" Arianna asked, curiosity evident in her voice.

"It reminds me of all the people we love," Jayden replied, his voice tinged with emotion. "Our families, our friends, all the people who mean the world to us."

Arianna nodded, a thoughtful expression on her face. "It's true. They're the ones who make life worth living, even when times get tough." Arianna herself was also in reminiscing mode with thoughts turned on happy moments of her existence with each of her mum, dad, and grandad. It is amazing how humans can recall the most simple and discreet moments with razor like accuracy. Arianna was feeling joyful inside by only recanting happy thoughts and moments as if her mind had locked negative thoughts within a high security prison. Internally her happiness was growing stronger and almost breeding with every breath she took. Parts of Arianna's being were reaching towards internal metaphorical explosion.

"And you know," Jayden continued, his heart pounding in his chest, "I can't help but feel like you're a part of that too. Like you have become a part of my life in a way beyond that I never expected. I want you to be always with me and a part of my future, no matter what happens to us, or where it takes us."

Arianna's breath caught in her throat, her eyes locking with his in silent understanding. Her fingers clenched and pupils dilated as she responded with "I feel the same way," whispering in her kindest voice. Speaking barely above a whisper, she continued "I never imagined that I could care about someone as much as I care about you." In that moment, as they sat together on the couch, surrounded by the echoes of their loved ones, Jayden and Arianna realized something profound. They knew that love was not just confined to the people in the photographs, but that it could also be found in the quiet moments shared between two souls, in the gentle touch of a hand, and in the unspoken words that passed between them. The room was burning with desire and the interconnected thoughts that were flying between them.

The room's ambient lighting cast a warm, inviting atmosphere, and the gentle white noise of the nearby city outside provided a soothing backdrop to their thoughts.

Arianna shifted slightly, her gaze drifting towards Jayden as she spoke. "You know, Jayden, I've been thinking," she began, her voice soft. Jayden turned to her, his eyes meeting hers with a curious expression. "What about?" he asked, his interest piqued. Arianna hesitated for a moment, her heart pounding in her chest as she gathered her thoughts. "About us," she admitted, her voice barely above a whisper. "About how much time we've been spending together lately, and... how much I enjoy it."

Jayden's breath caught in his throat as he listened to her words, a rush of warmth flooding through him at the realization that she felt the same way he did. "I feel the same, Arianna," he confessed, his voice filled with sincerity. "Being with you... it just feels right."

From the moment they drew their first breaths, Jayden and Arianna's lives were bound together by the invisible threads of fate, their paths intertwined in a dance of serendipity and coincidence that spanned the breadth of their existence.

Born mere days apart, they grew up side by side, their laughter echoing through the halls of their childhood as they navigated the trials and tribulations of youth together. From scraped knees to broken hearts, they weathered every storm hand in hand, their bond forged in the fires of shared experience and unwavering loyalty. Within the chaos of their everyday lives, they failed to see what lay hidden beneath the surface. It was a longing that pulsed beneath their skin like a dormant ember, waiting to be ignited by the flames of desire. For years, they had danced around each other, their hearts yearning for something more than friendship yet too afraid to speak the words that lingered on the tip of their tongues. Despite their unspoken desires, they remained steadfast in their commitment to one another, bound by the unbreakable ties of camaraderie and trust. Even when they had both been caught up in the natural progression of boyfriend and girlfriend relationships with other people, there was never real progression to the point they had all ended before they began. It was as if boyfriends and girlfriends respectively had come to simply fill an empty space.

It was not until they both found themselves here the cusp of the unknown; standing on the precipice of a new beginning, that they began to see each other in a different light. With each passing day here, their friendship blossomed into something deeper, a love that transcended the boundaries of mere companionship and soared to heights beyond their wildest dreams. Even as they danced further along the delicate tightrope of uncertainty, they remained hesitant to voice their true feelings, their fear of rejection outweighing the allure of possibility. The lust growing inside each of them was untamed and it was inevitable that it could only be kept at bay for so long.

For Arianna, Jayden was a tempest of raw passion and untamed desire, his every word and gesture igniting a fire within her that burned with an intensity she could scarcely contain. With each passing moment, she found herself drawn deeper into the depths of his gaze, lost in a sea of longing and ecstasy that left her breathless with anticipation. Within the tumult of their emotions, they remained hesitant to act upon the forbidden desires that raged within their hearts. Fearful of risking their cherished friendship, they suppressed their urges, burying them beneath layers of denial and self-restraint.

Despite their best efforts to resist temptation, the flames of passion continued to smoulder beneath the surface, their yearning growing ever more insistent with each passing moment. As they found themselves swept away by the tide of desire once more, they knew that they could no longer deny the truth that pulsed within their veins. As their eyes met once more, a silent understanding passed between them, their hearts beating in unison as they leaned towards each other, their moist lips meeting in a tender, tentative kiss. In that moment, everything else faded away. Primary personal doubts, even their doubts about doubts themselves, their fears, their uncertainties all dissipated, leaving only the undeniable truth of their growing feelings for each other. Time seemed to stand still as they lost themselves in each other, their hearts beating as one. Jayden felt a rush of adrenaline course through him, his senses heightened by the intoxicating taste of Arianna's tender lips.

Their lips joined again in a much longer embrace as they explored each other's mouths with more haste and less vigour. The Artificial Intelligent senses within the room itself could read the situation as well as any human would. The lights dimmed further, and romantic soundtracks started playing throughout the hidden speakers in the room. Even the door to the room ensured closure and pulled taught with an interlocking click.

When they finally pulled apart, both breathless and flushed, Jayden felt a sense of euphoria wash over him. He had never felt a connection like this before, a connection that transcended time and space as he knew it.

"I've been wanting to do that for so long," Arianna whispered, her eyes shining with emotion.

"Me too," Jayden replied, his voice calm and relaxed.

It was in that moment, as they sat together as one, on the edge of his bed, their fingers intertwined, Jayden knew that he had found something truly special in Arianna.

A soft welcoming smile now graced Arianna's lips, her eyes shining with affection as if she were the only girl in the world. "I think I'm falling for you, Jayden," she admitted, her voice filled with emotion.

Jayden's heart swelled with joy at her words, his own smile mirroring hers as he reached out to take her hand in his. "I think I'm falling for you too, Arianna," he whispered, his voice filled with love as he kissed her fingers gently and stared deep beyond her wide brown eyes and into her welcoming soul itself.

Chapter 19: The Political Chessboard

As the world braced itself for the upcoming election, the stage was set for a showdown between Sandronica Sprowl and Reebus, the incumbent leader of the Global Governance Council (GGC). With each passing day, the tension mounted, and the political landscape crackled with anticipation.

Sandronica Sprowl, the challenger, remained elusive. She was rarely seen in public and always shrouded in mystery. Her absence had only fuelled speculation about her intentions and strategies. Many had wondered exactly what game she was playing. Despite her low profile, whispers of her campaign echoed through the corridors of power. She garnered support from those who yearned for change and reform, especially as there were those who were not the biggest fans of the status quo. How many years can someone take of the same leader? with same ideas, and same rhetoric? People knew that a strong opposition was necessary to make people believe and hope for a better future.

Reebus himself, the seasoned politician, seemed to be everywhere at once, his presence looming large in the public eye. From televised debates to high-profile speeches. He had orchestrated a carefully choreographed campaign designed to highlight his leadership and accomplishments. With every move, he projected an aura of confidence and control, leaving no doubt that he was a formidable and worthy opponent. Behind the scenes, the battle for supremacy unfolded with all the subtlety of a high-stakes chess match. Strategists plotted and counterplotted, seeking to outwit and outmanoeuvre their respective adversaries. Every speech, every policy announcement, every media appearance was meticulously orchestrated to gain the upper hand in the race for power. The strategists for Reebus were well known figures in their own rights with names and faces familiar throughout. Sandronica's team were never to be seen, hidden sources of direction and misdirection powered from unknown sources.

As the countdown to the election continued, the political landscape remained turbulent. Reebus held a commanding lead in all of the polls. With each new survey released, his advantage seemed to grow, solidifying his position as the frontrunner in his race for re-election. The world watched in anticipation as the inevitability of another term under Reebus's leadership loomed ever closer.

In the halls of power at the GGC, whispers of uncertainty gave way to a sense of resignation, as even the most ardent supporters of Sandronica Sprowl acknowledged the uphill battle she faced. Despite her best efforts to gain traction and momentum, Reebus's overwhelming popularity seemed insurmountable, casting a shadow of doubt over her chances of victory, or even remaining competitive. There was still a great deal of hope with Sandronica's supporters throughout the world. Over twenty years of Reebus's grip had led to those who fall into the 'anyone but him' camp. Others would rather vote for a dead pigeon than Reebus. With this being the case, no matter how confident or guaranteed the victory would be it still required Reebus' campaign to be well ran and meticulously advertised throughout the world.

Reebus reclined in his luxurious office chair, a satisfied smirk playing at the corners of his lips as he chatted with Imelda Stravus, his trusted advisor and confidante. The latest poll data lay spread out on his desk, with wonderfully efficient data segments and holographic projections of the result easy to digest. The data detailing every facet of the projected result with voter turnout. The demographics and even reasons why people voted and for whom were clear to see. The numbers stated the likely election result would be 58% to Reebus and 42% for Sandronica Sprowl which was a clear and wide victory given the accuracy of the data set before them. Artificial technology was now so intrinsically linked in the world of politics that results could be plotted with accuracies of less than ha f a percent. The thrill of election night and not knowing who wculd be triumphant was a long-lost part of the electoral lardscape in these modern times. Unless there were to be late unexpected changes to policies, or to the likeability or trust of a political contender then only a lack of turnout in Reebus area strongholds could realistically affect the outcome.

Imelda chuckled; her voice filled with amusement as she studied the numbers. "It seems that Sandronica Sprowl's campaign is losing ground by the day," she remarked, a mischievous glint in her eye. "She doesn't stand a chance against you, Reebus."

Reebus's smirk widened into a grin, his confidence bolstered by the knowledge of his impending victory. "Indeed," he replied, his tone dripping with arrogance. "Sandronica is no match for me. She is grasping at straws; she would be desperate to salvage whatever shred of credibility she has left." as he laughed away as if a shared joke.

Imelda nodded in agreement, her expression reflecting Reebus's smug satisfaction. "I couldn't agree more," she said, her voice laced with disdain. "But just to be safe, I suggest we give her policies one final push – something to seal her electoral fate once and for all."

Reebus raised an eyebrow, intrigued by Imelda's suggestion. "And what do you propose?" he asked, his curiosity piqued.

Imelda smirked, a gleam of mischief dancing in her eyes. "If we were to leak information suggesting that Sandronica plans to raise the compulsory retirement age to eighty-two, it would surely be the final nail in her coffin," she explained, her voice filled with satisfaction. "It would alienate her from a large number of her remaining supporters and guarantee your victory in the election."

Reebus's grin widened into a predatory smile, his eyes alight with anticipation. "I like the way you think, Imelda," he said, his voice filled with admiration. "Get started on preparing Sandronica's message for distribution tonight. We'll ensure that she digs her own grave with her own words."
Imelda nodded in agreement, her lips curling into a wicked smile. "Consider it done, Reebus," she replied, her voice filled with a rasp of humour. "Sandronica won't know what hit her."
Imelda and Reebus had known each other over thirty years and were as close as people could be. They often thought the same, even dressed in similar fashion. Imelda had been there throughout Reebus's onslaught and rise up the political spectrum. Many years before when Reebus was just starting out it was Imelda who came to his aid when most in need. She was also the one whom ultimately helped him cross the political line when faced up against Killian Tredwell all those many moons ago. Imelda herself had her quarters right next to his and was more than just a confidant but a partner in all of the ruling observations and directives. She was the person whom he would turn to if there was a task that he wanted doing, no matter how big or small. It wouldn't matter how difficult the task was, or how legal its scope, Imelda would make sure it was done. Despite offering very complete and much needed guidance, Imelda also knew that if Reebus had made up his mind on something then it was not attempting to change. He was a stubborn man, supreme in power but not forgiving of anyone who were to step on his toes. Imelda had sacrificed much to follow Reebus, having to make many decisions in the past that ultimately made her choose him over her own family. It meant that at her very core was a brutal, clinical woman; someone who should never be crossed by anyone. Reebus himself had noticed many unusual events occurring the GGC which Imelda was clearly responsible for. He just let her do what she wanted, so long as it did not come back to affect him.

In one instance, Imelda had taken severe dislike to a well-meaning guard in her team. In an effort to be charming the guard had made a number of flirtatious remarks to her. This was not someone who interested her in any way, especially being a lowly GGC guard. After the first few quips and retorts from Imelda, the guard seemed to just 'disappear.' Not only did they disappear from within the confines of the GGC, but they did not appear back in their family home. Nor did the guard have further contact with any of their friends and family. If one were to start checking for his name inside the GGC tracking database, then no trace would be able to be found. This guard had effectively vanished from existence. Remaining guards chatted amongst themselves in private and discussed the situation. Never again did any of them speak to Imelda unless she spoke with them first. There was a hierarchy and order within the GGC, and it was not advisable to step out of line. It was long thought that Imelda was also responsible for many 'mishaps' on the outside world. Whether it be accidents, murders, or disappearances; you could bet that somewhere, somehow, Imelda had her footprint all over each tragedy.

Reebus leaned back once more in his chair in his office, a thoughtful expression on his face as he conversed with Imelda again.

'Any other business Imelda?" continued Reebus.

'Yes, I have some updates on your special project – that of Jayden and Arianna," mentioned Imelda in response.

The mention of Arianna and Jayden brought a flicker of interest to his eyes, and he listened intently as Imelda outlined her observations.

"It seems that Arianna and Jayden have developed quite a close relationship with Christina," Imelda remarked, her voice tinged with suspicion. "They could be trouble if we're not careful."

Reebus nodded thoughtfully, his mind already calculating the potential threat posed by the young rebels. "Agreed," he replied, his tone measured. "We'll need to keep a close eye on them and monitor their movements closely."

Imelda glanced down at the data on her tablet, her brow furrowed in concentration. "I'll ensure they are monitored closely, right away" she suggested, her voice firm. "We can't afford to let them interfere with our plans, not just yet anyway."

Reebus nodded in agreement, his gaze fixed on the screen before him as he considered their next move. "Good," he said, his voice filled with determination. "And once the election is over, we'll have the perfect opportunity to finalise our plans without anyone being aware."

Imelda nodded in agreement, a steely glint in her eye. "It won't be long now," she replied, her voice filled with anticipation. "Just a few more months, and then we'll be ready to execute the plan."

That evening, the flickering glow of the holographic screen illuminated the room as people across the city tuned in to watch Sandronica Sprowl's much-anticipated latest election broadcast. In living rooms and gathering places alike, eyes were fixed on the screen, anticipation hanging heavy in the air. Sandronica stood before the world, her expression resolute as she addressed the nation. "My fellow citizens," she began, her voice ringing out with authority, "I stand before you today as a candidate for change. Change that is long overdue."

As she spoke, the camera panned over the attentive faces of her audience, capturing their rapt attention and eager anticipation. Sandronica's message was clear, her words carrying the weight of conviction and determination.

"It is time," she continued, her voice unwavering, "to raise the compulsory retirement age to eighty-two. Our society is evolving, and our people are living longer, healthier lives. It is only fitting that our retirement policies reflect this reality. With the age at eighty-two people will have longer here to contribute to the vitality and stability of the human race, whilst still having more than enough time to enjoy their lengthy retirements on 'Serenity 1'"

A murmur of agreement rippled through the crowd of Sandronica's supporters, the significance of Sandronica's proposal not lost on them. It was a bold move, one that promised to reshape the landscape of retirement and redefine the parameters of aging in society but might not be a popular one.

Sandronica remained steady as she delivered her mandate, her words echoing with clarity and purpose. "Together," she declared, "we will build a future where every individual has the opportunity to thrive, regardless of age. A future where wisdom and experience are valued, and where the contributions of every generation are celebrated."

As the broadcast ended, the impact of Sandronica's message lingered in the air, stirring hearts, and igniting passions. For many, her mandate represented hope for a brighter future, a future where age was no longer a barrier to opportunity and fulfilment.

In the aftermath of Sandronica Sprowl's election broadcast, a wave of discontent swept through the city, leaving a trail of frustration and anger in its wake. For many, her proposal to raise the compulsory retirement age to eighty-two was met with vehement opposition, as it only added to the burdens already weighing heavily on their shoulders.

In dingy apartments and crowded streets, voices rose in protest, echoing the sentiments of those who felt betrayed by Sandronica's mandate. "How dare she?" they cried, their words laced with bitterness and resentment. "We can barely make ends meet as it is, and now she wants to make us work even longer?"

The anger was palpable, simmering just beneath the surface as people grappled with the harsh reality of their circumstances. With resources scarce and opportunities few and far between, the prospect of toiling away for even longer seemed like a cruel and unjust punishment.

Amid the uproar, whispers of dissent spread like wildfire, fuelling the flames of discontent. More and more people started to voice their opposition to Sandronica's mandate. "We won't stand for this!" they declared, their defiance ringing aloud and clear. "We'll show her come election day!"

For many, the choice was clear – they would cast their vote for Reebus, the incumbent leader who had promised stability and prosperity in times of uncertainty. Compared to Sandronica's lofty promises, his history spoke for itself, and for those struggling to survive, he seemed like the only viable option.

Across the globe, citizens grappled with a sense of resignation, resigned to the idea that Reebus's re-election was all but assured. From bustling metropolises to remote villages, conversations buzzed with resigned acceptance, as people came to terms with the reality of another term under his GGC's rule. As always there were pockets of resistance to the likely outcome for hope and fear are close allies in the electoral spectrum.

For Jayden and Arianna, the realisation of Reebus's inevitable victory was a worry. Despite their hopes for change and reform, the odds seemed stacked against Sandronica leaving them feeling powerless in the face of the political machine that Reebus had built.

As they watched the world around them seemingly resign itself to the status quo, Jayden and Arianna could not help but feel a sense of disillusionment wash over them. The promise of democracy seemed hollow in the face of Reebus's overwhelming dominance. It left them to wonder if true change was even possible in a world where the scales seemed so impossibly tipped. It genuinely felt that Reebus controlled not just the GGC, but the electorate and with it the entire world too.

As they discussed the looming election and the political landscape, a nagging question tugged at the edges of their minds, refusing to be ignored.

"It's strange, isn't it?" Arianna mused; her brow furrowed in thought as she turned to Jayden. "We've been here for weeks, and yet we've never seen Sandronica Sprowl anywhere in the GGC."

Jayden nodded in agreement, a thoughtful expression crossing his features. "You're right," he replied, his voice tinged with uncertainty. "I mean, you'd expect to see her around here more often and not hidden away from the GGC like this."

"I haven't even noticed any of her team here, and there's very little media or holographic advertising from her in the corridors around the whole complex.," said Arianna in reply, processing the harsh realities of what she was saying.

Arianna's mood darkened with concern as she considered the implications of Sandronica's absence. "Do you think something's happened to her?" she asked, her voice barely above a whisper. "Maybe Reebus has done something to her, maybe he has her hostage."

Jayden hesitated for a moment, his mind racing with possibilities. "I don't know," he admitted, his voice heavy with worry. "It's definitely strange. I mean, why would she hide away from the GGC, especially when the election is right around the corner?"

As they mulled over the mystery of Sandronica's absence, a sense of unease settled over them, casting a shadow over their thoughts. In a world where nothing was as it seemed, the sudden disappearance of a political candidate only added to the growing list of unanswered questions.

Chapter 20: The Secretive Cloakroom

As Jayden and Arianna wandered through the now familiar corridors of the GGC headquarters, their curiosity piqued by the mysterious surroundings, they stumbled upon a door that seemed to beckon to them with a silent allure. It was a nondescript door, tucked away in a forgotten corner of the building, its surface worn with age and neglect. There was something about it that drew their attention, something that whispered of secrets waiting to be uncovered.

"Have you ever noticed that door before?" Arianna asked, her voice hushed with intrigue as she gestured towards the uninspiring entrance.

Jayden frowned; his gaze fixed on the door as he tried to recall if he had ever seen it before. "I don't think so," he replied, his voice tinged with uncertainty. "It's strange, though. I could have sworn we've been down this corridor countless times, but I don't remember ever seeing that door."

Arianna nodded in agreement, her curiosity growing with each passing moment. "I wonder what's behind it," she mused, her eyes shining with anticipation.

Jayden hesitated for a moment, a nagging sense of unease gnawing at him as he considered the possibilities. "I don't know, Arianna," he replied cautiously. "I guess there is only one way to find out!" as he took a closer look at the guards' arms and noticed a familiar logo.

Arianna's brow furrowed in thought, her mind racing with imaginations competing for attention. "Maybe, tonight," she suggested, her voice filled with determination. "It wouldn't hurt to satisfy our curiosity, would it?"

Back in their room Jayden took a profound interest in a game of the world football league that had just started between New York United and Tokyo Dragons. It was not a game that Jayden had been overly concerned with in the past and Arianna was a little confused by his actions. "Why are you watching this?" she enquired.

Jayden smirked and told her "I'm doing some research as I think it will come in useful later on."

Arianna wanted to take the conversation further to fully understand what Jayden was telling her, but he was so engrossed in this event that she wasn't able to get his attention. She decided it was better to leave him be and instead went back into her room to have a bit of peace and quiet and look through some old holographic photo memorabilia and catch a nap whilst she could.

A couple of hours later Jayden woke Arianna and told her that it was now time to go. She quickly got herself smartened up and followed him out of the door.

"So, what's our plan? How are we going to get passed the guard, Jayden?" asked Arianna.

Jayden smiled at her and said, "Just leave it to me."

As they approached the guarded entrance to the secret door, Jayden then motioned for Arianna to stay back while he stepped forward to distract the lone sentinel. With practiced ease, he engaged the guard in a brief conversation, his words laced with charm and charisma as he deftly diverted the man's attention away from their true intentions.

"Hey, how is your day going? Did you see the soccer game tonight? It was crazy!," inquired Jayden.

"Yeah, it was a great game, one of the best I had seen and that goal, just wow. I have never seen a ball travel so far or so accurately," as the guard lost complete consciousness of events around him. Jayden had completely captured the guard's attention and intrigue and was beginning to fail at the basic guard etiquette and skills under 'guarding 101'. Jayden had noticed earlier that the guard had a 'New York United' tattoo down his arm, and he knew enough about football (or soccer as the Americans still called it) to be able to have a conversation.

Knowing that the game involving New York was on this evening was why he had decided to spend his night in front of the holographic screen. The guard and Jayden thus had a lot to talk about and his critique and analysis of the game was exceptional to a point where the guard was devouring every word.

Meanwhile, Arianna stood watch from a safe distance, her heart pounding in her chest as she waited for the signal to proceed. With each passing moment, the tension in her mind grew thick and foggy, the anticipation mounting as she neared her part in the objective. Finally, with a subtle nod from Jayden, Arianna sprang into life, slowly moving beyond the active conversation and sneakily through the door which the distractable guard should have been protecting. With practiced precision she was completely un-noticed and behind inside the mysterious room. Jayden had to work a bit harder for his chance to join Arianna. He continued to work hard on the football discussion knowing that this particular guard was a huge fan to the extent he could talk about nothing else. When Jayden pulled a football out of his backpack and started passing it back and forth with the guard it was a state of humour and distraction to anyone passing and becoming a commotion to all. The guard's direct command could see what was happening and called the football mad guard on his communicator. Whilst the guard was being chastised and scolded for the ball kicking, Jayden snook into the door to join Arianna without anybody noticing.

As Jayden and Arianna found themselves inside the secret room, their hearts racing with anticipation, they were met with a sight that defied their expectations. Instead of the hidden chamber harbouring dark secrets or clandestine operations, it revealed nothing more than rows upon rows of neatly stacked GGC uniforms, neatly organized on shelves. There were supervisor uniforms, guard uniforms and uniforms of operators and work associates of almost every element of the GGC operation. Arianna moved the uniforms on the racks looking for any sign of unusuality or mystique, but it was unforthcoming. These uniforms and all clothing within this room all seemed remarkably normal in every respect. There did not appear to be any secrets in this room.

Arianna let out a frustrated sigh, her disappointment palpable as she surveyed the mundane contents of the room. "This is it?" she exclaimed; her voice tinged with disbelief. "Just a storage room for uniforms?"

Jayden's brow furrowed in confusion as he took in the scene before him, his mind reeling with the implications of their discovery. "It doesn't make sense," he muttered, his voice barely above a whisper. "Why would they go to such lengths to hide a room full of uniforms?"

Before Arianna could respond, Jayden felt a tap on his shoulder, causing him to whirl around in surprise. Standing before them, her expression inscrutable, was Christina.

"Christina," Jayden stammered, his voice caught somewhere between shock and apprehension. "What are you doing here?"

Christina regarded them with a cool detachment, her gaze flickering between Jayden and Arianna as if sizing them up. "I could ask you the same question," she replied cryptically, her voice tinged with an undercurrent of suspicion.

Arianna's eyes narrowed as she took a step forward, her instincts on high alert. "We were just... exploring," she offered, her voice faltering slightly under Christina's penetrating gaze.

Christina's lips curved into a faint smile, but there was a glint of steel in her eyes as she spoke. "Exploring, hmm?" she mused, her tone laced with scepticism. "Well, it seems you've stumbled upon something rather interesting, haven't you?"

With a subtle flick of her wrist, Christina uncovered a concealed button on the wall, hidden amidst the rows of GGC uniforms. She then pressed and depressed the button with a soft click, and then a low rumble then filled the air before Jayden and Arianna watched in amazement as the ordinary uniforms began to swirl and twist, revealing a hidden passage concealed behind them.

Arianna gasped in astonishment, her eyes widening with wonder as she beheld the secret entrance revealed before them. "How did you...?" she began, her voice trailing off as she struggled to find the words to express her awe.

Christina offered them a wry smile, her demeanour betraying no hint of surprise at their reaction. "There's more to this place than meets the eye," she explained cryptically, her gaze flickering between Jayden and Arianna. "And it seems you two are about to discover just how deep the rabbit hole goes."

With a shared glance, Jayden and Arianna followed Christina as she led them through the hidden passage before them, the walls closing in around them like silent sentinels guarding their secrets. As they ventured deeper into the bowels of the GGC headquarters, the air grew thick with anticipation, each step bringing them closer to the truth they sought.

Finally, after what felt like an eternity of winding corridors and hidden passages, they emerged into a vast chamber bathed in soft, ethereal light. Before them stood a series of monitors and consoles, their surfaces aglow with data streams and holographic displays. Although there was flickering life in the room from all the electrical devices, there were no real people in the room they had entered. It was a very surreal feeling to be somewhere so important but also somewhere that was so quiet.

"This is the heart of the operation," Christina explained, her voice reverberating in the cavernous chamber. "The nerve centre of the GGC, where decisions are made, and destinies are forged."

"If you look on the screens of this station you will see something very interesting," said Christina to them both.

Jayden and Arianna peered into the monitor and saw a trail of words that were very familiar from the holographic news of the previous evening. They were the words from Sandronica Sprowl that had been displayed around the world in the last few days. The very words about increasing the retirement age to eighty-two and all the associated reasoning.

Alongside the words was a holograph itself, of Sandronica. At first this seemed nothing more than a captured media representation of what they had seen. Jayden looked more closely, and the screen had many other functions. You could change the colour of parts of the holograph, add textures and dimples to the skin or rotate the holograph to any position. The word entry could be modified with different sections of text. Jayden tried altering some of the text in the input stream to say, "I love monkey soup," and upon clicking 'speak' the holograph of Sandronica spoke those words in her recognised voice and even using the same facial and lip movements that had been associated with her. Looking further at the screens there were options to adjust every aspect of the face, the tones and hues and sharpness of every facet was evident. Away from the physical characteristics it was possible to adjust the voice tones and functionality of the voice in any way that the user would choose.

Christina looked at them both knowingly and tapped them on the shoulders simultaneously, "You have both just met the real Sandronica Sprowl."

Jayden and Arianna stood watching with their eyes wide with disbelief, Christina's words hung heavy in the air. They exchanged a bewildered glance, struggling to comprehend the magnitude of what they had just heard.

"A holographic representation?" Arianna echoed; her voice tinged with incredulity. "You mean... Sandronica Sprowl isn't real?"

Christina nodded solemnly, her expression grave as she met their gaze. "That's correct," she confirmed. "Sandronica Sprowl is nothing more than a carefully crafted illusion, a puppet designed to maintain the illusion of democracy while Reebus retains his grip on power."

Jayden's mind reeled with the implications of Christina's revelation, his thoughts spinning as he tried to make sense of the deception that had been perpetrated on the world. "But why?" he demanded, his voice tinged with anger and disbelief. "Why go to such lengths to deceive the people?"

Christina's eyes softened with understanding as she regarded them with a mixture of pity and sympathy. "Power," she replied simply. "Reebus and the GGC will stop at nothing to maintain their control over the populace. Sandronica Sprowl was merely a means to an end, a pawn in their game of manipulation and deceit. For some reason Reebus clearly needs more time in power, more time to control the GGC, more time to have control over the direction and order of the GGC."

As the weight of Christina's revelation settled over them, Jayden and Arianna felt a sense of urgency rising within them. "Why did you tell us this information, surely it would have been easy to hide away and keep this from us?," asked a confused Arianna.

"Sometimes in life you realise that being honest to people and letting them access and process their own thoughts and actions is the only way. Besides," as Christina paused for breath before continuing, "I value our friendships that we have built over the last few weeks and months. I do not believe it's right to hide things as important as this from those closest to you. There is more that I am aware of that you probably should know too, but you are going to have to discover these secrets yourselves."

The truth Arianna and Jayden had uncovered about Sandronica was staggering, but now they knew that there were still more secrets lurking in the shadows, waiting to be revealed.

"There's more?" Arianna asked, her voice tinged with a mix of curiosity and apprehension. Jayden and Arianna huddled together both appreciative and concerned by Christina's revelation and not knowing which way to turn.

"What else have we not been told? Why can't you tell us now? enquired Jayden.

Christina nodded solemnly at Arianna's question; her expression unreadable as she met their gaze. "Much more," she confirmed. "But I can't go into detail here. It's not safe, and you never know exactly who is watching .... or listening for that matter....", as Christina looked anxiously around the room.

Jayden exchanged a wary glance with Arianna, his mind racing with questions and possibilities. "What do we do now?" he asked, his voice barely above a whisper.

Christina's lips curved into a faint smile, but there was a hint of sadness in her eyes. "You need to find Hugo Bream in the GGC gym in the morning" she replied cryptically. "He'll help you uncover the rest of the truth. Tell him that Christina sent you and remember when he asks you the secret phrase, you must answer, 'Green Butterflies Eat Spinach.' It's the only way he will believe you."

"You need to go NOW!" ordered Christina as she could hear Imelda's GGC guards' approach down the corridor behind them, "I will distract them and you need to head back to your quarters.," as Jayden and Arianna took the opportunity to escape with the help of her distraction and left Christina to chat with her new guests.

Chapter 21: The Galactic Gym

Back in the safety of their quarters and with the door firmly closed and locked behind them Jayden and Arianna immediately flumped on the couch in front of them. Their nerves were still on edge and brains processing what had they had just learned and witnessed. It seemed that all the conspiracy theories around Sandronica Sprowl were in the case not just off the mark, but far less conspired than the actuality of a non-existent electoral nominee.

Jayden and Arianna exchanged a longing glance, but they knew that they had no choice but to trust Christina's guidance in their next investigatory adventure.

It had been a very long and quite stressful day and they were both extremely tired. With a second and then third check on the security of their quarters Jayden suggested that they should probably get some sleep whilst they could. Arianna's eyes broken by Christina's revelation just wanted to crawl into a warm and safe place and into the man she had grown to love more dearly than anything else in this world.

"Let's go sweetie.," directed a now calm and longing Arianna with the inevitable direction of the now shared bedroom. Her hand was held out as she needed Jayden to pull her up from her seat as all her weary adventures had taken their toll. Jayden grabbed her sleek and slender hand, pulling her up in manner like the most elegant swan. Jayden hugged her tightly as their feet stepped in unison towards the bedroom. Arianna and Jayden both sat on the respective edges of their sides of the bed. Jayden on the left and Arianna on the right. It was a night when closeness was a necessity as any day in this world could be the last. Arianna stepped out of her summery dress, leaving it in a heap on the floor. Her underwear was soon dispatched into the nearby washing collection tube. Jayden himself was more ruthless with his undressing at his side of the bed. His shirt, trousers and socks quickly dispatched to all corners of the room.

Arianna watched intently at her now nearly naked man. She continued to further undress with her black leggings rolled up and removed first, then a cheeky glance towards Jayden as her breasts were released from their daily prison deliberately and enticingly as he looked straight at her. Finally, she removed her knickers with her hand on each side by scraping then down her legs, but not forgetting to dispatch them into the washing collection tubes as her personality demanded. She then crawled under the covers wanting to both meet Jayden and her womanly desires as one. "Aren't you forgetting something?" quipped Arianna grabbing at his pants which remained the only clothing between them still attached. She yanked them away quickly, tenderly but firm. Her personality could not cope with filing these pants into the right tube, as it had gone beyond that point. Arianna knew what she wanted; what she desired, and what she must have, and she needed it right at this very moment. Arianna proceeded to begin a night of lust unlike any other with Jayden enjoying every part of her curvaceous body as she did equally with every part of his muscular frame.

The morning ambient light came into their room, designed to look, and feel exactly like sunlight coming between the trunks of a gigantic forest. Even the moving air and smells contributed to a realistic gentle natural environment. The settings on wake-up devices was now so proficient and advanced that rarely were alarms used in the final wakening. The bodies rhythms and sleep patterns monitored within the room and when a particular time of wakening was chosen the automated intelligence of room waking devices then delivered depending on personal preference the type of awaking one would prefer. It might be forest, seaside, even nightclub rave based if someone so desired. The customisation was endless, but the woodland wakeup was one of the favourites. With their bodies still aching from *all* their excursions of the previous day Jayden and Arianna exchanged a tender kiss before progressing with their morning routines. Teeth cleaning tablets and personal showers were followed by the clothes wearing process that accompanies each day. Once they were both dressed, they succumbed to the breakfast routine where their personal favourites appeared on the table in their selected morning slots without deliberation or noise. There was a quiet but satisfying feel throughout the room and they both looked content. After their energy refreshed for the new day before them, they knew it was time to progress in their quest for the truth.

Both Jayden and Arianna arose from their seats simultaneously and headed towards their room door. Upon opening the door shut behind them. As they made their way through the corridors of the GGC headquarters, Jayden and Arianna felt a sense of anticipation building within them. With each step, they drew closer to uncovering the secrets that lay hidden beneath the surface, and within trepidation expecting their encounter with Hugo Bream would be the key to unlocking further truths.

Finally, they arrived at the galactic gym room, where Hugo Bream awaited them. They had met Hugo a few times now but were only acquaintances and not yet, real friends. Christina, meanwhile, was very close with Hugo and if she had trust in him them then Arianna and Jayden should also extend that same respect to her confidents. With a further deep breath, Jayden stepped forward and spoke the words that Christina had instructed them to say.

"Christina sent us," he began, his voice steady as he met Hugo's gaze.

"And what animal eats away to get bigger?" retorted Hugo.

Arianna and Jayden looked at each other before Jayden blurted out "Green Butterflies Eat Spinach." In a calming and quiet delivery of words.

Hugo's eyes widened in recognition, and a knowing smile played at the corners of his lips. "Ah, I see," he replied cryptically. "Follow me."

Hugo and Christina had an enduring friendship that had gone on for over a decade. Hugo was not only her valued friend but also here confidant, the most trusted companion with whom she could share her hopes, fears, and aspirations for the future of space exploration. Christina had only a month ago appointed Hugo as her second in command for her new vision of the Space Exploration Program, but he still his time in the galactic gym room on regular intervals as his place of peace. Christina had asked him to go to the gym this morning, but he was unaware why.

With his keen intellect and strategic acumen, Hugo had already played a pivotal role in reshaping the direction of the Space Exploration Program, his insights and expertise guiding their efforts towards new ideas for discovery and innovation. Beyond his professional prowess, it was Hugo's unwavering dedication to their cause that truly set him apart. It was a commitment to excellence that earned him the respect and admiration of all who had the privilege of working alongside him. Hugo hated being in the limelight and Christina kept him away from any glare such that even within the reigns of the GGC headquarters he was a figure that almost never seen and hardly anyone really knew. He was now the brains and soothsayer behind Christina's flare.

After a few further but very uncomfortable pleasantries, Hugo now led Arianna and Jayden deeper into the gym room, where rows of exercise equipment stood in silent vigil. As they ventured further towards the very back of the room, Jayden and Arianna sensed that there was more to this place than met the eye, and they expected something to be lying around every bend.

As Jayden and Arianna followed Hugo's steps, they could not help but marvel at the state-of-the-art equipment that lined the walls. Yet, despite its impressive array of machines, the gym remained eerily quiet, devoid of the bustling activity one might expect.

"It's strange, isn't it?" Arianna mused, her voice barely above a whisper as they walked. "You'd think a place like this would be buzzing with activity."

Jayden nodded in agreement; his brow furrowed in thought. "Yeah, you'd think so," he replied, casting a thoughtful glance around the empty room. "I guess people don't really use gyms like they used to."

Arianna's expression softened with understanding as she considered Jayden's words. "I suppose you're right," she conceded. "With all the advances in health and fitness technology, most people can stay in shape without ever setting foot in a gym."

Jayden nodded in agreement, a thoughtful expression crossing his features. "Exactly," he replied. "Why bother going to a gym when you can get a full workout from the comfort of your own home? Besides, there are all kinds of pills and health machines that can reduce all the excess fat and control your muscle content, as well as look and feel."

Their conversation continued, with Jayden and Arianna reflecting on the changing nature of fitness in their world. Gone were the days of crowded gyms and gruelling workouts; now, people could achieve their fitness goals with ease, thanks to the convenience of home 'FITtslim' machines and other technological innovations.

As Jayden, Arianna, and Hugo ventured deeper into the deserted galactic gym room, a heavy silence hung in the air, broken only by the faint stir of the machines surrounding them with a background hum. Hugo's keen eyes swept over the empty space; his expression unreadable as he considered the implications of their surroundings.

"It's amazing, isn't it?" Hugo remarked, his voice low and contemplative as he addressed Jayden and Arianna. "An empty gym like this... it's the perfect place to hide secrets in plain sight."

Jayden and Arianna exchanged a wary glance, their senses on high alert as they absorbed Hugo's words. The notion of hidden secrets lurking within the shadows of the gym sent a shiver down their spines, and they could not help but wonder what truths lay concealed within its walls. Neither Jayden nor Arianna could see or notice any secrets or anything unusual despite looking in every direction.

"What kind of secrets?" Arianna asked, her voice tinged with apprehension.

Hugo's lips curved into a wry smile, but there was a hint of solemnity in his gaze as he met their eyes. "The kind that can change everything" he replied cryptically. "The kind that can shake the very foundations of the world as we know it."

Jayden's brow furrowed in confusion as he struggled to make sense of Hugo's words. "But why hide them here?" he pressed; his voice tinged with urgency. "Why not keep them in a secure location?"

Hugo's smile widened, but there was a glint of mischief in his eyes as he regarded them with a knowing look. "Because" he replied simply, "the best place to hide something is often right out in the open. What better place to hide secrets than in a place where no one would think to look?"

With a well-practiced hand, Hugo approached a particular fitness machine nestled in a concealed corner of the gym room. Jayden and Arianna watched with intrigue as he deftly inputted a series of intricate codes into the machine's interface, his fingers dancing across the keypad with precision. It was the furthest and oldest machine in the room and its position as the furthest from the entrance could not have been by coincidence alone.

As the final code was accepted, a mechanical labour of gears filled the air, and the machine emitted a beep as if awakening from a long slumber. Then, to Jayden and Arianna's astonishment, a section of the gym floor began to shift and warp, revealing a hidden spiral staircase concealed beneath.

Hugo offered them a knowing smile as he gestured towards the staircase. "Shall we?" he invited; his voice tinged with anticipation. With a shared glance, Jayden and Arianna followed Hugo down the spiralling staircase, their hearts pounding with excitement and apprehension. As they descended deeper into the bowels of the hidden chamber, the air grew thick with anticipation, each step bringing them closer to the truth they sought.

The staircase above them closed tight so even on the slightest chance of someone unusual entering the gym with a valid card, then walking down to the concealed room, and even with illusionary holograms in place, there was absolutely no way anyone could stumble across this staircase by accident alone.

Finally, they emerged into a vast chamber bathed in soft, blue light. Hugo turned to face them, his expression grave as he addressed Jayden and Arianna. "Welcome to the Earth Retirement Complex," he announced solemnly. "This is where the real secrets lie."

As Jayden, Arianna, and Hugo stood in the heart of the hidden chamber, bathed in the soft light from the monitors and consoles that surrounded them, Hugo turned to face them with a solemn expression.

"There's something you need to know," he began, his voice tinged with gravity. "Something that the GGC doesn't want the world to discover."

Jayden and Arianna exchanged a wary glance, their curiosity piqued as they awaited Hugo's revelation.

"It's about the Earth Retirement Complex," Hugo continued, his tone sombre. "A place where people above the age of eighty are sent to live out their days in luxury and happiness."

Jayden's brow furrowed in confusion as he struggled to make sense of Hugo's words. "I thought people over eighty were sent to Serenity 1," he remarked, his voice tinged with doubt.

Hugo shook his head, a sad smile playing at the corners of his lips. "That's what they want you to believe," he replied. "But the truth is far more sinister."

He went on to explain that the Earth Retirement Complex was a carefully guarded secret, hidden away from prying eyes and shielded from public scrutiny.

"In truth, the Earth Retirement Complex is nothing more than a luxurious guarded prison cage," Hugo explained. "A prison designed to keep the elderly out of sight and out of mind, while the rest of the world carries on as if nothing is amiss."

As Jayden and Arianna absorbed Hugo's words, a sense of outrage surged within them. The final realization and proof that the GGC had been lying to the people of Earth, manipulating them with false promises and empty assurances, filled them with a righteous anger.

As Hugo's revelation settled over them, Jayden could not help but feel a surge of curiosity. "So," he began tentatively, "does that mean everyone who was supposed to be sent to Serenity 1 is here in the Earth Retirement Complex instead?"

Hugo shook his head, his expression grave. "No," he replied, his voice tinged with sadness. "Only a select few are transported here."

Jayden frowned, puzzled by Hugo's response. "But why only a select few?" he asked, his brow furrowing in confusion. "And how does the Earth Retirement Complex cope with the numbers?"

Hugo sighed, his gaze drifting to the floor as he struggled to find the right words. "The truth is," he began slowly, "The Earth

Retirement Complex is not equipped to accommodate everyone who reaches the age of eighty. It's simply not feasible."

He went on to explain that the selection process for transport to the Earth Retirement Complex was highly secretive and tightly controlled by the GGC. Only those deemed to be of special importance or significance, or Reebus' favourites were chosen to be transported here, while the rest were left to fend for themselves in a world that was increasingly hostile and unforgiving.

"As for how the Earth Retirement Complex copes with the numbers," Hugo continued, "it's a delicate balancing act. Resources are scarce, and every effort is made to ensure that those who are chosen to come here are provided for."

Jayden nodded, his mind whirling with questions and concerns. The realization that only a select few were deemed worthy of being transported to the Earth Retirement Complex filled him with a sense of unease, and he could not help but wonder what criteria the GGC used to make their decisions.

Jayden's heart pounded in his chest as he posed the question that had been weighing heavily on his mind. "Hugo," he began, his voice trembling slightly, "what happens to those people who don't come to the Earth Retirement Complex? Do they go to Serenity 1?"

Hugo's expression grew profound, his eyes darkening with a mixture of sorrow and resignation. "Serenity 1," he repeated, his voice barely above a whisper. "Yes, there is a planet by that name, but nobody has ever lived there, it cannot sustain human life."

Jayden's eyes widened in shock, his mind struggling to comprehend the gravity of Hugo's words. "But then... what happens to all the others?" he asked, his voice barely audible.

Hugo's gaze bore into Jayden's, his eyes filled with a profound sadness. "I think you already know," he replied quietly. "They are disposed of."

A chill ran down Jayden's spine as the weight of Hugo's words settled over him. The realization that countless lives had been callously discarded, their existence erased without a trace, filled him with a sense of horror and disbelief.

As Jayden grappled with the enormity of what he had just learned, he felt Arianna's hand slip into his own, her touch a comforting anchor during the storm. Together, they stood in silence, their thoughts consumed by the grim reality of the world they inhabited.

Arianna's voice trembled as she posed the question that had haunted her since the moment she had set foot in the Earth Retirement Complex. "Hugo," she began, her words barely above a whisper, "can you confirm... did my grandad... was he... evaporated?"

Hugo met Arianna's gaze with a solemn expression, his eyes filled with a depth of sorrow that mirrored her own. Without a word, he simply nodded, confirming the devastating truth that Arianna had feared.

Arianna's breath caught in her throat as the weight of Hugo's confirmation crashed over her like a tidal wave. Tears welled in her eyes, blurring her vision as the reality of her grandad's fate washed over her.

"No," she whispered, her voice barely audible as she struggled to contain the torrent of emotion threatening to engulf her. "No, it can't be..."

Even as the words left her lips, Arianna knew deep down that it was true. Her grandad, the man who had been her rock, her confidant, her guiding light, was gone. There was nothing she could do to bring him back.

As the full weight of her grief threatened to overwhelm her, Arianna felt Jayden's arms wrap around her, pulling her close in a comforting embrace. Together, they stood in silence, their shared sorrow binding them together in a moment of profound loss.

For Arianna, the pain of losing her grandad was almost unbearable. With all the grief and heartache, there was also a flicker of determination burning within her chest. She knew that she could not let her grandad's death be in vain. She had to fight, not just for him, but for all those who had been unjustly taken from this world.

As the weight of Hugo's confirmation settled over her, Arianna felt a torrent of emotions swirling within her chest. She took a further breath, trying to steady herself as she grappled with the devastating truth she had just learned. Her grandad, the man she had loved and cherished, was gone, taken from her in the cruellest of ways.

Taking a moment to compose herself, Arianna glanced up at Hugo, her eyes filled with a mixture of sorrow and determination. "Hugo," she began, her voice steady despite the turmoil raging inside her, "who gets to decide who stays in the Earth Retirement Complex and who... who gets .....'permanently retired'?"

Hugo's expression grew solemn as he met Arianna's gaze, his eyes reflecting the weight of her question. "It's not a decision that is made lightly," he replied, his voice tinged with sorrow. "The selection process is... complex."

Arianna nodded, her mind racing with a million questions. She could not begin to imagine the criteria used to determine who was deemed worthy of being transported to the Earth Retirement Complex and who was condemned to meet a far darker fate.

"Is it based on age?" she asked, her voice barely above a whisper. "Or... or is there something else they look for?"

Hugo hesitated, his gaze drifting to the floor as he struggled to find the right words. "There are many factors that come into play," he explained carefully. "Age, yes, but also... influence, status, connections. Those who are deemed to be of special importance or significance are chosen to come here, while the rest..."

He trailed off, his words hanging heavy in the air as the reality of their situation sank in. Arianna felt a surge of anger rising within her, a burning fury at the injustice of it all. How could they play God, deciding who lived and who died based on nothing more than arbitrary criteria?

Chapter 22: Unveiling the Giants

Hugo's voice cut through the heavy silence of the room, drawing everyone's attention as he gestured towards a few separate individuals, each standing as a testament to human ingenuity and achievement.

"See that man over there?" Hugo pointed to a figure engrossed in conversation, his face alight with passion. "He's Arabeen Boult, the one who invented the holograph display and replication machine, revolutionizing communication as we know it." He spent decades developing and improving the highest of cutting-edge technologies, with improvements at every turn. His developments had led to him being one of the most famous and then richest people on the Earth. He was also really close to Reebus himself and involved in many projects for the GGC away from the glaze of the rest of society. Jayden and Arianna exchanged a look of awe, their minds reeling at the thought of the technological advancements he had both made and inspired that had shaped their world.

Hugo's finger then shifted to a woman standing nearby, her demeanour calm and composed. "And her," he continued, "She's Eleanor Traves, the brilliant mind behind the cure for breast cancer. Her work has saved countless lives and brought hope to millions. She's the lady who injected breast cancer particles into herself and allowed them to progress at the risk of serious illness or death... and then took her own developed cure capsules and proved to the world as to exactly what she had created."

Arianna felt a surge of admiration for this lady, her heart swelling with gratitude for the tireless efforts of scientists and researchers who had achieved this. Arianna was particularly thankful in this case as this cure had been used on her own grannie when before her mum was born and as a result might even be the reason why Arianna herself was able to be stood in this room today. A few tears eloped from her eyes in recognition of what this meant to her.

"And over there," as Hugo's finger pointed with a slow tenderness. "He is the most special of them all, that's Timothy Bream, or grandad as he is to me. He was my 'free pass' as they call it. When you first join up on GGC special projects then you are given some rewards for the stress and secrecy of the projects themselves. In this case we are allowed to bring people close to us into the Earth retirement facility rather than by designated for Serenity 1 like the others.", ended Hugo with a suppressed look on his face. It seems that the GGC could exert control over its employees in the most discreet and personal ways.

It was Hugo's final gesture that started to send a shiver down Jayden's spine. "And there," Hugo said, his voice tinged with reverence, "enjoying an extravagant lunch fit for a king, is Killian Tredwell – the first ever leader of the GGC."

Jayden's breath caught in his throat as he gazed upon the figure of Killian Tredwell, a man whose name was synonymous with power and influence. He had heard stories of Tredwell's rise to prominence, his vision for a better world, and the controversial policies he had implemented during his time in office.

As Jayden watched, Tredwell laughed heartily with his companions, his expression one of contentment and satisfaction. Beneath the facade of joviality, Jayden sensed a darkness lurking, a reminder of the secrets and lies that had shaped the world they now lived in. This was a man who had not just lived through the GGC, he was one of its creators, who conceptualised the singular world government itself.

"You might find it beneficial if you were to talk with him. He is an interesting enigma of a man and one whom has many stories to tell," added Hugo.

Hugo's suggestion hung in the air, casting a shadow over the room as Jayden and Arianna exchanged uncertain glances. The idea of speaking with Killian Tredwell, the legendary figure who had once led the GGC, filled them with a mixture of apprehension and curiosity.

"Are you sure that's a good idea?" Jayden asked, his voice tinged with doubt. "I mean, wouldn't he just brush us off or refuse to speak with us?"

Hugo offered a reassuring smile, his eyes reflecting a glimmer of determination. "It's worth a try," he replied. "Killian Tredwell may be a polarizing figure, but he's also a key player in the history of the GGC. If anyone can shed light on the origins of the organization, it's him."

Arianna nodded in agreement, her resolve firming as she considered the implications of Hugo's suggestion. "You're right," she said, her voice steady despite the lingering uncertainty. "We need to understand the full scope of what we're dealing with if we're going to have any hope of making a difference."

Tredwell looked up as they approached, his gaze shrewd and calculating as he took in their presence. "Well, well, what do we have here?" he said, his voice smooth and measured. "I wasn't expecting any visitors today."

Jayden stepped forward; his expression determined as he addressed Tredwell directly. "Mr. Tredwell, we'd like to speak with you about the beginnings of the GGC," he said, his tone respectful yet firm. "There are many tales I can tell, but who exactly are you and why do you want to know?", added a smiling calming face.

As Jayden opened his mouth to start his personal autobiography, Tredwell placed his right hand up signalling for him to stop. "It will not be necessary Jayden, nor you Arianna. I know more than enough about you two already. I am only surprised it has taken you so long to seek me out," added a knowing Tredwell.

"But...," as Jayden was about to question all that lay before him and exactly why Tredwell knew who they were. Tredwell intercepted like a king's guard. "Despite being forcibly tucked away behind forgotten doors, I still have many eyes and ears in the real world who enlighten me as to what is really going on. I like to understand what is going on out there and whether there is still hope."

Tredwell's eyes narrowed slightly, a hint of intrigue flickering behind his steely gaze. "So, you'd like to know about the beginnings of the GGC hey," he mused, his lips curling into a faint smile. "Well then, I suppose you'd better pull up a chair and make yourselves comfortable. We have much to discuss."

Seated across from Killian Tredwell, Jayden could not help but feel a sense of anticipation as he prepared to delve into the history of the GGC. With each passing moment, the weight of their conversation hung heavy in the air, the gravity of Tredwell's presence commanding their full attention.

Killian Tredwell was a glowing man. His face was much younger than his near one hundred years age belied. His mind was clearly bright and inceptual and his demeanour welcomed all and sundry to take a seat and discuss key issues of hope and despair. Killian wore glasses, not because of his vision being in any way deteriorated, but because it was an accessory that defined the Killian of old, and thus the Killian who sat there today. It was a fashion statement, or just a preference to be the wisest man in any room. The glasses delivered on this promise. The rest of Killian's frame was in good health, well fed, well-watered and he had no health concerns at all. This was a man enjoying his life in every way and his vibrancy suggested he still wanted to do more.

"Mr. Tredwell," Jayden began, his voice steady as he posed the question that had been burning in his mind, "why was the GGC set up in the first place? What led to its creation?"

Tredwell's gaze softened slightly, a flicker of nostalgia crossing his features as he settled back in his chair. "Ah, the beginnings of the GGC," he said, his voice tinged with a hint of reminiscence. "It feels like a lifetime ago."

Leaning forward, Tredwell began to recount the events that had led to the establishment of the Global Governance Council. He spoke of a world teetering on the brink of collapse, plagued by rampant population growth, dwindling resources, and escalating health crises.

"The Earth had reached its breaking point," Tredwell explained, his words echoing with a sense of solemnity. "We were at maximum capacity, stretched to our limits by the demands of an ever-growing population and the strain it placed on our planet."

As Tredwell spoke, Jayden felt a chill run down his spine, the weight of their reality pressing in on him from all sides. He had heard stories of the struggles faced by previous generations but hearing it firsthand from someone who had witnessed it firsthand brought a new sense of urgency to their plight.

"We knew that drastic measures were needed if we were to ensure the survival of our species. Individual country governments were too self-obsessed and selfish to the world they lived as they attempted to protect their own. National sharing and trading were reducing due to protectionism and hurting citizens through lack of choice and availability. Humanity was too successful and too selfish as it continued its rampant march towards destruction " Tredwell continued, his voice growing more impassioned with each passing word. "And so, the GGC was born – a beacon of hope in a world plagued by darkness. An organisation that took over all governing powers in order to try and be fair to all and strive to give a real chance of actions that could bring humanity back from the cliff edge it faced."

As Killian Tredwell recounted the challenges faced by humanity in the early days of the GGC, Jayden and Arianna listened intently, hanging on his every word. The weight of history pressed in on them, a reminder of the trials and tribulations that had shaped their world.

"Throughout our deliberations," Tredwell continued, his voice measured and deliberate, "we considered a multitude of options to address the pressing issues of population growth and resource scarcity. We knew that we needed to act decisively if we were to avoid catastrophe."

He paused, his gaze sweeping over Jayden and Arianna, as if measuring their reaction to his words. "One of the options we considered was the implementation of vaccines to reduce birth rates," he explained. "By incentivizing or mandating the use of contraceptives, we slowed the rate of population growth and ease the strain on our resources."

Arianna's eyes widened at these measures, as she had always wanted siblings but did not understand where the mandate had originated. She could not help but feel a pang of unease at the thought of governments dictating the reproductive choices of their citizens, even in the face of a looming crisis. This was not an easy decision to follow through on.

"But it wasn't just about controlling population growth," Tredwell continued, his voice growing more sombre. "We also sought to implement health advances that would reduce the consumption of food and drink required to sustain our population. By developing technologies and treatments that could extend lifespan and improve overall health, we hoped to mitigate the strain on our resources."

Jayden nodded thoughtfully, his mind grappling with the complexities of the situation. It was clear that the challenges faced by humanity were multifaceted, requiring a comprehensive approach that addressed both the root causes and the symptoms of their predicament.

"There were even suggestions around the GGC tables about introducing long since cured diseases to act as a life lottery to try and reduce the population expanse in some particularly condensed areas. I ensured that these proposals never came to light as they were by design a painful and non-merciful temporary solution to people living. You should not be penalised for simply being born as I would always phrase it.," added a thoughtful Killian.

"Then there was the question of voluntary euthanasia," Tredwell added, his voice tinged with solemnity. "We knew that we needed to reduce the burden on our planet, and some individuals expressed a willingness to sacrifice their own lives for the greater good. It was a controversial proposal, to be sure, but one that we considered nonetheless, and I believe still exists in some of the darker and shady corridors across the planet."

As Tredwell spoke, Jayden could not help but feel a sense of unease at the notion of individuals willingly giving up their lives to alleviate the burden on society. It was a stark reminder of the sacrifices that had been made in the name of survival, and the moral dilemmas that had accompanied them. Killian's words were profound as to the dark nature which must have accompanied the GGC high table. Being party to the throws of government certainly would have been a stressful occupation.

"Despite our best efforts to address the challenges facing humanity," Tredwell continued, his voice tinged with a hint of regret, "we soon realized that there were no easy solutions. The problems we faced were too complex, too deeply ingrained in the fabric of society to be resolved with a simple wave of the hand."

Jayden nodded in understanding, his mind racing as he considered the magnitude of the task ahead. It was clear that the challenges facing humanity were far from simple, and the solutions would require a level of innovation and cooperation that had never been seen before.

"We knew that we needed to think outside the box, to explore new horizons in search of a better future," Tredwell explained, his gaze fixed on the distant horizon as if searching for answers in the depths of space. "And so, we turned our attention to the stars, embarking on a bold new venture to explore the cosmos in search of a new home for humanity. Something that could bide us some time."

"As we set out on our journey into the depths of space, we were filled with hope and determination" Tredwell continued, his voice growing more animated with each passing word. "We knew that space itself was an immense, titanic adventure full of unknowns and likely failures, but we also knew that it was our best chance for survival."

"And so, we set out on our journey, guided by the promise of a new beginning and the hope of a brighter tomorrow," Tredwell concluded, his voice ringing with conviction. "For in the vast expanse of the cosmos, we searched for the key to our survival, but also for the boundless potential of humanity to overcome even the greatest of challenges. I woke up every day hoping and praying that it would be the day when our hopes would turn to reality, and humanity would be saved."

"Did you ever discover a planet that could support human life through the space program?" Jayden asked, his voice tinged with a hint of trepidation.

Killian Tredwell's expression softened, a weary smile playing at the corners of his lips as he shook his head slowly. "I'm afraid not," he replied, his voice heavy with regret. "Despite our best efforts, under my leadership we were never able to find a planet that could serve as a suitable home for humanity."

A wave of disappointment washed over Jayden, the reality of their situation crashing down around him like a tidal wave. For so long, he had clung to the hope that the space program held the key to their salvation, a light in a world shrouded in darkness. Now, faced with the truth of their failure, he could not help but feel a sense of despair creeping into his heart.

"We tried," Tredwell continued, his voice tinged with sorrow. "We explored countless planets, charting distant galaxies in search of a new home for humanity. In the end, our efforts were in vain, so far, at least. I know the program continues and I honestly believe that it will one day prove successful".

Jayden nodded in understanding, his mind swirling with a whirlwind of emotions. It was a bitter pill to swallow, the realization that their dreams of a better future had been dashed against the harsh realities of the cosmos. Even in the face of defeat, he knew that they could not afford to lose hope.

"We may not yet have found a planet capable of supporting human life," Tredwell said, his voice filled with quiet determination, "but that doesn't mean our journey ends here. We may have stumbled along the way, but we must not lose sight of the ultimate goal – to build a better future for ourselves and for generations to come."

Jayden's voice trembled slightly as he posed the question that had been weighing heavily on his mind. "Was the compulsory retirement program a last resort?" he asked, his gaze fixed on Killian Tredwell with a mixture of curiosity and apprehension.

Killian's expression softened; his eyes clouded with sorrow as he nodded solemnly. "Yes, it was considered," he replied, his voice heavy with regret. "We explored every possible avenue, exhaustively searching for solutions that would allow us to avoid such drastic measures. But it is not something I would ever agree to, as all life deserves a chance."

"It was then on what he perceived as my weakness that Reebus overthrew me. He knew I would not let it pass and he saw himself as the only person who could save humanity. A demigod if you like, believing in their own power.", continued Tredwell.

A heavy silence settled over the room, the weight of this conversation pressing down on them like a lead weight. For Jayden, the revelation was harsh; it was a stark reminder of the realities of their world and the sacrifices that had been made in the name of survival.

"We wanted to keep everyone as happy as possible," Tredwell continued, his voice tinged with sorrow. "That's why Reebus devised the Serenity 1 charade – to give people hope, to reassure them that their loved ones were safe and content in their golden years."

Jayden's mind raced as he processed Tredwell's words, a flood of conflicting emotions swirling within him. On one hand, he could not help but feel a sense of admiration for the ingenuity and compassion that had gone into creating the illusion of Serenity 1, a testament to humanity's resilience in the face of adversity. Although he could not shake the nagging feeling of unease that gnawed at the edges of his consciousness.

"And the holograph technology?" Jayden asked, his voice barely above a whisper.

Tredwell nodded; his gaze distant as he recounted the genesis of the AI calls that had become a lifeline for families separated by the cruel realities of the compulsory retirement program. "It was a small comfort, perhaps," he admitted, "but it allowed families to stay connected, to maintain a sense of normalcy in a world that had been turned upside down. Those Holographs are so real looking and are so advanced that they feel and sound exactly as if the real person was still there."

As Jayden absorbed Tredwell's words, a sense of resignation settled over him, the weight of their conversation pressing down on him once more. In that moment, he could not help but wonder if there was any hope left for a world that had been torn apart by greed, deception, and the unrelenting march of time? Or were they doomed to repeat the mistakes of the past, condemned to a future of uncertainty and despair?

Jayden's voice wavered slightly as he broached the topic that had been weighing heavily on his mind. "Do you have any regrets about what happened?" he asked, his eyes fixed on Killian Tredwell with a mixture of curiosity and apprehension.

Tredwell's expression softened; his eyes clouded with regret as he nodded slowly. "Yes, I have many regrets," he admitted, his voice tinged with sorrow. "There are so many things I wish I could change, so many mistakes that I wish I could undo."

As Jayden listened intently, a sense of empathy washed over him, his heart heavy with the weight of Tredwell's words. It was clear that the burden of their shared history weighed heavily on the former leader of the GGC, a testament to the toll that years of deception and manipulation had taken on his soul.

"One of my biggest regrets is that we didn't realize the severity of the situation sooner," Tredwell continued, his voice tinged with remorse. "We should have seen the warning signs, should have taken action before it was too late. But by the time we realized the full extent of the crisis, it was already upon us."

Jayden nodded in understanding, his mind racing with a whirlwind of thoughts and emotions. It was a sobering realization, the knowledge that their world had been brought to the brink of collapse by their own shortsightedness and complacency. Even in the face of regret he knew that they could not afford to dwell on the past. It was time to focus on the future, on finding a way to set things right.

"I also regret that we didn't trust the people with the truth," Tredwell added, his voice heavy with sorrow. "We thought we were protecting them, but in reality, we only succeeded in perpetuating a cycle of deceit and mistrust that has haunted us ever since."

Jayden listened in silence as Tredwell spoke, his heart heavy with the weight of their shared remorse. It was a painful realization, the knowledge that their actions had only served to further erode the trust between the people and their leaders. Even in the face of their mistakes, he knew that they could not afford to lose hope. They had to find a way to rebuild what had been lost, to be able to forge a new path forward based on honesty, transparency, and integrity.

Tredwell continued "Many other things just did not go to plan. We launched a new satellite drill originally designed to mine rocks and minerals from a distance to help with the capture of precious and scarce resources. Unfortunately, I made a mistake and rushed it into action before it was ready and instead of mining precious gems, it hit the city of Chicago causing great damage and death. We had to cover this unfortunate event up to prevent mass commotion and distrust – but that was a long time ago."

"And then there's Reebus," Tredwell continued as if interlinked on his thought. With Tredwell's voice tinged with bitterness. "His betrayal cut deeper than I ever could have imagined. To think that he would turn his back on everything we stood for, everything we had worked so hard to achieve... it's a wound that will never fully heal."

"But despite everything," Tredwell said, his voice filled with resolve, "I still believe that we can all be saved, and the answer is out there where everyone can live in prosperity."

Arianna and Jayden exchanged glances; their curiosity piqued by Tredwell's mention of Reebus's betrayal. They listened in, eager to hear more about the rift between the former leader of the GGC and his successor.

"How did Reebus betray you?" Arianna asked, her voice soft but insistent.

Tredwell's expression darkened, a shadow passing over his features as he recalled the events that had led to his ousting from power. "Reebus was once my protege," he began, his voice tinged with bitterness. "I took him under my wing, nurtured his talent, and groomed him to be my successor. He was a brilliant and clever mind, but also very cunning. When my back was turned, he showed his true colours."

Jayden leaned forward; his eyes narrowed with suspicion. "What do you mean?" he pressed; his voice edged with curiosity.

Tredwell sighed heavily, the weight of his words hanging heavy in the air. "Reebus saw an opportunity to seize power for himself, and he took it," he explained, his voice tinged with regret. "He orchestrated a smear campaign against me, spreading lies and misinformation to discredit my leadership and undermine my authority. When the time was right, he orchestrated a coup, ousting me from power and seizing control of the GGC for himself."

Arianna and Jayden exchanged a glance, their minds reeling with the implications of Tredwell's words. It was a shocking revelation, the knowledge that the man who had once been their leader had been betrayed by someone he had trusted implicitly. Even as they had struggled to process the magnitude of Reebus's betrayal, they could not help but wonder – what had driven him to such drastic measures?

"Why didn't you like Reebus?" Arianna asked, her voice soft but probing.

Tredwell's expression softened, a flicker of sadness passing over his features as he considered her question. "It's not that I didn't like him, I love him like my own son. He is the most special person I have left in this world." he replied, his voice tinged with regret. "It's that I couldn't trust him. Reebus is ambitious, ruthless, and power-hungry – qualities that made him dangerous in a position of authority. I saw the warning signs early on, but I chose to ignore them, believing that he had the best interests of the GGC at heart. It was a mistake that I paid dearly for."

Arianna and Jayden exchanged a look of joint belief; their resolve strengthening as they continued their conversation with

Tredwell. "What does Reebus want now?" Jayden asked, his voice tinged with suspicion.

Tredwell let out a humourless laugh, a bitter edge to his tone. "Reebus wants nothing but power" he replied, his gaze fixed on the two young rebels before him. "He'll stop at nothing to achieve his goals, no matter the cost."

Arianna frowned; her brow furrowed in thought. "But what does he want with us?" she asked, with her voice filled with urgency.

Tredwell's expression darkened, a shadow passing over his features as he considered their question. "There must be something about the two of you that Reebus either desires or he sees as a threat – maybe something that he believes could undermine his authority," he mused, his voice tinged with uncertainty. "If you can figure out what that is, you may be able to stop him."

Jayden nodded in agreement, his mind racing with possibilities. It was clear that they were up against a formidable opponent in Reebus. Even as they faced the daunting task ahead, he knew that they could not afford to back down – they had to find a way to outsmart the challenge before them and expose his true intentions to the world.

"Thank you, Killian," Arianna said, her voice filled with gratitude. "We won't let you down."

Tredwell offered them a small smile, his eyes filled with a flicker of hope. "Remember, the key to stopping Reebus lies within yourselves," he said, his voice filled with conviction. "Trust in each other, and never lose sight of what you're fighting for, and always keep hope as without it there is no tomorrow."

Chapter 23: Love is the Greatest Pleasure

As Arianna and Jayden returned to their quarters after their encounter with Killian Tredwell and the revelations that followed, a sense of nervous tension hung in the air. They exchanged glances, their minds still reeling from the weight of the secrets they had uncovered.

Can you believe all of this?" Arianna whispered, her voice barely above a murmur as they entered their dimly lit room. She was partly still stunned but also worried as to which eyes and ears might be watching and concerned that they might not be as alone as they hoped.

Jayden shook his head in disbelief, his thoughts still consumed by the gravity of their discoveries. "It's hard to wrap my head around," he admitted, his voice tinged with uncertainty.

Arianna sighed, sinking down onto the edge of their bed, her expression troubled. "What are we going to do?" she asked, her eyes searching his for answers.

Jayden hesitated, his mind racing with possibilities. "I'm not sure," he confessed, his voice laced with apprehension. "But we can't just sit back and do nothing, can we?"

Arianna nodded in agreement; her gaze unwavering. "We have to find a way to stop Reebus but I'm not sure what that will be" she declared, her voice filled with determination, but fear of the unknown that had a wide door opened in front of them.

Jayden reached out, taking her hand in his, a silent promise passing between them. "We will," he vowed, his eyes locking with hers. "Together."

Jayden sensed that Arianna needed reassurance and both needed escapism and to fulfil their desires. He had stared at her hunched on the bed with mind clearly elsewhere. "You are the most beautiful girl that I have ever seen," as Arianna's gaze switched towards him before continuing "You have eyes that make me travel to infinite worlds, and lips that remind me of the most delicate life." Arianna exited her slump and began to arch her body to face his in a more relaxed and welcoming way. "You say the kindest and sweetest things Jay," in her meek retort.

"I mean it Ari, you are so special to me. You make my world better by just being besides me. You are the one that I will always trust, the one whom has my back and the one whom holds my heart like putty in her soft and gentle hands.," as Jayden's words poured without processing directly from his heart. Arianna drew them closer for a gentle embrace reflecting her own appreciation of both his words and his own importance to her. Words faded away before them to leave both passion and lust lying underneath and both parties' desires needed to be quenched. Arianna and Jayden both discarding the strangling constraints of their clothes with abandonment, flinging accessories, outerwear and then underwear across all corners of the room. Wherever one would look a new garment sat freshly landed in finding it's new place to call home. Meanwhile atop of the bed continued the entrée of the meal that was undoubtedly to follow.

As they climbed into bed, their bodies pressed close, a mixture of emotions washed over them – mainly animalistic urges which reside at the root of nature itself. As they longingly grappled each other in the darkness, their love and resolve burning bright.

Their lips met underneath the covers in a tender kiss, igniting a fire that burned with an intensity unlike anything Jayden had ever known. It was a kiss filled with passion and need, a silent promise of the depths of their affection for one another. The air in the room filled itself with the raw smell of their desires. In that moment, as they lost themselves in each other's embrace, Jayden felt as though he were floating on air. Every touch, every caress was a testament to the depth of their connection, a connection that transcended the boundaries of time and space to a world where nothing else existed but themselves alone.

Arianna's fingers started tracing patterns across his skin, sending shivers of delight coursing through his body. Her touch was like a symphony, each note a melody of pure love and desire. Her fingers tracing the words "I Love Jayden" across the smoothness of Jayden's back. With recognition and understanding of her unspoken words he carved his own indulgent phrases on her back and then progressing to her smooth and curvaceous front as she could see and feel the tenderness and naughtiness of every word his fingers traced.

As they melted into each other, their bodies entwined in a dance as old as time itself, Jayden knew that he had found his soulmate in Arianna. Someone who understood him in a way that no one else ever could, someone who completed him in ways he had never thought possible. Their love was a force of nature, unstoppable and undeniable. It was a love that defied logic and reason, a love that transcended the boundaries of the physical world. With a contented sigh, Jayden once more nestled closer to Arianna, relishing the feeling of her soft curves pressed against his chest. Her skin was warm against his, a comforting presence that eased the tension from his muscles and calmed the turmoil in his mind.

Arianna shifted slightly, her hand coming to rest on Jayden's chest, fingers again tracing lazy circles against his skin. Her touch was like a balm, soothing away the lingering traces of fatigue and worry that clung to him like shadows in the night. He cupped each curve with nipples ever more erect and proceeded to explore every part of his partners' body with a tongue so lustful as if it had never been fed. Their bodies soon integrated as one and many hours of intimacy followed suit.

As time progressed and in the stillness of the bedroom, they lost touch with the realities of a harsh world. Their shared experiences, their laughter, their tears, all of it seemed to coalesce into a single moment of pure serenity.

Arianna drifted into a realm of dreams where the boundaries of reality melted away, leaving her free to wander through the corridors of her imagination. Amidst all the mist that shrouded her mind, she found herself enveloped in a vision of the future. It was a tapestry woven from the threads of hope and desire.

In her dream, she stood hand in hand with Jayden beneath a canopy of stars, their laughter mingling with the gentle rustle of leaves as they danced beneath the moonlit sky. Their love was a beacon that illuminated the darkness, casting aside the shadows of doubt and fear that lingered at the edges of their consciousness.

Together, they forged a life filled with joy and laughter, their days spent basking in the warmth of each other's embrace as they journeyed through the twists and turns of fate hand in hand. Their love was a fortress, impervious to the trials and tribulations that threatened to tear them apart, their bond growing stronger with each passing day. In Arianna's dream, they had built a home filled with love and laughter. It was a sanctuary where their children played amidst the echoes of their happiness with their voices a symphony of innocence and joy that echoed through the halls. Their days were filled with simple pleasures and quiet moments of bliss, their hearts overflowing with gratitude for the blessings that adorned their lives. Her dream of tranquil waters, sun-kissed shores, and boundless freedom. In this dreamscape, she stood upon the threshold of a house nestled by the shores of a great lake, its waters shimmering in the golden light of dawn. With each breath, Arianna felt the warmth of the sun upon her skin, its rays casting a luminous shine upon the landscape around her. The air was alive with the sound of birdsong and the gentle lapping of waves against the shore, a symphony of serenity that filled her heart with joy. As she wandered through the halls of the house, Arianna felt a sense of peace wash over her with a feeling of belonging that transcended the confines of reality. Each room held a promise of adventure and discovery, from the cozy nook by the fireplace to the sun-drenched veranda overlooking the lake.

Outside, the world beckoned with open arms, inviting Arianna to explore its hidden wonders and secrets with family days and great adventures with Jayden as they discovered the joys of nature's plants and creatures with every passing day. With each step she took, she felt a sense of liberation wash over her. It was a freedom born of the boundless possibilities that lay before her. In this dreamscape, Arianna was free to be herself. She could chase her dreams, to embrace her passions, and to carve out a life filled with meaning and purpose. Here, she was beholden to no one but herself, guided only by the whispers of her heart and the yearning for a life of true fulfilment. Although a dream, it was one that was once a reality for those people who belonged to Earth a number of centuries beforehand. Humanity it seemed had progressed so far that dreams are no longer future ensconced hopes but historically imagined retrospectives of what might have been. Maybe out there somewhere these dreams could yet become true, and life could transform itself once again - she could at least hope. As the years passed in the dream, they watched with pride as their children grew and flourished, their love serving as a guiding light that illuminated the path ahead. Within the chaos of their everyday lives, they found solace in the knowledge that they were bound together by love.

As Arianna drifted back to consciousness, her heart still heavy with the echoes of her dreams, her eyes averted back to Jayden whose eyes were now clamped shut, albeit with a comforting snore. His face blessed with inner peace and a glow of happiness that could not be masked. Maybe the epitome of life was ultimately where dreams lived. Rather than provoke further discussion or reaction to her alertness, she decided to let Jayden lie still and ensconced in whichever world his mind was currently visiting.

With a gentle kiss "Goodnight," she pressed her lips to Jayden's forehead

Jayden's peaceful slumber was softening and rejuvenating with his heart light, and his mind truly at ease. As sleep had claimed him, he had known that he was exactly where he was meant to be; wrapped in the arms of the woman he loved more than anything in this, or any other world. Jayden, unlike Arianna, had dreams and expectations based on future possibilities rather than spending wasted thoughts on what might have been. He was more a realist than a dreamer, but even despite their difference of dream carnations there was surely still hope that both Jayden and Arianna could have all their dreams fulfilled as one.

Chapter 24: Election Day Triumph

Election day dawned with a sense of anticipation that hung heavy in the air, as citizens from every corner of the globe made their way to the polling stations to exercise their democratic right. From bustling cities to remote villages, the spirit of democracy was alive and thriving, as people queued patiently to cast their votes.

In city squares and town halls, long lines snaked around corners, a testament to the unprecedented turnout that had gripped the nation. From bustling metropolises to remote villages, the fervour of democracy burned bright, igniting hearts and minds with the promise of change. Most voting now took place from within homely confines with technological patterned recognition and security allowing a few selections before accepting the electorate direction someone had chosen. Some people however liked to be seen and make a statement to the onlooking community and watchers. They wanted people to know and respect the voting traditions. Many people also wanted to show that they were prepared to vote against the incumbent Reebus and found fortitude in those that followed the same path. It was an experience and process that made people feel alive and respected in a world full of very little of either. Even just getting out of their apartment or complex, for a reason to get up that morning was more than incentive for some as it allowed their day to have meaning and purpose – things which were often lacking throughout the people in the world.

As the day now progressed, the turnout began to exceed all expectations, with a staggering 96% of eligible voters participating in the final electoral process. From early morning until late into the night, the polling stations buzzed with activity, as people lined up to make their voices heard and shape the destiny of their world. These polling station visitors were the merest fraction of the overall vote with the silent home bound technological majority incrementing the vote count with incalculable pace. It had been a long but important constitutional day; a necessity in the realm of the GGC but also likely to be an irrelevant one in terms of outcome that could change any direction the world had upon it.

As the sun dipped below the horizon and the final ballots were quickly counted, the results were announced to a waiting world. To nobody's surprise, Reebus emerged victorious with a resounding majority, securing a landslide victory with nearly 80% of the vote.

Cheers erupted across the world as Reebus's supporters celebrated their leader's triumph, their faith in his vision for the future reaffirmed by the overwhelming mandate of the people. From city squares to suburban streets, jubilant crowds danced and cheered, their voices ringing out in celebration of democracy in action. In New York itself large swells of the populous parked themselves in Central Park with fireworks and some other celebratory activities. Some food rations and alcoholic bottles were shared between the crowds as they seemed to enjoy the togetherness that this get together had made. There were so few times when people could be joyous and together as a crowd that even having the opportunity for a night of singing and dancing was a relief to most. It was going to be a long night for most; one where the harsh realities before them were forgotten or misplaced to allow one night of escapism and happiness to try and make things bearable again.

For Reebus, he saw it was a moment of vindication, a validation of his leadership and a testament to the trust and confidence that the people had placed in him. As he addressed the nation in a victory speech that echoed across the airwaves.

Reebus announced "I pledge to continue working tirelessly on behalf of all Earth citizens, to build a brighter and more prosperous future for generations to come. I am grateful for all your support. Together with my hard-working GGC colleagues and friends we will deliver on our promises. We will lower the age of retirement We will improve the nature and enjoyment of life for all of its inhabitants. I am here to serve you and to make our world a better place for you, your children and each of the generations that follows behind.," as his words were greeted by joyful raptures throughout all the parks and community get togethers. As the celebrations continued long into the night, the world watched on, united in the belief that democracy had prevailed, and that together, they could overcome any challenge that lay ahead. If only the world was aware of all the smoke and mirrors laid in front of them to deceive them all; the lies and counter lies that had made the election no more than a piece of entertainment with unchangeable direction with a plot that could never bring a satisfying ending.

The following day, Reebus sat in his quarters, his mind abuzz with the events of the day before. As the newly re-elected leader, he knew that he had once more full control of humanity. Somewhere in a corner of Reebus' mind he genuinely believed he had won fairly despite the evidence and control he had elsewhere. It was as if the ego of Reebus needed to stroke with regularity to keep him from stepping further over the line. Having controlled the policies and media around all candidates in the race and having the majority of the GGC in his back pocket then it was not a big surprise to his immediate staff. Knowing of Reebus' need to be commended they were all very eager to ensure he received their best wishes. His communication stream was endless with recorded messages of congratulations, comrades wishing to speak with him about issues of vested interest and the independent media types wishing to scoop any soundbite or titbits they could garner from the morning after the night before. Reebus was not in the mood for chat with people who could not contribute to his immediate goals but wanted to talk with the only person who could.

Reebus spoke to his AI communicator and told it to contact Imelda immediately and send her through to his quarters for a chat. Several minutes later there was a recognisable patter at the door and Reebus knowingly let her in. Carrying nothing but a communicator she progressed further inside the room and sat at her familiar position opposite Reebus' desk on a chair that was almost perfectly rounded to her body shape; after all it may have been Reebus' office and table, but this was very much *her* seat.

"Imelda," Reebus began, his voice tinged with satisfaction, "the election was a success beyond our wildest dreams. The mandate we have been given is a testament to the trust and confidence the people have placed in us. The GGC committee have also released funds destined for all of our election mandates.

Imelda nodded in agreement, a small smile playing at the corners of her lips. "Indeed, Reebus. The support we have garnered will give us the stability and momentum we need to move forward with our plans. It was very much needed and has put us in a very strong position."

Reebus leaned forward, his gaze meeting Imelda's with unwavering determination. "And speaking of plans, it's time we turned our attention to the Genesis project. With the election behind us, we finally have the time, breathing space and resources to devote ourselves fully to its completion."

"I want you to take all the funds from all of our mandates and use them to complete Genesis as quickly as possible.," said a decisive Reebus, "By the time anyone is aware of any missing credits it will be too late and we will have achieved our objectives.," added a forceful Reebus.

Imelda's eyes sparkled with excitement as she nodded in agreement. "Yes, Reebus. The Genesis project represents the culmination of years of research and innovation. It was a testament to our commitment to shaping a better future for all."

"How long does the project need to complete Imelda? What is the best estimate?," asked Reebus.

"Around two more months and we should be there, especially now that we no longer have to worry about where the funding is coming from," said Imelda as she laughed away to herself.

Imelda placed a reassuring hand on Reebus's shoulder, her expression one of unwavering support. "Together, Reebus, we will see the Genesis project through to fruition, and we will all enjoy a better future."

Reebus and Imelda sat for a while watching the media coverage of the electoral result and the celebration events throughout the world. They were enjoying the moment as days like these were few and far between. Reebus demanded a celebratory breakfast from his AI support bot and within a couple of minutes both Imelda and he were sat tucking into a most delicious breakfast of the finest produce existing anywhere in the world. Imelda then spoke up with news of interest to Reebus. "The retirement lottery is a great success Reebus. We had over one billion entries already, so we have a great deal of room for extra capacity through the retirement channels," she said excitedly.

"Very good Imelda, how about contacting the first fifty million or so and telling them the good news. With their 'lucky' winning friends and relatives that would mean around five hundred million people getting an early trip where they need to go.," said Reebus without an inkling of regret.

"Very Well," said Imelda. "I will make it so. The extra food, drink and other resources saved from this enterprise will help immeasurably with the current resource constraints of the failed western harvest. I will get to this straight away and set the wheels in motion." She continued.

At that, Reebus watched Imelda leave the room and as soon as the door slapped shut, he decided to action his next piece of business. With a decisive flick of his wrist, Reebus activated the intercom system, his voice ringing out with authority as he issued a summons to Jayden and Arianna, the two individuals whose presence had piqued his interest in recent days.

"Jayden, Arianna," he called out, his tone firm but kind. "Please come to my quarters at your earliest convenience. There are matters of great importance that we need to discuss." It was a message that echoed through the GGC. Although he could have contacted them directly; by summoning them so that everyone in the facility could hear allowed him double intent. Firstly, this was Reebus playing games, a power move that he could make them do anything he wanted, and they were powerless to avoid, and secondly should anyone see or be aware of them they would be hesitant to idly chat as all GGC employees knew that when Reebus says "earliest convenience" it is the very definition of 'immediately, without haste.'

As the message echoed through the halls of the GGC headquarters, Jayden and Arianna exchanged a glance, their curiosity piqued by the unexpected call from the leader himself. Suspecting something amiss but tied to Reebus' future no matter what they did, they set off down the corridors without care or abandon. As their footsteps turned one corner and another, they passed several important members of Reebus' inner circle, each waving them along the next corridor. Finally with their footsteps echoing against the polished floors as they made their way towards Reebus's chambers. Placing her head close to the communicator on his door, Arianna then took charge and alerted Reebus of their arrival. "Hi, its Arianna and Jayden and we are here to see you, as you requested," before waiting for the door in front of them to open. Reebus somewhat deliberately made them both wait for what felt like an eternity but was little more than a minute. The door then gave out a few clicks and cranks before opening from each side to reveal Reebus' quarters before them.

Upon their entrance, they were greeted by Reebus himself, his expression inscrutable as he motioned for them to take a seat. There were three seats prepared for visitors, but Imelda's seat looked uninviting and cold, so they positioned themselves between the two remaining options. "Thank you for coming," he said, his voice carrying the weight of authority. "I trust you both understand the gravity of the situation we find ourselves in."

"As you may be aware," Reebus continued, his voice measured and deliberate, "there are forces at play that seek to undermine the stability and security of our world. It is imperative that we remain vigilant and united in the face of these threats."

Jayden and Arianna exchanged a glance, their minds racing with questions and possibilities. What could Reebus want from them? How would their roles in the coming days shape the destiny of their world? What was he talking about here, we know that he is behind everything!?

Arianna sat before Reebus, her heart pounding with a mixture of fear and indignation. The question had been burning within her ever since she had learned the devastating truth about her grandfather's fate, and now, she could no longer contain her emotions.

"Why did you lie to me?" she demanded, her voice trembling with suppressed anger. "You told me that my grandad was alive, that he had been transported to the retirement planet – 'Serenity 1'. I know now that it was all a lie. Why?"

Reebus regarded her with a solemn expression, his gaze unwavering as he considered his response. He knew that the time for half-truths and deception was over, that Arianna deserved to know the truth, no matter how painful it may be.

"I understand your anger, Arianna," he began, his voice gentle but firm. "And for that, I am truly sorry. The truth is, I did what I thought was best for you, for all of us. The retirement planet, Serenity 1, was meant to be a beacon of hope, a sanctuary for those who had reached the twilight of their lives. As you now know, it was nothing more than a charade, a facade designed to maintain the illusion of peace and prosperity."

Arianna's eyes widened in disbelief, her mind reeling with the weight of Reebus's words. She had always believed in the vision of a better world, a world where her grandfather could live out his days in happiness and contentment. Now that vision lay shattered at her feet, replaced by a harsh reality that she could scarcely comprehend.

"Why?" she repeated, her voice barely above a whisper. "Why did you deceive us? Why did you send my grandad to his death?"

Reebus's expression softened, his eyes filled with a sadness that mirrored Arianna's own. "I wish there was an easy answer to that question," he said, his voice tinged with regret. "But the truth is, the world we live in is not always fair or just. Sometimes, sacrifices must be made for the greater good, even if it means betraying the trust of those we hold most dear."

Jayden's voice echoed through the spacious confines of Reebus's chambers, his words laden with a mixture of disbelief and indignation. He too had come to confront the leader of the GGC, to demand answers to the questions that had been gnawing at his mind ever since he had learned the truth about the elaborate deception that had been perpetrated upon the world.

Jayden began, his voice tinged with urgency. "And the retirement planet lottery, what is all that about?"

Reebus regarded them with a knowing look, his expression betraying a hint of unease. "I was wondering when you two would come to me with your suspicions," he admitted, his tone sombre.

Reebus held up his hands in a gesture of appeasement, "But you have to understand, the retirement planet lottery was never meant to be what it seemed."

Jayden's brow furrowed in confusion. "What do you mean?"

Reebus took a deep breath, steeling himself for what he was about to reveal. "The truth is the retirement planet lottery was just a way of helping the majority of people on Earth as quickly as possible. It was a cleverly crafted scheme to give people false hope while simultaneously hastening their 'departures' from Earth. It allows those who are the most in need of departure a chance to hasten that process without creating undue violence or attention. Besides, those who remain will benefit from the further access to resources they will be able to receive."

Arianna's eyes widened in horror as the implications of Reebus's words sank in. "You mean... it was all a scam?" she whispered, her voice barely above a whisper.

Reebus nodded gravely. "Scam is a harsh word, but yes, but it was more than that. It was a necessity to reduce the strain on Earth's resources by enticing people to want to leave voluntarily without anyone panicking and within the confines of the rules passed at the GGC. It was a plan, designed to cull the population while maintaining the illusion of benevolence."

Jayden's hands clenched into fists at his sides, his anger simmering just below the surface. "And this is all your idea?" he demanded; his voice laced with accusation.

Reebus hung his head in shame. "It is" he admitted, his voice barely audible. "However, you know the truth now and could just walk out of here and tell the whole world about what I have done, and I won't stop you!"

Arianna and Jayden sat in stunned silence, grappling with the enormity of the revelation that Reebus had just disclosed. The truth about the retirement planet lottery circus weighed heavily on their hearts, its implications stretching far beyond their wildest imaginations. As they exchanged troubled glances, a sense of dread settled over them like a suffocating shroud.

"I can't believe this," Arianna whispered, her voice trembling with disbelief. "If we expose the truth about the retirement planet lottery, the consequences could be catastrophic."

Jayden nodded in grim agreement, his mind racing with the potential ramifications of their actions. "The world is already teetering on the edge of chaos," he murmured, his tone heavy with concern. "If this were to come out, it could push Earth over the brink, and you would be responsible for that, not I", continued Reebus.

Their conversation was punctuated by a heavy silence, each moment filled with the weight of the decision that lay before them. On one hand, they had a moral obligation to expose the truth and hold those responsible accountable for their actions. On the other hand, they could not ignore the potential fallout of the violence, the unrest, the devastation that could be unleashed upon the world.

"We have to consider the greater good," Arianna said, her voice tinged with resignation. "As much as it pains me to say it, exposing the truth might do more harm than good."

Jayden nodded in agreement; his expression pained. "I hate to admit it, but she's right. The world is not ready for this kind of revelation. Not yet anyway."

Their minds bewildered moved onto the next subject of their disdain, although they were so deep into the hornet nest it almost no longer mattered. There were lies upon lies and deception behind each supposed truth. The path to understanding the whole picture of Reebus needed to continue and this was their chance.

"Why did you lie about Sandronica Sprowl?" he demanded, his tone laced with a hint of accusation. "You told the world that she was a real person, that she was our opponent in the election. Now we know the truth. She was nothing more than a holographic representation, a puppet to be manipulated at your whim. Why?"

Reebus regarded Jayden with a steely gaze, his expression unreadable as he considered his response. He knew that the time for further deception was over, that Jayden and Arianna had already crossed well behind the line of comfort.

"I understand your anger, Jayden," he began, his voice calm but firm. "And for that, I am truly sorry. The truth is, Sandronica Sprowl was a creation of necessity, a means to an end in a world teetering on the brink of collapse. We needed a figurehead, a symbol of opposition to rally against, and Sandronica served that purpose admirably, if I do say so myself", as a smirk appeared in the corner of his mouth.

Jayden leaned forward; her interest fully engaged. "But there are plenty of real people, of good people who could and should have had the opportunity to change the direction of the world and have their chance of dethroning you, so why? Why did you need to create her? "

Reebus's expression softened as he spoke, his words measured and deliberate. "Sandronica represented more than just a challenger to my leadership. She embodied the spirit of competition, the driving force behind innovation and progress. Without a credible opponent, people might have become complacent, and not believe there was a real election and the majority of people in the GGC who are not aware that she is not real. It helps me control the budgets and have total control of the future of the planet. I could not allow a real opponent as we could not take the chance that they might win."

Jayden nodded once again, beginning to understand the significance of Reebus's words. Even if you did not like Reebus himself you could not help but respect and be in awe of his intellect and cunning. He was a master of his kind and someone who would cross the line routinely if it meant his objectives were to advance.

Jayden thought in silence, his mind struggling to comprehend Reebus's words. He had always believed in the democratic process, in the idea that the people had the power to shape their own destiny. Now that belief lay shattered at his feet, replaced by a harsh reality that he could scarcely comprehend. Democracy on Earth appeared to have ended with Reebus' reign of power.

"Why?" he repeated, his voice tinged with frustration. "Why deceive us? Why manipulate the truth to serve your own ends?" Jayden already knew the answers after the conversation they had just had, but the implications of such deceit on so many levels led to him wondering whether humans are permanently flawed or just bred for selfishness and survival.

As Jayden and Arianna were still grappling with the revelation of the retirement planet lottery scam, the existence of Sandronica itself, and the clandestine retirement program that lay at the heart of the deception. All secrets and plans which cost millions of lives and the end of democracy itself. Reebus had gotten away with it all, and without anyone being aware of his deceit.

Arianna's heart sank as the full extent of their predicament became clear. "We can't tell anyone about the retirement plant, Sandronica or the lottery," she murmured, her voice barely above a whisper. "Not just because of the consequences, but because... because there is no other option."

Jayden's expression mirrored her distress, his eyes filled with a mixture of anguish and resignation. "We're bound by the same silence that has kept this program hidden for so long," he admitted, his voice heavy with regret. "We can't risk exposing it, not when so much is at stake."

Their conversation was punctuated by a heavy silence, each moment filled with the weight of their newfound knowledge. They had stumbled upon a truth that was too dangerous to share, a secret that had the power to unravel the very fabric of society if it were ever brought to light.

"It's not about protecting ourselves," Arianna said, her voice trembling with emotion. "It's about protecting everyone; the people who need hope, the ones who believe in the promise of a better future."

Jayden nodded in solemn agreement, his mind racing with the implications of their collective decision. "We have a responsibility to safeguard the stability of the world," he said, his voice tinged with determination. "Even if it means bearing the burden of this secret for the rest of our lives."

Reebus's expression softened with the reality that faced all in the room. He listened to Arianna and Jayden's word and realisation as his openness had worked exactly as he hoped and expected. His gaze now filled with a sadness that mirrored Jayden's own. "If someone else were to become leader then not only would they become aware of the horrific truth, but they would also have a burden of despair that nobody but myself can understand.'

"Besides, if there were any leader but myself then I can assure you that the human race will be extinct in the next few years." added Reebus.

Chapter 25: The Genesis Warehouse

Jayden and Arianna discussed at length how their arms were tied in every facet and aspect of their knowledge about the truths presenting themselves to the people of the world. There was nowhere to go, there was no way out or anything they could do to make things right. A heavy noose now positioned itself around their respective necks which seemed taught already but knew that Reebus could pull tighter towards inevitable strangulation at any point.

Despite all that weighed their minds there was still concern that there were more secrets in Reebus's power than had presented themselves so far. They knew not where to look, or what to look for and were reliant on others to present new metaphoric and literal tunnels to explore.

For Jayden and Arianna, the next two months was a whirlwind of investigation and discovery as they delved deeper into the secrets surrounding the GGC. In the aftermath of his landslide election victory, Reebus seemed to retreat from the public eye, shrouding himself in an aura of silence and mystery that left many wondering what he was planning next. Gone were the days of high-profile speeches and public appearances; instead, Reebus seemed content to fade into the background, his presence felt only in the quiet corridors of power where decisions were made behind closed doors. The general public just got on with their lives as if nothing had changed since the election day.

Since the election itself one thing had progressed – the intensity and frequency of the retirement lottery broadcasts and advertising. People were never more than a few metres or a few minutes from a presentation or carefully designed words and images to take an unsuspecting person away from their harsh reality. The first winners started to flow through the process. Interviews with winners before they set for departure with whole families in tow. Each would be carrying key possessions and to all intense purposes a holiday atmosphere of fun and happiness was all that could be seen. As the weeks passed and the first winners began to arrive, there became interviews from Serenity 1 with some of the lucky ones. Holographic images and presentations of wonder and awe of the greatest place anyone could possibly go. The GGC knew how to play the propaganda card to greatest effect and was no more than a similar recycled media exercise they had used for the eighty-year-olds some weeks earlier. Jayden and Arianna knew the obvious truth behind the curtain but could only turn their backs and look in other directions; this steamroller could not be slowed or stopped.

Millions upon millions of people started to win the retirement lottery on weekly and sometimes a daily basis. Whole families and likeminded groups of people disappeared from communities worldwide to be 'retired.' The GGC required the signing over of any property they were leaving in exchange for the luxurious new properties awaiting them on Serenity 1. Winners even got to assign their colour schemes and preferences in advance of leaving which made the experience more comforting and real. Earthly residences that were left behind were empty for at most a few days before the GGC had reassigned them to crowded or unhoused others. It was very much like a cultivating or farming activity designed to grow, harvest and replant except the crop was to be humanity itself. There was a little more food and water available with less mouths for planet Earth to feed, however the difference it made was not enough to raise the quality of life of too many people. Every time when new lottery winners were being read out on the holographic nightly feed, Jayden and Arianna would change channels, turn on music or turn everything off. They may be aware of what was happening, but they did not need to be reminded daily of impending death sentences to poor people who were expecting new beginnings. Separately, the effective cull of the eighty-year-old section of society continued unabated as Reebus's free flowing extermination of life continued beyond unimaginable limits. Still, the world was unaware; people still lost in their own worry rather than trying to look beyond into the ruling GGC whom were 'helping' them. In many ways it was the perfect magician's sleight of hand with a card never quite in the pocket as expected.

Jayden comforted Arianna one night as her tears flowed relentlessly down her face. They both secretly wondered if Reebus was right all along and wished that instead of being a part of his web of lies, albeit with food and resources to dream of; perhaps it would have been better to be an unsuspecting pawn in the confines of a crowded deprived London street - still believing there was hope. Hope itself was evaporating rapidly from Arianna's mind with every day that passed.

For those who had supported him, Reebus's sudden disappearance from the public spotlight was cause for concern. Many had hoped for bold action and decisive leadership in the wake of his victory, but instead, they were met with silence and uncertainty. What was Reebus planning? Why was he keeping it hidden from view? Maybe something had happened to him? It was a genuine concern. Little progress was made on most of his promised initiatives, despite having funding secured and approved. It was as if he had taken his eye off the ball at the worst possible time. The world needed a focussed Reebus at the heart of its engine room. Without his progressive decisions then it was likely the world would fall even further from grace and the lives of its populace would worsen still.

As days turned into weeks and weeks turned into months, Reebus remained elusive, his whereabouts unknown to all but a select few. Rumours swirled about his intentions, some speculated that he was laying the groundwork for a transformative agenda that would reshape the world as they knew it, while others whispered of darker motives and hidden agendas that threatened to undermine the very foundations of society.

Despite tireless efforts, the elusive further secrets of the GGC remained just out of reach, shrouded in a veil of secrecy and intrigue. Every lead that Arianna and Jayden pursued seemed to evaporate into thin air, leaving them with more questions than answers. They themselves had no idea where Reebus was, or any idea of whatever activities were happening behind the scenes. As Jayden and Arianna both pored over a swathe of documents, laboriously trailing through the GGC archives, and sifting through mountains of data, they found the most solace in each other's company, their shared passion for uncovering the truth binding them together in ways they never imagined possible. In the quiet moments between their investigations, their love blossomed as far as mortal limits would allow, growing stronger with each passing day until it became an unbreakable bond that defied all odds. In the stillness of the night, as they lay entwined in each other's arms, Jayden and Arianna found refuge from the chaos of the world outside. Their whispered conversations echoed with laughter and shared dreams, their hearts beating as one in perfect harmony. In each other's presence, they found strength and courage, knowing that together, they could conquer any obstacle that stood in their way. They looked into each other's eyes, lost in the depths of their love, Jayden and Arianna knew with certainty that they were meant to be together. They started to believe that maybe all the truths out there had been discovered and there was nothing left to uncover around the GGC or Reebus. With each passing day, acceptance of the situation grew. The dangers, the uncertainties, the unanswered questions that loomed large on the horizon. They were completely immersed into the GGC lie but had allowed their hearts to accept these lies in a way that allowed them to breathe without being constantly pulled into an unsustainable cavern of despair. Within the chaos and confusion, they found moments of peace and serenity in the simple act of being together. They took long walks through the corridors of the GGC, hand in hand, their footsteps echoing in the quiet stillness of the secure facility. They shared stories and laughter, dreams and fears, their bond growing stronger with each passing moment. They even had date nights where they used the holographic entertainment devices to turn their quarters into relaxing ocean scenes, mountainous retreats, and historical romantic moments. Each virtual scene composed with appropriate, sometimes historical clothing and provided food from the automated chef machine in their abode. They were enjoying life the best they were allowed to do so. They focused on the here and now, cherishing each moment they had together, determined to make the most of the time they had been given. For in the end, they knew that love was the only thing they could control themselves. With life often so unfrequented by such good things they decided they decided to make on whilst it was possible.

One day when Jayden and Arianna had just been enjoying themselves having a very tasty GGC sandwich "buffet," they left their quarters on a gentle stroll. They were looking out across the bustling and noisy New York landscape, watching people get on with their daily lives. They could see all realms of life at play. Some people walking smartly and hurriedly to waiting jobs, others sat in the corners of streets, clearly desolate and desperate with the hands they had been dealt. On looking closely, you could see the whole circle of life in one Brooklyn scene; from young babies and families finding the smallest available corner of central park to play; to a group of older individuals dressed up smartly probably on their way to retirement. The scene before them would be repeated across the rest of the world.

Arianna and Jayden then had a tap on the back. It was Christina who excitedly had information to share. She had sought them both out and then led them to a quiet corridor where nobody was eavesdropping distance. Christina took Jayden and Arianna aside in the corridor and whispered, "You need to check out the Genesis Warehouse."

Christina's words hung in the air, a tantalizing promise of hidden truths waiting to be uncovered. Jayden and Arianna exchanged a glance, their curiosity piqued by the mention of a Genesis Warehouse. It was a term they had never heard before, but the urgency in Christina's voice left no doubt that it held significance.

"What is the Genesis Warehouse?" Arianna asked quietly, her voice tinged with excitement and apprehension.

Christina's expression grew solemn, her eyes betraying a hint of uncertainty. "I'm not entirely sure" she admitted, her tone grave. "But I've heard rumours today when I walked by Imelda Stravus's office. They were talking of a facility hidden beneath the remaining waves of the Atlantic basin; a place where secrets are kept, and truths are submerged. I don't know what lies within its depths, but I fear and hope that it may hold the answers we seek."

"We have to find it," Jayden declared, his voice firm with determination. "Whatever it takes, we have to uncover the truth."

Christina nodded in agreement, her expression grave but resolute. "I'll do everything in my power to help you," she promised. "The Genesis Warehouse is a mystery and not sure what you will be getting yourselves into."

That night and under the cover of darkness, Jayden and Arianna crept through the shadows, their hearts pounding with a mixture of excitement and trepidation. They again crept through the galactic gym room and found themselves recalling the exact sequence of button presses to open the facility that lay below them. Venturing down the staircase and back to the room they had visited only once before. Here within the Earth retirement facility, they were determined to seek out Killian Tredwell again and attempt to uncover whatever secrets he may hold about the Genesis Warehouse.

As they neared the entrance to the facility, they paused, their senses on high alert as they scanned their surroundings for any sign of danger, or rogue GGC guard. The night was silent save for the distant clatter of machinery; a constant reminder of the world that lay hidden away beyond the building.

With a silent nod of agreement, Jayden and Arianna pressed on, their footsteps muffled by the soft carpet beneath their feet. They moved with purpose and determination, their eyes scanning the darkness for any sign of movement.

Finally, they reached the entrance to the facility, a looming structure that rose up from the ground like a silent sentinel. With one final careful glance around the room to ensure that they were not being watched, Jayden and Arianna slipped inside, their hearts pounding with anticipation. The interior of the facility was eerily quiet, the only sound was the grind of machinery that echoed through the corridors. Jayden and Arianna moved cautiously whilst listening to the echoing walls off the walls of the chatter up ahead where Killian Tredwell resided.

They reached the room where Killian Tredwell resided; a small chamber tucked away in a remote corner of the facility. With a nervous glance at each other, Jayden and Arianna pushed open the door and stepped inside.

Killian Tredwell was sitting at a desk humming, his expression unreadable as he regarded them with a mixture of curiosity and suspicion. "What brings you here?" he asked, his voice calm but tinged with wariness of a long day.

Jayden and Arianna exchanged a look, their resolve steeling as they prepared to confront the man who may hold the key to so many secrets. "We need to talk," Jayden said, his voice firm with determination. "About the Genesis Warehouse."

Tredwell's eyes flickered with curiosity as Jayden and Arianna broached the subject of the Genesis Warehouse. He listened intently as they explained their suspicions and their desire to uncover the truth hidden within its depths.

When they finished speaking, Tredwell leaned back in his chair, his expression thoughtful. "The Genesis Warehouse," he repeated, his voice tinged with nostalgia. "It's a concept that never came to fruition, a dream that was never realized, but maybe things have changed?"

Jayden and Arianna exchanged a puzzled glance, their brows furrowing in confusion. "What do you mean?" Arianna asked, her voice tinged with uncertainty.

Tredwell sighed, his gaze drifting to the window as he spoke. "The Genesis Warehouse was meant to be a place of preservation, a sanctuary for the plants and foods that were in danger of extinction," he explained. "It was a project that we had hoped would ensure the survival of our world's most precious resources."

As Tredwell spoke, Jayden and Arianna felt a sense of disappointment wash over them. They had been so certain that the Genesis Warehouse held the key to uncovering the truth about the GGC's secrets, but now their hopes had been in vain.

"But why keep it a secret?" Jayden asked, his voice tinged with frustration. "Why not tell the world about it?"

Tredwell shook his head, his expression grave. "The world was not ready for such a concept," he replied. "We feared that if the truth were to be revealed, it would only lead to chaos and unrest. The Genesis Warehouse remained hidden, a secret known only to a select few. Just imagine if anyone caught wind of such an idea. They would loot and steal every resource of consequence for their own gain. It is something that if it exists – it needs to be protected at all costs."

Tredwell's gaze softened, his eyes reflecting the weight of the world's burdens. "Perhaps it is time for the truth to be revealed," he said with his voice barely above a whisper. "Perhaps humanity is ready to face its destiny and to embrace the legacy of the Genesis Warehouse and forge a new path forward."

On returning from the meeting with Tredwell, Jayden and Arianna returned to their quarters to contemplate what was next.

Chapter 26: Secrets are Punished

Reebus had been away for a number of weeks working for the advancement of some of his projects with Imelda but had decided to come back to the GGC late one evening. He snook in quietly with very few aware of his reappearance. On greeting a few of his key staff he progressed further down the corridors until he came to his private quarters. He skulked inside without saying a further word. As soon as he felt homely, he climbed into his waiting bed and after a short period of settling in - started to fall asleep. Reebus had been a very busy man and even he needed to rest. Tomorrow would be a big day as he had plans to action and people to see.

The following morning Reebus awoke all refreshed. He flicked a few screens on his personal device, removing the immediate and recent messages from view. He then navigated to a personal folder where several audio files resided. On scrolling down to the third file and after a quick automatic glance to ensure nobody was watching, he set it to play some previously recorded audio. He sat focussed and listening intently to the conversations that had been recorded through various surveillance systems. They were conversations recorded through the tracking devices that Imelda had placed on Arianna and Jayden to keep a close watch on their exploits. Some of what had been captured was very enlightening. His eyes narrowed with focus as he overheard Tredwell's recent chats with the Jayden and Arianna; his mind racing with memories long buried beneath layers of ambition and power. He had heard these recordings for the first time a few weeks ago but had needed time to think about any further course of action. This is why Reebus had returned once more to the central hub of the GGC as he had things that must be taken care of.

The recordings had Tredwell's words echoing through the hidden chambers of Reebus's mind, unlocking doors to a past he had long tried to forget. Although all the conversations were full of snippets and key conversations, it was the one he was particularly drawn to -the talk of the accident in Chicago; the catastrophic event that had torn through the heart of the city, leaving devastation in its wake. For Reebus, it was more than just a tragic event, it was the day that had forever altered the course of his destiny.

As he listened to Tredwell recount the details of that fateful day, Reebus felt a surge of emotion welling up within him. He remembered the anguish and sorrow that had consumed him in the aftermath, the pain of losing his parents in the blink of an eye. Yet, amidst the chaos and destruction, there had been a glimmer of something else. A seed of determination that had taken root in the depths of his soul. New information had presented itself as one of the most unusual gifts. For years, Reebus had buried his grief beneath a facade of strength and resolve, channelling his pain into a relentless pursuit of power. Now, as he listened to Tredwell's words, he felt something stir within him long-buried sense of anger and retribution.

The failed experiment in Chicago had not only claimed the lives of countless innocents. It had also taken his parents from him, leaving him orphaned and alone in a world torn apart by tragedy, and until he heard this recording, he had no idea why it had occurred. It felt like many years of hidden lies were finally falling into place. Not being a very forgiving man made any new information that was of personal value to Reebus a very dangerous thing.

Reebus, along with two of his closest and most trusted guards made their way down the corridors like a secretive clan. Entering the gym area and walking the well-known path down to a place he had visited so often. Although he had not been here so frequently of late, over the years it was a place where Reebus had learned and discussed many of his most extreme ideas, with someone whom he both respected and had loved dearly. Progressing further after triggering the staircase down to what lay below, the three cloaked figures lay sight on their ultimate destination --the Earth Retirement facility. The journey felt like a pilgrimage, a solitary quest to confront the ghosts of his past and seek solace in the words of an old friend. As the door to his personal quarters was opened, there stood before Reebus was his old master, Killian Tredwell.

As he approached Killian closer, Reebus felt a sense of trepidation wash over him. The facility and corridors were silent, the air heavy with the weight of years gone by. It had been nearly a decade since he had last seen Killian, and the thought of facing him now filled Reebus with a mixture of anticipation and dread.

Reebus hesitated for a moment before lowering his cloak so he could be seen in all his might. There was a brief pause before Killian, sitting in a chair by the window realised the identity of his latest visitor.

"Reebus," Killian said, his voice quiet but filled with warmth. "It's been a long time."

Reebus nodded, unable to speak as he took in the sight of his old master. Killian had aged since they had last seen each other, his once-strong frame now frailer and more stooped with the weight of years. His eyes still held a spark of the same fierce determination that Reebus remembered from his relative youth.

"I heard about the election," Killian continued, gesturing for Reebus to take a seat. "It sounds like you are elected once more.... you were never someone who would give up power without a fight", as he smirked knowing from the personal experience of battles long since gone. Reebus nodded, grateful for the small gesture of kindness. "Thank you, Killian. But that's not why I am here, there are things we need to discuss. Things from our past that cannot be ignored any longer."

Killian's brow furrowed in confusion, but he nodded, sensing the gravity of Reebus's words. "Of course, Reebus. What is it that is on your mind?"

Reebus took a deep breath, steeling himself for the words that were about to come. "I need to know about the failed experiment that hit Chicago. I need to know what really happened that day, and most importantly why?"

Killian's eyes widened in surprise, but he nodded slowly, as if recognizing the weight of Reebus's request. "It's a long story, Reebus. I will tell you everything. For the sake of the truth, it has been such a long time."

As Killian began to recount the events that led to the catastrophic failure of the mineral mining experiment in Chicago, Reebus listened intently, his heart heavy with the weight of the truth.

"It started as a simple experiment," Killian explained, his voice tinged with regret. "We were exploring new methods of mineral extraction, hoping to find a more efficient way to extract valuable resources from the Earth's crust."

Reebus nodded, his mind racing with memories of the past. He remembered hearing about the experiment as a child, but the details had always been shrouded in secrecy and never talked about when he was around.

"We thought we had taken every precaution," Killian continued. "But something went wrong. The drill malfunctioned, causing a chain reaction that destabilized the entire area."

Reebus's heart sank as he listened to Killian's words. He had always suspected that there was more to the story than he had been told, but hearing the truth laid bare was more painful than he had ever imagined.

"And the people of Chicago?" Reebus asked, his voice barely a whisper.

Killian's expression darkened; his eyes clouded with sorrow. "They were innocent victims, Reebus. They had no idea what was happening until it was too late. We did everything we could to contain the situation, but we were fighting a losing battle."

Reebus closed his eyes, his mind filled with images of the devastation that had torn through the heart of Chicago. He could still hear the screams and still feel the overwhelming sense of loss that had consumed the city in the aftermath of the disaster.

"We tried to cover it up," Killian admitted, his voice heavy with shame. "We thought we could protect the truth from the world, but in the end, it only made things worse."

Reebus nodded, his jaw clenched with anger. He had spent years searching for answers, trying to uncover the truth behind the disaster that had claimed the lives of so many innocent people. Finally, he had now found them. They had been right in front of him all this time, with the man who had saved him and taken him under their wing. The sequence of events was not sitting well with Reebus' as he was beginning to realise that he too was a pawn in the world and was only part of the GGC due to the events being described. It was indeed ironic that Reebus's power derived from that very day of the accident but also now that a few decades later the same technology discovered as a result of that accident was now only used in one place on Earth. It was, in essence, the same machine that now sends all eighty-year-olds to their destination.

"I'm sorry, Reebus," Killian said, his voice filled with remorse. "I wish there was more I could have done to prevent it, but it was just one of those fateful things."

Reebus shook his head, his eyes filled with anger. "So, was it just a coincidence that you happened to meet me and take me under your wing?"

As Killian's confession hung heavy in the air, Reebus felt a surge of conflicting emotions wash over him. He had spent so many years searching for answers, longing for closure, and now that he had finally found them, he was not sure how to feel.

"I've spent my whole life trying to understand what happened," Reebus said, his voice raw with emotion. "But I never imagined that you were the one behind it all."

Killian bowed his head, his expression one of profound regret. "I know that nothing I say can ever make up for what happened, Reebus. But I want you to know that I've spent every day since then trying to make amends."

Reebus stared at Killian, his mind reeling with the weight of his words. He had spent so long harbouring anger and resentment about the incident, but now, faced with the reality it made things even more intense.

"I was told about you, Reebus," Killian continued his voice barely above a whisper. "About the boy who lost everything in the wake of the disaster. My advisors sought you out, hoping to find a way to make things right."

Reebus felt a surge of disbelief wash over him. He had always believed that he was alone in the world, that nobody cared about the orphan boy left in the wake of the tragedy. Now in hearing Killian's words, he realized that he had been wrong.

"Why didn't you come forward sooner, to tell me the truth?" Reebus asked, his voice tinged with frustration.

Killian sighed, his shoulders slumping with the weight of his guilt. "I wanted to, Reebus. I was afraid of what might happen if the truth came out. I thought that by burying the past, I could protect you from the pain of knowing the truth. I thought that time would heal your wounds, and you would be okay."

Reebus shook his head, his eyes burning with anger. "You should have told me, Killian. You should have given me the chance to make my own choices, to decide for myself what I wanted to believe."

"You mean the same way that you have given the world's populace the opportunity to understand about Serenity 1, this 'lottery', Sandronica Sprowl and all the other things you have engineered Reebus?", said Killian in a forceful retort. Reebus appeared unmoved as if no blood were flowing through his body, he was immune to these double standards as he had justified himself as being always right and that they were totally different situations. Reebus was correct that the scenarios were totally different; on one hand the death of a few hundred people by accident versus the deliberated culling of millions upon millions of innocent people. Both situations involved lies, but the intent was not on the same scale, not that Reebus had any empathy or sympathy for what Killian had done.

Killian's tone then softened as he reached out a hand, his expression one of pleading. "I know that I can never make up for the mistakes of the past, Reebus. I truly hope that someday, you can find it in your heart to forgive me."

"I don't think I can forgive you, Killian," Reebus said, his voice barely above a whisper. "But now I have control over decisions and big decisions have to be made. It's only fair that we find a solution......, nay punishment for what you have done."

Reebus's voice cut through the air like a knife, his words heavy with adrenaline. As he locked eyes with Killian again, he felt a surge of conflicting emotions wash over him. He had spent so long grappling with the pain and anger of his past, but now, faced with the man who had played a pivotal role in shaping his fate, he knew that he had to decide. Although his mind had ran scenarios around Killian's fate numerous times over the course of the last few weeks, one outcome always prevailed; Reebus was not and never has been a forgiving man and he was not about to start now.

"Killian," Reebus said, his voice firm. "I need to take you on a journey as you have served the GGC well over the years", as Killian looked on hopeful of where he was being taken.

"It is time you visited Serenity 1..... Permanently.", continued Reebus with the force and emotion of an executioner.

Killian's eyes widened in shock, his expression one of disbelief. "Reebus, please," he pleaded. "I've spent my whole life trying to make amends for the mistakes of my past. You cannot kill me; it was an accident and one that I have tried to make up for." Killian was scrambling for words, for compassion, sympathy, and empathy. He was, however, dealing with a man monster whom he knew had none. It was always Reebus's way or nothing as if a spoiled child still stood before him.

Reebus shook his head, his resolve unwavering. "I'm sorry, Killian. But this is the only way to ensure that justice is served."

As Reebus spoke, he could see the weight of his words sinking in, the realization dawning on Killian's face. He knew that his fate was sealed and there was little if anything he could do to change this. He turned towards the hi-tech wall and looked at himself in the mirror for one last time. The scars of age and history on show for one final time. He then took off his most precious jewellery; a ring that he was given on the first day as the leader of the world and placed it on a table in front of him. One of the guards now placed his hand on Killian's shoulder and turned him in direction to face his new destiny. As Killian was escorted away by the guards, he could not shake the sense of betrayal that gnawed at him from within. He had devoted his life to the GGC, to leading humanity into a new era of prosperity and progress. In the end, all his efforts had been for naught. The person whom he had loved and cared for more than any other was the very person to stick the proverbial knife in his back.

"Reebus," Killian called out, his voice tinged with bitterness as he turned to face the man who had once been his protege. "Why? Why did you go behind my back and overthrow me as the leader of the GGC?"

Reebus met Killian's gaze with a steely resolve, his expression unreadable. "I did what needed to be done," he replied, his voice devoid of emotion. "You were never going to be strong enough to make the toughest decisions."

Killian's eyes narrowed in disbelief. "That's not true," he protested. "I did everything in my power to guide humanity towards a brighter future. I made sacrifices, and difficult decisions, all in service of the greater good."

Reebus shook his head, his expression hardening. "Your methods were flawed, Killian," he said, his voice cold and unforgiving. "You were not prepared to reduce our population by any methods to save humanity. You were too soft and too weak."

Killian felt a surge of anger welling up inside him, his fists clenched at his sides. "And you think you have what it takes to lead?" he spat, his voice dripping with contempt. "You, who have manipulated, lied, and betrayed your way to the top? You are no better than the tyrants of old, Reebus. No better than those you claim to oppose."

Reebus's expression remained impassive, but Killian could see the flicker of uncertainty in his eyes. "Perhaps you're right, Killian," he said, his voice barely above a whisper. "Perhaps I have made mistakes, done things that I'm not proud of. But I did what I believed was necessary to save humanity from itself. If that means sacrificing everything, even my own soul, then so be it."

"Take him away," Reebus said, turning to his guards. "And make sure he is escorted to Serenity 1 immediately, to begin processing for his 'Journey."

Chapter 27: A Stranger Beckons

Jayden sat in his quarters, the soft warming glow of the holographic internet casting a flickering light across his face. He scrolled through page after page of search results, his eyes scanning for any mention of the Genesis warehouse. Despite his efforts, the elusive facility remained shrouded in mystery, its secrets hidden from prying eyes.

Frustration gnawed at Jayden as he continued his search, his mind racing with unanswered questions. Why was the Genesis Warehouse kept hidden? What secrets lay buried within its walls? Most importantly, how could he uncover the truth?

Like so many times before it felt that despite being so close to truth's door, they were lost in finding exactly where to go next and needed some help along the way. Arianna too spent her time looking for leads and information, but it was a futile battle to find the information that was needed.

Then one morning, just as Jayden was about to give up hope he heard a loud bing from his communicator. Having received tens of beeps a day then there was no rush to view what would present itself this time as it was probably something insignificant. After completing a conversation with Arianna about historical battles in the Roman empire, he brought up the new message on his holographic display. As the message fizzed into action in front of them. The sender's callsign read "Affected18," a name that was all too familiar to both Jayden and Arianna after their earlier adventures in London and piqued his curiosity, at once.

Intrigued, Jayden opened the message, his heart pounding in anticipation. The message was brief, containing only a couple of simple lines of text: "I know about the Genesis warehouse. Meet me at the coordinates attached."

Jayden's pulse quickened as he read the message, his mind racing with possibilities. Would they finally get to meet

'Affected18'?;and how did they know about the Genesis Warehouse? More importantly, could they help they uncover its secrets?

With a sense of adventure, Jayden replied to the message, "We will be there as soon as we can" before sending the encrypted response back through the layers of the darkest web to whomever and wherever 'affected18' was located.

After they had agreed to meet at the specified coordinates. They knew that this could be the breakthrough they had been searching for. It was the key to unlocking the truth about the Genesis warehouse and whatever secrets it held.

As Jayden and Arianna made their way through the corridors of the GGC headquarters once more, their footsteps echoing against the polished floors, they could not shake the sense of conclusion that hung in the air. The message from 'Affected18' had injected new energy into their quest, and they were eager to follow any lead that might bring them closer to the truth about the Genesis warehouse.

As they rounded a now familiar corner, they spotted an ever-sparkling Christina approaching from the opposite direction. Her expression was a mix of curiosity and concern as she caught sight of them.

"Jayden, Arianna," Christina greeted them, her voice tinged with warmth. "What brings you both here?"

Jayden actioned for Christina to huddle into a quiet space at the side before revealing the information they had discovered. "We received a message from someone called 'Affected18'," Jayden explained, his excitement palpable. "They claim to know about the Genesis Warehouse and want to meet us there."

Christina's eyebrows shot up in surprise, her eyes widening with intrigue. 'Affected18?' she repeated, her mind clearly racing with possibilities. "I've heard rumours about them. They are a notorious figure in the underground network, known for their expertise in uncovering and revealing GGC secrets."

Arianna's eyes widened with excitement, her pulse quickening at the thought of finally getting some answers. "Do you think we can trust them?" she asked, her voice tinged with uncertainty.

Christina's expression grew serious as she considered the question. "It's hard to say," she admitted. "But if they're willing to reach out to you, then they must believe that you can help them in some way."

Jayden nodded in agreement, his mind already racing with plans for their meeting with 'Affected18'. "We need to find out what they know," he declared, his voice filled with determination. "We now need to find a way of getting to those coordinates!," added Jayden trying to find a way to fulfil their objectives.

Christina nodded, her eyes alight with excitement. "I'll come with you," she offered, her tone resolute. "Together, we'll uncover the truth about the Genesis warehouse and put an end to the secrets that have plagued us for so long. I have access to a GGC space car so that might be able to solve your transportation problems too!"

The three friends agreed to grab a few essentials for their trip, as you can never tell how a trip might develop. They made sure to include enough snacks and drink with a change of clothes and a few other essentials. Jayden and Arianna returned to their quarters to begin the process and Christina headed to her quarters.

"You can never be too prepared for an adventure," said Arianna in her typical organised manner. "I can pack your bag too Jayden if you like?" as she looked at him knowingly as it was a rhetorical question of the type she often asked. Jayden sat on the couch as Arianna busied around him packing essentials, as well as some items that Jayden would argue were not quite as important. It was best to let her get on with it as this was one activity where she was best left on her own. They were now ready to leave and upon exiting their quarters they met with Christina at the agreed meeting point near the GGC private space car port. The three intrepid adventures loaded their possessions into the storage boot at the side of the car and then hopped into their respective plush seats. Christina in the drivers' position, but all three of them together at the front of the pure silver vehicle. Its smooth, shing exterior reflected the reflection of the hangar lights.

Christina's fingers danced across the holographic controls, inputting the coordinates for their destination in the middle of the vast Atlantic Ocean. The location they had plotted seemed to be that of nothingness itself and all three wondered whether it was going to be a fool's errand of a trip. With a jolt, the engines thrummed to life, filling the cabin with a low, steady vibration. As they ascended into the night sky, the lights of New York below faded into the distance, replaced by the glittering expanse of stars that stretched out before them like an endless tapestry. The world still offered beauty in all directions – if only you knew where to look. The journey was filled with a mixture of awe and trepidation as they hurtled through the darkness of space, the only sound the steady thrum of the engines and the startup of the ship's systems.

Arianna glanced out of the window, her eyes wide with wonder as she watched the stars streak past, their light casting a gentle lit patterns passing over her face. Beside her, Jayden sat with a determined expression, his mind focused on the task ahead. Despite the darkness, they looked out of their windows at where the vastness of the Atlantic Ocean had once been. It was now a dry and desolate shelf with occasional plant life and greenery. The desalination and water capturing devices that were commonplace had long since sucked away the large volumes of sea water that had previously lay there. Occasionally in the deeper troughs there were bodies of water looking like lakes or miniature seas, but very different in size to the ocean that once lay beneath. The world had changed a great deal over the centuries, but the last hundred years had been the most brutal and damaging of them all. As they approached the coordinates the depth and size of one such lake like water body came before them. They were heading towards what was probably the deepest point in what was left of the Atlantic Ocean itself, the point where humanity hadn't quite found a way to destroy in its entirety. Arianna just keep looking at each other with words unable to make the way out of their mouths.

Christina's voice broke the silence, her tone calm and reassuring. "We're almost there," she announced, her eyes fixed on the navigation display. "Prepare for descent."

As they hovered above their destination, the lights of the space car dimmed, casting the cabin in a soft, ambient state. The tension in the air was palpable as they descended towards the ocean below, the surface looming closer with each passing moment.

With a gentle thud, the space car touched down on the calm waters of the remnants of the Atlantic Ocean, the waves lapping gently against the hull. Jayden, Arianna, and Christina exchanged a glance, their hearts pounding in unison as they desperately arched to uncover the secrets that lay hidden beneath the surface.

After floating for a few seconds Christina nudged a few colourful buttons and levels on the control panel and the space car transformed into an ocean ready craft. It is frame sealing away any air gaps and engine redirecting in an outer frame towards the back of the space car. After another nudge on a flashing button, Christina exclaimed "I've always wanted to try this function, but never thought I would!" as the space care dipped beneath the surface of the water and powered down to whatever lay below.

The sleek space car descended gracefully beneath the surface of the Atlantic Ocean, its reinforced hull cutting effortlessly through the water. Inside, Jayden, Arianna, and Christina watched in awe as the vibrant marine life danced around them, their colours shimmering in the dim light filtering down from the surface above. There were creatures before them that they had never seen and long since thought extinct in the world they had lived. "If life can survive here then maybe there is hope for us all," whispered Arianna glowing with hope.

Christina's voice broke the silence, her tone sombre as she gestured towards the ocean floor. "The oceans have changed drastically over the past century," she explained, her eyes scanning the desolate expanse around them. "The relentless demand for water led to the proliferation of desalination plants, sucking the oceans dry and leaving only small pockets of water behind." As they delved deeper into the murky depths, the world outside the windows transformed into a mesmerizing underwater landscape, filled with towering coral reefs, swaying seaweed forests, and an endless array of exotic sea creatures. It was as if the life in the ocean had been aware of its water being stolen in passages of environmental theft around the world and had retreated to the area of the ocean where their lives had the best chance of survival. The sea creatures' fate was entwined but similar to humanities fate. The sea life's resources had also dwindled and been eroded to a point where their life sustaining sea water itself was at crisis point and life itself was retreating into an ever-smaller life sustaining trench. Eventually when the water dissipates from this and other remaining trenches across the Earth then the natural conclusion to their lives would be reached, as with similar battles going on for all lifeforms left on the lands elsewhere and above. Arianna pressed her face against the glass, her eyes wide with wonder as she took in the breathtaking sights unfolding before her. "It's incredible," she breathed, her voice barely above a whisper.

Christina nodded in agreement; her gaze focused on the navigation display as she guided the Space car through the underwater depths. "Let's Just wait until we see what's waiting for us at the bottom," she replied, a hint of excitement in her voice.

As they descended deeper into the now darkness, a faint light appeared on the horizon, drawing closer with each passing moment. Jayden's heart quickened with anticipation as he strained to catch a glimpse of what lay ahead.

Suddenly they emerged into a vast underwater cavern, bathed in the soft, ethereal light of bioluminescent algae. The walls of the cavern were adorned with strange, otherworldly formations, their shapes twisting and whirling in the gentle currents.

In the centre of the cavern, nestled among the world's last types of coral reefs and sea anemones, was the tip of a towering structure unlike anything they had ever seen before. Its smooth, metallic surface gleamed in the soft light, casting long algae fuelled shadows across the cave floor.

Arianna gasped again as she took in the sight before her, her eyes wide with wonder. "What is that?" she asked, her voice filled with excitement "Whatever it is, It's huge, it's incredible" she had continued.

Christina smiled, her eyes shining with anticipation. "That, my friends," she said, "is the entrance to the Genesis warehouse."

Jayden, Arianna, and Christina all looked in wonder as they surveyed in detail the structure they could see before them. It seemed that the top of this behemoth was some sharp and detailed points and the chassis thickened as it progressed downwards. The structure progressed to the bottommost floor of the seabed but appeared to continue below whilst still widening. Whatever this Genesis warehouse was, its only visible part was the proverbial tip of the iceberg; there was much to discover below the surface. The space car hummed softly as Jayden, Arianna, and Christina looked for the right place to land, before noticing a large circular hole to the side. It appeared to be an air pocket, or chamber where anything landing or visiting this structure must go. A parking bay or deliveries entrance as many would say. The space car progressed through the hole which became a chamber and then once inside it closed behind them. All water was flushed away back outside the tank and the car dropped gently towards the bottom of the chamber until all water had dissipated and only air remained. Christina now turned the space car back into its normal travelling mode and drove it forwards and brought it to rest at a small landing pad adjacent to what appeared to be the main entrance to the Genesis structure. Christina, Arianna, and Jayden exited the space car and grabbed their earlier packed bags from the storage hold. As they stepped out onto the platform, their eyes scanning the dimly lit surroundings towards the entrance that stood before them. They had parked in a landing bay made for about twenty vehicles; most spaces currently occupied in what must be a busy place. Within the carpark there were all kinds of maintenance and delivery vehicles which must have been parked for a long time with various kinds of moss growing across their exteriors.

As sense of anticipation hung in the air, a noise could be heard from the entrance ahead. It was the quiet workings of the machinery around the door mechanism which had been locked in an airtight hold. Arianna glanced nervously at Jayden, her hand tightening around his as they stood together, ready to face whatever lay ahead, and whatever may exist behind that door. Christina just stood there looking towards the door, knowing that whatever was coming could never be unseen.

Suddenly the door sprung open, and a shadowy figure emerged from the darkness, The figure then moved silently towards them with a purposeful stride. Jayden's heart skipped a beat as he instinctively stepped forward, shielding Arianna from any danger.

As the figure drew one step nearer, they could see that it was not a threat, but rather a woman dressed in a sleek uniform, her features obscured by the dim light. She approached them with a confident air, her gaze steady and unwavering. "Welcome, Jayden, welcome Arianna, and Christina – so glad you've made it!"

"Who are you?" Christina demanded; her voice sharp with suspicion as she eyed the newcomer warily.

The woman paused for a moment, her expression unreadable, before finally speaking in a low, melodious voice. "My name is Nova," she said,," her tone calm and measured. "I'm here to guide you through the Genesis Warehouse."

Chapter 28: Earth's Library

Nova stood before Jayden, Arianna, and Christina, a vision of beauty and intellect. In her late twenties, she exuded an aura of confidence and grace that captivated all who beheld her. Her lustrous hair cascaded in waves of ebony silk, framing a face adorned with features of exquisite symmetry. Her eyes, pools of sparkling sapphire, held a depth of wisdom far beyond her years.

Dressed in attire that blended sophistication with effortless style, Nova wore a tailored ensemble that accentuated her slender figure. A sleek, form-fitting blouse of ivory silk hugged her curves, complemented by a pair of tailored trousers that tapered elegantly at her ankles. A statement necklace adorned her slender neck, its delicate chains adorned with shimmering gemstones that caught the light with every movement.

Nova's presence commanded attention, her every gesture imbued with a natural poise and confidence. As she spoke, her voice was melodic and captivating, its timbre carrying a hint of mystery and intrigue.

With each word, Nova painted a vivid picture of their surroundings, her intellect and insight guiding them through the corridors of the Genesis warehouse. Her knowledge was boundless, her intellect razor-sharp, and her wit quick as lightning.

Jayden exchanged a glance with Arianna, a flicker of uncertainty passing between them. They had hoped to meet 'Affected18' but whom was this 'Nova'. She was not someone that they had expected and was a mysterious woman which only added to their sense of unease.

Christina studied Nova intently, her eyes narrowing in suspicion. "How do we know we can trust you?" she asked, her voice tinged with doubt.

Nova smiled faintly; her eyes gleaming with an inner light. "You don't," she replied cryptically. "But if you want to uncover the truth hidden within these walls, you'll have to take that risk."

Beyond her beauty and brilliance, it was Nova's compassion and empathy that truly set her apart. Her eyes held a warmth and kindness that spoke of a soul attuned to the needs of others, a heart that beat with a fierce determination to have influence in the world. As Nova led Jayden, Arianna, and Christina through the entrance of the Genesis Warehouse, a tense silence hung in the air, broken only by the rhythmic sound of their footsteps echoing against the metal floor. Jayden glanced nervously at Arianna, his mind racing with questions about the mysterious woman who now walked before them.

Suddenly, Nova paused, turning to face them with a solemn expression. "There's something I need to tell you," she said, her voice soft but resolute. "I am the one you know as 'Affected18.' I reached out to you because from my holograph search scans I saw that you were searching for the truth, and I believed that together, we could uncover it. There is a lot of things I can show you today if you will let me."

Jayden's eyes widened in surprise, his mind reeling at the revelation. Arianna gasped softly beside him, her hand tightening around his as they exchanged a bewildered glance. Even Christina seemed taken aback, her expression a mask of disbelief as she had expected 'Affected18' to have been some kind of rebellious scummy gun slinging superhero man, not the feminine epitome of style and sophistication that stood beside them.

"But why?" Christina demanded; her voice tinged with suspicion. "What do you hope to gain from all of this?"

Nova met Christina's gaze evenly, her eyes shining with determination. "We need to preserve and nurture all elements of the world," she replied firmly. "The greedy cannot deplete us into extinction."

"We're with you," Jayden said firmly, his voice ringing with conviction. "Whatever it takes, we'll help you and I'm sure the GGC is behind all this injustice."

Nova barely reacted to Jayden's comment which seemed either strange or very accepting of the realities of the situation. She led them all down one set of stairs to a large door that stood in front of them. Nova, obviously well averse in the functions and workings of the structure keyed in a few numbers and then with a retina and fingerprint scan the bulky door started to open on her command. As the door slid to the side it opened up a small chamber where she actioned them all to step into. The bulky door behind closed on them and they were now in a self-contained chamber. Whooshes of air and a sprinkling of vapour droplets then circled the room and then ended as soon as it had begun. "What was that," asked Jayden who did not fully comprehend what was occurring. "In order to protect the life within here from external factors such as disease and bacteria, measures need to be taken to ensure we are all sterile and free from potential threats to nature.," as Nova explained the situation. The door facing them now began to slide open and the vast room before them was about to be unveiled.

As Jayden, Arianna, Christina, and Nova stepped into the first room of the Genesis warehouse, they were greeted by a breathtaking sight. Rows upon rows of towering shelves stretched out before them, each one packed with an astonishing array of plant and vegetable species. It was a garden fit for the gods themselves, as if every species they could imagine was in view. Jayden's eyes widened in wonder as he gazed around the vast chamber, taking in the sight of plants he had only ever read about in books. Arianna's breath caught in her throat as she spotted species, she had thought long extinct, their vibrant colours a stark contrast to the sterile metal surroundings.

Christina's expression was one of awe as she surveyed the room, her mind racing with the implications of what they had discovered. Nova stood beside her, a look of quiet satisfaction on her face as she watched their reactions.

"This is incredible," Jayden breathed, his voice filled with tenderness. "I never imagined there could be so many different types of plants in one place."

Arianna nodded in agreement, her eyes shining with excitement. "It's like stepping into a whole new world," she murmured, reaching out to touch the leaves of a nearby plant with trembling fingers. Each of the plants looked healthy and in their prime. One area of the room had thousands and thousands of fruits and vegetable bearing greenery in layers and rows of different state in their crop lifecycle. It was a sustainable farm of nature and the fruits that it could bore.

Christina studied the shelves intently, her mind whirling with the possibilities. "Imagine the knowledge contained within these walls," she mused, her voice tinged with awe. "There could be species here that hold the key to solving some of our greatest challenges."

Nova smiled softly; her eyes alight with satisfaction. "That's exactly why I brought you here," she said, her voice quiet but resolute. "These plants are more than just a collection of species, they're a treasure trove of knowledge, waiting to be unlocked."

After a while perusing the contents and nature within the room, Nova ushered them to another staircase where they all ventured further down into the depths of the warehouse, deeper into the Earth's crust. A similar routine as before occurred with the next large door opening only to blast and scatter vapour droplets eliminating any bacterial threat as before. The second door eventually opening and a further journey into humanity had begun. As they stepped through the doorway into the second room of the Genesis warehouse,

Jayden, Arianna, Christina, and Nova found themselves surrounded by a vast expanse of shimmering tanks filled with crystal-clear water. The air was cool and moist, carrying the faint scent of salt and marine life. Some enormous tanks were pure water alone, others embedded with sea life and further ones of different mixtures of liquids that were connected to pipes leading up to the room where all the plants had been seen in the previous room. It was an advanced self-watering system to ensure that the natural life above was kept in its pristine state. Looking closer there was filtration and purification systems with waters entering through beneath and above. A maze of interlocking pipes seemed to offer carriage of the precious liquid throughout the confines of the entire warehouse.

Arianna's eyes widened in amazement as she took in the sight before her. "Water," she breathed, her voice filled with wonder. "So much water."

Jayden nodded in agreement, his gaze sweeping over the endless rows of tanks. "It's like an aquatic paradise," he murmured, his voice tinged with awe.

Christina studied the tanks intently, her mind racing with possibilities. "This must be a sanctuary for marine life," she mused, her eyes alight with excitement. "Look at the diversity of species, there's everything from tropical fish to deep-sea creatures."

"There's fresh water, salt water in almost endless supply for everyone, everything." Said Nova.

Nova smiled with her eyes gleaming with satisfaction. "Water is one of the most precious resources on Earth," she said, her voice filled with reverence. "And yet, here it is, preserved in abundance to ensure future existence of life."

As they moved through the chamber, they wondered further at the variety of marine life on display. Vibrant schools of fish darted through the water, their colours shimmering in the soft light. Exotic creatures with colourful scales and delicate tendrils drifted gracefully through the tanks, their movements mesmerizing to watch.

Jayden, Arianna, and Christina stood amidst the vast expanse of water-filled tanks in the second room of the Genesis Warehouse, they exchanged surprised glances.

"This is... unexpected," Jayden remarked, his voice filled with astonishment.

Arianna nodded in agreement, her eyes still scanning the rows of tanks. "I thought the Genesis project was primarily focused on preserving plant life," she said, her brow furrowed in confusion.

Christina's gaze swept over the shimmering waters, her mind racing to make sense of the situation. "It seems that the scope of the project is broader than we initially thought," she said thoughtfully. "Perhaps the preservation of water resources is also a key component."

Nova, who had been observing their reactions quietly, stepped forward with a smile. "The Genesis project was conceived as a comprehensive effort to safeguard Earth's biodiversity and essential resources," she explained. "While plants and seeds are certainly a crucial part of that, water is equally, if not more important to the sustaining of life on our planet." Nova continued further, clearly enjoying the reaction and excitement her tour was presenting to her guests. Like before they found the next staircase and like before ventured down before coming to the third room of this enormous extravaganza of life. Again, they went through the rigmarole of being tormented by gusts of air and being blasted free of all potential life affecting elements they were carrying.

The third room door now opened before them and was about to surpass their preconceived expectations once again. This time, they found themselves surrounded by towering shelves stacked with an astonishing array of rocks and minerals, each meticulously catalogued and arranged. Some of the inventory was melted down into its purest forms, others were just stacked in huge piles of its rawest mineral form.

Arianna's eyes widened in amazement as she took in the spectacle before her. "I had no idea there were so many different types of rocks and minerals," she exclaimed, her voice filled with wonder.

Christina nodded in agreement, her gaze moving from one display to another. "It's incredible," she remarked. "I never imagined that the Genesis project would include such a comprehensive collection of Earth's geological treasures."

Nova then gestured towards the back end of the room and continued with her sightseeing monologue, "Towards the back of the room behind those closed metallic doors are elements considered unsafe for humans in terms of proximity. Things that emit strong doses of radioactivity, various types of toxic gases and other things that are dangerous if used in the wrong way. Access to that area is limited to only those people with the right protection and safety protocols."

Nova, who had been observing their reactions throughout, stepped forward to offer an explanation to their whispers. "The preservation of Earth's geological diversity is just as important as safeguarding its plant life and water resources," she explained. "Rocks and minerals play a crucial role in supporting ecosystems and providing essential nutrients for life to thrive."

As they continued to explore the room, Jayden, Arianna, Christina, and Nova were awestruck by the sheer magnitude of the mineral cache. From sparkling crystals to rugged igneous rocks, each specimen held a story of Earth's geological history, preserved to discover, and appreciate.

As had become the pattern, Nova ventured further and down a further staircase. The three friends followed closely behind not quite realising exactly how deep beneath the ocean's floor they now were. As Nova explained that there were still more revelations awaiting them, they were once again blasted by the air and vapour particles on the chambers entrance. The fourth door slid open just like the others. They had entered another massive chamber, and as the doors slid shut behind them, they were greeted by the background noise of whirring machinery and the soft glow of fluorescent lights.

"This is the heart of the Genesis project's energy infrastructure," Nova announced, gesturing toward the colossal power generator at the centre of the room. "What you see before you is not just any generator, it's a revolutionary fusion reactor capable of generating immense amounts of clean, renewable energy. It is designed so that it can power every part of the facility, every lifeform, light, and operations within. We also have a backup facility and can generate further energy from outside through solar panels."

Jayden's jaw dropped in astonishment. "I've read about these new ultra-fusion reactors, but I never imagined seeing one in person," he exclaimed. "This would provide enough energy to power entire cities!"

Nova nodded, her expression grave yet hopeful. "Indeed. With this reactor, we have the ability to harness the power of the sun itself, unlocking virtually limitless energy without producing harmful emissions or depleting finite resources."

Arianna looked at the intricate web of pipes and conduits that snaked around the reactor, transporting superheated plasma and coolant to and from the core. "But how does it work?" she asked, her curiosity piqued.

Nova smiled, stepping closer to the reactor to explain. "At its core, a fusion reactor uses the same process that powers the sun in nuclear fusion. By fusing together lightweight atomic nuclei like hydrogen isotopes, we can release vast amounts of energy with minimal waste."

Christina nodded; her eyes alight with understanding. "And the best part is, fusion reactors produce no greenhouse gases or radioactive waste, making them a truly sustainable source of almost limitless power."

Nova led them all deeper still down to their fifth level since they had entered the warehouse many hours before. Each of them was tiring mentally as much as physically as their minds had been taken to the most extreme and unimaginable of places. On the next level familiarity again took charge with procedures in place to ensure the protection of whatever is inside now a matter of expectancy and routine.

On entering the fifth zone, they were met with a sight that took their breath away. Before them stretched a vast network of large but separate areas. This time it was so vast they were spread over a number of floors which was to take hours to explore. Each separate area housed a menagerie of life and biome unlike anything they had ever seen before. The air was alive with the sounds of nature. Loud birdsong mingled with the soft rustle of leaves, the gentle lapping of water, and the distant calls of creature's unseen. Everywhere they looked, they saw animals of every shape and size, living in harmony within their native habitats. There were savannah planes with large African mammals such as lions, zebras and giraffes present and enjoying their days. Symbiotic and non-destructive species were often kept in the same confines but predatorial animals like lions were kept apart. A maze of technological virtual barriers existed which were connected to controllers located somewhere inside each animal's body.

"Each animal has a defining chip from birth. Each zone limits the areas where all those chips can go to, or it sends a high frequency increasing pulse as they attempt to go further beyond their own confines. It has been tested to work with One hundred percent effectiveness meaning that we can create biomes with limited natural losses through hunting and maintain the intricate balance of the environment. They are all fed through feeding stations delivered from above at regular times and it keeps them all happy and in good health," Nova divulged as it she had been reading from a card.

Nova's eyes widened with wonder as she took in the spectacle before her. "It's like a modern-day ark," she breathed, her voice filled with awe. "A sanctuary for life in the midst of a changing world. We have sanctuaries for almost all animal types that have been on the Earth, even those that have been close to extinction. Over the next three floors, with a little bit of imagination you could find yourself almost anywhere on Earth.

Jayden nodded, his heart swelling with pride at the realization of what they had accomplished. "This is the heart of the Genesis project," she explained, her voice tinged with emotion. "A place where every species has a chance to thrive, protected from the dangers that threaten their existence. "Nova further explained that even the days and nights are simulated here with the use of backdrop lighting with simple technological weather conditions generated and simulated with automated rain and wind making everything feel more natural to each inhabitant.

Christina's face lit up with excitement as she surveyed the diverse array of creatures around her. "It's incredible," she exclaimed, her eyes shining with wonder. "I never imagined we'd see something like this in our lifetime."

Arianna, too, was moved by the sight before her, her heart overflowing with gratitude for the opportunity to witness such beauty and diversity. "It's like stepping into a living, breathing reinvention of the world" she murmured, her voice barely above a whisper.

As they wandered through the corridors of the underground complex, Nova, Jayden, Christina, and Arianna marvelled at the wonders that surrounded them. From the majestic lions to graceful giraffes they had already seen, from playful otters to elusive snow leopards, from the smallest insects to the largest of all mammals. Every corner held a new surprise, a new testament to the resilience and adaptability of life on Earth. It was like a living breathing zoo, except it was located deep beneath the Earth's crust and away from the bulk of humanity who might have tried to harm it.

They were now so far under the sea all senses were lost. The air conditioning and distribution machines made every floor as pleasant as the outside world. Gentle breezes and subtle scents of freshness passed through every layer and floor that they visited. With every turn and every glance, the Genesis project turned more elusive and extravagant and around the next corner was no exception.

"Prepare to witness something truly extraordinary," Nova exclaimed, her voice filled with anticipation. "Inside these chambers lies the culmination of years of research and innovation culminating in the rebirth of previously extinct animals."

Jayden, Christina, and Arianna exchanged excited glances; their curiosity floored by Nova's words. Together, they followed her as she pushed open the doors, revealing a sight that took their breath away.

Before them stood a sprawling laboratory, filled with state-of-the-art equipment and bustling with activity. Scientists moved about with purpose; their eyes alight with excitement as they worked tirelessly to bring new life into the world.

Nova led the group to a series of observation windows, through which they could see into a series of large, climate-controlled chambers. Inside, they caught glimpses of creatures long thought to be lost to the annals of time. Animals such as dodos, mammoths, and even some of the smaller dinosaur types of the distant past.

"It's like something out of a science fiction novel," Christina exclaimed, her voice tinged with wonder.

Nova nodded, her smile widening with pride. "Thanks to advances in genetic engineering and cloning technology, we've been able to recreate these animals from DNA samples recovered from fossils and other sources. It's a testament to the power of human ingenuity and the resilience of life itself."

As they watched, mesmerized, the scientists carefully monitored the progress of their creations, ensuring that each one was healthy and thriving in its new environment. It was a delicate process, fraught with challenges and risks, but the rewards were immeasurable. Here was the chance to witness the rebirth of species long thought to be lost forever.

For Jayden, Christina, and Arianna, it was a moment of inspiration, a reminder of the limitless potential of science and the boundless wonders of the natural world. As they stood together, gazing out at the creatures that roamed the chambers before them, they knew that they were witnessing history in the making. It was something that would have once been deemed impossible.

"This place is so huge," said Arianna, and Christina chipped in "There really can't be anything else left to see, can there?" as they all realised the enormity of everything that had come before them today. Nova led them away from the advanced research labs and down further into more winding staircases and then to the entrance of yet another room. Not for the first time what greeted them was to be a breathtaking sight. First there was the noise of chatter, of people talking happily; people sounded like they were playing and enjoying life. As the door opened to reveal its secrets, they were engulfed by the sight of thousands of young people with their faces illuminated by soft light, filled the chamber with laughter and conversation. It was a scene of vibrant energy and youthful exuberance, a stark contrast to the sombre atmosphere they had encountered on the surface of the Earth.

Jayden and Arianna looked around the room noticing face after face and the joy and delight that was on show before abruptly turning focus to one figure who stood out from the rest. There was an imposing silhouette that radiated power and authority.

This figure was making its way towards them from the distance. As the figure drew nearer, Jayden's heart skipped a beat, his mind struggling to comprehend what he was seeing.

"Reebus?" Arianna recoiled; her voice tinged with disbelief.

The man nodded, a faint smile playing at the corners of his lips, but his attention was not on Arianna, Jayden or even Christina; "Nova, it's good to see you," he said, "Thank you for bringing them to me.," his voice deep and resonant.

Nova's expression softened at the sight of this man before her, with eyes betraying a mixture of pride and apprehension. "Father," she replied, her voice filled with emotion. "I've missed you.," as she gave Reebus a gentle hug.

Reebus chuckled, a twinkle of amusement in his eyes. "I could say the same for you," he replied whilst looking over the triumvirate of shocked eyes that faced him..

Chapter 29: Running Away from Reality

Arianna and Jayden were still in a state of shock when Reebus stepped forward; his gaze fixed on Jayden and Arianna with unwavering intensity. "Welcome," he began, his voice echoing through the chamber with quiet authority. "Good to see you again Jayden, and you too Arianna. I bet you are starting to wonder what all of this is about," he said rhetorically, "You have been brought here for a purpose; a purpose that I have long been preparing for."

Jayden and Arianna exchanged puzzled glances, their minds racing with a whirlwind of questions. What could Reebus want with them? What role did they play in his grand design?

Reebus's lips curved into a faint smile as he regarded them with a knowing expression. "You see, my dear Jayden and Arianna" he continued, his voice tinged with a hint of amusement, "the Genesis project was never simply about preserving the flora and fauna of Earth. It was about something far greater, it is my vision of renewal, of rebirth."

"Jayden, Arianna," Reebus began, his voice resonating with conviction, "I want to tell you about Genesis. It is a project that goes beyond politics, beyond borders, beyond anything we've ever imagined."

As he spoke, Reebus painted a vivid picture of a world where the preservation of life in all its forms was not just a priority, but a sacred duty. He spoke of the need to protect not just animals, minerals, and vegetables, but also the very essence of humanity itself., covering the hopes, dreams, and aspirations that define us as a species. Stood before Jayden and Arianna was a genuine leader of thoughts, someone who actually seemed to have a plan for a future beyond all the smoke and mirrors and web of deceit seen so far.

"At the heart of Genesis lies the belief that every living being has value, every ecosystem has a purpose, and every voice deserves to be heard," Reebus continued, his words carrying the weight of conviction and determination. "But to achieve this vision, we need more than just good intentions. We need strong leadership, unwavering commitment, and the courage to face the challenges that lie ahead."

"Jayden, Arianna," Reebus began, his stare unwavering as he addressed them directly. "I chose you both personally for a reason. You embody the spirit of youth, daring, and creativity that the Genesis project requires. You have shown resilience in the face of adversity, and a willingness to question the status quo. People with your attributes will be needed as we progress towards our goals"

Jayden and Arianna exchanged glances, a mixture of surprise and curiosity playing across their features. They had not expected to be singled out in such a manner, but the gravity of Reebus's words stirred something deep within them.

"You are not alone in this endeavour. There are thousands more like you who have been chosen to join the Genesis project. Some of them are currently in their quarters, preparing for the journey that lay ahead, others you can see before you now in this very room.", he continued as his arms waved in both directions as if lighting their focus across the people and conversations happening behind them.

Jayden and Arianna exchanged surprised glances, the magnitude of Reebus's revelation sinking in. Thousands of others, all chosen for the same purpose, all bound together by a shared vision of hope and renewal.

"These individuals come from all walks of life," Reebus continued, his voice carrying a note of pride, "each possessing unique talents and perspectives that will be invaluable as we embark on this journey. Together, you will form the basis of Genesis, the pioneers of a new world."

"Reebus," Jayden began, his voice tinged with apprehension, "what journey are you talking about?" exuding a puzzled look on his face.

"Jayden my boy, we are all going on a journey into space. We are leaving the Earth behind in the search of a new planet where we can start humanity again. You are very lucky to be a part of this project and should be forever thankful to be here." explained Reebus.

Jayden responded with concern as this was not a plan he had ever planned, nor one he had any input or control over, "But, what about my mum? What will become of her?"

Reebus regarded Jayden with a mixture of empathy and resolve, understanding the depth of his concern. "Your mother will be taken care of, Jayden," he assured, his tone gentle yet firm. "She, along with others who are unable to join us on this journey, will be provided for and supported back on Earth. You have my word on that."

Despite Reebus's reassurance, Jayden could not shake the feeling of unease that settled in the pit of his stomach. "But Reebus," he persisted, his voice tinged with urgency, "Your word hasn't exactly been particularly trustworthy or believable in anything you have done. How can we just run away from Earth in its hour of most need? That cannot be the path for humanity, can it? There must be another way, a way to help everyone, not just those of us on Genesis."

Reebus regarded Jayden with a thoughtful expression, acknowledging the sincerity of his words. "You're right, Jayden," he conceded, his tone contemplative. "You have every reason not to trust me, but I sense you know why I have done everything I have in order to save our species. We will not turn our backs on Earth, nor can we ignore the plight of those who remain behind. Sometimes in order to build a better future, we must take bold steps and embrace new opportunities. By going on this adventure we will give humanity a second chance, better odds if you will of not only survival but in flourishing throughout the galaxies beyond."

Jayden pondered Reebus's words, grappling with the complexity of the situation. While he understood that Reebus's perceived necessity of forging ahead with the Genesis project, he could not shake the feeling of responsibility toward those he would be leaving behind.

Nova joined in the conversation before taking a deep breath, gathering her thoughts before continuing. "It's like the biblical story of Noah's ark. About a tale of survival and renewal in the face of cataclysmic change. Just as Noah built an ark to save humanity and preserve life in the midst of a great flood, your vision for the Genesis project embodies a similar spirit of resilience and hope."

"Is there anything we can do to help the rest of them?" Jayden asked, his voice laced with worry. "To ensure that they have a chance at a better life, even if they cannot join us on Genesis?"

Reebus regarded Jayden with a sense of admiration, impressed by his compassion and resolve, but deep down saw his compassion as a weakness. "We will do everything in our power to support those who remain on Earth," he vowed, his voice echoing with conviction. "

In a rare moment of quiet introspection, Reebus sat down with Jayden, the weight of the world heavy on his shoulders. There was a truth he needed to share, a revelation that had been weighing on his mind for far too long.

"Jayden," Reebus began, his voice filled with a mixture of sorrow and determination, "there's something I also need to tell you. A truth that has been hidden for far too long."

Jayden looked at Reebus, his brow furrowed in confusion, sensing the gravity of the moment. "What is it, Reebus? What truth do you speak of?"

Reebus took a deep breath, steeling himself for what was to come. "When your father was killed in that tragic accident almost twenty years ago it was brought to my attention by several of my sources. I became aware of the situation you were in. It reminded me of my own past, of the pain and loss that I had endured. In that moment, I felt a deep sense of pity for you, Jayden, in recognition of the suffering you were about to endure. I wanted to make things easier for you and help you out wherever I could."

Jayden's eyes widened in surprise, his mind reeling at the revelation. "You mean to say that you knew about my father's death all along?"

Reebus nodded solemnly. "Yes, Jayden. I knew right from your lowest moments till the time when you walked into my office at the GGC.. Your situation had moved me to take action. I wanted to reach out to you, to offer you guidance and support in your time of need. Just as Killian Tredwell had done for me so many years ago, I wanted to take you under my wing, to help you navigate the challenges of life and find your place in the world."

From the moment of Jayden's father's tragic death, Reebus had kept a watchful eye on the young man, recognizing in him a potential that was too great to ignore. He had seen the fire of determination burning in Jayden's eyes, the resilience and strength of character that had carried him through the darkest moments of his life.

And as Jayden grew and matured, Reebus watched with growing admiration, impressed by his unwavering commitment to justice and his unyielding sense of purpose. He knew then that Jayden was destined for greatness, destined to play a pivotal role in the future of the world. Unbeknown to Jayden but Reebus had whole data archives of Jayden from his earliest years until the present day. Jayden had been watched by society throughout his life through all conversations, movements and even items he had bought. In some regards Reebus knew Jayden better than he knew himself.

It was not until Jayden and Arianna's daring break-in at the GGC Warehouse that Reebus knew the time had come to act. It was the final trigger for his overall assimilation plan, the catalyst that would set into motion a chain of events that would change the course of their lives. If the break-in had been by almost anyone else then the end result would have been to provide them with a quick and decisive path to the retirement planet along with their families; but for Jayden, and by association Arianna, it created a very different outcome. It was then that Reebus had reached out a hand to Jayden and Arianna in his own way; gradually offering them a part of the inner sanctum of Reebus' new world of which today was the final part of the induction process.

As Reebus spoke and explained the situation and historical attachment to Jayden, his words seemed to hang in the air, each syllable pregnant with meaning. Jayden and Arianna listened intently, their hearts pounding with a mixture of bewilderment and comfort.

"And now, as your assimilation is completed" Reebus continued, his voice low and solemn, "Today is the time to progress with Genesis, it will allow us all to have a key role in ushering a new era of prosperity and abundance for all mankind."

Jayden and Arianna exchanged stunned glances, their minds reeling with the enormity of Reebus's revelations.

Reebus decided to let everyone have some space as some of the revelations and discussions must have come as quite a shock. He left Arianna and Jayden comforting each other and Christina also on their inner circle of shock. Meanwhile Nova simply performed her daily activities by preparing and ensuring everything was in its correct place. She was a very organised and capable girl who had fulfilled the role her father had given to her in bringing Jayden and Arianna to Genesis. As Nova walked away from the trio her facial similarities and demeanour seemed almost an exact replica of her own father, something that had not been obvious until this point.

The door behind Reebus opened once more and Imelda Stravus walked in. She was looking smart and very focussed. As soon as Reebus noticed her he signalled to come to his side.

Reebus asked her for an update on a number of matters which seemed to relate to each of the compartmental areas of the Genesis project. He was questioning the completeness of the enormous zoological library of animals on board, on the state of the energy systems, the complete amount of water on board and whether all the expected human arrivals were on board. Imelda confirmed positively on each of Reebus's questions, and he looked at her with a knowing glance of approval.

After glancing around the room once again, Reebus turned back to Imelda until she was aware of his glare. Reebus then signalled to Imelda with his hand telling her that "It's time", his voice tinged with anticipation. "Prepare the final checks, Imelda. We are ready to begin. I will see you in the control room in the next half hour."

Chapter 30: One Last Hope

Whilst Reebus was preparing to set his plan finally in motion, He instructed that Christina be being escorted to her new quarters through the many floors and spaces with the structure. One particular guard who seemed quite friendly led her away. She was looking solemn and unknowing of the future ahead. As the guards stationed in front of her opened one door there stood a truly massive living space, but all was not quite what it seemed.

As Christina made her way through the massive dormitory within the Genesis project, she could not help but marvel at the sheer scale of the space. Rows upon rows of beds lined the walls, stretching as far as the eye could see, their simple yet functional design a testament to the efficiency of the living quarters.

At first glance, the dormitory appeared relatively empty, with only a few people scattered about, sitting on their beds, and engaged in quiet conversation or deep in thought. As Christina walked further into the room, she realized that appearances could be deceiving. For hidden within the walls of the dormitory were thousands upon thousands of pull-out beds, both low and high, neatly tucked away against the walls like pieces of a puzzle waiting to be assembled. With a simple flick of a switch, the beds would slide out effortlessly, providing sleeping quarters for the countless individuals who called the dormitory home.

It was a remarkable sight to behold with beds rising high into the air three deep, their sturdy frames supporting mattresses of varying sizes and thicknesses, each one tailored to the needs and preferences of its occupant. The higher beds requiring an automated lifting machine or AI helper to escort the human occupant into its sleeping quarters. Not that the people here seemed to mind any difficulties reaching their beds; in fact, the room seemed full of a genuinely happy group of people. These people had probably been recruited to Genesis by choice; or as an alternative to what faced them in the real world, not by stealth, lies or deceit as was Christina, Jayden, and Arianna's journey.

As Christina looked around further, she realized that this seemingly empty space was, in fact, teeming with life in a bustling community of individuals from all walks of life, brought together by a common purpose and shared sense of camaraderie.

For many, the dormitory was more than just a place to sleep. It was a sanctuary, a refuge from the chaos and uncertainty of the outside world. Here, amidst the towering beds they found solace and companionship, forging bonds. Already personalisation factors had taken place throughout the room, sometimes adding a touch of colour, and often having printed photocards of loved ones within view of their chosen beds. It was unusual to see so many photocards and physical printouts in a world so technologically based that holographs had become the norm.

As Christina was led further through the dormitory, her attention was drawn to a group of familiar faces that she had not seen in quite some time. They were individuals she had encountered during her time at the GGC headquarters, though they occupied relatively low positions within the organization's hierarchy. Surprised to see them here in the heart of the Genesis project, Christina approached with a curious expression on her face. "Hey," she greeted them, her voice tinged with surprise. "What are you all doing here? I haven't seen you around the GGC headquarters in weeks."

The group exchanged hesitant glances before one of them spoke up, a nervous smile playing at the corners of their lips. "Oh, Christina, it's good to see you," they replied, their tone slightly evasive. "We were reassigned to work on a special project here at the Genesis project. It is all a bit hush-hush, you know? We are glad you made it here too." Christina's eyebrows furrowed in confusion at the vague response. She could not shake the feeling that there was more to the story than they were letting on. After all, why would individuals in relatively low positions within the GGC suddenly be reassigned to such a high-profile project like Genesis?

Before she could press for more information, the group quickly changed the subject, deflecting her questions with practiced ease. "Anyway, how have you been, Christina? It's been a while since we last saw you."

Caught off guard by their sudden shift in conversation, Christina hesitated for a moment before offering a polite smile. "I've been good, thanks," she replied, though her mind was still buzzing with questions.

A separate member of the Genesis project's staff hurried over to Christina, a look of urgency etched upon their face. "Christina, I'm sorry to interrupt, but there's been a change of plans," they explained quickly, their voice rushed and breathless. "On the orders of Reebus we have a different place of residence prepared for you. We need to move you there immediately." Surprised by the abruptness of the interruption, Christina glanced back at her former colleagues, a sense of unease stirring within her. They exchanged worried glances, their expressions mirroring her own apprehension.

"Wait, what's going on?" Christina asked, her voice tinged with concern. "Where are you taking me?"

The staff member hesitated for a moment before responding, their tone guarded. "I'm sorry, Christina, I can't give you all the details right now. It is a matter of security. Rest assured; we have everything under control. We just need to ensure your safety."

Though her instincts told her to push for more information, Christina knew that now was not the time. With a nod of resignation, she followed the staff member and the original escort guard as they led her away from the dormitory, her mind racing with questions and uncertainties. Christina was then led through a few more corridors before arriving at a quieter more peaceful living area with separate rooms.

"This is your quarters Christina, please make yourself comfortable.," said her guide as he unlocked with his passkey "Your biometrics and fingerprints are already assigned to your room so you should be able to come and go as you please from now on," added her guide.

"But why was I escorted her under guard?" asked Christina somewhat perplexed.

"You are not under guard at all. You are a member of the Genesis project and will be of significant value to everyone on board. It is just an escort policy we have so that people do not get lost in the huge confines of this facility.," added the guide which someone calmed her earlier concerns.

As Christina stepped into her designated quarters, she could not help but marvel at the ingenuity and innovation that had gone into their design. Though incredibly small in size, her living space was a marvel of modern technology and comfort, carefully crafted to make the most use of every inch.

The walls were lined with sleek, multifunctional furniture that doubled as storage units, their minimalist design adding to the sense of spaciousness despite the limited square footage. A compact automatic robochef nestled in one corner, equipped with state-of-the-art appliances and cleverly concealed storage compartments. In the centre of the room, a comfortable seating area beckoned invitingly, its plush cushions and soft throws providing a cozy spot to relax and unwind after a long day. A large window stretched from floor to ceiling, offering a breathtaking view of the surrounding landscape. It was a reminder of the beauty and wonder of the natural world outside. Although the view appeared to be real it was clearly an extremely advanced holographic display which she then found could be configured a set to any landscape or theme she desired. She tweaked the settings to that of a scenic mountain landscape which brought immediate peace to her mind.

Her quarters also had an integrated smart holograph virtual reality system with realistic avatar that controlled everything from lighting and temperature to entertainment and security with a simple voice command. With just a few words, she could adjust the lighting to create the perfect ambiance, queue up her favourite music playlist, or even activate the security sensors to keep her safe at night. As Christina settled into this new residence, she was introduced to a state-of-the-art virtual reality holographic replicator system tailored to her needs. It was capable of creating near-lifelike holographic representations of anyone she desired, complete with their voice, personality traits, and mannerisms. Excited by the possibilities, Christina wasted no time in exploring the capabilities of the system. With a few simple controls, she summoned a holographic representation of her favourite singer, their image shimmering into existence before her eyes. It was as if they were standing right there in the room with her, as she played one of the greatest ever concerts with Christina as the entire audience. It could be configured to an exact song or moment that she wished to hear, or even access holographic preferences of people who would share them with her. The system did not stop there. With a few more commands, Christina could summon holographic representations of people that she knew; her mother, her relatives, her friends, and anyone she could imagine. Each hologram was meticulously crafted to embody the essence of the person it represented, their personality traits and quirks faithfully recreated down to the smallest detail. Where all of these traits and images were attained from Christina did not really understand but it led to underlying thoughts in her mind about individuals being watched, scanned, or recorded throughout their everyday lives with no knowledge of this occurring. Christina's mind did not want to delve too deeply into the record or creation, but just wanted to feel like she had family around her so succumbed to the experience. It surreal, as she interacted with these lifelike holograms, each one a faithful companion and confidant, ready to fulfil any whim or desire she had. Whether she wanted to engage in lively conversation, seek advice and guidance, or simply enjoy the company of her loved ones, the holographic companions were always going to be there, eager to lend a listening ear and a helping hand, or just be a servant to whatever she needed at a given point in time.

For Christina, who had spent so much time away from her loved ones in pursuit of her dreams, the Virtual Reality Holograph (VRH) system was a welcome godsend. It was a lifeline connecting her to the people and places she held dear. Although it might be a fictitious path into those she knew, VRH was also comforting and would allow her to seemingly reconnect with anyone from her life or from history; whether they were living or dead. She adjusted the device settings to let the VRH become like her own mother so it could start communicating with the dulcet tones that made her both teary and homesick. It reminded her of the days gone by when she was able to find personal solace in routine conversations with her mum long before her GGC days -and long before her mum had sacrificed her own life; dying due to lack of available clean drinking water when she had saved everything she had for Christina. Using the VRH system this way was something that will cause positive and negative memories with equal measures.

As Christina settled into a comfy looking seat, her mind was consumed by thoughts of Jayden and Arianna. She had grown close to them over the last few months and in many ways they had become new family. She wondered where they were or what Reebus was doing with them, and why was she escorted away separately? She hoped they would have quarters close to hers and really hoped she could see them soon. Lost in her thoughts, Christina found it difficult to relax. She paced back and forth across the room, her mind racing with worry and uncertainty. What if something had happened to them? What if they were in danger? Despite her best efforts to push aside her concerns, Christina found herself unable to shake the feeling of dread that gnawed at her insides. She knew that she needed answers, and she needed them soon. She could just leave her quarters and start wondering around but she did not know where to go, through the maze of corridors and levels and more significantly was tired beyond imagination. Exhausted from the tumult of emotions swirling within her, Christina finally succumbed to the pull of sleep. She had moved over to her fresh bed still fully clothed and fell asleep within a few seconds of her eyes closing; her body too weary and her mind too heavy with the weight of the adventures that had filled the day.

For a while, she drifted in the hazy space between wakefulness and dreams, her thoughts consumed by visions of Jayden and Arianna. She saw them wandering through the corridors of the Genesis project, their faces set in determined expressions as they searched for answers amongst the danger around them. Whether this was real or just a vivid dream it was impossible to tell. Just as she began to slip into a deeper sleep, Christina was jolted awake by a familiar sound which increased in volume as she perked up from her slumber. Christina felt into her pocket for her communication device which vibrated away with an urgency that made her heart skip a beat. With a reflexive glance around to ensure no one was watching, she slid it out and answered the communication without looking at the caller's source.

"Hello?" she said, her voice hushed with anticipation as her eyes opened wider with each moment. "Christina, it's Hugo," came the voice and then image on the other end, breathless with excitement. "We've done it! I We have appear to have discovered a new planet, one that can sustain life. And it is closer than we ever imagined!"

Christina's eyes widened with disbelief, her mind racing with the possibilities. A new planet with a fresh start for humanity. Here was a chance to start moving everyone from the Earth to the new planet."

"That's incredible, Hugo," she replied, her voice barely above a whisper. "Where is it? How soon can we get there?"

"We're still analysing the data, but preliminary estimates suggest that it's within reach of our current technology and is a place we could regularly send transportation ships to." Hugo explained, his voice tinged with excitement. "We're already preparing to send an expedition to investigate further, but we wanted to inform you right away. This could be our chance to populate a new planet and save the Earth. Can you please alert Reebus and tell him the good news and get back to me with our next steps as soon as you can", as a swathe of cheers and screams of happiness could be heard from large groups of the space exploration teams located around Hugo. Christina's team had done it, they had achieved the ultimate discovery, one that would lead to the salvation of Earth's populace and allow them to become a multi-planetary species. In amongst all the joy Hugo was lifted up on the shoulders of some of his team members and at that the communication to Christina terminated abruptly, possibly because of a dropped or broken communicator.

With the conversation ended, Christina's grasp of reality came back in play. Her heart had been swelling with hope at the thought of a new world, a second chance for humanity to thrive. The reality then set in; she needed to tell Reebus immediately of the discovery and prevent his plan from going ahead. There appeared to be another way of saving and progressing humanity and all it needed was a bit of time to action. Christina looked at her communicator and ushered the words "Call Reebus" as she tried to contact Reebus directly, but the connection could not be made. She tried again and again but it failed as before as if Reebus did not want to be contacted. She persevered again trying to call Imelda and then other members of Reebus' inner circle, but it was a futile task. Not one of them picked up; nobody was willing or able to answer her call for help -the most important call that they would ever miss. With time of the essence, Christina realised that technology was betraying her this time and needed to find another way to get through to Reebus. She looked at the side of her entry door where some basic schematics of the whole facility were written in print. Noticing particularly the area labelled as the 'Control room' which was where she expected Reebus might be. She ripped the schematic off the wall and prepared for the fastest run of her life.

Chapter 31: Five Seconds Late to the Party

Christina's heart raced with excitement as she burst out of her quarters inside the eighteenth floor of the vast Genesis structure. Unlike traditional building segmentation, the eighteenth floor here was the number of the floor in a downwards direction from the top. Christina had not thought about how many floors were in the whole structure. On Christinas's immediate mind was the number twenty-six, the location of the control room on the schematics she had before her. It was coloured in bright red and looked to be a very important. Christina knew she had to travel eight large floors downwards and then hope that her hunch about Reebus being there was correct. She was relieved that the travel was in a downward direction at the very least but had no time to wait. Her footsteps echoed with each stride down the corridor as she hurried towards the steps. With one of Reebus's guards securing level eighteen she ran towards him shouting that "I need to speak to Reebus" with the guard gesticulated downwards saying "He's in the control room"

Christina was relieved that the thoughts she had about Reebus's location were proven to be correct. She paced downwards, taking the manual route rather than attempting to wait for a lift. Christina wanted to be in control of her own footsteps and destiny rather being made to wait for something that was infrequent at the very least.

With each step downwards her anticipation grew, filled with the knowledge that the space program discovery could change everything. The fate of humanity might rest in her hands. She was determined to deliver the news to Reebus as soon as possible.

Reebus stood in the command centre of the Genesis Project, his gaze fixed on the vast array of monitors and projections that lined the walls. Imelda stood beside him, her expression one of quiet resolve as she surveyed the bustling activity around them. The build up to something historic and life changing was encapsulating the entire room. The room was silent except the occasional beep from some of the displays and gadgets. Reebus firmly asked "All systems checks please Imelda"

Imelda nodded, her fingers flying across the control panel with practiced efficiency, moving several levers up and down and turning some buttons on and others off. After a few short moments she efficiently responded, "All systems are online and operational," her voice steady despite the magnitude of the task at hand. "We are ready to initiate the launch sequence on your command"

There were about ten of Reebus's team in the control room as well as Jayden and Arianna who were there on personal invitation to witness history. Reebus's lips curved into a faint smile as he thanked Imelda with a mixture of admiration and gratitude. Together, they had worked tirelessly to bring their vision to fruition. It was chance to create a new world, a new beginning for humanity. The two of them had been building the Genesis facility together for nearly two decades. The idea behind the project was to provide a way for humanity to reinvent itself if and when needed. It was to ensure that whatever the future brought that the human race would prosper. The project was no more than a backup plan originally as it was originally expected that mankind would find solutions quite quickly to the problems it faced. At the time there was unwavering hope that the space program would delivery results eventually. Time and resources were pouring deeply into the discovery of new worlds. As time had gone on, only a chosen few would know of the existence of the project. Reebus and Imelda had needed to keep full control of the GGC to ensure that funding channels could continue to allow the construction of something more advanced than humanity had ever witnessed before. Through the years many GGC employees and key ministers had uncovered what they had seen as embezzlement of government funds. On presenting the evidence to Reebus these telltales had mysteriously disappeared or found themselves on fast track to retirement. Some of the lucky ones had become insiders within the Genesis project ranks. Recruitment had progressed over the last twenty years for key personnel to propel the project along at speed. Focus had then switched to the collection of all aspects of the water, food and minerals that were found inside the vast library they stood in today. The creation of different biomes to allow native animal types followed as soon as the water and food infrastructure was proven to work. Then key scientists developed genetical advances allowing long extinct creatures to be recreated.

It was only recently that the younger human subjects who mostly now filled the residential quarters were recruited. Imelda and Reebus had used the last few months since the election result to analyse all human data available. They had picked the best people at all kinds of skillsets and attributes. The best people from mathematics, engineering, even social interaction, and attractiveness amongst hundreds of key data points. The world's compulsory education system had not been about learning, it never had been but more about supplying skill data to Reebus in order for him to propel the natural selection process. Educational competence along with natural DNA genes had allowed millions upon millions of the worlds populace to be rated, ranked, and then chosen to be a part of Genesis as it was today. The selected Genesis participants were then taken by Reebus's special teams and brought directly to Genesis; they were told that they were recruited for key GGC initiatives and would be well looked after. These chosen 'candidates' mostly rejoiced at being able to escape from their difficult home situations, seeking a better future in any way that lay ahead. The opportunity to be well paid and fed as part of a hi-tech research facility was a dream to most. These recruits had still not discovered their overall purpose to the current day. In true Reebus style, they had been told a few half truths about their families being looked after as well only part of the truths behind Genesis itself.

"Initiate the launch sequence," Reebus crowed, his voice echoing through the command centre with quiet authority. "It's time to leave this world behind and begin anew."

As Imelda input the final commands into the control panel, a hush fell over the command centre, the air crackling with tension and excitement. Outside above the structures massive cave doors began to open and in doing so revealed the tip of the large Genesis spaceship to the sea above it. As the cave doors moved, they caused an incredulous thunder and rumble above as the boundless expanse of the ocean beyond was revealed.

Starting with a low frequency hum, the engines of this would-be massive spacecraft roared to life. The powerful thrusters started to propel the vessel skyward with breathtaking speed. As the ship soared through the ocean's protective layer above and then into the air, it started to leave the Earth in its wake. Reebus and Imelda watched on with quiet satisfaction, their hearts filled with hope for the future.

"We've done it," Reebus said, his voice loud and composed. "We've taken the first step toward a new beginning of a world of endless possibilities, where humanity can thrive and prosper once more."

Imelda nodded, her eyes shining with unshed tears. "Yes," she replied, her voice choked with emotion. "And it's all thanks to you, Reebus. You had the vision, the courage to see it through. Now we are beginning our journey to a brighter tomorrow."

As Christina ran into the control room with a number of guards in trail she approached Reebus now out of breath from her marathon run to get there. Christina prepared herself to speak, catching breath as she went. Outside of Genesis everyone could hear huge unimaginable bangs, creaks, and explosions along the path where the gigantic structure had left its previous home deep inside the Earth.

"I have incredible news, Reebus," Christina exclaimed, her voice tinged with excitement. "My team has made a groundbreaking discovery. We have found a new planet -one that can sustain human life!"

The room fell silent as Reebus, and his advisors absorbed Christina's words. Outside they were witnessing a path of destruction which tore through the layers of the Earth to its central core creating an explosive cataclysm of a level that had never before existed. As Christina saw the grim effects of the situation out of the command window, her heart sank with despair and mind chatter. How could they have been so blind to the consequences of their actions? How could they have allowed their pursuit of progress to lead to such devastation?

Tears streamed down Christina's cheeks as she bore witness to the destruction occurring around, her mind struggling to comprehend the magnitude of the devastation unfolding before her. Earth, the cradle of humanity, now lay broken and in parts. Its once-great cities getting reduced to nothing more than rubble and dust. The Earth was fragmenting into hundreds, thousands, or in fact millions of pieces. As each moment passed billions of people were sent to their permanent 'retirement' – what lucky recipients of this latest lottery they were. There was never going to be a recovery from this, civilization on Earth as it had existed for thousands of years was to be no more. The reality of Earth's destruction sank in for all in the room. Jayden and Arianna felt the weight of grief and despair bear down upon them like the most gruesome devil. With the immediate knowledge that their families had perished in the cataclysmic event, the pain of loss consumed them, leaving them reeling with a potent mixture of anger and sorrow. They both ran over to Christina which allowed the three friends to at least share the burden of this insane grief.....

A few hours later in the dimly lit confines of their quarters aboard the Genesis spacecraft, Jayden and Arianna sat side by side, their hearts heavy with the crushing burden of lost loved ones. The silence between them was deafening, punctuated only by the soft sound of their laboured breaths and the distant rattle of the ship's purring systems. Arianna's hands still trembled with emotion as tears streamed down her cheeks, her anguish palpable in the quiver of her voice. "They're gone, Jayden," she whispered, her words choked with sorrow. "Everyone we loved everything we knew -it's all gone."

Jayden's chest tightened with a visceral ache as he struggled to contain the overwhelming tide of emotions threatening to engulf him. With clenched fists he fought to suppress the rising tide of anger and despair that threatened to consume him whole. "I can't believe it," he muttered, his voice thick with emotion. "They were supposed to be safe. We were supposed to protect them."

"My Mum...... your Mum.... Our Mums!" as Jayden's face streamed with tears facing his true love. After a few more tears Jayden continued "Arianna Stafford," as he used her full name to ensure the singleness and sincerity of his next sentence, "I Love you more than the world." Amid their shared anguish, Jayden and Arianna had at least found solace in each other's presence.

For Christina, the margins of life were much thinner, and she had nobody to turn to. With a brief knock on their door, she joined them in their quarters with the three of them snuggled as one. All three friends had tear-streaked faces and hearts heavy with grief before leaning into one another, drawing strength from the unspoken understanding that bound them all together. As they grappled and processed the devastation of Earth's destruction, they could not help but draw parallels between the cataclysmic event and the insidious underpinnings of the retirement program orchestrated by Reebus. Though the circumstances differed, both tragedies were rooted in the choices made by the very man who had promised salvation and prosperity.

The destruction of Earth was a harrowing reminder of the consequences of unchecked power and hubris, a stark testament to the devastating impact of Reebus's relentless pursuit of control. In his quest for supremacy, he had overseen the demise of an entire planet, condemning billions to an untimely end in pursuit of his own selfish ambitions.

Similarly, the retirement program -concealed behind a facade of benevolence and promise -was just a tool of manipulation and subjugation, designed to rid the world of its elderly population under the guise of providing them with a paradise in their twilight years. Yet, beneath the veneer of false promises lay the sinister truth and reality; those deemed expendable were callously disposed of, their lives sacrificed in service of Reebus's insatiable hunger for power.

In both instances, Reebus's choices had unleashed unimaginable devastation upon the world, leaving calamity in their wake. Whether through the annihilation of Earth or the clandestine execution of the elderly, his actions had irrevocably altered the course of humanity, leaving a scar upon the fabric of reality that would never fully heal.

As Jayden, Arianna and Christina contemplated the parallels between these tragedies, they were struck by the sobering realization that Reebus's thirst for dominance knew no bounds, just as it never had. He had proven himself to be a force of unfathomable destruction, willing to sacrifice anything, and anyone, in his relentless pursuit of power. Although the Earth had been shattered, a brief light shone with humanity still enduring aboard the Genesis. As this huge spaceship pressed onward into the unknown, they all knew that they carried with them the legacy of their fallen world. With it, any potential future of humanity relied on the inhabitants of this ship alone.

With all the devastation and horror that was occurring, Christina thought about Hugo, and his horrific but instantaneous death. She knew that she would never see her trusted friend again and also realised that he had not even had chance to send the location of the discovered planet before this apocalypse had begun. Despite the amazing planetary discovery of the team she managed, they had no idea in which direction they should travel in the search for a viable planet to call home. The knowledge, data, and analytics behind all the space exploration voyages had seemingly been destroyed for eternity. Christina turned her gaze away from the shattered remnants of Earth, wiped away tears and tried to focus instead on the path ahead. For though their journey had begun with destruction, she hoped that it would end with renewal, a new beginning among the stars, forged from the ashes of their former home.

The search for a new planet to call home had well and truly begun......

Epilogue

Reebus stood before the window in his large quarters, his gaze fixed upon the shattered remnants of Earth below. A faint smirk played upon his lips, a subtle expression of satisfaction that belied the magnitude of the devastation that lay before him. To an outsider, it might have seemed callous, even cruel, to revel in the destruction of an entire planet. To Reebus, it was the culmination of a meticulously crafted plan. It was a triumph of ambition and cunning that had been years in the making. As he surveyed the wreckage and flying rocks below, Reebus felt a surge of power coursing through his veins. With a heady rush of exhilaration that left him intoxicated with the taste of victory. For too long, he had laboured in the shadows, biding his time, and laying the groundwork for his grand design. Now, as he looked upon the shattered remains of Earth, he knew that his moment of triumph had finally arrived. It was a scene of utter chaos and destruction. The once vibrant planet reduced to shattered dreams and lost hopes. Yet, amidst the wreckage, Reebus saw an opportunity, It was a chance to forge a new world in his image, free from the constraints of the past and beholden only to his own desires.

For Reebus, the destruction of Earth was not an act of malice, but rather a necessary step in the pursuit of his goal: absolute power and control over the fate of humanity. In his eyes, the sacrifice of billions was a small price to pay for the chance to reshape the world according to his own vision. It was a vision of order and dominion that would brook no dissent or opposition. As he continued to stare out upon the shattered pieces of Earth, Reebus felt he had completed a significant goal. It was a moment of triumph which would be a vindication of all his efforts and sacrifices, and a harbinger of the new world that he would soon bring into being.

Reebus then looked through his old messages and found one from his head of engineering at the start of the Genesis project who had sent an electronic communication that stated "It is my belief that if this structure is ever used as a spacecraft as designed then there is a very high risk it may fracture the Earth to a point where the Earth core may become destabilized and may even cause destruction of the planet itself. We need to ensure that we fill the Earth support structure with layers of carbon fibre and protective sheeting to ensure this could not happen. Please advise next steps. Peter Stafford."

As Reebus scrolled this message further his response was shown. "Excellent work Peter, I am proud of your skill with this matter and would like to reward you. Please ensure not to tell anyone else your findings at this stage as I do not want any alarm to be caused, so have arranged for you to have a special reward for your excellent work. Regards Reebus."

It was not a coincidence that Peter was never again seen on the project from the day of that communication, his "Retirement" happened very quickly when some of Reebus's closest guards provided the necessary push and covered up any loose tracks with his family. Reebus made sure to delete this message and all related to it before putting his device down with haste.

Reebus then went to get showered and changed. As he brought his towel to his body to dry himself, he looked in front of his mirror whilst admiring the tree-shaped birthmark on his chest. It reminded him of some of his wilder days when he was raw and reckless that had required Killian to cover up from the public glare.

It was then that In the silence of his own quarters, Reebus looked pleased with himself and whispered a single word; a word that echoed through the depths of space and time, a promise of things to come:

"Genesis."